THE PITTSBURGH HAMLET

RON SHAFER

ISBN 978-1-0980-0995-3 (paperback)
ISBN 978-1-0980-0996-0 (digital)

Christian Faith Publishing, Inc.
832 Park Avenue
Meadville, PA 16335
www.christianfaithpublishing.com

Author's photo by: Cassie Clouse

Printed in the United States of America

To my family—Mom, Dad, Bob, Dick,
Jim, Larry, Wayne, and Sue

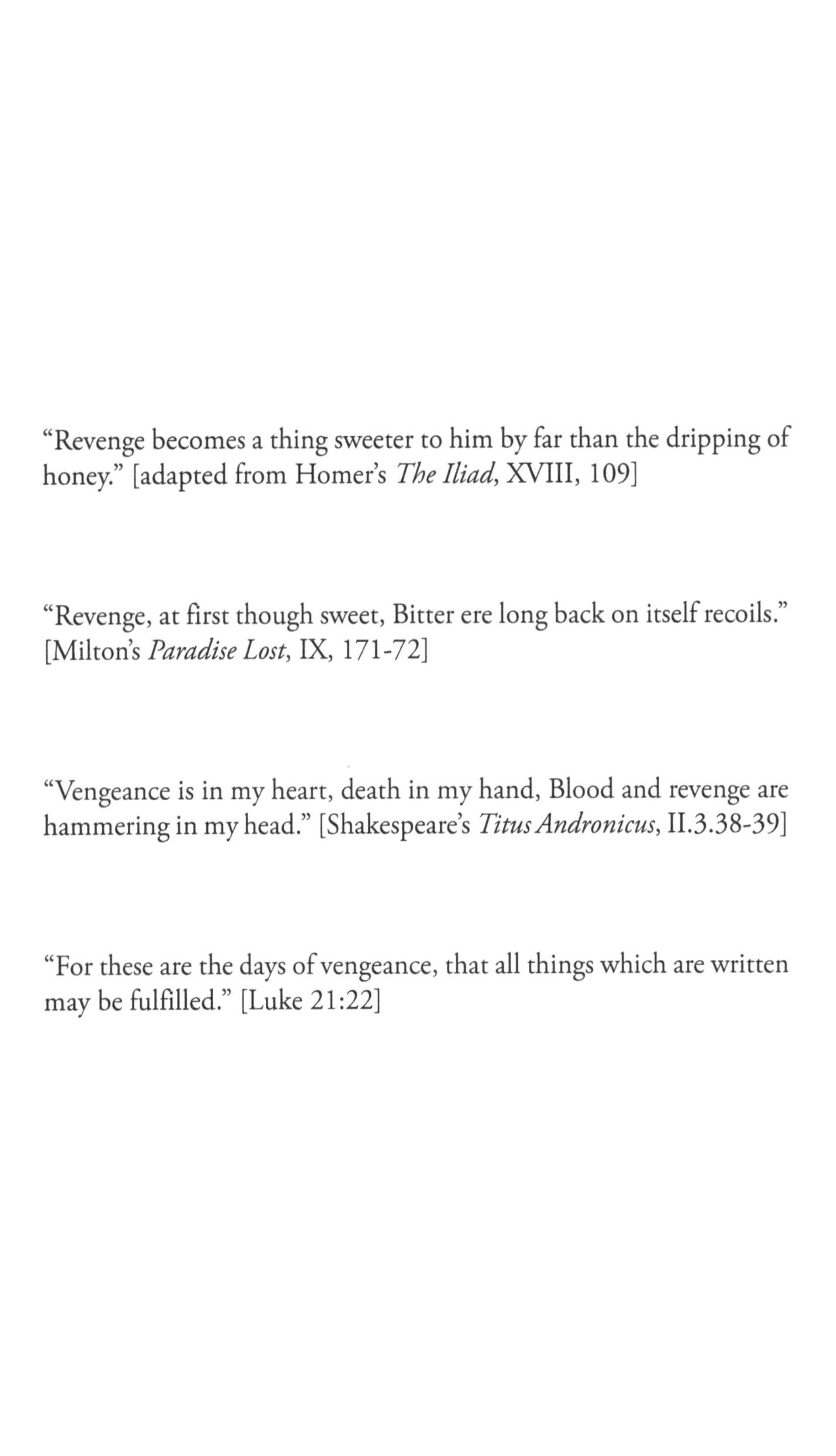

"Revenge becomes a thing sweeter to him by far than the dripping of honey." [adapted from Homer's *The Iliad*, XVIII, 109]

"Revenge, at first though sweet, Bitter ere long back on itself recoils." [Milton's *Paradise Lost*, IX, 171-72]

"Vengeance is in my heart, death in my hand, Blood and revenge are hammering in my head." [Shakespeare's *Titus Andronicus*, II.3.38-39]

"For these are the days of vengeance, that all things which are written may be fulfilled." [Luke 21:22]

CHAPTER 1

"Revenge should have no bounds!" The line from Shakespeare's *Hamlet* exploded in Abe Badoane's brain with the power of a .300 Magnum rifle shell. As he sifted through a pile of compost in the upper strawberry patch behind his house, Abe's mind had wandered to a lecture he once heard on the Bard's great tragedy. The professor's comments had made such an impact that to this day Abe could paraphrase it. "Revenge is the major theme of the play. It is achieved in *Hamlet*," the Carnegie Mellon professor had opined, "when the evil king pours poison into the ears of the innocent dupes around him. That verbal poison is so powerful that it distills their brains to swill. Once that happens, the victims are incapable, first, of cognitive function and, as a subsequent consequence, any sort of future self-determination."

With their brains sucked out, Abe thought to himself, drawing the back of his hand across a sweaty brow, *they embody T. S. Eliot's hollow men:*

> *We are the hollow men*
> *We are the stuffed men*
> *Leaning together,*
> *Headpiece filled with straw.*

That's it! The evil king Claudius inches his plot forward by injecting poison into the brains of the underlings around him.

"Does the course of revenge have any boundaries?" one of the female students had queried. "I mean, does Shakespeare speak of its limits?"

The professor prided himself on his hasty response: "Revenge should have no bounds!"—the famous line from *Hamlet.*

Would such a strategy work in Abe's case? *Might I too poison the minds of the stooges around me, distill their peon brains to swill, and fill their idiotic headpieces with straw? Why not? Venom achieved my ends in the past. I merely have to select the right victim, the right moment, the right poison. The proper course of revenge is exactly what I need to get even with Jude and Cory for their conspiratorial act of war—reading about the most precious and zealously guarded secrets of my sick, private life!*

Especially the shameful molestation when I was an innocent child—O! horrible! O, horrible, most horrible! Especially the death of my dear wife whom I abused so terribly, whom I loved with all my heart, and whom I destroyed with my monstrous hate, which I can never control, and now they know of this and have trumpeted it abroad. O, horrible! O, horrible, most horrible! Most especially the death of my dear, dear son, that bright-eyed little jewel baby, bright as the morning sun, beautiful as the child Moses lifted from the Nile and given to me, unworthy me, and then just as quickly taken from me, cruelly swept away, and of this, even this, Jude and Cory now know and have blabbed abroad with their sword-sharpened tongues—O, horrible! O worse than horrible! O infinitely worse than most awful horrible! You are right, Mr. Shakespeare—revenge for that atrocious act should have no bounds, absolutely none! I'll do my work in mine or kirk! Revenge I'll have, in rose bush lurk!

The next day at the end of lunch break in the mushroom mine, Abe motioned for Tina Reynolds, Duke Manningham's sexy on-off girlfriend, to come and talk to him. He was standing alone at the lunchroom vending machines, smiling as always.

"Tina, I want to give you a heads-up on this. You've heard about the nude pictures of Cory making the rounds in the mine. Have you seen them?"

"Yes, I've seen the pig. I keep telling people she's no angel!" Her hands went to her hips. "I knew I was right all along."

"Come on, Tina. You have to admit she's a beautiful woman. She'd give *Dukes of Hazzard*'s Daisy Duke a run for her money any day of the week."

"Ha! You haven't seen other folks' goods." She stood erect and pulled her shoulders back. "And not just me. You've seen Beavers and Bonnie in low-cut tops. Those babes would hold their heads up high in Raquel Welch's company!"

"I'm not interested in arbitrating the mine's most-beautiful-body contest. But one little matter does touch you and touch you dearly."

"You gotta be kidding. I don't think so. I hate both Jude and Cory."

"Cory's spreading rumors that both Duke and Jude want only her and not you." Abe hastily swept his eyes in front of him. "Or any of the other women in the mine for that matter."

Tina's eyes flashed fire like a bollock dagger in the sunlight. "The floosy!"

"That's not all. Cory said that, after Duke's had her, 'he won't even look on Tina the slut.' That, my darling, is a direct quote."

Tina's nostrils flared. "Let me at her!"

"Take it down a notch and listen to the rest. Cory went on to say, 'Once you've plowed the princess, who'd splay the pig?'—another direct quote. Can you imagine she'd say that about you? Several of us were there when she said it."

"The whore! Who does she think she is! I ought to tear her hair out!"

"Don't take it lying down." *Though she will be!* Abe stopped talking, put his finger to his lips, and looked across at the lounge as if deep in thought. "As I see it, you can fix her wagon once and for all."

"How? I hate her."

"Get back with Duke, and you know in what way I mean. Make her jealous as the dickens. That's how I'd fix her. Surely you haven't forgotten the good times you and Duke have had."

Tina looked forlorn. "Duke's turned goodie-goodie on me." She shook her head back and forth—a worried woman. "He wouldn't come on to me even if I tried."

"I don't believe that for a second. You're forgetting who you are and the goods *you* have!"

Tina looked at Abe's darting eyes. "Okay, snake eyes. Let me hear your plan. I know you've got one up your sleeve!"

"Get him to take you to The Inn and get a couple beers in him. Tell him you need a friend to cheer you up because of some problem you have. Any problem."

Tina wrinkled her brow, already contemplating Abe's idea.

"Start slowly, and it won't be long till you have him. Now that he's been off the booze a while, he'll get drunk more quickly. He'll be on an empty stomach, so that too will help your cause. Once you get the booze in him, you'll be leading him by the nose."

Tina smiled broadly.

"And you can do anything you want—absolutely anything! After all, revenge should have no bounds."

"Maybe so. That might just be the way to get my revenge on that flirty floozy!" Tina wrinkled her brow. "But who's to say I can even get one beer in him? He's holier than Saint Sebastian these days!"

After work the next day, Tina met Duke in the parking lot. Totally exasperated, he wanted Cory desperately and mused on her often. *I know from the nude pictures that she's fair game, but how can I bed the babe? Jude's with her constantly!*

"Hey, Duke. You're the picture of torment these days," Tina began, smacking her gum. Duke was seated in the driver's seat of his snazzy '57 Chevy, Tina standing by the car door. "What happened to Mr. Confidence?"

"Just a little frustrated. No big deal. What's it to you?"

"Well, let's go get a fast drink. My mom just got superbad news about her biopsy. We can cry in each other's beer."

"No! You know I'm off the beer. Don't tempt me!"

"Come on, Duke. Show some pity for an old friend." Tina dabbed a moist eye. "I need someone to talk to. My mom's in bad shape. I gotta be strong for her, and right now I don't have the strength to do it. Come on, be a friend! One or two beers ain't gonna hurt you."

"I don't know."

"I promise to keep a good eye on you. If you don't want to drink, that's okay. I just need someone to talk to." She looked at her watch. "I only have a short time. I gotta be home when Tony gets off the bus. I'm a horrible mother, I know, but at least it will never be said that Tony is a latchkey kid."

As she spoke, the top buttons of her blouse were unbuttoned. Duke was at the steering wheel, and she leaned over as she spoke. He didn't mind at all that his gaze was not subtle. Nor did Tina.

"Hop in."

CHAPTER 2

At The Inn, Tina coyly eased into her beer-drinking ploy, knowing Duke would most likely resist. "I'll guzzle just one beer, and then we'll be on our way. I appreciate your bringing me here." She took a large gulp of beer. "You see, my mom just found out she has breast cancer. Several of the women in my family have already died of that." Another large swig of beer. "My two favorite aunts passed earlier this year. It runs in our family." Tina held a hand to her breast and finished her beer. "Duke, I'm so scared."

"I'm sorry to hear that. What a terrible disease!"

She shed a timed tear and finished her beer. "Wow, I forgot what it's like to drink beer on an empty stomach! I haven't eaten all day." She laughed loudly and knocked over a salt shaker as though starting to get tipsy. After she drank some more, she slurred her speech. "This beer's shitting me. I mean hitting me!" She laughed uproariously.

Duke pointed to a large eight-point buck mounted on the opposite wall. "See that? I shot that puppy two years ago." He held up his draft beer and took another giant gulp. "I was going to throw it out, but Ben said he needed another mounted animal for his restaurant, so I gave it to him, and he hung it there. Pretty nice rack, wouldn't you say?"

"Very nice." She pulled her shoulders back. "Almost as nice as this one. Where'd you shoot him?"

"Smack dab in the heart. That big old boy went down before he knew what hit him. I'm as good with a gun as the Indians pitching ace, Doug Jones, is with a baseball." Duke drained his beer and started a second one. "You know he broke a record last night—had his fourteenth consecutive save."

Tina looked away.

"I know—you could care less about baseball. It never did interest you." Finishing his beer, Duke slid closer to Tina, who put her hand on Duke's upper thigh. When he wasn't looking, she unloosened another blouse button and pulled down her bra.

Though he's feeling good, he seems uptight and preoccupied. Maybe I can loosen him up with some jokes. "Gotta a question for you. How did the IUP football player die while drinking milk?"

"I haven't a clue."

"The cow fell on him! Ha! Ha!"

"That was a good one, but Jude would kill you if he heard that."

"Heck with him!" She swept her hand through her hair. "How about this one. What do you say to a Pitt football player who's dressed in a suit?"

"I don't know, but now you're picking on Pitt. I like the Panthers."

"Here's what you say. Will the defendant please wise?" She purposely slurred her speech. "I mean rise. Ha! I think that's a riot!"

Duke laughed hard and finished his beer.

"Here's one more. How many of the freshmen football players in Jude's class does it take to replace a lightbulb?"

"I have no idea."

"None. That's a sophomore-level course!"

This one struck Duke's funny bone. He laughed so hard that other people in The Inn looked in their direction.

A master at playing the enchantress role, Tina easily aroused him. *Another beer or two, and I'll have him!* She put her arms around him and snuggled closer. By design, she had, upon entering The Inn, led him to the high-backed corner booth, facing away from the others. Though they were in a public setting in broad daylight, they had a fair amount of privacy.

"Hold me, Duke. I'm so afraid. Put your arm around me." She pulled his arm upward and placed his hand on her breast. "I don't want anything to happen to these golgeous beauties. It would kill me if I'd get breast cancer too." The slurred speech worked perfectly.

"Ah, these 36-Cs! Lovely, lovely," he said, fully aroused.

She slid her hand up his thigh. "That's my man!"

While Tina was with Duke at The Inn, Abe was still at the mine, killing time until he could "accidentally" bump into Bull Chestnut in the parking lot. Jude later learned how Abe managed this perfectly timed meeting with Bull. Barry Kepple, an employee in the security camera department, gave Jude two important—and very helpful—film clips. The first clip clearly showed Abe "hanging out" (as Jude noted in his journal). Walking in the parking lot after work this particular afternoon, Abe had gone to his car, waited a bit, and then walked back inside, depositing his lunch bucket and thermos on the lounge sofa.

A second inside camera showed him waiting in the lounge as various stragglers punched the time clock.

Abe anxiously watched as people rounded the far corner on their way to the exit time clock. When Bull was in sight some distance away, Abe hurriedly exited the building again. He walked toward his car for the second time, drew near to it, and then made a gesture as though he had forgotten something. He entered the mine just as Bull was walking away from the clock.

"Hey, Smiley, what are you doing here? I thought our crew was the last one leaving."

"No, you're not. I just knocked off too. Paperwork, voluminous amounts of paperwork, for the boss. You know how it is."

"Why are you coming into the mine when we're headed out?"

"Forgot my lunch box. Wait till I get it, and I'll walk you to your car." Abe went into the lounge to pick up his lunch box and thermos. "Why are you late today?"

"Our crew just finished in room 21. We had to git some of the mushrooms to the packhouse for evening delivery—another big deadline. You bosses are always giving us these damn deadlines. Have you seen the women coming out? They are not happy campers. I thought Meg the Keg was going to have the big one."

Walking in the parking lot toward Bull's car, Abe mused on his strategy. "Bull, did you know that the Shawmut Railroad Bridge up the river made the front cover of the national *Trains* magazine back in 1855? I just saw a copy of the magazine in the Armstrong County museum the other day." *A little bit of sugar makes the medicine go down, and helps me get some venom in this clown.*

Sharing several pieces of like trivia, Abe cast himself as the innocent man of eclectic interests. *But now it's time to get down to business with Mr. Brain-Dead. Let's go!* "Did you ever do anything with the nude photos I showed you?"

"Yeah, I showed them to Duke. Didn't he tell you?"

"I haven't talked to him."

"I gave the pictures to Duke, and he found out that the picture is definitely of Jude and Cory. It's Jude's watch and sweatshirt, Cory's jewelry, and—get this—the picture was taken in Cory's bedroom."

"Come on, Bull. How could anyone possibly prove that?"

"Duke did."

"How? What did he do—stop by the Mohneys and say, 'Hey, I'm here to take a hasty look at Honey Hot Pants's hive?'"

"He was at Cory's house working on Saturday morning, and when everybody was outside, he went into the house to take a whiz. While he was in there, he thought maybe he'd dash upstairs to take a look at queenie's bedroom—you know, just a quick look-see. There was the exact furniture that was in the photograph—same bed, dresser, bedspread, pictures on the wall—the whole shebang. The nude photo was definitely taken in Hot Pants's bedroom. No doubt about it, chief."

Abe reached out and clasped Bull's shoulder. "Unbelievable!" *You are one dumbass, Bull! You remind me of what Mark Twain once said—"Never argue with stupid people. They will drag you down to their level and then beat you with experience." How true of you, but still you could prove useful!* "So you scored some points with Duke in showing him the photographs."

"Scored some points! Are you kidding? He thinks I'm a genius, and he thinks it won't be long until he's made Hot Pants, thanks to our good teamwork. Like John 'Hannibal' Smith says, 'I love it when a plan comes together!'" Bull unlocked his car door. "*The A-Team* is my favorite program. Do you watch it?"

"Yes. I admire Hannibal's smoothness. Okay, back to business. Want to hasten things along a bit?"

"Well, I guess I could help out a bud. How?"

"I have the answer right here." Standing with his back to the mine entrance, Abe nonchalantly pulled out a folded piece of paper. "Cory was writing a note during lunchtime. I didn't pay particular notice since chick notes aren't my thing. Well, when Cory walked out of the lunchroom, she folded it up and put it in her helmet. Now for the interesting part. Without her realizing it, it fell out of her helmet when she put it on. One of the girls picked up the note and glanced at it. Not being a friend of Cory—and seeing it contained some very juicy information—she gave it to me, though I'm not sure why. Guess she thought I'd find it interesting."

"What's this got to do with Duke?" Bull opened the car door. "We ain't into reading chick notes, as you call them." He tossed his lunch bucket on the seat. "Why are we talking about this? You're wasting my time, man. Give me a break. I gotta run." Bull started to get in the car.

"Slow down. This note has everything to do with Duke. Read it yourself." Abe gave the note to Bull.

Duke,

Sorry I've been giving you such a rough time of late. I was blinded a bit when Jude came on the scene, but now I realize how much I love you and want you. The nude photos are of me. I won't lie about that any longer. I want you, Duke. In that picture of me, I kept imagining that Jude standing behind me was you instead. Do you know the joy that gives me? The very idea turns me on! Can you meet me this evening? I want to share with you what I've shared with Jude. Everything.

I can't wait any longer. It's got to be tonight. I'll explain later why this is so urgent. Please don't let me down!

Your true and penitent love,
Cory

CHAPTER 3

What won Bull over was the penmanship. He knew Cory's handwriting and especially her signature—that long rolling *C* at the start of her name, which finished with the distinctive bottom loop. *This is Cory's handwriting—no doubt about it!*

"So what do I do with this, Abe?"

"Show it to Duke"—*Fast thinker!*—"and score some more points. Duke's at The Inn right now. He thought this might be the night when Cory would make her move. She was winking at him all afternoon and really came on to him in the lunchroom when Jude wasn't looking." Abe carefully folded the note. "I thought she was going to proposition him right there!"

"Who's he with at The Inn?"

"That's the problem, but you're the man to handle it. He's with the buxom broad, and you know she'll pitch a fit if Duke walks out on her. If I know Tina, she's probably hanging all over him right now. When you get to The Inn, figure out some way to get this note into Duke's hands and tell him he needs to leave immediately."

"Tina will go crazy if I try to pry him loose from her. What excuse would make him leave Miss Hot-to-Trot? What do I do—just walk up to him and say, 'Hey, Duke, come with me and watch the highlights of the Orioles game'?" Bull thought for a moment about his flippant comment. "Speaking of which, did you know that their fourteen-inning game last evening broke the record for longest game ever?"

"Stay focused, Bull. Who cares about the Orioles or even the Bucs for that matter? We have important business here. Now make up something. Tell Duke it's an emergency. Just get him out of there. As soon as he reads the note, you won't have to talk him into anything. It'll make him a bubbling caldron of hormonal ecstasy!" Deep in thought, Abe's laser eyes scanned the distant horizon. "Here's something else—make sure he digests the content. Tina might have him so drunk that he won't know what he's reading."

"Can you imagine Tina? She'll kill me."

"Who cares about Torpedo Tits? Yes, she'll be mad, but so what? She'll get over it. Hey, if you play your cards right, you'll be having the good time instead of Duke. Don't delay. Cory's wants this to be the big night since she's got the perfect excuse."

"What's the perfect excuse?"

"Jude's tied up with his grandma this evening, so Cory's free as a bird to fly where she wants. Don't blow it, cool guy."

"Okay, Abe. Duke's gonna thank you till the cows come home!" Holding the note like a flaking parchment, Bull recklessly drove to The Inn.

Abe watched him run to his car. *Poison in Bull's ear turns his brain to swill. Duke gets drunk on beer, with Cory gets his fill.* Abe haughtily smiled to himself. *I too love it when a plan comes together!*

One part of the evening scheme remained. Abe had chosen this night to make his move since Jude and his grandma had planned to be away—that all-important key to the plan's lock. *Jude had delayed seeing an aunt out in Worthington, and tonight's the night when he and Grannie Rosetta will make their visit. I overheard Jude and Cory's conversation about this at lunch: "I just can't keep putting Grandma off, babe. Thanks for understanding."*

Jude had been riding his motorbike a lot of late. At the university, he had little chance to explore the scenic rural roads, but back in Armstrong County, he often took off, Cory seated behind him, to drive the country roads with abandon like a high-plains drifter. Soon he learned them all—the Boggsville Road, the Winfield Road to Sarver, Nicholson Run, the Worthington road to Slate Lick, Sportsman, Yellow Dog, Wilson, Sistersville, Dutch Hollow, South Scenic Drive. Many had become favorites in a short time. He and Cory had even ridden his bike to work a few times.

The next part of the plan, also important but less complicated since it was straightforward and involved no human variables, centered on Jude's motorbike. Abe drove past the home of Jude's aunt in Worthington to be certain that he and his grandma were there. *Sure enough, there's Jude's car parked along Bear Street, just above the Snyder-Crissman Funeral Home. So this is Jude's evening out with Grannie! This is a high tide I must catch and ride. Shakespeare, you were so right. "There is a tide in the affairs of men Which, taken at the flood, leads on to fortune." Well, this high current serves my purpose well indeed!*

He next drove over to Jude's grandma's farmhouse, parked the car behind the shed so it wasn't visible, and looked around for Jude's motorbike, which he found parked in the shed. Abe grabbed his wrenches and, in a single minute, had accomplished his mission—loosening the front wheel.

The front wheel will wobble off on the bumpy dirt roads, no doubt about it! On smooth roads, an experienced cyclist would instantly detect the shimmy, but on dirt roads, filled with washboard bumps and pock-marked with potholes, the wobbling will be less noticeable, especially if one is driving recklessly on a do-or-die mission. Jake Atwood recently told me that the front wheel of his motorbike had fallen off when he was riding trails in the woods above the Allegheny River at Reesedale. When I asked if he had detected the shimmy in the front wheel before the accident, he said no. "When your bike is bouncing all over creation, you don't feel a shimmy, even a bad one!"

Based on that anecdote, Abe proceeded with his plan. Completing his task, he looked to make sure no one was around. *Excellent! My revenge plot inches along!*

The serpent slithered away.

Chapter 4

The whole plan was predicated on one likely move on Jude's part—his riding to Cory on the motorbike once he learned of her trouble. To Abe's way of thinking, that was probable. *When Jude hears of Cory's dilemma, he'll seek the most expeditious way of rescuing her. He'll be forced into it since time will be of the essence.*

Abe got back in his car and drove away. *So now on to the next detail in my master scheme.* Abe knew Cory was at home. Since Jude and his grandma were making visits that evening, she had indicated that she would use the evening to get caught up on house chores. Abe had overheard Jude and Cory talk on their way to their car after work. Cory's comment was especially relevant. "Now that we're fixing up the outside, it's high time for me to tackle the kitchen cupboards. You've done your part in getting the farm back to order. Now it's time for me to do mine. Those cupboards are a mess!"

Abe picked up the phone and gave Cory a ring. *She's home this evening without Jude. I'll adopt the pose of the penitential sinner tired of dallying in the fields of sin.* "Hi, Cory, this is Abe. I've been feeling awful since I turned down your invitation to go to the Strawberry Festival at the Center Hill Church." *Not really!* He paused for a moment as though overcome with emotion. "That's caused me to do some pretty serious thinking. You must be praying because I've been feeling rotten in my spirit and under tremendous conviction of late." *I'll pause again and fake a cough, as though I'm stalling for time.* He coughed and blew his nose. "Do you think Pastor Wyant would talk to an old sinner man like me?" *This will get her!* "It's high time I got a few things straightened out between me and the Man Upstairs. Do you know what I'm talking about?"

"Yes, I do know." A lilt in her voice, Cory was unable to suppress her excitement. "Of course, Pastor Gabe would talk to you, Abe. In fact, he'd be delighted!" *I can't believe it!*

"What about this evening? Can you give him a ring to see if he might want to talk to me on such short notice? I'm afraid that if I don't act while I'm in the mood, I'll get cold feet and back out as I always have in the past." *Here's the perfect line!* "That's my pattern—to slither away like a coward from the heavy things life drops in my lap."

"I understand. I'll give Pastor Gabriel a ring right now. Sit tight and I'll get back to you as soon as I can. I think he'll be able to see you since, like most pastors, he seems to specialize in short-notice interventions."

Immediately Cory called Gabe. Pastor Wyant had been lamenting the Jim Bakker scandal and the fallout for pastors. "Cory, I'm up to my eyeballs in all this distressing news, especially its negative impact on the Christian church. Talking to Mr. Badoane will give me a welcome break. Maybe I can rescue a lost sheep or at least witness to him." Pastor Gabriel looked at the open Bible on his desk. "I'll be sure to quote Psalm 37:23 to him. I've been meditating on this verse as I prepare Sunday's sermon. Here it is. 'The steps of a good man are ordered by the Lord, and He delights in His way.' Listen to this next verse. 'Though he fall, he shall not be utterly cast down; for the Lord upholds him with His hand.' Isn't that good? I'll tell Mr. Badoane that though he's fallen—like all of us—he has not been utterly cast down or, even more, cast off. I'll be in my church office. Just stop by. Good outreach, Cory. Praise God!"

"That's a wonderful thought, Pastor, truly comforting." *I hate to be Debbie Downer!* "But I would remind you that there's real deceit and wickedness in this man. Jude and I know him to be brilliant, so please don't underestimate his dark side."

"Your reference to wickedness and deceit reminds me of another verse."

"What is it?"

Gabriel Wyant leafed through the Bible on his desk. "Here it is. Psalm 36:3–4: 'The words of his mouth are wickedness and deceit. He has ceased to be wise and to do good. He devises wickedness on his bed; he sets himself in a way that is not good. He does not abhor evil.'"

"You know I'm not a judgmental person, Pastor. In fact, I hate critically minded, negative people, but that verse describes Abe Badoane perfectly. We need to be a harmless as a dove but wise as a serpent."

Cory hung up from talking to Pastor Gabriel and called Abe immediately. "He really wants to talk to you, Abe. He's heard so much about you, especially from Chuck Claypoole."

"That's great, Cory, but one thing." Abe hesitated briefly. "Are you and Jude busy this evening? I'd like for you to be present and introduce me to your pastor. You know, until I get my feet wet. You don't have to stay during my talk with the pastor." *This next point will get her.* "Actually, I'd prefer that you wouldn't be present when I bare my heart since, being such snake in the past, an audience is the last thing I need when I unpack my burdened soul." *Abe, you are good!* "What I'm trying to say is that I could use a little support for the beginning difficult moments." *What a serpent I am!* "You wouldn't believe the butterflies I have. Maybe I'm experiencing the conviction of a sinner's conscience!" *Now that phrase had a nice turn!* He paused again, faking a wave of emotion. "Do you think that's what I'm experiencing?"

"What's convicting your spirit is between you and God. I can't speak about that, but I do know the inner turmoil I feel when I've done something wrong. Unfortunately, Jude's away this evening, so he can't go, but I can join you. Will you settle for little ole me?"

"Aw shucks, I had hoped to have Jude by my side." *What a liar I am!* "We have so much in common, and he's like a son to me, but that's all right. You can at least introduce me to your pastor since you're the one who's known him for years. Oh well, maybe it's better this way. As a total stranger—I've never even met the guy—I'd feel awkward walking in on him without a friend present. It means a lot that you'll introduce us. Thanks, Cory. You'll never know how grateful I am." *And sneaky too!* "Do you want me to pick you up so we can ride together? Is that all right?"

"Perfect!"

"Good. I'll be over in a short while." *Swill that brain, for that's my gain. Your fight's in vain. Like Satan I reign!*

About the same time Abe was making the arrangement to pick up Cory, Bull was pulling into The Inn. He saw Duke seated in the back corner with Tina draped all over him, squirming voluptuously. Even at a distance, Bull knew that Duke was nearly drunk. *I bet Gorgeous has him fully aroused too. That never takes much with Duke!*

Bull walked over to them in the corner. *I hope he's at least decent! I put nothing past these animals!* "Hi, Duke. Hi, Tina. How you guys doing?" Duke flashed him a look of disgust. "Hey, Duke, look at this. I've got something you'll want to see." He waved the note in front of Duke's eyes so quickly that Tina, who had leaned forward for a quick peek, wasn't able to read the words. "Judging from the shape you're in, you'd have trouble reading it."

"Wha…you have thar?" His speech was slurred, but after a moment, he spoke again. "Can't you see I'm oc…cu…pie…busy?" He slid his hand down Tina's blouse as he reluctantly eased her off his lap and stood up, making sure his shirt was hanging out in front.

When they walked a few steps toward the door, Duke, stumbling, whispered in Bull's ear, "You better have gud reason…for dwagging me away. She hottest toy box…in world! I've never seed her on fire like this. Even in pooblic." He gently hit Bull on the arm with his fist.

Bull again waved the paper. "Get a grip!"

"What's…with freaking note…dumb arse? Lemme see." He ripped it out of Bull's hand so fast that he tore off the corner. "I ought to…dick you…deck you right now."

"I do have a good reason. Look at this. Sober up, jackass. You can't even talk right!"

At the door, Duke struggled to focus his eyes but, with Bull's help, managed to read the note.

He looked at Bull through bloodshot eyes. "Is this…joke?"

"You don't know Cory's writing, you moron? She's waiting for you to pick her up on Cheechak Road. Right now! Are you hearing me? Focus, man! Do you know what I'm saying?" Bull looked at

Duke in disgust. "Way to get yourself drunk! The biggest night of your life, and you're blowing it. You think Tina's hot? Wait till you get your hands on whory Cory."

"Slow down! What you mean...waiting? Where she waiting?" Duke struggled to comprehend Bull's news. "Why she waiting? How you know...she there? You mean now...right now?"

"She's on Cheechak Road."

"How you be so sure?"

"Because of the plan, you dimwit. Wait here. I need to get some coffee in you." Bull went to the counter to order a coffee while Duke stepped out on the porch to peruse the note again and get some fresh air.

In a moment, Bull rejoined Duke, coffee in hand. "Here. Drink this. Abe told me that he'd be on Cheechak Road and pulled off at the side of the road. He'll fake trouble with his car—a flat tire or some damn thing. You drive by and just happen to come upon Abe and Cory. They'll be on their way to church, so Abe can talk to the preacher dude—what's-his-face. Abe's going to tell you and Hot Pants to go visit Pete while he fixes the car. Ain't it a brilliant plan?"

Duke broke in, "Abe Badoane in church! The roof would fall over...fall in! I don't believe...that plan for second."

"Yeah, he is, man. That's the beauty of it. Says he wants to talk to the pastor and reform his snaky ways. Cory's riding along to introduce him to preacher man."

"Right now?"

"Yes, for the tenth time! Abe says they have a meeting set up with the pastor. They're on their way to the church. That's why you have to go." Bull held the coffee to Duke's mouth and made him take another drink. "You gotta get your behind sobered up!"

Duke sipped the coffee, brushed his hair back, and buttoned his shirt, all the while thinking about the note. "Let me read this again."

"Yes, it's Cory's writing. Quit doubting! When you see her and Abe at the side of the road, make up a story. Like you're on your way to see how Pete's doing. Abe will be doing something with the car. You give Cory a lift. Say you're going to visit Pete for fifteen minutes while Abe fixes the car."

"Yeah—that's a good excuse."

"But instead of stopping to see Pete, you can take Honey Hot Pants to Beatty's Mill. She wants this to be the big night since she's completely free. You saw her note."

"Why's she free?"

"Because of what I said. Criminently, you're being dense! I already told you. Jude and Grannie Rosetta are visiting some loser aunt in Worthington. Now don't blow it and git going! While you're gone, I'll take your place with Tina." He gestured obscenely. "I've got the ace to do it. Hear what I'm saying?"

"Any loser…could hump her!"

As Duke walked to his car, Bull yelled over his shoulder, "And hurry! This will require the work of an outstanding man. Get it? *Out* and *standing*. Ha-ha!"

Thinking he was probably running late, Duke drove fast to Cheechak Road. He had chugged several beers but was not as drunk as Bull had deduced. *I've got to get myself sobered up! Wish I hadn't drunk those last couple of beers!* As he drove along, he slugged down the coffee, combed his hair, and nervously adjusted his shirt.

Soon he neared Cory's house and saw Abe's car pulled to the side just as Bull had said. Duke got a smile on his face. *That sneaky SOB really did plan all this!* He looked in the car mirror to make sure he was presentable and put a cough drop in his mouth.

He pulled alongside Abe's car. "What's up, Abe? And what's Cory doing with you?" *You are one sexy woman!* "I just on my way to see Pete. I haven't been with him mush. Seeing him last Sarday—we did a couple jobs—put me in the move—I mean mood—to see him again." Duke knew he wasn't speaking clearly and was wise enough to slow the pace. *I have to do a better job at acting sober. Wish I had another freaking coffee!*

Later Abe wrote about the encounter in his journal:

> Duke was just sober enough to be convincing. He managed to pull it off, but his slurred speech nearly gave him away. It was his excuse that was so perfect—seeing Pete. Good-hearted Cory was

> so grateful that he was again stopping by to cheer up her dad. In *King Lear*, Shakespeare describes such an innocent, easily duped person, "Whose nature is so far from doing harms That he suspects none" in others (1.2.184–85). Well, that is so true of innocent Cory too. She can't comprehend the evil in people like Duke or me. Also, Duke's working the previous weekend on farm chores warmed Cory toward him a lot, as did his good help when she had fallen against the stack of trays in the mine. She was probably so focused on getting yours truly, the repentant old sinner, to church that she didn't look critically at Duke. She was sucked in by my subterfuge as a rainbow trout in Buffalo Creek sucks in the wormy bait. Swill the old brain—key to my gain!

Abe looked with disgust at his tire. "I have a flat tire. Look at this! Must have picked up a nail." *They don't know I leaked air out of the tire before picking up Cory—ha! Ha!* "Why don't you and Cory stop by to say hello to Pete while I fix this? I have a trunk full of junk, so I'll be a while, but that's all right, as I need the time to think about what I want to say to preacher man. I have more than a few ducks to get in order!"

"Sure you won't dant… I mean don't want me to stay? I can give you a hand."

Duke, you are such a dumbass. At least try to talk right! "No, Duke, you go along and say hi to Pete. It's nothing for me to fix a simple flat. I've done it scores of times. Give him my regards!"

I have to stop garbling my words! "What do you think I should do, Tina?" A loud cough. "I mean Cory!"

"It's nice of you to offer to help Abe, but if he really does have this under control, then you could talk with Dad for a few minutes. He'd sure like that, and you could see Zoe again. Remember how you made a fuss about our new family member last Saturday? It's up to you—stay here and help or see Dad. If you want to see him, I'll ride along."

"You go, Duke," Abe broke in. "Don't hurry. I'll need nearly a half hour to fix this. You do your deed as I'm on the way to do mine. Besides, you'll enjoy it a lot. You'll see how good a deed like that feels." *You're so drunk, Duke, that my clever double entendre went right over your head!* "When you guys return, Cory and I will go to the church. Fill him in on the details, Cory. He won't believe that sinner man has an appointment with the preacher."

"Okay. If you're sure you don't want a hand, I'll go. Cory, get in. We'll see your dad for a few minutes."

He looked at her wantonly as she entered his car. At first, she did not guess that he had been drinking or pay particular note to his ravishing eyes. The cough drop covered up the beer smell; and the drive, the coffee, and the conversation had substantially sobered him.

Duke sped past the lane into the Mohney farm instead of pulling into it.

"Hey, where are you going? I thought we were stopping to see Dad!"

"Right!" Duke stepped on the accelerator, and away they flew down the road.

What's the idiot doing? "Slow down! I had one wreck with you. I don't want another!"

CHAPTER 5

Duke was puzzled by Cory's reaction. *If she wrote the note and wants this to be our big night, why the surprise act?* "Yeah, we'll stop to see your dad in a minute." *Woman, you are confusing me!* "I wanted to take you for a spin…in car…since it's all jazzed up. You no comment…on all the changes? How about the Hooker Headers? They're hot as a real hooker. I'm hurt you didn't notice."

"Yes, your car's more beautiful than ever." Uneasy, Cory squirmed in her seat and reached for the dash to steady herself as Duke rounded a curve at high speed. "Please slow down. You're driving like a maniac."

Duke slowed the car.

"Thank you. I still have flashbacks about our wreck. *If I play along and don't panic, maybe he'll turn around and go back to my house.* "What are some of the other recent additions?"

"Look at these sexy red lights under the dash. They give the car a cozy, warm feeling and make a person want to hang out here. Abe calls it ambient lighting, whatever the hell that is. What he said exactly was, 'The ambient lighting is'"—Duke said the next words very slowly because he knew he'd be tongue-tied if he didn't—"'softly lum-in-if-er-ous…and e-voc-a-tive.' I actually looked them up to see if they're real words. Heck's fire if they ain't! Those are actual words! Why can't the freaking guy just speak English? Well, I'll say it my way—the new lighting's nice, and I like it!"

"You certainly have gone to a lot of trouble." She held the dash as they rounded another curve.

"Thanks. I think it's the new Slomaster Muffler that might be my favorite. I love the deep pretty sound it makes when it gets turned on." He looked at Cory lasciviously. "Lots of things make deep pretty sounds…when they get turned on."

She looked away. *The sex motif is everywhere—like the car freshener with the well-endowed naked beauty, which Duke spun backward when I got in the car. He thinks I didn't see him do that, but I did!* Cory also looked at the performance parts stickers which were plastered over the windows. *No surprise—more alluring women! This disappoints me since I've been working so hard to make him less carnally minded. I've often told him, "You have to get your mind out of the gutter, Duke. A healthy sexual appetite's one thing—and there's nothing wrong with it if properly controlled—but you're obsessed! You're becoming a sex addict!"*

They drove along the country roads for a short distance, and then Cory said, "Don't you think we should get back? Abe will have the flat fixed by now."

"Take it easy." By now, Duke was very perplexed. *I thought the bit about going to church with Abe was a ruse, something she said to the old man to save face. Surely, in picking her up, I did exactly what she wanted. After all, the content of her note is unmistakable. Why, then, is Madam Coy sitting over there against the door and not hanging all over me with wandering hands like tigress Tina?* He flashed a quick glance at Cory. *I guess she's starting with her religious act. The guys say she always begins that way. But why? All right, I'll be patient and play along. The greater the saint, the greater the sinner. Or ever how you say it!*

"Please slow down!"

"Relax. I just want to take you for a short spin. You need to hear the sound of the new Cherry Bomb glasspack muffler when I get on the open road. They purr like a kitty." He cast a wanton glance at her. "Just like you. They really get heated up. Just like you."

Cory crossed her legs and angrily looked straight ahead.

"Don't be mad, kitty!"

When Bull reentered The Inn, Tina confronted him. "Hey, what's up? Where's Duke? He was my date for the night! What do you mean coming in here and ripping him away from me? He was ready for action—and then some. He was at last the old Duke. Who do you think you are?"

"Sorry, sweetheart. He stood you up. Whory Cory gave him the nod. Seems Don Juan Duke is going to get it together with her this evening. Jude took his granny out to Worthington, so while they're having dessert in the living room, Duke will be having his dessert in the back seat of his '57 at Beatty's Mill. Come on, Tina, you know he's been gunning for the prize forever."

Tina slammed herself into the booth and angrily placed her elbows on the table. "That little whore!"

"Stop being so mad and face the facts."

Her chin resting on her hands, she craned her head sideways and spoke, "How's he ever going to pull that off? He couldn't touch Cory with a ten-foot pole."

"He'll take care of that!" *Wonder if she knows what I'm talking about!* "Here's the plan. Duke's going to go by Abe's 'accidentally' broken-down car on Cheechak Road and offer to pick her up. He's going to tell her that they'll pay her old man a short visit while the snake fixes his car. Once he has her in his Chevy, he'll soon have her. Get it?"

"That little slut. I hate her guts!"

Fortuitously—or "providentially," to use the language of the Center Hill folks—Blanche, one of Cory's good friends at the mine, was seated at a table in the vicinity of Bull and Tina at The Inn. Listening intently to their every word, she learned of the trap that had been laid for Cory. *Duke is planning to assault Cory without Jude nearby to protect her!* Blanche excused herself and went to the pay phone to make some calls.

A moment later, Blanche was speaking with Pete Mohney on the phone. "Is Cory there?"

"Cory went to the church with Abe Badoane."

"I see." *So Pete fell for the ruse.*

"When you called," Pete continued, "Zoe—that's our dog—came running near and sat on the floor beside me. He started whimpering in the strangest way. That was crazy! What's going on with Zoe?"

"Thank you, Mr. Mohney!"

Next, Blanche called Jude's grandma's home. No answer. By this time, fighting panic, she thought of Pastor Wyant. "Yes, Blanche," Pastor Gabriel said a moment later. "I'm waiting for them here at the church. Actually, I thought Cory and Mr. Badoane would be here by now. Cory had said they'd arrive in a few minutes."

"Well, I've got bad news. They're not coming." Blanche quickly told him of Cory's immediate danger. "Pastor Gabriel, I fear the worst."

"Did you know that Jude and his grandma are making pop calls over in Worthington this evening to see Jude's aunt?" He nervously paced the floor. "Do you have his aunt's phone number?"

"No, I don't."

He gave her the number. "You'll call her then?"

"Whatever you prefer, sir."

"I do prefer that so I can go to prayer. Thank you very much."

Blanche called the aunt immediately. "Jude and Rosetta left my house some time ago," Aunt Jacquie explained. "Rosetta wasn't feeling so perky, so they went home. They've decided to come back some other evening."

Blanche again called Jude at the farm, and this time, she reached him. *Praise God, he answered!* "Jude, this is Blanche. I'm one of Cory's friends at the mine." A pause. "Good. I thought you'd remember me. Listen carefully. I have something very important to tell you. I'm at The Inn having dinner with some of my friends." She faced away from the dining area and lowered her voice. "We're seated near Bull and Tina. Well, I overheard Bull tell Tina that Duke plans to seduce Cory this evening at Beatty's Mill. They could even be there by now. Duke was drinking a lot, so I know Cory's in trouble. Hurry, Jude! You don't have a second to spare!"

CHAPTER 6

Numerous questions immediately went through Jude's mind. *How can Cory be with Duke? She'd never consent to this! Did Duke abduct her? Such a stupid act is unlikely even for animal man! Unless he's back on the booze.*

Either way, Jude knew he had to leave for Beatty's Mill immediately, but he also realized that the winding road to the stream encompassed several curvy miles which took an agonizingly long time to traverse. *A short but rough bike trail runs through the woods and connects the two dirt roads I'll be traveling—the Worthington/Slate Lick Road and the Beatty's Mill Road. If I turn off the first one and dash cross-country on the dirt path to the lower one, I can shave off several precious miles. And many crucial minutes!*

Only one detail worked against Jude's hastily devised plan. *The guys tell me that the rough shortcut trail down the hillside hasn't been used much in recent years and is barely passable.* He remembered Ray's comment at lunch one day: "The teenage boys are now older and don't use the bike trail as they did when they were younger. That would be a hazardous run. I wouldn't risk it!"

All this went through Jude's mind in a flash. He donned his helmet while racing for the bike in the shed. Seconds later, he sped off in a whir. During the first few miles, the wheel wobbled only slightly since the nut on the bolt had not worked loose. Had Jude possessed his normally calm mind, he most likely would have noticed the slight shimmy. He sped along at breakneck speed, adrenaline flowing and caution thrown to the wind. *My beloved Cory's in real danger, and nothing else matters, not even my own safety!*

Meanwhile, as Duke neared Beatty's Mill, he said he wanted to take a walk. "Let's park the car and go down the bank to see if we spot any trout."

"Duke, let's go. Abe will surely be done with the car by now. I don't want to keep him or Pastor Gabe waiting. Pastor was kind enough to arrange his busy schedule to see us. I don't want to disappoint him."

"In a minute."

"Please, let's go. Why are we taking so long to get back? You're acting so strange. Why do you keep looking at me that way?" She adjusted the gap in her shirt to make sure her bra couldn't be seen. *Why's he staring at me so much? He's driving me crazy!*

"As soon as I check to see if they've stocked the stream, we'll leave." *Wonder if the pitched tents will still be there? That's where I can enjoy Madam Hard-to-Get! I've seen the photos. She is one hot babe!*

Once out of the car, Cory felt less trapped. *The evening air might sober him and bring him to his senses. I didn't realize it at first, but I know he's been drinking.* She picked her steps carefully along the dirt path leading to the stream. *His head might clear, and that will improve my chances of appealing to his previously reformed moral sense. Also, if Duke tries anything while I'm out of the car, I can flag a passing motorist or maybe run away. Better to be free by a stream than trapped in a car!*

Young boys, Huck Finn and Tom Sawyer-style, had pitched tents farther down the creek in a wooded area, which back in the summer had been the setting for endless exploits and carefree fun. Ashes from campfires and crudely sharpened sticks, used for roasting hotdogs and marshmallows, were scattered around a firepit and testified to the good times which had been shared by people of all ages along the slowly meandering stream. Cory had no way of knowing that Duke's ulterior motive was to use one of the tents for his own style of amusement.

However, no tents were pitched this evening. *No matter*, Duke thought. *My '57 has been the setting for lots of good times in the past. It'll work just fine!*

To this point, Duke's conduct, from Cory's point of view, had been in the main civil and rational. *Except, of course, for the sexual innuendoes and wanton glances, but that's Duke and more or less par for the course. But I don't understand his motive in bringing me to Beatty's Mill, and his serious lapse in judgment in reverting to drink earlier in the evening is terribly disappointing to me.* She saw a dead fish along the stream and thought of Frans Snyders's painting *Fish Stall*, which hangs in the Stage Hermitage in St. Petersburg. *This decaying fish on the ground reminds me of the fish in Snyders's painting—white-bellied, lifeless, ghastly. I have that painting in one of my art books.* She again looked at Duke walking in front of her. *Though he's stumbled a couple times, he isn't staggering like a drunk, but it's his spirit which is decaying and white-bellied and ghastly! Still his small talk about Dad and Zoe seemed sincere enough and his desire to see them perfectly natural. Is it possible that two conflicting spirits, which I see in Duke right now, can coexist in the same fevered brain? I have no recourse but to rely on that Christian mind-set of the ages—be wise as a serpent but harmless as a dove.*

She was relieved when Duke spoke, "Well, we better get back to Abe so you can make your church visit."

"Thank you. I don't want to keep Pastor and Abe waiting."

They finished their climb up the hill and were getting in the car when, all of a sudden, Duke said, "Wait. Before we take off, look in the back seat. You haven't seen the new seat and carpet. I'd like your opinion."

Cory knit her brow, unable to suppress her frustration. "Come on, Duke. We have to go! I don't want to miss this chance to have Abe see Pastor Gabe, nor have you seen Dad for the couple minutes you promised. You said we'd go!" Her face was flushed, her tone angry.

"I'm not leaving till you see my handiwork."

He had already taken his place in the driver's seat and fastened the seat belt—at least that's what she thought when she heard the click of the metal belt clasp. To keep from prolonging the ordeal, she reluctantly agreed. *I might as well go along with him. This doesn't seem too suspicious.* "Just a fast glance and then you promise to go, right?"

"Scout's honor!"

She opened the back door and bent over to take a brief look. *I'll take a fast peek at the seat and carpet.* "It's very nice."

"Touch the floor," Duke said, "and see how soft it is. I put in the new fancy plush carpet." When she bent over to touch the floor, he came up behind her and, like a flash, pushed his body firmly down on hers. When she collapsed on the seat, he fell on top of her, gyrating and rocking his hips and feeling her breasts. "So soft, kitty—so very soft!"

Cory squirmed to free herself, but the more she wiggled under him, the more she aroused Duke. She screamed hysterically, "Duke, what are you doing? Get off me right now, you animal!" *What's he going to do?*

Locking the back door on her side so she couldn't open it and run, he bodily lifted her up and sat her on the seat and then crawled in and sat tightly against her. Duke put his right arm around her shoulder and placed his left hand on her upper thigh. He looked directly at her, the cough drop no longer disguising the scent of beer on his breath. "Come on, Cory. I'm tired of your games. Let's bypass the…pious act and get down to business. I've seen the lovely proof, and I know a woman's handwriting when I see it."

"What in the world are you talking about? What proof?" She jerked his hand from her thigh. "Get your hand off me!"

Her resistance increased his lust, as did the fragrance of her perfume and the agitated squirming of her body. When he began to try to touch her, she firmly pushed him away and slid against the door. He tried to kiss and fondle her, but she turned from him and huddled tightly into the corner of the seat, her feet and thighs pulled against her chest, her eyes tightly shut. Duke backed away from her.

Praise God, he slid away from me! Has he come to his senses, and is he going to stop being an animal? Are we going to go now? She opened her eyes and looked at him. He rose up and rested his right knee on the seat and his left foot on the floor and then pulled off his T-shirt.

His huge arms and shoulders are rippled with muscles! What's he going to do?

He unbuckled his belt and pulled down the zipper of his jeans, paused, and said, "I've seen your goods. It's time for you to see mine. Take off your blouse. It won't be just a quick feel this time."

"No!" she screamed. "Quit acting like an animal! What's gotten into you? Duke, you're scaring me! You know I'm a virgin, and I'm going to stay that way!"

"Virgin? I don't believe that fairy tale for a second! You call me animal, eh? You want to see what an animal with equipment like this can do?"

He put his hands in her blouse and violently pulled them outward, ripping off all the buttons and instantly exposing the deep cleavage of her breasts. "Very nice. Exactly as I thought. Ready for some pole-vaulting? I'll happily supply the pole!"

He pulled his jeans down to his knees.

CHAPTER 7

By this time, Jude had left the main road and headed down the mountain trail that linked the two roads. Although the pronounced wobbling of the wheel had worsened, he attributed the increased jerkiness of the ride and the difficulty of keeping the bike upright to the reckless speed on the bumpy terrain. He spoke of the experience in his journal:

> I was flying down the hill and concentrating so hard on keeping the bike on the trail and away from trees that I never considered the fact that the wobbling was caused by the loose wheel instead of this mountainous obstacle course. Needless to say, in panic mode the whole time, I wasn't thinking rationally!

Nearer the bottom of the forest trail, the violent shaking of the wheel was more severe as the bike careened from side to side across deep ruts, rocks, and fallen branches. Although the nut had wobbled loose from the bolt, the wheel was still temporarily attached to the bike. *I can barely keep my bike upright, but once I jump the stream, I'll be in the smooth grass on the other side. Then this infernal wobbling will stop!*

Back at the church, Pastor Gabriel had activated the prayer chain. Never one to perpetuate rumor, he had heard his clergymen colleagues hint that prayer chains had, on rare occasion, degenerated into gossip grapevines. *That will never happen in my church!* Though the prayer request for Cory was clearly urgent, he kept the details to a minimum. "I lack all the facts," he explained to the first person on the prayer chain. "But I know that her need for immediate prayer is real. Apparently, she's been abducted by a man crazed with lust. Please pray for dear Cory. She definitely needs it." Many of these western Pennsylvania people, believing firmly in the power of prayer, bowed their heads or fell to their knees moments later.

This transcendent dimension of Duke's abduction was manifest in another unusual way to Pete. *Zoe has been behaving very strangely ever since Cory went out the door. He's so anxious!* A while later, Zoe began a strange barking fit. In hearing this commotion, Pete kept looking to see if someone was driving up the lane. *There's no other plausible explanation. What's agitating him so much?* After the revelation in Pittsburgh many weeks later, they at last understood Zoe's unusual behavior.

But that was future, and now was very now. Especially at Beatty's Mill.

In the back seat of his car, Duke stared at Cory's heaving breasts, which she had covered with her arms. He grabbed her arms at the elbow and savagely pinned them to the sides of her head, thrusting out her upper torso and exposing her more fully. "You bunny! Where are the *Playboy* photographers when they're needed?"

"Please stop, Duke, you're hurting me!" she began to scream loudly, thinking that the nearby motorcyclist might hear. *Might it possibly be Jude? Please, Lord, let it be!*

At the bottom of the hill near the edge of the stream, Jude aimed his bike at the center of a mounded ramp which daredevil boys had built years earlier to clear the narrow eight- to ten-foot stream. His original plan had been to ride the bike down the trail, jump the stream, and speed up the bank and along the road to Duke's car. Jude hit the mound dead center—a direct hit—but the smashing impact of the wheel against the ramp jarred the wheel completely off the bike. Seeing the wheel detach in midflight over the stream, Jude acted instantaneously and vaulted over the handlebars to avoid falling on the cartwheeling bike. Temporarily dazed, he crashed to the ground in the tallgrass a few feet beyond the bike!

Back at the car, Duke had put his hands on his underwear to take them down when Cory, screaming in her huddled seat in the corner, gave him a savage kick to the groin—another direct hit. Doubling over in pain, he howled in primordial rage and fell facedown into the seat. "You rotten bitch!"

Jarred to his senses by the repeated screams, Jude struggled to his feet, regained his balance, and made a mad dash up the hill. *At least the car's only a short distance away, but will I make it in time?*

When Duke raised himself up, he cupped his groin with his left hand and, towering over her, gave Cory a crushing blow with his opened right hand. She saw it coming and quickly jerked back and upward, causing the blow to catch her lower jaw and throat instead of the side of her face as he intended. She hit the window with such force that she was immediately knocked unconscious.

Duke hurriedly pulled down her jeans and panties and started to mount her just as Jude, breathless, arrived at the car. He grabbed Duke's legs and violently jerked him out of the car. Duke fell facedown on the ground as Jude collapsed backward on to Duke's legs. His position advantageous, Jude scampered to his feet first, fell on Duke's back, and got him in an all-or-nothing headlock. To keep from having Duke land one of those lethal fists, Jude body-hugged him viciously. *This is my only chance to survive a brawl with this hulking madman*!

"Get off me, you bastard! Let me up or I'll kill you!"

Though Jude was clinging tightly to Duke's back, Duke, by brute strength, heaved both of them to their feet. When he tried to swivel around to shake Jude off and regain a secure stance, Duke lost his footing in the tangled jeans at his calves. Keeping his arms tightly wrapped in a death-grip headlock, Jude rode him around in an awkward wrestler's pirouette. In his falling downward twist, Duke violently crashed his head into the back fender. Temporarily dazed, he fell to the ground with a thud.

Seeing his chance for escape, Jude instantly jumped into the car and started the engine. *This is my only chance! I've got to get away right now!*

CHAPTER 8

"Cory!" Jude yelled as he turned his head backward. "Are you all right?" No response. *Come on, keys! Turn!*

With his jeans still snarled around his legs, Duke struggled to his feet and tried to run the few steps to the door but tripped just as his outstretched hand firmly grasped the driver's door handle. "Stop right now, or I'll kill you!"

Like a driver at the starting line of the Indy 500, Jude sped away, dragging Duke some thirty feet through the loose roadside gravel. When he let go of the handle, Duke somersaulted in several rapid-fire rolls and violently slammed into a tree. The spinning wheels of the '57 shot a cloud of spraying dirt, grass, and gravel into his mouth and eyes. Jumping to his feet and screaming like a maniac, Duke watched as Jude squealed the tires and raced up the road.

Duke again faced the wild cherry tree, coiled his left hand into a massive fist, and sledge-hammered the tree with a vicious swing, the jagged bark knifing into flesh, blood, and bone. Wiping dirt from his eyes with his right hand and spitting out gravel, he screamed hysterically, "I'll kill you, Hepler! I swear I'll kill you!"

His hands trembling so much that he could barely grasp the wheel, Jude drove at a perilous speed for a half mile and stopped the car at the side of the dirt road. *My hands have never shaken like this my entire life!*

Seminaked and sprawled on the back seat, Cory lay facing downward on the seat with her head jammed against the door, awkwardly tilted toward the front. With her left leg bent at the knee, her hip was lifted slightly off the car seat. *She's completely unresponsive no matter how much I yell and try to rouse her!* "Please come to, Cory! Regain consciousness, my love!" Then a groan. *She's stirring! Maybe she's coming to!* "Cory, can you hear me?" *I shouldn't shake her in case she injured her spine or neck, so I have no recourse but to gently touch her.*

Jude looked into her face. *She seems all right except for a red mark on her chin and throat where Duke's open hand struck her.* Continuing to examine her injury, he stole a glance at her body. *Her jeans are down to her ankles, and though she must have been unconscious when Duke tugged at her panties, she had continued to clutch them tightly with her right hand. Her left hand had probably gone up to defend her face against the coming blow. Yes, I think that's what happened. Though unconscious, she continued to cling tightly to her panties with her right hand. That's why they remain in place at the right and pulled down on the left, leaving them on a diagonal and completely exposing her raised left hip.*

Jude wrote at length of this moment in his journal:

> I felt like a voyeur as I looked at the whitest flesh I had ever seen in my life—silky, smooth, perfectly rounded, and shining in the sunlight as though illuminated by a strobe light. The phrase 'the magnificent grandeur of statuesque perfection,' which I had recently come across in one of my art books on ancient Greco-Roman statuary, flashed in my mind. Her forbidden beauty made me gasp. I couldn't breathe! I had never seen anything so stunningly beautiful in my life.
>
> I thought to myself, *Cory, I want to gently glide my hand along your ivory-smooth hip and caress that Scopas-like beautiful perfection, but I know that would be wrong, since it would be taking advantage of you in your compromised state. But, my love, how beautiful you are! Forgive me that thought as you lie there in distress, but I am, after all, a man. How in awe I am! How I want you!*

Like a baby at sleep, her face was angelically peaceful. When I lowered my eyes to her body again, I was, for a brief moment, crazily reminded of the time years before when I examined Michelangelo's sketches in the Ashmolean Museum in Oxford, England, the world's largest collection of original drawings by the Italian genius. Given special permission to study these priceless Sistine Chapel ceiling sketches, I had experienced a kind of catharsis as I pored over them. The verger—or maybe he was a librarian of some sort—stood by me and carefully monitored my handling of the drawings to make sure I observed all the decorum intricacies.

The verger had been momentarily called to the door by a colleague. With these men behind me and my body hovering over the sketches at my breast, I surreptitiously glided my hand softly across the blank white surface of one of the drawings. I couldn't believe I was touching something so precious, so beautiful, so forbidden. *Michelangelo's hand rested right here! On this spot! I am touching what he touched!* Though it lasted for a split second, the experience had hit me with tremendous force. *I am at one with Michelangelo as my hand glides over this utterly forbidden white expanse!*

I roused myself from my fleeting memory and looked again at the naked beauty in front of me, that other forbidden, even more lovely white expanse of insanely gorgeous flesh. I gently and slowly reached my hand toward her hip. I paused. *Touching her erotically would be very wrong. Surely, I can refrain from adulterating our love with lustful fondling.* Though aroused even amid the trauma, I drew my hand back and simultaneously thought of the time when Cory referred to Ophelia's song in *Hamlet*: "Before you tumbled me, You promised me to wed!" Well, you haven't been tumbled, and you'll be the chaste maid on your wedding day!

Then jolted to reality, I remembered our circumstances. *My beloved Cory's in danger and desperately needs help, but I can't take a beautiful woman into the emergency room with her panties down! Flailing tongues would grind that juicy tidbit in the gossip mill for months!*

I had no choice and, deep down, was happy that was the case. I had to dress Cory and get her to the ER immediately. I pulled her jeans up her legs and allowed my hand to approach the side of her naked hip—porcelain smooth, whiter than sun-blanched snow, but warmer than Zoe's sun-heated back. I was again in the Ashmolean Museum touching the priceless and forbidden white space. Gently, softly, clandestinely, my feather-light hand slid down the side of her hip. With my eyes closed, I grasped the top of her panties and—flower-soft—began to slowly pull them up. Gently, tenderly, caressingly.

As I did so, I glanced almost accidentally through the back window. Madly running toward us at breakneck speed, Duke was only seventy-five feet away!

CHAPTER 9

Jude leaped back into the driver's seat and, for a second time, rocketed down the road. *In the rear-view mirror, I can see Duke's enraged face, flared nostrils, engorged carotid arteries. What an animal! He's completely winded from the long sprint, his eyes narrowed to death-survival slits. That face reminds me of the journal entry I made the first time I saw him by Cory in the mine: "Three jagged slits chiseled in granite." Exactly—except I should have said "hacked in granite"!*

Duke screamed hysterically as Jude raced away in a cloud of dust. "Damn you! Stop! Come back here!" Though by now fifty feet away, Jude beheld the primordial rage as though it were inches from his face. He sped away and drove the car down the road a couple miles and stopped at a secluded spot where he finished dressing Cory. She was now fully clothed, as he noted in his journal:

> My integrity—and Cory's honor—remained intact. But my hands trembled violently. Both Cory and I had tangled with real evil and barely escaped. Back at the wheel, I drove along, but the image of Duke's monster face—three jagged slits hacked in granite—was never once out of mind. I've never seen hatred like that before—inhuman, Neanderthal, nauseously hideous. As often as possible, I looked back at my dear Cory. "I love you, honey. Please be all right. Lord, help her to repress this awful experience."

Jude raced immediately to the Armstrong County Memorial Hospital where he pulled into the ER lot. Once parked, he sprinted to the triage nurse to explain that he had a woman in his car who had been struck unconscious by a vicious blow to the face. A group of nurses and paramedics immediately sprang into action and, moments later, wheeled Cory into the ER.

Cory slowly regained consciousness. The right side of her face, which had hit the window, had by now developed swelling and bruising that was as bad as the throat and chin area. Assessing the viciousness of the hit, the doctor instructed her not to move.

When they carted Cory away for x-rays, Jude stepped to the nurses' station to make two fast phone calls, one to Pete Mohney and the other to Pastor Gabriel. "We're waiting for results from the x-rays," Jude explained to Pete. "The doctor doesn't seem to be too concerned." *I'll minimize the blow for Pete's benefit.* "The big thing is the shock to her system. She's conscious but not responsive. To this point, we see only superficial injuries, mainly the bruise to her throat and the side of her face."

"How did they end up at Beatty's Mill? I thought Abe and Cory were headed for the church." Pacing the darkened den of the farmhouse, Pete struggled to comprehend the words that Jude had fired into his brain. "You say Duke did this to my Cory? Surely you don't mean Duke. Not Duke Manningham. Why, the man's been like a son to me!"

"Yes, he did. Going to church with Abe was the plan, but it seems Duke had a severe lapse in moral judgment. I'm trying to break this to you gently, Pete. But you need to know the truth." *Okay, Pete, here goes.* "He tried to rape Cory. I got there in the nick of time!"

"I can't believe it! He's been another son…here on the farm. He really helped Joey and me a lot." Pete stifled a sob and paused to get his emotions under control. "Why? Why would he do this to Cory? He never laid a hand on her." Pete threaded his fingers through his hair and shifted legs. "I asked her lots of times if he was a gentleman around her…well, because a person hears things."

"There are a lot of unanswered questions. When I have some details, I'll be in touch. I'm letting you know about this in case you want to come and see her."

Although the x-ray revealed no serious bone or neck injury, the doctor nevertheless had two real concerns: Cory's listlessness and the severity of her headache. "The swelling to the side of her face and her throat and chin area are superficial. That's not a real cause for alarm. But the severe headache and continued unresponsiveness, on the other hand, are different matters. Right now, those are my main concerns."

The ER doctor tried to get Cory to speak, but when she remained silent, he determined that she was likely in shock. He also wondered, after further examination, if the swelling might affect her speech. "That too might be a problem."

Jude immediately responded, "Do you think there could be possible internal damage to the throat and vocal chords? That would be awful. Cory's a beautiful singer."

"We won't know until we see the results of further tests. I will let you know that later. As I say, what concerns me now is her lack of response." The doctor bit his lip in thought. "I have no other choice but to admit her for observation."

While the hospital personnel made preparations for her admission, Jude was temporarily alone with Cory in the ER bay. "I love you, sweetheart." He brushed the hair from the nonswollen side of her face and gently slid his fingers across her hands and forehead. He bent over to kiss her. "Cory, I love you. Please be all right!"

He looked down at her waist and thighs and could not resist the passing thought of the loveliness he had seen there a half hour earlier. *That beautiful flesh right there under her denim jeans. I touched it—stove-warm, porcelain-smooth, and lightning-bolt white!*

Once up in her room on the third floor, Jude took a seat at the side of Cory's bed. When the nurses asked Jude to step out of the room so that they could tend to Cory, he walked to the corner lounge at the end of the hall.

From the lounge, he looked across the vale and was surprised to see in the distance the domed knoll of Center Hill. *There it is, the hill at the middle of our beloved Center Hill village. How often have we walked across it!* He scanned the horizon. *Over there on the faraway ridge to the left is our beloved Vinlindeer, the ridge above the farms which offers the view over the valley—that ridge which has been the scene of our countless hours together, that ridge where I have held and passionately kissed the most beautiful woman on the face of the earth. Cory, please be all right. God, please heal her!* He brushed a tear from his cheek. *How did we get ourselves into this mess? What's our exit strategy? I'm totally confused!*

Walking back to Cory's room, he thought again of the seriousness of their situation. *I'm not even sure there is a way out!*

CHAPTER 10

The next morning before they entered the building to punch the mine time clock, Abe Badoane clustered in the parking lot with a couple of Duke's friends: Bull Chestnut, Smitty Reeves, Al Bates, Hank Jamison, Blassie Grafton, Skeeter Dowling, and Huddy Weaver. On this particular morning, the men were talking about their wives and girlfriends.

"One thing is certain," Skeeter continued. "No one will ever pull the wool over my wife's eyes. She is one sharp babe."

"You think she's sharp? Listen to this," Huddy replied. "Here's what I've found out. If we're in an argument, and my girlfriend begins by saying 'first of all,' I've learned that I have one option—run for the hills!" The guys laughed. "She's about to resort to her research, gathered data, and flip charts, and I'm on the verge of total destruction!"

"Ha! Ha!" Good-natured laughing could be heard across the parking lot.

This discussion could prove useful! "Speaking of altercations with the fair sex," Abe rejoined, "what about Duke's incident at Beatty's Mill last evening?"

A couple of the men had heard about it while several others had not.

"Here's what happened," Abe began. "I was pretending to repair my car along the road to Cory's house when Duke, according to our little plan, came along and took Cory with him."

"How'd she end up with Duke?" Hank asked, puffing on his cigarette. "You said earlier that she was supposed to be going with you to church."

"Because she thought I was fixing a flat, and Duke said he'd take her to her house for a quick visit with Pete while I changed the tire. He gets along well with Pete Mohney. That's the one part of the story that's true. The rest of it was a setup—every single, clever, wonderful detail."

Smitty corroborated the story. "I saw Duke late last evening too. Get this. He called me from a farmer's house near Beatty's Mill. I had to drive the whole way down there and pick him up so he didn't have to walk home. On the way back, we stopped at The Inn for a drink. He was holding his left hand, which was already starting to swell. I wouldn't be surprised if he broke a bone in it." Smitty paused to take another drag on his cigarette. "I'm telling you the guy was mad as a hornet. He swore nonstop the whole way to The Inn. But he wouldn't go to the hospital to have it checked. 'Hell no! Just get me a beer!' You can hear wild man say it."

"I don't know much about that part," Abe continued. "What I do know is that Duke was trying to get it on with Cory at Beatty's Mill. The college professor arrived just in the nick of time. They tussled and—can you believe it?—Jude made our champ a chump. Yes, my boys, Duke the stud was made a fluke and dud! That's only half of it. I heard from Carla, a nurse friend of mine who was with Cory in the hospital, that Cory is pretty badly beaten up."

"How'd that happen?" Skeeter interrupted.

"Duke slugged her!" Abe resumed. "That's how! Well, Jude's an enraged animal because of it. Carla overheard Jude say that he was going to do something to get back at Duke. She quoted Jude. 'Duke will pay for this!'"

In his usual fashion, Abe studied the faces of the men to carefully note their reactions. "If Jude had had a gun with him, I think he'd have shot Duke right there at Beatty's Mill. Carla says she's never seen a man hotter under the collar than Jude." Abe again stopped to observe the body language of the men. *With a few deft words, I can work this conversation to my decided benefit. Words in the ear are like poison in the cup. They will slowly swill their brains and gobble all sense up! Okay, kiddies, here comes your next gulp of poison.* "Wonder what he plans to do to get back at Duke?"

"Jude might be mad as the dickens at Duke," Al Bates interspersed. "But don't think for a moment that wild man's not just as mad. Jude really humiliated him, and now Duke's got to deal with all the razzing. You should have heard the women at the Inn last night when word got out about why Duke's face was scraped, his head swollen, his shirt torn, and his hand bandaged. You know the gossip train!"

"Yeah, I know about that!" Blassie broke in. He addressed Al and Smitty. "You guys weren't at The Inn, so I'll tell you how the women hard-assed him." He mimicked a female voice. "'Duke, I thought you were the tough guy in the mine! You got beat up by a wimpy college prof—ha!' And then Meg the Keg chimed in, 'With that goose egg on your head, you gotta a real reason for being called *egghead*!'"

"You should have heard Bingey Platt," Hank broke in. 'Hey, Romeo, Jude's been in Cory's pants. Why haven't you?' I'm telling you, everybody in the whole joint was laughing their heads off at poor Duke. I thought he was going to bust up the place!"

As he stood there with the men in the parking lot, Abe knew that he had only a few minutes to further work the conversation to his advantage. *Clearly, the next part of my master plan centers on Jude's revenge on Duke. That act, whatever form it takes, will provide the impetus for Duke to get back at Jude once and for all. The important thing this morning is to get the men to focus on Jude's wrath instead of Duke's. Okay, boys and girls, it's time to center this discussion on Jude's revenge. Yes, Mr. Shakespeare, revenge should have no bounds!*

"Yes, I know Duke's pride is hurt," Abe began. "But that's a transient emotion. You don't think that Jude's wrath is far greater? Let me educate you." *Okay, guys and dolls, time for another giant gulp of poison. You won't be capable of refuting the hard logic—yes, the venomous poison—I'm about to pour into your gullible ears!* "You're forgetting the central defining fact—Duke tried to rape Cory. Can you imagine what went through Jude's mind when he saw Duke on top of her, trying to deflower his darling? Carla overheard Jude's ranting and raving and is convinced that he's planning some form of retaliation." *I'm winning! They're caving already!* "Duke's pride is hurt—I grant you that—but Jude's Cory is hurt worse, far worse. Which kind of anger most often leads to revenge? Gentleman, allow your erudite colleague to educate you about the fundamentals of revenge psychology. Duke will cool down in a day or two when he realizes that it was wrong to try to rape Cory. In fact, he'll even feel remorse for what he did to a very good woman. On the other hand, Jude will get madder by the day. Don't underestimate his anger. Because his beloved was seriously threatened, he'll do something to get back at Duke." *I can taste victory! They're getting sucked in and dropping like flies!* "Cory's face looks like Robin Givens's face."

"Just who is Robin Givens?" Bingey interrupted.

"Mike Tyson's wife," Abe patiently replied. "Tyson recently beat the crap out of her. I saw a picture of her on TV the other evening. He must have really slugged her. All right, back to our situation. I don't have a clue as to the form of Jude's retaliation. You gents can be the ones to spot it, but keep an eye out for it, and do let me know if you suspect anything." He checked his watch. "Good soldiers, once more to the breach. It's time to deflower some mushrooms!"

"Yeah," Hank quipped. "Bet we'll do better at deflowering mushrooms than Duke did Cory!"

CHAPTER 11

When the men went as a group to the mine entrance, Abe motioned to Bull Chestnut and pulled him apart from the others. They lagged behind as they walked across the parking lot.

"What's going on?" Bull asked.

"Interested in making some extra cash?" Abe waved a couple brand new $100 bills in front of Bull.

"What'd you have in mind, sneaky snake?"

"I said, are you interested in making a couple hundred bucks for a single minute's work?"

"Lay it on me, big guy."

As they strolled toward the entrance, Abe draped his arm around Bull's shoulder. *I'll start with some small talk.* He chatted first about current events, starting with the terrorist bomb that took down the Pan Am jet in Lockerbie, Scotland. "Now there's Hurricane Gilbert's damage in Jamaica. It ripped the place apart." *Enough on that. Now, stooge, we come to brass tacks!* In the parking lot, Abe gave Bull the details of his part of the plan and concluded their conversation when they arrived at the mine entrance a few moments later. "I'll give you the rest of the details later, but that's all you need to know for now. Remember what I said—not a word to anyone. The plan is perfect. I've thought through every detail."

Bull looked again at the money. "I promise. I'd love to blow the rear end out of these beaucoup bucks! I screw up a lot but won't blow this!"

Before entering the building, Abe looked around at the placement of the security cameras in the parking lot and mine entrance.

I wonder if there are any uncovered areas. That's an important detail I need to check. Yes, that could be the lynchpin.

When a number of the workers gathered to drop their lunch boxes in the lunchroom at the start of their work day, several of the women approached Duke.

"Hey, mighty one, I saw you coming out of the men's locker room earlier. How's come you put your helmet on so gently?"

"Marge, did you see the back of Duke's car? There's a dent in the back fender. What in the world caused that?"

"Duke, my uncle's starting boxing classes at the YMCA next week. Maybe you ought to sign up and learn a few pointers for your second round with Jude."

On and on they joked with Duke. Most of it was good-natured fun, though a couple of the women, laying for Duke, dipped their sarcasm in venom. He laughed off their ribbing the best he could but, deep down, was boiling. He coiled his right hand into a massive fist.

By now the reasons for his anger were twofold. *I can't believe Jude beat me in our quick fight. I just couldn't shake off the wimpy college prof. That hurts the ole ego!* But he knew the scuffle was a fluke. *In a legitimate fight, Jude doesn't have a chance.* He looked at his coiled fist. *One blow with this right hand, and—like Big Bad John—I'd send him to the promised land!*

But the other matter that really angered Duke was the morass with Cory. *What's going on? I'm convinced that, before Jude happened on the scene, she wanted to be with me. I think she wants me in that other way too. I saw that look in her face when she saw me in my underwear at Beatty's Mill. It's a real woman who gazes like that! And I've also seen the photos and the note. So why then is she playing coy? We had such a perfect setup at Beatty's Mill—right location, right timing. I just don't get it!*

Nevertheless, there was no denying that her anger and hurt the previous evening in the car were real. *When we were parked by the stream, she was the pure and good Cory I've always known. Does this mean that the photographs and the note, despite their seeming authen-*

ticity, are bogus? There's no other explanation, but if they're counterfeit, then like the dumbass I am, I assaulted the loveliest woman on the face of this green earth. Why did I do that? Because I'm a screwed-up mess!

Soon Duke's guilt started to equal the anger. *Who produced the photographs and notes with such cunning? Did someone make a clever trap that I fell into? Who's playing with my brain, and how could I be so dumb to get sucked in like this?* The longer Duke stewed on these events, the more his blood boiled.

Meanwhile, walking hurriedly out of the lunchroom, Abe nearly collided with Morley Spencer, one of the men who worked with the security system, including the video cameras positioned throughout the mines.

"Hello, Morley, how are you? I've wanted to talk to you for a few days and hoped I'd bump into you. But not literally as we almost did!"

"Hi, Abe. See me about what?"

"About the new security system that's been installed. You know my love of technical things—electronics, photography, and such gadgetry. All of it intrigues me." *He's another stooge I'll suck in completely!* "I take it that the new security precautions are cutting-edge modern?"

"Yes, they are, and speaking of modern, did you know Microsoft just released its MS DOS 4.0? I think that's amazing. Well, our new system is pretty high-tech too. There's no denying it. If you want to take a peek, stop by my office someday. Either Barry or I can give you a quick overview." Morley checked his pocket calendar. "In fact, my afternoon's slow. Got anything going on today?"

"No, just routine stuff, but I can spring free a few minutes. Are you sure this would suit? I don't want to put you out."

"Today's good, Abe."

"I'll only take a few minutes of your time. Thanks, Morley. I really appreciate this. I'll likely call you this afternoon." He started to walk away. "Oh, I just thought of a joke I meant to tell you. I remember how you said at lunch one day that you play computer chess."

"I do. I love it."

"I found this quote by an Emo Philips. He said, 'A computer once beat me at chess, but it was no match for me at kickboxing!'"

Morley laughed. "Good one!"

"Okay. I'll likely give you a ring this afternoon." *Another move in chess. Why bless when I can mess!*

CHAPTER 12

A short while before these events transpired at the mine, Jude, granted special permission to clock in an hour late, stopped to visit Cory at the hospital on his way to work. While in Cory's room, Dr. Buck swung by on his morning rounds. Cory's night in the hospital, Jude learned, had not been good since her headache had intensified. By morning, the fierce pain had become a real concern to Dr. Buck.

Out in the hall moments later, the doctor discussed Cory's condition with Jude. While he was very sorry to see Cory uncomfortable with her headache, Dr. Buck was pleased that the report on her throat was good. "The neck and throat injury don't alarm me. That will most likely heal in a few days, during which time Cory will likely have a raspy voice. She also said that her shoulder which struck the window is a bit sore. It took a hit when she had been hit in a wreck with the same man a while back."

"So at least this much is good news."

"I agree. And the swelling on her face is not all that bad, so as things stand now, the main thing I'm keeping an eye on is her intense headache. As I said, that's understandable given the blow she took." Dr. Buck stopped speaking and looked in the room to see if Cory was listening to their conversation. He lowered his voice. "But we do need to watch it."

Jude listened carefully to the doctor's report and then drew Dr. Buck a few feet away from Cory's door so they were out of earshot. "Dr. Buck, excuse me. I couldn't help but read your obvious body language. I think you have more of a concern about her headache than you're letting on to Cory. Am I right?"

Dr. Buck thought for a moment. *Patient privileges and privacy rights are a real consideration in medicine these days. How much do I say?* "You're very perceptive." He decided to keep it general. "Developing a headache after a blow like she took is to be expected, but the intensity of her headache troubles me. The pain should be decreasing by now—at least some. I'll keep an eye on it and prescribe a pain pill for her in the meantime."

"Thank you, Dr. Buck."

"You're more than welcome." Dr. Buck started to walk toward the nurses' station but turned again to face Jude. "You're the literary scholar, right?"

Jude chuckled. "Well, I guess you could say that."

"Cory told me that you're getting your PhD in literature and that you're writing your dissertation on Shakespeare. You might find it ironic for me to say that I've read a fair amount of literature in my time, even struggled through a couple of Shakespeare's plays. They were heavy sledding at times, but I persevered. I found some of them, especially the language, fascinating."

"Really? I'm impressed. Maybe you'd be interested in the production of *Hamlet* at the Three Rivers Shakespeare Festival coming up in a few weeks. A friend of mine out at Center Hill, Professor Charles Claypoole, is codirector. His helping with the production has generated quite a lot of local interest, even among those who don't give a hoot about Shakespeare!"

"Yes, I know the professor. I treated him in the ER, if I remember correctly. Can you please send me information on the coming production? My wife and I saw Shakespeare's *Much Ado about Nothing* at the Pittsburgh festival last summer. It was one of the best plays I've ever seen. The repartee between the main characters—I forget their names—was superb."

"The characters were Beatrice and Benedick. Shakespeare was at the top of his comedic genius when he wrote those late comedies. Yes, I'd be delighted to send you the details."

"Thanks. You can give the info to my secretary, Sarah Jane, okay? Thank you very much."

"You're welcome, Doctor, and thanks for what you're doing for Cory."

Back in Cory's room, Jude resumed his talk.

"So how are you feeling now?"

"All right except for this killer headache."

"Maybe I should tell some jokes to get you laughing."

"Are you kidding? The pain to the side of my face is terrible when I smile. I can't imagine a hearty laugh. Don't you dare!"

"How about a witty comment?"

"As long as it isn't too witty!"

"This happened at work one day when we were in separate lunchrooms. During that, lunch Abe quoted Alexander Pope's famous line: 'To err is human, to forgive divine.' And just that fast, Huddy shot back, 'But to blame it on someone else shows management potential.' He cracked the place up!"

"That is hilarious."

It's good to see her smile. The lifting of her spirits is worth the brief twinge of a laugh pain. Another witty comment will do her good! "Here's another funny thing that I heard at that lunch table. Blanche, Gail, and Joyce were talking about washers and dryers, and out of the blue, Blanche said, 'Wouldn't it be great if we could put ourselves in the dryer for ten minutes and come out wrinkle-free and two sizes smaller?'"

"That is also a riot!" Seeking for words to say what was really on her mind, Cory straightened her sheet. "Jude, I was thinking about Duke before you came in this morning. What's going on with him? He's impossible to figure out. He's been wonderfully decent and gentlemanly for weeks on end, and then you show up, and he reverts to ever-increasingly bizarre behavior. He was a madman last evening." She shuddered as she recollected the horror of the previous evening and pulled the sheet across her chest. "I've never been more afraid in my life."

"As you should have been. I hate to think what would have happened had I not arrived when I did."

"There's the thought that worsens my headache! I know this pain will pass in a couple days, so I'm not really bothered by that. I'll just have to bear it, but what's going on with Duke, and what do we do about it?" She pulled the sheet to her chin.

"I wish I knew, Cory. I wish I knew." Jude gently stroked his hand across her forehead and kissed her. "I can't tell which of my emotions is the dominant one—love for you or anger at Duke."

"Boy, do I understand that! I too wanted to kill him as I lay in the ER last evening, but we must be careful. That's the thing that's been on my mind the most." She smoothed a wrinkle in her sheet. "We're called to love our enemies and pray for them. You know what I'm talking about, but it's really tough to forgive a guy who tries something like that. He really hurt me." She again gently touched her throat and the side of her face. "I hurt my shoulder a bit too. I only banged it slightly when Duke rolled his car, but then the same shoulder took a hit when I ran into the tier of trays in the mine. Now I jammed it into the window when he hit me!" She stopped speaking and rolled her shoulder. "But for all it's been through, it doesn't hurt that badly."

"At least that's a ray of light in the dark." *She speaks of forgiving. "How smart a lash that speech doth give my conscience!"* "Yes, I know we're supposed to forgive, but I also know how much I love you and how far I'd go to protect you."

A short while later, he kissed Cory and departed for the mine. "Goodbye, my love. Duty beckons, but how I wish it didn't!"

CHAPTER 13

Except for the intense headache, Cory spent a fairly decent morning at the hospital. Pastor Gabriel stopped by for a short visit and informed her about a recent occurrence with Old Mary. "She's also in the hospital. At the end of the corridor in room 214. She had another of her 'spells,' as she calls them."

"I probably should stop by to say hello. The doctor wants me up and walking around a bit, so that would give me some good exercise. Knowing Old Mary as I do, I'm sure she'd enjoy a visitor. Do you think it would be all right if I saw her?"

"Yes, I do." The pastor nodded. "I just came from there. She actually seems fine."

"You say she had one of her spells." Cory rubbed her temples. "I don't know what they're like, though I've heard people refer to them in the past. Is it very serious?"

"She had trouble speaking this morning. She couldn't get her words out when she was talking to her neighbor Joyce, so Joyce called for the ambulance. The ER doctor admitted her for tests. As I say, this isn't the first time she's experienced this, but she's talking now as though nothing happened. We say with Ezra that 'for a little while, grace has been shown from the Lord our God' (Ezra 9:8). Praise God for His marvelous grace to this ever-faithful woman! I'm sure she'd love to see you."

Cory tried a weak smile and gently touched the side of her face. *Seeing Old Mary would get my mind off last evening. I'd like to see her.* "Thank you, Pastor, for telling me. I'll walk down there after bit."

That afternoon in the mine, Abe followed up on his promise and gave Morley Spencer a phone call. "Morley, this is Abe."

"Hi, Smiley. Are you going to pay me that visit this afternoon?"

"Yes, if it still suits."

"Now would be a perfect time."

"Excellent, I'm on the way. Can't thank you enough, Morley. This is very kind of you."

Moments later, Abe Badoane checked out the new security system at the mine. He feigned interest in the whole operation but, from the start, was particularly riveted to Morley's comments on the security cameras. *I want to know about their operation, strategic placement, and, above all, the extent of their usefulness in my current scheme. I need to steer the discussion to the way I can use them.* "Looks as though the system covers all the important areas like the entrance to the mine or the packhouse or the pasteurization rooms."

"Got it all covered. Every square inch."

"That's impressive. I suppose it has to be that way, or it's not much use. A chain is only as strong as its weakest link, and a security system as strong as its vulnerable area. Is that the logic?"

"Very good, Abe. You're exactly right. In the past, the cameras didn't canvass the plant so completely, but the security company insisted doing it this way because of pressure from the insurance company."

Morley showed him the operation and the control center. "I'm impressed with the thoroughness of the coverage. Well, you've shown me the new system. I guess that does it." Abe feigned to leave but paused. "By the way, I didn't pay much attention to some of these monitors. May we take a fast peek at these?"

"Of course."

Abe swept his eye across myriads of monitors. "The cameras truly do cover the entire operation."

"Yes, they do. Even the entrance at the top of the hill, the gates, and the parking lots too. As I say, the insurance company mandated thorough coverage."

"Really? You have even those areas covered. May I see those monitors?"

"Yes, of course. They're the ones over there on the end."

Abe looked at his watch. "Wow, time has flown as I've checked this out." When Abe got up for a closer look at the monitors, his knee gave way, and he stumbled slightly into Morley's desk. "Darn knees! They're getting worse by the month."

"I didn't know you had so much trouble with your knees. That probably comes from spending too much time on them in the cold, or maybe I should say with those delicious strawberry plants?"

"That probably hasn't helped, but I've actually had trouble with my knees since I was a young boy."

"Too many bike wrecks?" Morley laughed.

"Or other incidents one can't control." Abe bent his leg a couple times to work out the kink. "Well, I've enjoyed this. I'll take a fast peek at the other monitors, and then I best get back to my darlings."

"Which ones, the ladies or the mushrooms?"

"All of the above!" As Morley pointed toward the monitors, Abe looked with postured nonchalance at those cameras which covered the parking lots. *The whole lot is covered by cameras. Darn! That means my master plan for revenge can't be set among the parked cars as I had hoped.* He looked again at two of the monitors. *But that one area at the end of the lot running along the woods is seemingly out of range of the cameras. Better take a closer look.* He gave the entire range of monitors one last scan before departing, even moving his head as he appeared to sweep across them, but the whole time his eyes were riveted to the parking lot monitors. *Now I can ascertain the size and location of the area not in surveillance range. That's the single-most important detail!*

"Morley, this has been fascinating. No wonder you like your job!"

"I wouldn't go that far, but it is a job, and it's better than working in fifty-six-degree temperatures day after day year after year."

"Thank you, friend." Abe flashed his characteristically large smile. "Oh, I owe you a joke. I only told you one this morning."

"I liked it. The one about the kickboxer and the computer. I wrote it down, so I remember to tell my wife."

Abe thought for a moment. "This isn't a joke. It's just a comment which I heard on the Johnny Carson show on the ten-year anniversary of Elvis's death last August. 'If life were fair, Elvis would still be alive today, and all the impersonators would be dead!'"

"So true! Some of them are pretty bad, and I do miss the king of rock. Keep 'em coming, Smiley. At least someone around here has a sense of humor."

As he departed the security office, Abe puzzled about the best way to execute the next part of his plan. *I have to devise a convincing reason for Duke to go after Jude. If Duke's vengeance, no matter its nature, is sufficiently nasty, it may well cause Jude and Cory enough anguish that they would leave the mine for good. I don't actually care if Cory stays or not. I can tolerate her, though my detestation of her increases because of her family's past conspiratorial role against me. It was the Mohneys who turned my wife against me and made me lose my child, so a plague on their whole house! I say with Jesus, "Your house is left to you desolate!"*

His interior monologue continued as he departed Morley's office and drove back in the mine. *The real way to get at her is through lover boy Jude—the real object of my wrath. I must come up with a plan so malicious that he would run for the nearest exit, with or without his beauty-queen girlfriend. If Jude left the mine, Cory most likely would not be able to endure the hard work without him around. Or if she stayed on, she'd be a sitting duck and have to endure the daily "slings and arrows of outrageous fortune." In time, Cory would reach her breaking point and, like Jude, get out of Dodge and find a better lodge. He needs the final kick, as does his blonde-haired hick!*

But this evil heart! Why do I constantly destroy and mangle and disrupt? I long to be free of this hateful heart! But how does one cut his mind-forged manacles?

CHAPTER 14

One formidable problem faced Abe. What could make Duke come after Jude and, by extension, Cory? Ensconced in his study, he ruminated on the topic incessantly. *There's the rub. Rape had been the obvious ploy, but that avenue failed me, at least for the time being. What a disappointment—it was so perfect! What else, besides her, does Duke really like?* He tapped his pen on the desk pad and then fingered the binding of his leather journal. *His '57 Chevy—obviously! If Jude were to do something to that car, maybe sabotage it in some way, Duke would be instantly riled. Jude, of course, would never lay a finger on Duke's car, but framing him is a distinctly juicy possibility. If Jude could be made to look guilty for damaging it, Duke would spring into action like a crazed madman. Now that is a plan! Abe, you are one sneaky snake!*

He began to consider more seriously the idea which he had intimated to Bull earlier. *The area just off the parking lot next to the woods may work after all. Out of the range of the security cameras, the partially secluded area, as I noted in Morley's office, provides the perfect setting. Bull could sabotage the car—say, hammer in a chrome hubcap or smash out a taillight—without being picked up by the cameras. He could slip up the hill through the woods, do the dastardly deed in seconds, and escape without being seen. Marvelous! I merely have to identify the location and nudge Bull the stooge to execute it. Come, dummy. Time to gulp your poison!*

Walking up to the strawberry patch, Abe continued to reflect on his plan. *But why would Duke park his car along the woods? That makes no sense, especially since the tree sap would play havoc with the new finish on his hot rod-converted car. Now that is a problem!*

That afternoon in the mine, Abe puzzled over this next hurdle. Had men or women passed him during those moments, they would have seen a man deep in thought, forehead creased, eyes darting about and cutting into whatever they looked at with acidic penetration. Mine employees spoke to one another about the phenomenon. "What's a thinker like him doing here? The only other guy with a brain like that is Jude Hepler." And another: "I'm telling you, intelligence hangs on the man's face. The guy intimidates the crap out of me!" Yet another: "His mind was made to grapple with libraries, not fizzle away in dark limestone tunnels!"

Having assimilated tons of knowledge and the accumulated wisdom of the ages across his life, Abe nevertheless was currently relegated to noting which strawberries in the rows and which mushrooms in the trays were harvest-ready. Morley Spencer spoke for the entire mass of employees: "What a waste of a first-rate brain. This guy wouldn't even back down from Einstein!"

Meanwhile, Jude's world revolved around Cory. On his way home from work that evening, Jude passed Pete, who was at the end of their lane, picking up the mail. "Hi, Pete, how are you, and what's the latest on Cory? I'm going to the hospital to see her as soon as I grab a bite to eat."

"She told me on the phone that she's had a decent day, but the headache's still pretty bad. I hope the doctor gives her something to kill the pain. It was actually worse this morning and hasn't improved through the day, far as I know." Pete bit his lip and looked toward the cloud-obscured sun. "Good thing you came along last evening when you did. That was a close call!"

"Yes, I think God's fingerprints were all over that rescue. Thanks to Joey, I had learned about the bike trail through the woods leading to Beatty's Mill Road. That saved me the precious minutes I needed to rescue her. If I hadn't used that shortcut—well, I hate to think what would have happened."

I can't talk about my dear Cory and this friend-turned-enemy. Though I need to face the facts, that's something I can't talk about! "How's the bike? Much damage?"

"No, not really. One of the guys at work helped me load it on to his flatbed truck. I was surprised to see that just the front fender was bent—quite a bit, in fact—but that's nothing. The deep grass along the stream cushioned the blow. Far as that goes, I don't care about the appearance of that old bike. I just want wheels to ride the wind." He cast his eyes upward to Vinlindeer. "But I must say, riding horses up there with Cory has become our new favorite."

Deep in thought, Pete looked down at the ground and hesitated before he spoke. *How can I talk about what's really on my mind?* "Jude, I just can't believe it. What came over Duke? He was like a son to me. Why would he do this to Cory? He often told me how much he liked and respected her." He looked carefully into Jude's face. "Don't be hurt by this, Jude, but I think the guy was in love with her. Maybe still is!"

"I have no idea, Mr. Mohney. It's a true mystery that really bugs me." Jude glanced at his watch. "Well, sorry to be rude, but I better get running. I want to spend as much time as possible with Cory before visiting hours end. They've gotten very strict about them."

"I know. They have."

Jude started to pull away but thought of something else he wanted to ask Pete. "Oh, by the way how's football practice going for Joey? I often think about that. Any chance the coach will use his talent this season?"

"Too soon to tell. But to this point, Joey hasn't been encouraged. He says that the coach only plays his favorites. According to Joey, the other running backs and benched players are decent athletes, but they don't get a crack at the starting lineup. Who knows? He may not be all that good, but he'd just like a chance to play, and I do see his point. He's still at practice."

"We need to encourage him to hang in there. 'All things work together for good.' Cory and Gabe tell me that constantly."

"Thanks, Jude."

While Abe conspired and Jude hurried to the hospital to see his beloved, their friend Charles Claypoole and the director of the upcoming *Hamlet* production, Winston Armrose, talked back stage at the Stephen Foster theater in Pittsburgh before assembling the cast for the late-afternoon rehearsal.

"We're getting down to the wire, Chuck. What final areas do you think require some sprucing?"

"On the whole, I'm very pleased. But before we get into that, let me ask you a question. Did you see that *Cabaret* closed at the Imperial Theatre in New York after 262 performances? What a run!"

"Yes, I saw that, and I noted that *Madame Butterfly* and *The Phantom of the Opera* were the big winners at the Tony Awards. Okay, enough about performances in New York. Let's talk about performances in Pittsburgh!" Winnie looked at his clipboard and some notes he had scrawled. "I was thinking of our conversation the other day concerning Claudius and Laertes. You said you were going to speak with your minister about it. Did you?"

"Yes. After that rehearsal, I spoke with Gabe Wyant. He was the gentleman who sat in on the final minutes of that rehearsal."

"Yes, I saw him at the back of the auditorium. What did he think?"

"He was impressed and agreed with our take on Claudius. Though he's a simple country preacher, he's a gifted thinker, very gifted. Because his field is theology, he spends a lot of time thinking about the nature of evil."

"I see."

"Gabe's theological and philosophic perspective is very informed, to say the least. He said it was Shakespeare's depiction of evil that drew him to the great tragedies. One of his seminary profs was a real aficionado who introduced Gabe to the Bard's tragic vision."

"I wish I had had a few moments to talk with him. Did he have any suggestions?"

"Not really. He thought we should keep tacking in the same direction, but come to think of it, Gabe did offer one comment about Claudius's interaction with Rosencrantz and Guildenstern, which I found quite valuable."

"Please continue."

"Remember how we said we needed to make Claudius a more formidable force in the play, especially when one on one with Laertes?

We had agreed that Laertes, in the presence of the king, was too forceful and assertive."

"Yes. I think the dynamic between them now is much better. The youthful courtier was virtually fawning in that last rehearsal, and Claudius the cunning snake charmer. Don't you agree?"

"Yes, completely, but I say we do the same thing when Claudius interacts with Rosencrantz and Guildenstern. This was Gabe's main point. Claudius the king has to be more charming with them, his demeanor more relaxed and cheerful. These are gullible stooges who, in the presence of this vast intelligence, are easily manipulated. Claudius's intelligence has to be foregrounded so that his showdown with Hamlet later in the play—brilliant mind pitted against brilliant mind—is nail-bitingly intense and dramatic. What do you think?"

"Excellent, Chuck. You instruct the three of them—Claudius, Rosencrantz, and Guildenstern—about this suggestion. I suggest we start today with the scenes when Claudius speaks with them."

At this point, Charles went on stage to speak with Rick, Marcel, and Austin, the three actors cast in these roles. Summarizing his discussion with the director, he offered a few pointers. "What we're concerned about here is demeanor, tonal modulation, and delivery of lines. Rosencrantz and Guildenstern, when you interact with the king, show more respect and deference, maybe even a bit of fear. He is the powerful king who overwhelms and even intimidates you. One sideways glance from him, and you're sent packing from court, your tail between your legs, sipping third-rate tea in your rotting manor house in distant Dorset. That's the power he exudes. Understand? Excellent!"

They picked up the practice at this point in *Hamlet* when Claudius speaks with his courtier friends, Rosencrantz and Guildenstern. Seated in the audience, Charles and Winston watched the brilliant Claudius go to work on the courtiers. As the king walked and talked with the men, he put his arm around their shoulders, patted their backs, even flashed his toothy smile. When it came time for Claudius to part company with the courtiers, the king tipped his hat, the superior personage obsequiously condescending in a classic manipulative gesture. Rosencrantz and Guildenstern were temporarily taken aback, for the king—the feared, all-powerful, capricious potentate—had, with this gesture, just turned social decorum topsy-turvy.

As the scene on stage progressed, Charles and Winston resumed their discussion. "The men are wax in his hands," the director opined, stretching his legs forward and couching his head in his folded hands. "They don't have a chance against such formidable evil." He sketched in the margin of his notebook, a mannerism when tense. "Who does? King Claudius is brilliant. I tell you, Chuck, a powerful personality of this sort—malevolent, toxic, and calculating—scares me silly. He is absolutely brilliant."

"Right you are. Who could stand up to that awful and sinister intelligence?"

Later in the afternoon Charles and Winston smiled at the conclusion of a virtually flawless rehearsal.

"We're almost there," Winston began. "I'm starting to think we might be ready for opening night after all!"

"It's been quite a ride. We just might have a hit on our hands. Let's keep our fingers crossed. One never knows how these productions turn out. I've seen some real surprises across the years."

"Yes, one needs to anticipate the unexpected. But surely we've done our part unless a greater power than we can contradict intervenes to thwart our intent."

"I caught your adaptation of Shakespeare's line in *Romeo and Juliet*. But sometimes the fault is too recklessly attributed to that divine and Greater Power. Sometimes it's in ourselves. To wit, I give you Cassius, 'The fault, dear Brutus, is not in our stars But in ourselves.'"

Winston thought for a moment and straightened the papers on his clipboard. "By citing *Julius Caesar*, you're saying that evil originates in the human heart and not always external forces. Is that your point?"

"Yes. In fact, Edmund mockingly makes this very point in *King Lear* when he states that we shift blame to 'spherical predominance' and 'planetary influence.' He says we blame the stars and even planet alignment when we and we alone are responsible for our dissolute behavior and author our own demises. How subtly we humans shield the real culprit—the deeply sinful human heart! That, by the way, is a recurring theme in my preacher's sermons."

Winston tapped his clipboard and rose to his feet. "I guess that's the place to which Shakespeare came five or six years after *Hamlet*. Remember the riveting and universal question which his King Lear asks: 'Is there any cause in nature that makes these hard hearts?'"

"Yes, these hard hearts—like Claudius's limestone-hard heart. And like the hearts of others too!"

CHAPTER 15

As Claudius spoke with Rosencrantz and Guildenstern on a Pittsburgh stage, Abe Badoane headed back into the mine after his discussion with Morley Spencer. Having settled on the car-sabotage plan, Abe searched for Bull Chestnut. A short while later, he saw him at the packhouse, but Bull was surrounded by people at the time. *Darn! Well, I'll have to catch Mr. Dimwit another time!* An hour later, Abe passed his crew. *What luck I'm having! He's again in the middle of conversation with several of the pickers, and I can't lure him away without creating suspicion. I have no recourse but to bide my time.*

In a short while during a run to the packhouse, he passed Bull when, at last, he was alone. "Hey, Bull, see these two brand-new $100 bills? They're yours for the minute's work I spoke to you about earlier." Abe held up one of the bills in Bull's face. "That's a pretty easy way of tucking Mr. Franklin in your wallet."

"Lay the details on me, old man."

"We need to frame Jude so we can get his butt out of here once and for all. He's driving our good buddy Duke crazy." *Quit playing with yourself, idiot!* "Here's something else. Have you seen how the managers suck up to Jude? Pretty soon he'll be running this place. I hate how Jude thinks he's better than you guys simply because he's on the fast track for his PhD and will soon end up with a cozy professor job. I'm tired of him making fun of all of you. Especially, Duke and you."

"Who? Me? The preppy prick makes fun of me? I don't think so!"

"Yes, you! Haven't you noticed how he humiliates you guys by using big words you don't even understand? He does that on purpose.

Especially around you, Bull. He's putting you down. He's mocking you to your face, and you don't even realize he's doing it. I use big words to educate and expand people's vocabulary. He does it to show off and put down."

"The pwick!" Bull took off his helmet and slicked his hair. "I hate that!"

"You should not make fun of your coemployee Bonnie. She can't help it if she can't pronounce her *r*'s. Your sense of humor is sophomoric."

"What? Speak English! You're worse than Hepler!"

"Never mind! Okay, here's the plan." *Okay, sonny boy, time for some poison.* "We can help out Duke by getting rid of Jude. Deep down, Cory has real feelings for Duke. She'd get together with him again instantly if Jude were out of the picture. My little plan in the long run, you see, is actually a way to help Duke, not hurt him."

As they spoke, Abe walked with his arm around Bull's shoulder.

"How are we going to do this, Smiley? This better be good. If Duke finds out, my butt's toast. And if my butt's toast, your butt's not happy either! It won't be pretty, and you won't have that sneaky snake smile on your face."

"Shut up and listen. Your silly threats don't intimidate me!" Abe's laser stare bore into Bull's eyes. "We're going to stick with the plan I spoke about earlier, and it's now time to give you the specifics. Duke's car will be parked along the edge of the wood. You come up through the trees, bang in his rear taillight, and put a big dent in the rear mag wheel. You'll be doing Duke a favor, and it will take less time than it takes for you to unhook Beaver's bra."

Bull smiled, but not for long. Abe watched him squirm and shake his head back and forth. "I don't know, Abe. Sounds pretty risky to me."

Waving the money in front of Bull's face, Abe knew he had to go to work on him. *This could be a bit harder than I first thought, but no problem. Each man has a price, their brains turned to swill. Dumb Bull I'll now entice, His mind with poison fill.* "Don't be so indecisive. The road of life is littered with squirrels that couldn't make up their minds." *Good! He's smiling. Maybe he's coming around.* "Let me fill you in on some facts. The rear taillights are the last thing Duke hasn't replaced on his car, and the driver's side left mag wheel already has a blem on it. He's been saying for ages that he's going to replace those parts."

"I know. You'd think his car had leprosy."

"He even priced those parts. The only reason he didn't purchase them is because I keep making him stall."

"Why are you doing that?"

"Because I've been looking at these taillights and hubcaps for weeks and finally found them at a parts store in Pittsburgh last weekend. I already have them at the house."

"You do? Why'd you buy parts for Duke's '57?"

"I'm going to give them to him as a gift—a way of repaying him for repointing the bricks on the upper part of my chimney last fall. With my bad leg, I was afraid to go that high up the ladder, so Duke helped me out. When we're done with our little masterpiece plan, his car will be in mint condition. I'll even help him install the new ones. It will take us a grand total of twenty minutes, and you, my friend, will be a whole lot richer." *And dumber than my chimney bricks! You know what, Bull, I've given this a lot of thought, but I don't think being an adult is going to work for you!*

"You're making this sound pretty good."

"Pretty good!" *Of course, it does to you!* "We'll be doing Duke a favor, genius, and pocket a fast $200. Plus—here's the big one—Jude will be framed. It's win, win, win for us. Come on, Bull. Are you a man?"

Bull looked down at his feet.

"If you don't want to do it, fine." *Come on, stooge. Come around!* "There are plenty of guys who would jump to have two pictures of Mr. Franklin in their wallet for a minute's work." Abe again waved the bills in front of his face.

"How will we ever be able to pull this off? The last place Duke would park his '57 is under those trees that drip sap. The guys complain all the time about that gicky stuff ruining the finish of their cars and trucks. You'd never in a hundred years get him to park there."

"Leave the details to me, Einstein. I'll tell you when we can proceed. Just keep your mouth shut, and be sure to wear gloves so you don't leave fingerprints."

"If you say so."

As Abe gave Bull a pat on the back and tipped his helmet when parting, Bull noted his ear-to-ear smile. *The guy's always smiling!*

"Relax. The plan is perfect. We might even do it this afternoon. Just sit tight and wait for me to let you know."

"If you say so, boss."

I say so, dumb hoss!

CHAPTER 16

At the Armstrong County Memorial Hospital, Cory's severe head pain continued. When making his rounds early the next morning, Dr. Buck asked Cory about the medication he had prescribed the previous day. "Has the headache subsided?"

"Not really." She hesitated. "To be honest, I'm a long way from normal."

"The CT scan revealed no blunt-head trauma. That's the good news. The powerful pain medication should give you further relief from the pain, but I started with a small dose. Have you had any side effects from it? Any nausea, for instance, or other symptoms?"

"No, I haven't, Doctor. No symptoms. At least nothing…I'm aware of just yet."

"Good. The side effects of these meds are a real nuisance for some patients. *But, Cory, somehow you don't look yourself.* "Then I'll increase the dosage since the headache hasn't subsided. I started with a low dosage so I could observe possible side effects. We'll keep you on it through the day, and if you still experience no side effects by late afternoon, I'll discharge you. I'm sure you'd rest more comfortably at home than here."

"Thank you, Doctor."

"You should take off work a couple days and get some rest. Do you have sick days at the mine?"

"Yes. I have some…ah, sick days coming."

"Do you have a way home?"

"Yes, I do. Jude's coming…here…from work this afternoon."

"Good." *What's going on with your speech?* "That will give us time to prepare discharge papers and monitor this pain pill."

"Is it all right if I walk around until he comes? I'd like to go down"—she paused—"hall to see…someone…who? Yes, Old Mary. She was…ad-admitted yesterday. She's a good friend."

"Yes, walk around as much as you want." *Cory, why the hesitations when you talk?* "The exercise will be good for you. Just don't overdo."

"Thank you so much. The care here has been ex…exc…very fine."

"You're welcome. Helping patients is our job." *Oh, yes, I just remembered.* "By the way, Jude told me about the production of *Hamlet* in Pittsburgh coming up in a few days."

"Yes, he told me. He…mentioned it to you. Are you…planning to go?"

"Well, I'm thinking about it. And I'm sure you won't miss it."

"Not for the world. I'll be front and center! I love"—a pause—"the woman, Hamlet's girlfriend. I can't think…of her name." *I don't believe this! What's going on with my memory?*

"I'm not the one to ask." He looked at the floor in thought. "Is it Desdemona? No, that doesn't sound right. Not Juliet. It's Ophelia, isn't it?"

"Ophelia. Of course. She's one of my…favorite characters. I'm going to…shadow her so I can be her"—another longer pause—"I want to…the word means play her part if she's sick." *Like me!*

"You want to be Ophelia's understudy?"

"Yes, that's it—understudy! I'll be Ophelia!"

"Ha! Well, goodbye, Cory. Remember. Take it easy and no fast head movements. Give yourself some rest. That was some hit you took yesterday. That's likely what's affecting your memory. That too is normal."

Cory enjoyed talking to the doctor but was disturbed, as she spoke with him and the nurses later, that she had trouble finding the right words. Her pain started to pass, but occasionally she had trouble concentrating. *Why am I disoriented, almost as if I have a touch of vertigo?* "I feel a bit woozy in the head," she explained to the floor nurse. *It was probably the blow to my head. Maybe I'll take a short nap before going down the hall to see Old Mary.*

Meanwhile, at the mine, Abe left the women on his crew and went to his locker to pick up an article which he had read the previous evening on the damaging effects of bright sunlight on fresh car paint. The article stressed the importance of keeping a newly painted vehicle out of bright light to prevent discoloration. *Excellent! I found what I need—ammo to persuade Duke!* With a copy of the article in hand, Abe hustled down the corridor to the room where Duke's crew was picking mushrooms. *Sure enough, there he is, massaging his sore left hand. What an impulsive, hulking bruiser!*

Pulling alongside, Abe yelled, "Duke!"

"What's going on?"

"Take a look at this. You just painted the hood of your car to get rid of some of those stone chips, didn't you? I only saw your car at a distance, but even from across the lot, it looks really sharp."

"Yeah, I did. The paint's barely dry."

"That's what I came to talk to you about. You need to read this article. It says that having a freshly painted car in bright sunlight is the worst thing you can do if you use the new PPG Deltron paint. Isn't that the kind you used?"

"Yeah. It's the latest brand. Nothing but the best for the Duke's baby!"

Abe pretended to read from the article. "A freshly painted vehicle should be kept out of bright sunlight for at least forty-eight hours to prevent discoloration and possible peeling. While PPG Deltron Clear produces the best automotive finish in the business, it is susceptible to damaging ultraviolet rays during the first forty-eight hours after application."

"I've never heard of that before."

Dropping the magazine article to his side, Abe thought to himself, *Swill, baby, swill!* "Do you realize that it's ninety-five degrees outside and that Allegheny County recorded fifteen days straight of temps at or above ninety degrees? Cleveland just recorded its highest

June temperature on record. You're crazy for keeping the fresh paint in that scorching sun."

Duke decided to go on the defensive. "I never had trouble before. Do you know how many cars I've painted? I don't need anybody's advice on how to paint a car. Besides, most guys think the hot sun helps dry the paint and is good for the finish."

"You never parked a car with this new PPG Deltron Clear paint in such scorching sunlight, nor did you care about those clunkers as you do your beloved '57. In my opinion, the love of your life deserves better treatment."

"You're serious, aren't you?"

"Of course, I am. Hey, it's no skin off my back, but the perspicacious thing to do is to get her out of that blazing sun."

"What is perspick—heck's fire, what does that mean? Use English, Abe. Your big words piss me off! Besides, where would I park the car? The whole freaking lot's in the sun."

"What about under a roof somewhere or in the shade trees?"

"No parking's allowed near the buildings in the shade. I got in trouble for parking there in the past. Talk about being reamed! I almost got a three-day vacation for using one of the kahuna's parking spaces!"

"If I were you, I'd come up with something. I bet that paint's bubbling up right now. In this heat, it will be peeling off in a day or so. You just watch. Hey, maybe I'll take a close-up and call it 'Moonscape: Craters Visible to the Naked Eye.'"

"Shut up! Where can I park?"

"I told you. In the shade trees along the woods."

"Yeah, I guess I could do that. I don't think the trees would drip sap in the couple hours until quitting time. Maybe there's some open spaces between the trees. Do you have a minute to keep an eye on the chicks while I dash outside? Watch 34-B. She's been mouthy again. It'll take me just a couple minutes to move my car."

"Well, I've got someplace to go, but I'll keep an eye out if you make it fast. Take off, but don't lollygag around. And remember—you owe me!"

Abe waited for a while at Duke's crew and, upon his return, drove back to where Bull was working. *So far, so good. Now on to the second part of my plan and use of the brainless one.* He motioned for Bull to come to his mule.

"Hurry up. I only have a minute."

"What's up?"

"The plan. *The* plan, moron. Remember the plan? It's on. Duke's already moved his car to the edge of the lot near the woods. Sometime within the next hour or so, find an excuse to leave the crew and take care of your business. Can you find an excuse to cut out? What will you tell your boss? I want to know." *Because I leave nothing to chance with a loser like you!*

"That won't be a problem. I have to go to the storeroom to pick up some new handles for the crap bushels. While I'm doing that, I'll slip out the back door, run along the woods, and come up the hill through the trees. Are you sure the car will be there?"

"Yes."

"I want my money."

"Do the deed, and you'll get your ducats."

"I don't think so, big guy. Fork it over now or no deal. I'm not overly fond of this idea. No matter what you say, I think it's dangerous."

He gave him one of the two crisp $100 bills. "Don't blow it, Bull. Keep your gloves on. There can't be any fingerprints. If you do this fast, you'll be back on the job in fifteen minutes."

Bull held the bill to his lips. "I hope you're not crazy, Abe. If we screw up this plan, we're both dead meat."

"It's not going to fail. You'll get this second bill when you complete your minute's work."

Abe returned to his crew while Bull, a short while later, circled down around the side of the parking lot, came up through the woods, and in a matter of seconds, smashed in the right taillight and gouged a deep, ugly dent with his ball-peen hammer in the rear hubcap nearest to the woods. As he ran down the hill through the briars and milkweed, he fingered the $100 bill in his pocket. *In the long run, Duke will be grateful. He'll install the new ones Abe already bought.*

Bull ran so fast that he nearly tripped on a root. *Geez, I gotta watch what I'm doing! By tomorrow Duke's car will be like new.*

Bull paused at the bottom of the hill and looked at the $100 bill. *You're beautiful! Now to get my other picture of Mr. Franklin!*

CHAPTER 17

Hoping they could mount a memorable production, Charles and Winnie Armrose focused ever more intensely on the *Hamlet* rehearsals, especially since they had just learned that a couple of the city's influential drama critics would likely be present for the impending dress rehearsal. Because of this ever-increasing preoccupation with the play, Charles was unaware of the recent developments in Jude's and Cory's lives—namely, Abe's insidious desire to ruin them and the sabotage of Duke's car. While he had learned the shocking news of Duke's attempted rape, he lacked knowledge of subsequent details, such as the effects of the pain meds on Cory.

At the time, thus, Charles did not appreciate the uncanny parallels between the storyline in *Hamlet* and the events playing out in his dear friends' lives, nor did he have the slightest inkling of what was about to happen at the theater in Pittsburgh. For now, one thing was front and center in his life—presenting a production of *Hamlet*, which somehow explored the play's ingenious philosophic and psychological underpinnings. *At best, modern audiences and readers miss and, at worse, completely misunderstand these massively complicated internal themes. This cannot—this will not—happen in our production! I need one more conversation with Gabe, that "endless fount of knowledge," as Jude calls him! Possibly there are things I don't understand about the play's brilliantly subtle exploration of good and evil.*

Before departing the Stephen Foster theater early that evening, Charles gave the pastor a ring. "Hello, Gabe. I was hoping we could continue our discussion of Shakespeare's *Hamlet.* I greatly benefited from our earlier exchange and am more than ready for part two. Does this evening still suit?"

"I'm waiting and primed!"

"Wonderful!"

"How can I help?" Gabriel began their discussion a short while later. They were seated in Pastor Gabriel's parsonage study and surrounded with pictures and memorabilia of the Holy Land. "I wouldn't pass up a chance to talk about *Hamlet*. I'm really excited to see the play. Martha and I have our tickets already."

"Good. Let's hope you won't be disappointed." Charles looked around at the mementos on Gabriel's desk. "I see you're still displaying your photos and keepsakes from your Holy Land tour."

"Yes, the experience lives on in my heart," he said, fingering a pebble he picked up by the Sea of Galilee near Capernaum. "Had I shown you this cross?" Pastor Gabriel picked up a silver jewel-encrusted cross and chain which was draped over a photo of the Temple Mount. "Take a look at this." He handed the cross to Charles.

"This is beautiful. How did you come by this? Martha doesn't often wear such lovely jewelry."

"You're right. Well, there's quite a story behind this cross."

"I'd love to hear it before we get down to business."

"One afternoon in old Jerusalem, we were trampling the huge flagstone rocks of the Via Dolorosa, the supposed path Jesus trudged on the way to Calvary. Because we were deeply moved by the experience, as all pilgrims are, my head was bowed as I walked in prayer and meditation, when out of the blue, while looking down, I saw this cross wedged deep in the crevasse between two large stones."

"Amazing!"

"It had probably lain there for ages as it was covered by dirt. Just one of its little encrusted jewels faintly caught the sun's rays and gleamed through the grime for that split second as I stepped over it. Think of everything that came together for me to see it—exact right slant of the afternoon sun, perfect angle of the cross to reflect it, my eye in the right position to catch that faint sliver of refracted light, my happening to look at the precise moment, and so on. It's mind-blowing, Chuck—mind-blowing! Well, I dug it out with the pen in my pocket—a kind of archeological dig really—brought it home, and had it cleaned at Adam's Jewelry Store. Look how it glistens."

"It's a beautiful cross."

"Yes, it is. But for me, it's the symbolism that's meaningful."

"In what way?"

"The way the cross was trampled across the years—totally neglected and abandoned. Tens of thousands, probably hundreds of thousands, trekked over it, indifferent to its lonely existence down there deep between the rocks." He gently ran the back of his finger across it and nodded his head toward the wall painting of Jesus on the Cross. "Just as they're indifferent to the real Cross."

"Yes, I see your point. Nice analogy."

"Okay, enough on that, important as it is. Let's get to the matter at hand. Remember that I saw just a snippet of the *Hamlet* rehearsal the other day, so expect little help from me. You're dealing with some gifted actors there by the way. Do you normally bring in that many equity actors?"

"There are more than usual. Winnie's shooting for an A-1 production." After taking another sip of coffee, Charles resumed, "I'd like to talk about Claudius and the way Ophelia and Hamlet stand up to him. When you think about it, they both have very different reactions to the authority figures in the play. Ophelia is totally compliant to her father's and the king's wills, mere putty in their hands." Charles ran his finger around the rim of his cup. "Voiceless and powerless, she ends up becoming a self-destructive nonentity by the end of the play." Charles paused in his recitation.

"I see your point," Gabriel acquiesced. "Please continue."

"The patriarchal control barons who surround Ophelia destroy her utterly. Their evil influence is insidious, but from one perspective—and I know there are alternative views here—she bears a certain amount of responsibility."

"In what way?"

"She acquiesces to their demands instantaneously by choosing the path of compliance to these overreaching authority figures. In the process—this is the part that bothers me—she turns with seemingly little hesitation against her true love, Hamlet. She allows herself to be pitted against him and chooses allegiance to her father and the king over allegiance to the prince. I know some would find this interpretation controversial, but others would see it as a viable reading."

"Maybe tenuous to some," Gabriel responded, "but you make a convincing case. I've often read the play in a similar light. I recall Ophelia's line to her father: 'I shall obey, my lord.' I think that's her line." Gabriel fingered the silver cross on his desk. "From the moment of that shocking pronouncement, she sides completely with Polonius against Hamlet. That is a most revolting and instant turn against her beloved."

"Exactly."

"She repels Hamlet's subsequent gestures of love, even though she says"—Gabriel paused to pick up his copy of *Hamlet* and leafed to the passage—"he 'importuned me with love in honorable fashion.'" The pastor continued looking at the lines of the play. "She even says here that he spoke with 'all the holy vows of heaven.' If Hamlet was that good of a man and if she realized that his overtures of love were that genuine and heartfelt—she even implies godly—then why would she side with the foolish father against the wise lover?"

"I hadn't thought of it in quite that way, but you're definitely buttressing my claim."

"Love is supposed to bear, believe, hope, and endure all things, but she sells Hamlet out in a heartbeat. That moment of unlove seemingly bothers her not a bit." When Gabriel pushed the silver cross and Galilee pebble together, the cross turned upside down on the pebble. "I find this very fascinating, Charles. Please continue. I need to know where you're headed."

"To this terminus. Hamlet reacts in a very different way. He's been instructed by his father, the Ghost, to remember his command to retaliate, kill, and destroy. The Ghost advises the most godless counsel imaginable—the old eye-for-eye mentality. It goes like this: I was wronged, so you seek vengeance on the person who wronged me. Although I suffer horribly and am condemned to walk the earth, I now want the same thing for you. You see how the Ghost insists on adherence to the old ancestral, tribal voice of revenge? Do you see my point, Gabe? His parental request is stupid and pagan. Why would the ghost wish such a horrible fate on his highly intelligent and artistic son? That is flat crazy!"

"Yes, I see your point. I find this riveting."

Charles paused and sipped his coffee to further formulate his thoughts. "The ghost's offering counsel to Hamlet parallels the situation with Ophelia since it shows another controlling parent trying to order the steps of his child. In the process, the ghost deprives Hamlet of his right to autonomous, and indeed normal, self-determination." Charles wiped his lip with a napkin. "But note the stunning contrast. By blinding following the counsel of her father, Ophelia destroys herself and their beautiful love. She never agonizes one bit about turning against her beloved Hamlet. How very disturbing that she sells him out in a heartbeat!"

"You're right. She never hesitates."

On a roll, Charles continued his analysis of the play. "Hamlet, on the other hand, questions the parental counsel and even tries to oppose it, thereby choosing a different path altogether. He zealously seeks to reject the ancestral path of revenge, seeing its stupidity for what it is. Hamlet, rather, tries to get to the bottom of things with a play instead of inflicting destruction with a sword. Do you see my point, Gabe?"

"I do."

"To ferret out the truth, he chooses art over warfare, opting for cultured civilization over ancient aggression. In the Danish society of his day, that is surely a radical departure from the social norm."

"You need to write a book on these very scintillating insights!"

"Of course, Hamlet doesn't succeed in the end. He fails miserably, in fact, and that to me is so very tragic, but let's give him credit for nobly trying to fend off the evil tribal voice that has been the scourge of mankind from time immemorial. That's why his demise is so terribly sad. This noble and heroic man—of angelic sensibility, mind you, and of exquisite artistic temperament—becomes a mindless butcher. How very tragic! Ophelia's description of Hamlet as having 'been loosed out of hell,' is accurate in the extreme. It is indeed a terrible falling-off. No wonder I'm disheartened every time

I enter Hamlet's world. He was so close to making it! Why couldn't he have been a stronger man?"

Pastor Gabriel nodded in agreement, the corner of his mouth curled upward in a faint but distinct smile. "That's quite the summation. I couldn't phrase it so eloquently, but I must admit to agreeing completely with your interpretation. What then is your question? How can I offer any insight that you haven't already considered? In my book, you've thoroughly covered all the bases!"

"I interpret the play through a scholar's literary—and I guess I could say psychological—lens, but the play obviously makes a powerful religious statement too. It's those spiritual underpinnings that I have trouble disclosing. That's the question I put to you. As a trained theologian, how do you read the play? Can it be read along religious lines, or is that contriving an interpretation? I'm too skeptical these days to ferret out such an exploration. There's the rub! If you want a specific question, here it is. Is the cement of this play undergirded with biblical rebar?"

"Nice metaphor! As I say, I think your analysis is dead-on accurate. Hamlet tries to follow his internal compass, that 'still small voice,' as his moral guide through the impenetrable Danish jungle of power politics. Instead of declaring war against Claudius as both his ancestors and peers have always done, he tries to ascertain the king's culpability by staging a play. How magnanimous of Hamlet! That really is a marvelous decision on his part. Everybody else would pick up a sword and start swinging like Peter in the Garden of Gethsemane. Not Hamlet. He concocts the idea of the play and instructs Horatio to observe, not swing. How fascinating, how very Christlike! Bravo for Hamlet! No wonder I admire the aspiring young prince!"

"So well put, Gabe! So good!"

"However, after *The Murder of Gonzago*, during which he surmises Claudius's guilt, he chooses the path of vengeance and destruction instead of forgiveness and love. To use the expression which I heard from one of the teenagers at youth group the other evening, 'He lost it!' I laughed when Mitch said that! Well, for me, the staging of *The Murder of Gonzago* is the turning point in the play, the all-important fulcrum. Hamlet is radically changed from this point on. How very sad his demise! Am I tacking in the direction you desire?"

Charles nodded in agreement as he slowly stroked his beard. "Spot on."

"Claudius needs a savior so that he can repent of his crime, not a murderer who revenges it. Up to the point of ascertaining Claudius's guilt and complicity, Hamlet is clearly on the right path. However, once he determines the king's guilt, he surrenders to his base impulse and chooses the Danish sword of war. He should have wielded the banner of peace, as he had learned from the immortal Reformers at Wittenberg. You comprehend?"

"Perfectly!" Charles enthusiastically responded. "Let me see if I have this right. You think that Hamlet, at the beginning, wisely followed his own conscience against the formidable voice of ingrained culture. His problem then is forsaking that inner compass, which had to this point astutely guided him through the dark political jungle. He abandons that still small inner voice of truth—to use your metaphor—and follows instead the worn and bloody path of ancient tribal warfare. That is Hamlet's tragedy. You're perfectly right—the angelic artist becomes a murdering thug! How foolish, how sad!"

"That's how I read the play." Gabriel picked up the cross on his desk and leaned back in his chair. "The play formulates a profound question with marvelous relevance for all times. That's why I think your production will be a hit. It poses that enduring conundrum—who or what is going to determine your destiny? Mind you, I'm saying this from a preacher's point of view. The play looks each viewer/reader in the face and asks these profound questions: Are you going to be self-determining, thereby forging your own destiny—as Hamlet did for a time—or are you going to lie down and allow the culture to pitilessly bulldoze you into whatever contorted and heinous shape it wants? Sorry, Charles, for that mixed metaphor, but I think that's the question at the heart of the play. It's that abandonment of self that in the end is so very tragic."

"Don't worry about your mixed metaphors. I see your point. All right, I'm with you so far, nor did I get lost in the God talk. Could you speak further about Hamlet's girlfriend, Ophelia?"

"I agree with what you said, but I don't use your big scholarly words to say it! If Hamlet follows his inner conscience as the determining, ordering center of his life—at least he does so for a time—Ophelia never does. She must have had a beautiful love relationship of some sort with Hamlet, but because her father and brother ordered her to forsake him and shut up the doors of her affection, she complies instantaneously and foolishly betrays her true love. That abandonment of her inner compass, which occurs early in the play, immeasurably contributes to Hamlet's suffering. Can you imagine Juliet turning against Romeo? Or Desdemona against Othello? Or Cordelia against her father? Never! These are strong women who never waver."

"Fascinating, Gabe!"

"From a minister's point of view, Ophelia represents the mass of people who are too weak to forge their own destiny and, instead, drift along with the mindless blind crowd." Placing the cross back on his desk, Gabriel searched for the right words. "Her self-betrayal is instant and pitiful, whereas Hamlet's is gradual and immensely tragic."

"This makes perfect sense, Gabe. You're offering deeper insights than all the professors I've ever heard combined!" Charles finished jotting a note on his pad. "Yes, very helpful. I knew your insights would be excellent. I can't wait to share this with Winnie."

"Hang on. There's more. Now let's probe the religious connection a bit more deeply since that's what you wanted. The culture says that we should be strong in ourselves, but the Bible says that we should be strong in the Lord and in the power of His might. Hamlet and Ophelia try to machete their way through the Danish jungle in the energy of the flesh, but the Bible says to do so through reliance on the Comforter. Neither Hamlet nor Ophelia, in the end, make it, though Hamlet tries nobly and comes close. In a moment of awful weakness, he gives in and reverts to the ancestral voice of revenge. It's that act of retaliation that undoes both of them. At least that's how I read the play. It polarizes reliance on the inner music of the soul against the external static of the world. Or to recapitulate our dominate theme, Shakespeare in this play pits the personal code against the ancestral code. Like so many of the Bard's characters, Hamlet and Ophelia find themselves at this biggest of life's crossroads."

"You remind me of your teachings on the Reformation," Charles said, during a pause.

"I hadn't thought about that, but indeed there is a correlation. Let me see if I make the connection you have in mind. The Reformation was that time in the history of mankind when self-determination came to the fore. People started to rely on their rational intelligence and their own critical thinking skills instead of the enslaved and weary reliance on cultural forces, especially the corrupt institution of the church—that all-controlling center of people's lives. This new awareness and cultivation of reliance on the inner conscience is deeply scriptural. In fact, Christ spoke of this when He said that 'the kingdom of God comes not with observation.... For indeed it is within you.' Remember that astounding statement in Luke 17?" Gabe tapped the small Galilee pebble with his pen. "If it's possible to make the messianic kingdom, which lies within the heart, the basis for self-determination, then we'd do well to use it as our plumb line of truth instead of the world's ever-trending philosophies. Better to set one's course by the North Star, instead of the doctrinal ships that restlessly bob on a nighttime sea."

Charles continued to jot down a few notes in his notepad. "Yes, I completely agree! This reminds me of the flesh-spirit dichotomy of Paul's letters. If I recall, that's a recurring theme for the apostle Paul, but it's here that I run into trouble. I just can't put my finger on the relevant verses that speak to this."

"I see what you're after. Here's one example. Remember what Paul wrote to the Galatians: 'For the sinful nature desires what is contrary to the Spirit, and the Spirit what is contrary to the sinful nature. They are in conflict with each other.'" Gabriel reached for his Bible and started leafing through its pages. "The play depicts the epic battle between these two natures, the flesh and the spirit."

"Perfect. That's exactly what I want. Is that where the verse stops? Is that Paul's main point?"

"No, it isn't." Gabriel had found the Galatians text and ran his index finger down the page. "Here it is. Paul goes on to say that the sinful nature and the spirit 'are in conflict with each other so that you do not do what you want.'"

"That's it! That's it exactly. That's precisely what I want! 'No other answer can I make but thanks and ever thanks!'"

Later that evening, Pastor Gabriel, writing in his journal, spoke of his meeting with Charles:

> Charles and I had an enlightening discussion on *Hamlet* this evening. How he enhances my understanding of Shakespeare's dramaturgical genius! I especially found our interpretations of Hamlet and Ophelia fascinating, but one thing I didn't have a chance to emphasize is the sad fate that befalls Ophelia. It's her decisions early on that cause her eventual madness. She's a perfect embodiment of a dominant biblical theme: create your destiny while you're free because the time will eventually come when you will no longer be free to decide and will instead have no recourse but to live out the tragic consequences of devastating past choices. When people get to that state, they have no recourse but to spend their lives in a succession of dungeons. Unless—and this is why the Gospel truly is good news—they make Christ their Lord and Savior.
>
> That's one point, but there's another that I didn't get a chance to make. It centers on Hamlet's moral free fall. Once he learns of Claudius's guilt, he should have chosen the path of forgiveness, mercy, grace, and love. His abdication of this typical Christian response during his course of vengeance lies at the root of his demise. Some of this I alluded to, but I never got around to speaking about the Mark Twain quotation that hangs on a plaque in my study. I was just coming to it when I was interrupted by that phone call and

then forgot to make the point. Twain once said, "Forgiveness is the fragrance that the violet sheds on the heel that has crushed it."

For a man not perceived as an apologist for the Christian faith, Twain hits here on an amazing insight, and what a lovely notion it is! Had Hamlet taken the Christlike course of action when he felt Claudius's foot crush down on him, the perfumed aroma of merciful love would have emanated from him like a crushed violet. But by the end of the play, his conduct reeks of rank carnage instead of sweet perfume. Made for heaven, this once noble prince of Denmark acts with the vengeance of a demon. How sad, how very sad! Shakespeare, you said this so epigrammatically in Sonnet 94: "Lilies that fester smell far worse than weeds." Because Hamlet was the exquisitely beautiful lily, the stench of his corruption is very great indeed. I must pass along these additional humble thoughts to the professor.

CHAPTER 18

After taking another stronger-dose pain pill that afternoon, Cory walked down the long hall to see Old Mary. Because the pain in her head was still quite intense, she welcomed the distraction. "I'm getting cabin fever in this little room!" she said jokingly to a nurse.

Moments later, she peeked her head into Old Mary's room so as not to disturb her if she was napping. Old Mary was wide awake and watching television. "Hi, Mary. How are you? Feeling…any better now?"

"Yes, I am, Cory. I'm doing much better." She turned off the TV and smiled broadly at Cory. "At least I can get my words out now! My goodness, but that was awful this morning." Old Mary gestured with a sweep of her hand for Cory to come in and sit in the chair beside her. After she sat down, she looked at Cory for a moment without speaking. *Something's not right here. Though in the hospital, Cory's hair is more unkempt than need be, and she looks distraught. I hope I can suppress my shock.* "I heard about your awful incident with that bad man at the mine."

"Oh, I'll be fine. Just a br-bruise to the face and a…king-size headache to go with it." Cory folded her arms and looked away, a vain attempt to deflect the memory of the trauma.

"Yes, I can see the swelling. You must have taken a pretty hard blow." She gently shook her head back and forth. "I feel bad that you endured such a horrible thing. What strange times we live in!"

"Yes, the bad man hit me pretty hard, but it's nothing. Really."

"Where did it happen?"

"Down at—I'm not sure. I can't say the name of the place. Where we always...went to swim. Where the people go to fish on the first day of trout season."

"You mean Paradise Beach on the way to Crooked Creek?"

"No, the other one. By the bridge off the Worthington Slate Lick Road."

"Oh, Beatty's Mill?"

"That's it! Sorry, I guess the blow...affected my memory." *Beatty's Mill! Time to change the subject!* "I wonder if this is a good time...a good time for you...to fill me in on the ro-rose vision." Cory massaged her temples. "You promised to tell me...tell me the entire dream...someday."

"Yes. As you can see, I'm not real busy now!" Old Mary looked intently at Cory but said nothing. *Something's not right with that girl!* "Can you hand me my Bible? It's there on the stand."

Cory gently picked up the Bible from the bedside stand—crowded with a glass, a Styrofoam water pitcher, a box of tissues, and the phone.

"Here it is," Cory said, placing the Bible in Old Mary's gnarled fingers. *Her hands are amazing—swollen knuckles, arthritically bent fingers, shiny smooth skin on the fingertips, purple and brown splotches on the backs. They would make a lovely painting, but picking up my art brushes is the last thing I feel like doing now!*

"Take it out, please."

The Bible was zipped inside a green canvas cover with the poem "Footprints in the Sand" embossed on the front cover. Gently fingering the Bible, Cory read the poem on the cover. "I love you and would never leave you. During your times of suffering when you see only one set of footprints, it was then I carried you." *But not carry you every single moment,* Cory thought to herself, reflecting on the Beatty's Mill horror. *Was I carried or abandoned that evening when I was in the back seat with Duke? Have to think about that one!*

Carefully opening the zipper, Cory took out a maroon-colored Bible and handed it to her. As Old Mary thumbed through the pages, Cory was close enough to see that they were worn with age. *Many of the pages have pencil markings, and countless verses are boxed in neat pencil lines. The woman has pored over those pages so much that they're as transparently thin as tissue wrapping paper!*

Old Mary continued to leaf through her Bible. "It's in here with lots of other notes and things." A bookmark fell on to her lap. "Oh, look at this lovely painting of a hummingbird." She lifted up a piece of painted, carefully stitched silk from her bedsheet. "My son picked this up in England on one of his visits." She held the bookmark close to her eyes to examine its beauty. "It's hand-painted by the noted English artist Mirlarna Armstrong. Isn't it lovely?"

"Yes, it is. Same name, *Armstrong*, as our beloved township. I mean county."

Old Mary held up the small rectangular piece of silk cloth on which was painted the most beautiful hummingbird Cory had ever seen. "I keep the painting of the hummingbird in my Bible next to this verse in Song of Solomon. I should read it for you. You have a second, don't you?"

Cory rolled her neck back and forth. "In here, I have lots of time!"

Old Mary focused her eyes and held the Bible closer to her face. "These old eyes aren't focusing so well these days." She leafed through the worn pages. "Yes, here's the verse. I have it marked." The verse was surrounded with a thin pencil box. "'The flowers appear on the earth, the time of the singing of birds is come.' I just love this idea. The beautiful woman in the Song of Solomon is so much in love that she sees blooming flowers and singing birds everywhere she looks. Mirlarna Armstrong's hummingbird represents that perfect love, a love made in heaven. What a pleasant thought—this time of the singing of birds. Well, this bookmark has always represented that happy time when bluebirds sing, lovers love, and all's right with the world."

Cory reached out to touch the smooth fabric. "It's a beautiful work of art."

Old Mary continued leafing through her Bible. "I keep so many treasured notes and such items in this Bible that it's a kind of museum! Wait a minute. It's here somewhere. I'll find it. Yes, here it is. Take a look at this." She held up an old pencil sketch, the edges brown and flaking, the creases frayed.

"What is that? It's ancient!" Cory watched Mary carefully unfold it with her arthritic hands. "You look like you're handling... an ancient man...manu...old paper!" Cory looked at her fingers, this time in action. *Her fingers are much more crooked than I realized!*

"This is a sketch I made of an eagle when I was a little girl. It's an important part of the rose vision." She held it up for Cory to see and then handed it to her. "You wouldn't think it would be important, but it is."

"This relates to the rose vision? Really? Please te-tell me about it. I love the in...the intri...the...the good detail in your sketch." Cory laid the sketch on her lap and, after massaging her temples, examined it closely. "You were quite...the drawer once upon a time." She traced her finger along the fine pencil line of the sketch and handed it back to Old Mary.

"No, not much of an artist, but this feeble little sketch relates to the vision." Old Mary carefully laid the drawing on her lap and prepared to tell the story. "Though the original vision of the rose came to me decades ago, to this day, it's vividly etched in my brain. I could never forget it." She looked again at the drawing and straightened its one bent corner. "All right, here goes. Once when I was a little girl, I had a vision, or maybe it was a dream. I guess I don't really know the difference. Anyhow, in my dream, I was on the bridge in Kittanning watching the pigeons and looking down at the Allegheny River. I was walking over to Market Street from my aunt's house on Franklin Avenue in Applewold." Old Mary paused to take a sip of water. "My mouth's dry from not talking much."

Placing the glass back on the stand with her wobbly fingers, she continued, "The dream came to me after we had spent a day in Pittsburgh touring Oakland. I was with my mother and father looking at stained-glass windows. The one I liked the most was the Stephen Foster window of the beautiful dreamer. It was astounding to me. Well, when I went to bed that evening, I couldn't get the picture of that beautiful woman and her lover out of my mind. I couldn't stop thinking about their story and the beauty of that song. You see,

Mama sang 'Beautiful Dreamer' most of the day after seeing the window. By the way, the artist who painted the stained-glass windows in the Stephen Foster Memorial Museum was Charles Connick. I remember the name because he made such an impression on me."

Old Mary took another drink of water to moisten her throat. "Well, as I walked along in my dream, I saw two lovebirds standing and talking near the middle of the Citizens Bridge in Kittanning. It was a beautiful summer evening, and the crescent moon and stars were shining brightly. The young man and woman were such a beautiful couple and so in love that I couldn't stop myself from just standing there and looking at them!"

"This dream is…so real!"

"Very! The girl, the one I call the beautiful dreamer, wore a long light-blue dress which went clear to her feet and set off her long blonde tresses. He wore a tan suit, and each of them held an English Crimson Glory rose, my very favorite. Can you believe that the details of a dream can be so clear? The blossoms were"—Old Mary paused to read from a caption at the bottom of her sketch and pushed her glasses upward—"shapely, velvety, deep red, and endowed with a real rose fragrance." Years later, I copied this from a book I have on roses called the *Rose Expert* because it offers such a perfect description of the roses I saw. Well, in my dream, the girl held her rose to her breast, and he held his toward her. They exchanged the roses, kissed them, and then—this is the part I see over and over—dropped them into the Allegheny River."

"This is a beautiful dream!"

"I'm coming to the amazing part. I leaned over the bridge and watched the red roses float down the river side by side. At first, they were sort of close to each other but then drifted apart. I was so sad to see them separate. The back one kept trying to catch up, but it couldn't. The front one tried to slow down, but it too was swept along by the current."

"I can just imagine them…drifting downstream."

Old Mary put her head back, completely immersed in the details of the dream. "I watched the roses bounce along, bumping into floating driftwood and nearly run over by a motorboat. The young lovers stood on the bridge and watched the roses. I can see them there plain as day." Old Mary closed her eyes and brushed a tear away. "The lovers are always there, propping their elbows on the green railing of the bridge. They watch until the roses float downstream and are gone, gone forever. The lover stands behind his beautiful beloved, and he always holds his arms around her as he whispers sweet nothings in her ear. They are so much in love! So beautiful!" Old Mary paused and looked at Cory. "Sorry if I'm boring you. I guess you didn't want all that when you asked me to tell you the whole dream!" Again, Old Mary laughed.

"Please keep going. Th-this…is, ah, fas…fascinating. Tell me more."

"Then there was a lapse of time or maybe a change of scenes. The roses were now separated but still within sight of each other as they neared a city with lots of tall buildings. I've always figured it was Pittsburgh. One rose was slightly downriver from the other and separated from its mate by a floating clump of branches and debris. The roses were a little frazzled since their journey had been long and difficult." Mary paused for a moment to take another sip of water. "I know all of this must sound unbelievable. By the way, I'm giving you the whole thing at one time, but the dream came to me in small pieces across many years."

"It's amazing," Cory broke in. "Please continue." Cory listened intently, but her eyes momentarily glazed over, and she had trouble concentrating. She looked at the door as though someone were entering the room and even started to speak. "Is there someone…" No one was there. She stopped talking and again faced Old Mary.

"Are you all right, Cory?"

"Yes, I'm fine." *But not really*. "Thank you. Please go on." Cory struggled to focus on the story. "So what happened to the roses? Please don't stop. It's so sad that they…were sep-separated." Cory bowed her head and wiped a tear from her eye. "Being apart is…so very difficult. Things in love should never be—what's the word?—ripped apart. They shouldn't have to endure something so awful. I don't like it…that the roses split. From each other. I didn't like that part. The roses should be together—always and forever!"

Old Mary gently placed the folded paper on her lap and peered at Cory, who stared out the window and fidgeted with her straggly hair. She ran her finger along the crease of the sketch. *Cory, what's going on in that head of yours?*

CHAPTER 19

Old Mary lifted her eyes to Cory, who by now stared out the window. *Dear Cory*, she again thought to herself. She glanced at the call button by her side. *Should I call for a nurse? But what would I tell her? What could she do?* She felt it best to stop the narrative. *Why tell her this beautiful dream when she is not herself?* "Well, I think that's all I should tell you now, Cory. I'll give you the rest when you're feeling better and aren't so tired. I think that's best."

"No, please con-continue. I want to know about the roses. I need to know what happened to the roses. Those beautiful flowers that were separated. Sep-separated from each other so long, and they never thought they'd get back together, and they endured such hard times! Please don't stop!"

I'm not so sure I should keep going! "All of what I was saying happened in the Allegheny River right above the Point in Pittsburgh. I forgot to say that. Then in my vision, a large paddleboat draws near the two roses. You know those large riverboats that cruise up and down the three rivers. I've always remembered that the word *Liberty* was written on the side of the boat. I don't remember the boat's second name."

"The *Liberty… Belle*?" Cory broke in. "I think that's the…name of one of them, but I'm not tr-trusting my memory much right now." Cory again looked out the door.

"Goodness, that's it!" *Cory, why do you keep looking toward the door?* "I didn't think this old brain would recognize the name, but I'm sure that's it. You mean when I was a little girl, I saw in my dream an actual boat, complete with its right name, that I didn't even know existed? That is something! Yes, the *Liberty Belle.* I'm sure that's it. Well, in my dream, the boat paused near the fountain as its large paddle wheel churned the water. I remember being very nervous because the one rose was drifting nearer and nearer to the paddle wheel and was going to be destroyed in seconds! The other rose was up the river a short distance, but it too was aimed right for the paddle wheel. That also made me sad."

"This is awful! What...what happened to the roses? Please say...they'll be all right!"

"Then I heard a booming voice, the only sound I heard during the dream. It said, 'The Comforter is coming, the Comforter is coming!' I couldn't tell where the voice was coming from, maybe from above. And just like that, this large wing appeared, which I thought was part of a bird. I never saw the whole object, mind you, only the wing. Well, this bird, or whatever it was, swooped down and snatched the rose closest to the wheel in the nick of time and then picked up the other rose too. It flew away with the two beautiful roses floating along like on a breeze."

"This is an unbelievable dream!" Cory interrupted, looking again at Mary's sketch. "I see it so...vividly in my mind that I could paint...a picture of it."

"The two roses were carried away." Old Mary again ran her smooth fingers along the crease of the paper. "It seems like that might be the end of the story, but it isn't. The flowers were flown to the Point by the fountain and were there wrapped in a garland chain made of lily of the valley flowers. Don't ask me how that was done. Goodness' sake, I guess anything's possible in a dream! I only saw the roses after they had been wreathed in a lily of the valley garland."

"I'm am-amazed...at the detail!"

Old Mary paused for a moment. *How strange dreams can be!* "Dreams can be very strange. Look how unusual the pharaoh's two dreams were—one of fat and scrawny cows and the other of plump and wasted ears of corn! Remember the dreams Pharaoh told Joseph? I taught those Bible stories to generations of Sunday school children at the Center Hill church. Well, the whole thing was very vivid to me—the roses, the lily of the valley garland, and the edge of the wing. My dream is as strange to me as Pharaoh's dream, but I don't have a Joseph around to interpret it!" Old Mary stopped speaking and picked up the picture of the wing. "Well, that's it, child—the dream I've had ever since I was a little girl. Have you ever heard anything like it?"

"Was it a onetime dream, or was it a—" Unable to come up with the word, Cory paused.

"Are you asking if I dreamed the whole dream in one long sequence, or did I dream it piecemeal across years?"

"Yes, that's what I'm…trying to say. I can't…get my words out!"

"Maybe you were trying to say *recurring*?"

"That's what I'm trying to say." *Why can't I think right?* "Was it a recurring dream? The same dream…coming to you over and over?"

"The entire dream was not recurring. In fact, I dreamed the entire dream only a couple times, but I'd get snatches of it here and there across the decades. Snippets recurred, I guess you could say." Old Mary adjusted her head on the pillow. "I still see the rose when I dream at night, and sometimes I see the handsome couple standing in each other's arms on the Kittanning bridge." She closed her eyes. "I love to dream of them and to be in their world. Every night when I go to bed, I hope I'll dream of the lovers, standing under the stars and the crescent moon." *Old Mary blotted a moistened eye.* "They look just like the couple in the Beautiful Dreamer stained-glass window in Pittsburgh. Sometimes I see the roses tumbling into the water, and at other times, the tall buildings appear. The part of the dream I see the most—I'm not sure why—is the inside part of the large bird's wing with one of the roses visible in the background. That's what the sketch is of. Take another look."

Cory took the sketch from Old Mary and again examined the fragile piece of paper. "You show only…part of a wing here and not"—another awkward pause in Cory's speech—"not the…not the…the whole bird." *What's going on with my speech?* "Is that because you see just…just part of the wing…in your dream?"

"Yes. As I say, I never see the entire bird, just this very large and protective wing." She brushed her hair from the side of her face and gazed again at the picture. "I keep calling it a bird, but I only saw the inside part of its huge wing."

"What do you think is the meaning of the dream? What's its sig.... what it's about? Why has it...recurred...across so much of your life? Dreams have meanings. Sorry to ask so...many questions!"

"I wish I knew, Cory." Old Mary stopped speaking and looked directly at Cory. *Something is not right with you, my dear friend—too many pauses, overall nervousness, irrational glances out the door. Why should I tell her all the beautiful details of this dream when she's not in her right mind? On the other hand, it might serve as a needed distraction.* "The part that amazes me the most is how the dream of the rose links to you. Well, to you and Jude, I should say."

"To me? To us? Mary, what are...you talking about? How could I...be part of this dream? You had the first part of it decades before I was even born! How could I be in it...part of it?" Cory rubbed her temples and forehead and again rolled her head. "You're about to tell me this...this important thing, and my head aches so much I can't even...I can barely con...concen...focus right. I'm getting st-stabbing pains in my head. Right here." She pointed to the top of her head. "I'm getting so forgetful...and can't talk right!"

"I'm so sorry, child." *Do I stop now? Should I call a nurse? I'm afraid, my dear, you need help!* She hesitated, but Cory gestured for her to continue. "Maybe I should stop now."

"No! I want...hear. What happens to them...the lovers? I mean the roses."

"It's the link with you that has made the dream even more baffling to me. Well, let me explain." *Child, are you sure you're able to comprehend?* "This brings us to the important part, and you're smack dab in the center of the action. Of course, that amazes me too. But maybe I should delay telling you since you're not feeling so well."

Just then, a nurse walked into Old Mary's room. "There's a man in your room, Ms. Mohney. He came to take you home, and Dr. Buck is also there to check on you before you leave and go over your discharge instructions. Sorry to be so urgent, but you know these doctors—always in a hurry!"

"All right, I'm coming. Thank you so much…so much for telling me." She turned to Old Mary. "I'm so sorry, but I have to go. I wish it didn't…have to go now…no choice. I really want to hear… hear this next part of your dream. But my head…is hurting. Let's talk soon, okay? I'll be praying for you." She furrowed her head in deep concentration. "What is it I'm to pray for? Why you here?"

Old Mary again looked at Cory and paused before answering. *I'll say this carefully.* "They thought I had another ministroke, but I'm sure I didn't. My mind's sharp as ever!" *Right now, we need to be concerned with your mind, not mine!*

"Oh yes, you did tell…you did say that. Goodbye, Mary."

Old Mary watched Cory go out the door and stared in that direction a long time. *Cory, Cory, there's far more going on with you than a severe headache!*

CHAPTER 20

Up in her room a few moments later, the doctor examined Cory before discharging her. The nurse gave her another pain pill and covered a few discharge instructions. Moments later, Jude and Cory were headed down Freeport Road toward Cory's farm.

"You're early," Cory began. "I didn't expect you…for a while. But I'm sure glad to see you!" She leaned over and kissed him on the cheek.

"The boss allowed me to leave early to pick you up. Very nice of him, wasn't it?"

"Yes, very."

"So tell me about your day," Jude began. "How are you feeling?" *What's going on with Cory? You're obviously not yourself!*

"Nothing I could put my finger on," he wrote in his journal that evening. "Just a faraway look in her eyes, an indescribable listlessness, and that slovenly appearance. The Cory spark was definitely missing!"

"Well, not much happened at the hospital today. I found out that Dr.—what's his name?—I'm talking about my doctor—is planning to go to…to Pittsburgh to see the production of…of *Macbeth.*"

"Dr. Buck. So he's planning to go to see *Hamlet.* You said *Macbeth,* silly person!"

"*Hamlet*? When did they change the play?"

"Cory, what are you saying?" Jude looked piercingly at her. "We've been reading the play in the evenings for a couple weeks. We've talked about *Hamlet* by the hour, and Charles has spoken with us numerous times about the rehearsals."

As they rode along, Jude continued small talk and noted Cory's increased hesitations while speaking. Feeling that she needed rest and should not be bothered with idle chitchat, he soon stopped talking altogether and rode along in silence. *What am I to make of Cory's mental lapses and halting speech? Forgetting the doctor's name was an atypical slipup for my ever-astute girlfriend, and in her defense, she has seen several doctors since her arrival at the ER. Getting their names confused, especially in the wake of a head trauma, thus, is no major cause for alarm. Forgetting the name of the play, on the other hand, demonstrates an incoherence that deeply troubles me. Possibly there was greater head trauma than the doctors realized or tests revealed?* Glancing at Cory who had her eyes closed and head reclined on the top of her seat, he prayed in silence as they drove along.

As they passed the Smith farm in Center Hill, Cory lifted her head, opened her eyes, and looked around. "My head's killing me, and I keep…having these weird thoughts." She paused momentarily and looked blankly at Jude. "I have a question. When I got the name…of the play wrong…why did you yell at me?"

Her face was completely expressionless. "Her eyes were blank and lusterless," Jude wrote in his journal that evening. "I nearly wrecked the car!"

"What are you talking about?"

"No use being…so mad about it." She looked straight ahead and, in a moment again, turned to Jude. "You're getting more and more like the bad man every day."

"Who's the bad man?"

"He tried to rape me!"

"Duke? You think I'm like Duke? Cory, what are you saying?"

"You men! You just sit there in silence…while I'm fighting to keep…head on straight. I could use a bit of loving encouragement!"

"Cory, what are you saying?" *Lord, help me. She's divided from herself and her poor wits!* "I'm not mad about anything. I love you, sweetheart." *Cory, my beloved, what is going on with you?* "I've never loved you more than at this moment!" The first unkind words Jude had ever heard her utter, they shook him to the core. *Her mental lapses speak of a more serious malady, a much worse malady, than I first realized! What should I do?*

"Just be quiet. I'm tired fighting…with you all the time. Take me home." She sat sulkily in the front seat, rubbed her temples firmly, and then laid her head back on the seat. After a moment's silence, she spoke again and uttered the statement—"that awful statement," according to Jude's journal—"I want to talk to Mom."

The statement hit Jude with the force of a crushing blind-side tackle by Jack Lambert, the famous Pittsburgh Steelers linebacker. *Cory, your mother's been dead for years! What is causing her irrationality, and more to the point, what should I do about it? Should I take her back to the hospital right away?*

When they pulled in the driveway, Cory saw Zoe sitting on the porch as though waiting for them. *Good!* Jude thought. *Zoe will comfort her as he always does and maybe restore her sanity.* He carefully watched her get out of the car and walked to Zoe, who came running in her direction. Zoe began licking her hands wildly and rubbing his side against Cory's legs. His long-lost friend had returned. *Perfect! Zoe will jolt her back to reality. This is exactly what I hoped would happen. Thank You, Jesus!*

"Jude, look at that…adorable dog! Wonder…where he came from!"

Eliot, you were so right in "The Waste Land": "I had not thought death had undone so many!"

CHAPTER 21

A tear formed in Jude's eye as he looked at Cory's expressionless face. *She registers no joy at arriving home or seeing her beloved Zoe! She doesn't even know Zoe!* Standing on the walkway beside her, he was momentarily speechless as he looked into her empty eyes. *She returns my gaze with that patient-etherized-upon-a-table look and stumbles along but doesn't see. Cory, how crazy to say it at a time like this, but you remind me of Gloucester's line in King Lear—"I stumbled when I saw." That's you, my dear!* Jude wiped a tear from his eye with a handkerchief. *Any minute I expect her to say, "Who are you, and what are you doing here?" What is going on with my beloved Cory?*

"Oh no," she said as she stepped on to the porch after their slow meander down the sidewalk. "I forgot my Bible and sketch pad. I wanted them for this evening." She put her hand on Jude's arm and warmly smiled at him. "I think they'd calm me down, and goodness knows, I need something to settle me down. It's as though I can't think straight, and I know I haven't been making sense. Please forgive me for all the dumb stuff I've been saying." She smiled warmly and pecked him on the cheek. "Did I actually say I didn't know Zoe? Of course, I did!"

Jude nodded.

"Come here, you adorable dog!" She warmly hugged Zoe. "I can't believe this! Fortunately, I'm fine now."

"I'm more than a little relieved. That was very scary!" *And I'm very confused! Just what is going on?*

She stopped for a moment, again put her hand on Jude's arm, and asked, "Can we drive out to the mine? I'd like to get my Bible and sketch pad. It would only take me a minute to dash into the locker room to pick them up."

That, my darling, is a disconcerting request! You need the rest and calm of your home, not the added disturbance of a trip to the mine immediately after discharge! On the other hand, your last statements have been totally coherent, and you have certainly emerged out of the world of madness. At least for now. "Sweetheart, don't you think you need to lie down and take a nap? You took a hard hit yesterday, and it's obviously affected you. Without meaning to upset you, I need to remind you that you've said some pretty incoherent things. I really think your body needs some rest. We can get those things later." *She's not agreeing with me. I know her body language.* "Do you understand my point?"

"No, I don't."

Jude tried one last time. *I need to get her in the house immediately so she can rest.* "I think you need to lie down. Don't you think that would be best?" *She's wrinkling her brow in agitation. Precipitating another outburst or spell of incoherence is the last thing I want to do, but she has talked rationally during the last minutes and seems normal again. Maybe I should go along with her plan. On the other hand, a trip to the mine would delay my talk with Dr. Buck, and that, as soon as possible, is absolutely imperative. It's a real quandary for me!*

"I want to go to the mine."

Jude tried one last time. "I wish you'd get some rest."

"But I really want to go. My Bible's in my locker, and I want to get the sketch I started. I think working on that this evening will make me feel better. I know I haven't been making sense. Honey, this has been awful. I feel that I'm trapped in a theater of the absurd play in my own brain and that I've been writing my own absurdist play! Can't you see my point?"

"I'm not so sure." *But that was a super intelligent response—very impressive, in fact! She really does appear to be normal again and smiling in her loving beauty-queen way. Maybe work on one of her sketches is the exact thing she needs after all this duress. Having said that, I can't gloss over her scary irrationality! I'll propose a compromise, and maybe she'll settle for that.* He clasped her arms with his hands. "Why don't you go in the house and lie down? After I grab a cool glass of water, I'll go out to the mine to get your Bible and sketch pad. That way, you get both your rest and the things in your locker. It's win-win!"

"Thanks, Jude. That's very kind of you, but listen to yourself. You can't go in the women's locker room! Do you have any idea what those women would say if they caught you in there? 'Hey, ladies, here comes peeping tom the pervert!' I'll be fine really. You can stay in the car while I run into the locker room. It will take me less than two minutes, and then we'll be gloriously alone for the evening!"

Against his better judgment, Jude agreed to make the trip. *I'm afraid I might come to regret this, but I can see that reading her Bible—her mainstay strategy during her too-frequent storms—and drawing too might be the very balm she so desperately needs.* Jude lifted his eyes to faraway Vinlindeer. *Plus, there isn't a better alternative since denying her request might set her off again. Still, a big part of me thinks this is crazy!*

"If you insist." With a resolve to keep a close eye on his beloved Cory, Jude headed, unknowingly, for the mad scene in the parking lot at the mines. *I have no way of knowing what lies in store, but in the foggy recesses of my own fevered mind, I feel like Daniel headed for the proverbial lion's den!*

CHAPTER 22

When they arrived at the mine toward the end of the workday, Jude circled around to the main entrance to drop Cory at the door. She had been speaking rationally en route—of Van Gogh's personal struggles and her progress on cleaning the kitchen cupboards—so Jude, though still wary, entrusted her to make the fast trip to the women's locker room to retrieve her Bible and sketch pad.

The errand will take her only a few minutes. More than that, reading David's psalm this evening in her own beloved Bible will comfort her, just as it did during our five-year separation. "Whilst memory still holds a seat in this distracted globe." God, please stabilize her distracted globe—and mine too in the process—and restore it to health again!

"Goodbye, my beautiful dreamer. I'll be waiting here at the door. Maybe we'll go up on Vinlindeer later in the evening."

"Lovely idea, just what the doctor ordered. Ha! Ha!"

"Maybe we could ride the horses?"

"Perfect! See you in a jiffy, my love." She flashed her warm smile, then gave him a peck on the cheek and a pat on the thigh.

Workers were scurrying across the parking lot as Cory exited the car and dashed toward the entrance.

Fortunately, Cory didn't bump into anyone. Good! This is one time when it's best for her not to get tied up in conversation. Though terribly shocking, her mental lapse was temporary, and now—hallelujah—she seems fine again. Jude reclined in his seat and drummed his fingers on the car dash. *She is moments away from rejoining me in the car and returning home for a quiet evening of reading, drawing, or walking on*

Vinlindeer. He continued to finger-tap "You are my sunshine, my only sunshine." *Yes, this will work out for the best, but what a mad siege it was!*

Waiting idly, if anxiously, in the car, Jude looked across the parking lot and saw a group of men encircled around a car at the edge of the woods. He didn't pay particular notice to the gathering since workers frequently huddled around their vehicles to briefly chat before going their separate ways. *But more people are clustered together than usual. Wonder what's going on.*

Prior to Jude and Cory's arrival in the parking lot, Skeeter Dowling had exited the mine and gone to Duke's car to check out the new paint job. An accomplished pro at detailing, Skeeter wanted to examine the finish of the new Deltron paint on Duke's '57 Chevy. Seeing the smashed taillight and the dented Cragar S.S. Mag wheel, he immediately called to a couple of his friends who were getting into their cars. "Hey, guys, get your butts over here. You won't believe this. Someone hurry and fetch Duke!"

"He's still in the mine," one of the men yelled across the lot. "His crew's working late."

A group of men gathered at the car and began to chatter.

"Would you look at that!"

"Duke's gonna blow a gasket!"

Very shortly, Abe Badoane was among them. "I've never seen anything like this," Abe joined in the conversation. "Who in the world would do something so awful? Do you know what that Cragar Mag wheel cost? Looks as though someone smashed a hole in it with a ball-peen hammer."

"Somebody's really laying for Duke," one of the men said.

Good—the exact comment I wanted some stooge to make! Time for some brain swill. "Someone here, you think?" Abe nonchalantly asked. "Maybe some outsider came out of the woods and did it. Surely none of the mine employees would do something like this!" *Swill, you losers, swill!*

"Yeah," Skeeter agreed.

"Don't kid yourself," Blassie observed. "Duke's had his share of enemies over the years. It's not like you to forget the civil war we had here in the past when this place was a pit of vipers!" Blassie looked at Abe in disbelief as he spoke. "Surely you remember that Duke was in the middle of it, and your nickname may be 'Smiley' now, but back then, more than one person called you the *snake*!"

"He's right, Abe," Smitty joined in. "You called that turmoil the whiskey rebellion since it started because of the heavy drinking in the mine. You're the one who said Duke was the hardest drinker of all." He turned and looked directly in Abe's face. "What do you mean that someone here wouldn't have done this?" Smitty again examined the damage.

Abe's intent was to steer the banter toward an allegation. *Chessboard, chessboard, which piece to move? Knight, queen, rook, or pawn—which does behoove?* "But those troublemakers left years ago. Everything's been pretty quiet lately, and Duke is one reformed man. You have to agree with me that this place has been quiet as a morgue. I mean, who has it in for Duke now?" *Let that sink in, my boys.* "Cory's on the verge of making him into a preacher man, and you have to admit, she's well on the way to success. Remember the old adage—the greater the sinner, the greater the saint."

"How about the college professor?" Bull asked. "Don't forget that Duke was doing just fine with Cory Mohney till Hep showed up. Those guys don't get along like two peas in a pod."

"Or the little incident at Beatty's Mill last evening," Skeeter added. "I wouldn't call that pretty quiet."

"Yeah," replied Smitty, "you guys are right. The whole atmosphere has changed around here in the last couple weeks."

"I know one thing," Al commented. "Duke's been a mess."

"Jude's over there by his car," Bull said, catching Abe's fast snake-eye wink and sly nodding toward Jude. "Let's see what Hep has to say."

Wonderful. This is better than I anticipated. I figured Jude had gone for the day to visit Cory in the hospital. Abe looked in the direction of Jude's car. "The professor's a very smart man. Better get him over here to survey the damage. He'd be the kind to offer some slippery answer and cut out before you get a chance to grill him properly."

"Boss is right," Smitty concurred.

"You need to proceed cautiously," Abe resumed, "since we want his answer here in the presence of objective witnesses and not over there by a biased girlfriend. It's never wise to underestimate the intelligence of an enemy who, because of his cunning and manipulative nature, plays gullible people who don't even know they're being played."

"I agree," Blassie commented. "Hank, let's pay the professor a visit."

Hank and Blassie started walking in the direction of Jude's car. Making certain none of the men were looking at them, Bull elbowed Abe and whispered in his ear, "This is working out real good, ain't it?"

"Shut up, jackass!" Abe furiously whispered.

During this exchange at Duke's car, Jude's anxiety increased by the minute. *Why hasn't Cory returned? Did something come up, and is she all right? If I go in and stand outside the women's locker room, maybe I'll bump into someone who has info on Cory's whereabouts.*

Jude stepped out of his car and started walking toward the door to check on Cory when two men, Hank and Blassie, dashed across the lot in his direction. Not wanting to get tied up in conversation at such an inopportune time and thinking the two men were headed for the mine entrance instead of him, Jude began to walk quickly toward the door. *I need to know where my Cory is—right now!*

"Well, bless my soul," Abe said to the men standing by Duke's car.

"What's that, Smiley?" one of the men asked.

"When Hank and Blassie neared Jude, the professor immediately started going in the other direction. I'm not exaggerating. Look at that! He's still trying to get away from them, and now he's almost running toward the building. Why would Jude go in the other direction when they're yelling at him to stop?" *It's so much fun to manipulate you jackasses!*

"Look at him go!" Bull concurred.

"Does he have something to hide?" Abe resumed. "I can't tell from here—you young bucks have better eyes than I—but is that a look of guilt on his face? When Jude looked back at Blassie and

Hank, I saw a face as red as the strawberries I passed around during lunch."

"Let's get him over here so we can question him," one of the men stated, an edge of anger in his voice.

"If you think it's necessary," Abe flippantly said. "But whatever you're going to do, do it fast. I have better things to do like checking my darling strawberries. Standing around on this hard concrete is killing my bad knees." Abe hobbled a few steps to fake the intensity of his leg discomfort.

A couple other men started toward Jude, Hank, and Blassie. One of them yelled, "Jude, get over here! We want to talk to you."

By this point, Jude was beside himself. Because his beloved Cory had not come out of the mine, he kept looking toward the door to see if she was in sight, but still no Cory. *If I could get my head inside the building, I could look down the hallway and possibly see her or talk to someone who had.* The men stood side by side to barricade his path to the door.

"Hepler, stay here," Hank shouted. "We want to talk to you. How come you keep walking away from us? You seem awful jittery."

"You wouldn't be hiding something, would you?" Blassie sarcastically added.

"Like a ball-peen hammer!" Hank's comment was dipped in acid.

Back at the car, Abe intently watched the proceedings. "Is it my imagination, or is Jude trying to hightail it out of here? I'm amazed that he doesn't act like a man and come and talk to us! They're trying to get him over here, but he's scrambling in the opposite direction!"

"He better git his ass over here," Duke's good friend Huddy yelled. Hudson Weaver, known to all in the mine as *Huddy*, was getting angrier by the minute. So certain was he of Jude's guilt that his eyes glared hate, and his jugular vein vined down his neck like a thick rope. With a reputation of being the angriest and most violent man in the whole mine, Huddy had instigated several brawls during the earlier "whiskey rebellion." Because crushing blows from those huge fists had put more than one man out of commission, several of the workers in the mine, in fact, likened him to "Big Bad John," the eponymous character in the famous Jimmy Dean pop tune from the early '60s. One of the women—always assumed as either Bonnie or Beavers—had written the lyrics out and pasted them on the lunchroom bulletin board: "Huddy, this is for you. 'A crashin' blow from his huge right hand / Sent a Louisiana man to the promise land, Big Bad Huddy.'"

But that aggressive behavior had, however, become more or less a thing of the past as Huddy, under the influence of his new girlfriend, was of late more temperate and generally more likeable. *That being the case,* Abe reasoned, his index finger tapping his lip, *Huddy's anger in this situation is somewhat unusual. Never mind, I'll play it to my advantage!*

When Huddy started walking toward the small group by Jude's car, Jude saw him coming. *His massive curled fists, with their pendulum swing, look like steel wrecking balls!*

"Guys," Jude said to Hank and Blassie, "I'm waiting on Cory. She's not well and was talking like a madwoman a little while ago. I've got to get her home and into bed."

"To sink the shaft? I understand that!"

"Yeah, a run of the rod would be great!" Another laughed. "Especially with the beautiful one!"

"I don't mean that!" Jude raised his voice. *How they botch the words up to fit to their own thoughts!* "I just picked her up from the hospital, and she was completely out of it. I brought her to the mine so she could dash in and get a couple things out of her locker." Jude turned his gaze from the men to the group assembled by Duke's car. "What's going on over there? Why's everybody upset, and what are you doing around Duke's car?"

"Why don't you just take a little hike over there and see for yourself?"

"Look, men, I need to get Cory home. I'm worried about her."

By this time, Huddy arrived at Jude's car. "Maybe you have a good reason to be worried about your own butt, and just maybe you're using Cory as a lame excuse." Huddy's fist was curled into a tight ball.

Yes, a steel wrecking ball, Jude thought.

"Come and take a look at Duke's car and tell us what you know!" Huddy spoke with such anger that he sprayed spit on Jude's shirt as he spoke.

"What are you talking about?" Jude implored.

"Someone smashed the taillight and rear hubcap of Duke's car!" Huddy retorted. "Duke's going to be hotter than blazes when he finds out what happened! Why are you standing there trying to look innocent?"

"Okay, I'll come over and take a look, but let me peek inside to see if Cory's coming. I need to explain to her what's going on and let her know that I'll be right back."

"Maybe you should take a peek over here first!" Huddy savagely yelled at Jude, who had by this time started inching toward the door. Huddy vise-locked his massive hand around Jude's shoulder and violently pushed him toward Duke's car. "Now get going!"

At Duke's car, Abe continued to work his plan. A few moments before, he had inconspicuously pulled Bull aside and whispered in his ear. Then Abe, a moment later, spoke loudly enough for all to hear. "I can't believe it. Why doesn't Jude come over here and join us? That's very strange. Bull, you're standing there not saying a word. Does it look fishy to you?"

"If he's done this," Bull responded, "he needs to pay the price. I don't know if he's guilty or not, but it's darn suspicious that he's dragging his feet!"

"Something's rotten in Denmark," Abe responded.

Cory's delay was terribly worrying to Jude since by now she had plenty of time to return to the car. *If she doesn't see me when she exits, she'll be worried sick, but seeing me in the middle of a full-blown argument would be even worse and possibly trigger more delusional thinking. Oh, my Cory, "O rose of May!"*

Jude again tried to appeal to the men's good sense. "Guys, I really do need to stay here by my car. Cory was talking nonsense on our way to the mine. Can't you be reasonable and understand that?"

"You'll be talking nonsense if Duke gets ahold of you," Smitty said. "The longer you delay, the more you're making yourself the prime suspect in this little drama. Look at this from our point of view. Am I right that in the last twenty-four hours it was you who had a little scuffle with Duke?"

Blassie continued the argument, "He's right. Wouldn't that make people wonder just a little bit if you had something to do with the damage to his car? You, college professor, are the primary suspect."

When Jude saw that Cory was not coming, he had no recourse but to walk to the mob of people at Duke's car. *How, just how, did I ever end up amid this paragon of animals, whom I will trust as I would adders fanged? Wonder why I feel like the quintessence of dust! Now there's a mystery! Wonder why I've lost all my mirth—another mystery! Well, I'll take a fast peek, settle this matter in a second, and be here when my Cory, whom I love passing well, exits.*

As Jude approached the car, he clutched his breast. *But thou wouldst not think how ill all's here about my heart, but it is no matter.*

CHAPTER 23

Jude's plan was to quickly examine the damage to Duke's '57, establish his innocence, and then scurry back to the car. *After all, I was at the hospital picking up Cory and therefore have an airtight alibi. Once I quickly establish my innocence, I'll rush her away from this madness! But for now, I need to face the rubberneckers at Duke's car!*

Standing in the center near Duke's '57 Chevy, Abe wore a fatherly smile on his face as Jude approached. "He's coming at last!" Abe said. "But did you ever see a guiltier face?" *Swill, baby, swill!* "Look at him!"

"He really does," Blassie agreed.

Jude, Huddy, and Al walked together towards Duke's car. His fists still clenched, Huddy spoke first, "Hey, prissy professor. Take a look." He gestured toward the taillight and mag wheel. "The assembled jury thinks you might know something about this!"

"Yeah," yelled another. "Who else but Hepler has tangled lately with Duke?"

"You should see Duke's sore head," shouted one of the women.

A picker standing beside her friend agreed. "Yeah. Duke's head hurt so bad today that he kept his helmet off. Wonder how he got the goose egg?"

Another shouted, "We heard you made him so mad that he slammed his fist into a tree and broke his hand!"

"Look," Jude interjected, "I don't know a thing about the damage to Duke's car since I wasn't even here. Cory was in the hospital, and I left the mine to pick her up. The boss let me go early and arranged for someone else to drive my crew out of the mine. Any of the women will vouch for me. How could I have done this when I wasn't even here?"

Jude spoke with great feeling. *I'm angry that I'm being charged for a crime I didn't do, and the last thing I want to do is rile these men and pit them against me, especially at a time when Cory so desperately needs me!* He again looked toward the mine entrance. *Is my Cory all right? I can't spot her in this large mob, which is obstructing the entryway.*

"Get a little closer here and take a look, Jude," Abe remarked. "That's all we ask. We don't want any trouble." *Like hell! Conscience and grace, to the profoundest pit!* "We just want you to answer a couple questions, thereby proving your innocence. Surely you see the validity of our concern."

Jude walked closer toward the rear of the car to examine the damage. *I see a couple women from my crew who can verify my early departure. Once they do that, I'll be free to find Cory and leave immediately, and it won't be too soon!* He wormed his way through the large crowd and stood at the back of Duke's car, mere inches away from the damaged taillight. Abe and Bull positioned themselves behind Jude.

"Let me see," Bull said. "I haven't had a close look. I saw the new intake carburetor Duke put on last week but haven't seen the wheels or the superhot Hooker Headers. They sure do put out when riled up. *Like someone else I know!* Bull looked over at Beavers, one of the women with a less-than-sterling reputation. *Yeah, sweetie. I'm talking about you!* Bull shoved his way through the crowd and, in the process, purposely pushed into Abe, who—momentarily knocked off balance—bumped into Jude, whose hands flew out on the trunk of Duke's car. "Excuse me," Bull said. "I tripped."

"Well, maybe I should get a better look too," Abe said. As he bent over to examine the taillight, Abe extending his hand for support, placed it on Jude's. *That looked innocent enough!* "Excuse me. I'm trying to get a better look."

Gratified that this part of the plan had succeeded, Abe sought next to keep the situation from getting out of hand. *Framing Jude is the centerpiece of my little enterprise, but I have to do this subtly so that I appear to be Cory and Jude's ally.*

"Brenda and Izzy," Abe said, "could you women testify to the truth of what Jude said? Did he depart early this afternoon?" *I've called on two women of good standing on Jude's crew. They get along well with him and will rush to defend him. Okay, girlies, that was your cue! Don't be botching your lines!*

"Yes," Brenda said. "He left about two for the hospital to pick up Cory. Jake Cogley filled in for him and drove us out of the mine." Of excellent reputation, Brenda was the perfect person to defend Jude. "Jude's telling the truth."

Izzy agreed. "That's right. I was there when he left. The whole crew saw him go. He couldn't have done this because he wasn't even here, so you guys are barking up the wrong tree!"

"Brenda's right. You're treating Cory awful—just awful! I feel so bad for her."

Abe carefully monitored the proceedings. *Okay, boys and girls. It's now time to ratchet up the manipulation.* "We all know by now about the incident at Beatty's Mill last evening. Seems Duke tried to get a little too cozy with Cory. Jude happened along just then and in a brief scuffle banged Duke's head into his car. You see the damage here." He pointed to the damaged fender. "And we all know about Duke's hand too. Those are the simple and incontestable facts. We further understand that Jude, seeing Duke atop his beloved, had motive to get back at Duke. Stop and imagine in your mind what that would have looked like to Jude."

"Had my man been there, he would have shot first and asked questions later!" Izzy interrupted. "This is Armstrong County, and he's big on true justice—the real stuff!"

"You're right," Abe resumed. "From Jude's point of view, Duke had tried to rape Cory or have sex with her. Here's where it gets tricky because we don't actually know if it was consensual or not. Ascertaining the answer to that is a 'touchy' problem, if you catch my pun. After all, we know about Cory and Duke's relationship back in the spring. They were getting pretty cozy-cozy in the weeks prior to Jude's arrival at the mine, and let's be honest, Duke, like a giddy little schoolboy, was once again on his well-honed trajectory toward yet another conquest. Part of that, I admit, may be speculation, but one thing is certain—Jude is mad as a hornet and thinks revenge should have no bounds."

Like a seasoned lawyer, Abe set forth the points of his argument. "Brenda and Isabel, let me get this straight. You say that Jude had gone to the hospital to pick up Cory. We can easily prove if Jude was on such a mission since we have your word and the word of your crew associates, and many witnesses at the hospital, moreover, could corroborate the veracity of this story. We assume then that part is true." *I've been so friendly and kind to this point that I could be taken for Jude's father, but more to the point, I've convinced them all that I—this mushroom picker-turned-lawyer—am giving Jude a consummately fair hearing. On to the next point: turning the fickle mob against Jude. This is the fun part of the game—manipulating people, molding them like sculptor's clay. Brains to swill. That's my thrill. Now the kill. As I will!*

"What we don't know," Abe resumed, "is what Jude did once he came into the parking lot. He would have had plenty of time to smash Duke's car prior to driving away." He turned to the anxious Jude. "What you've presented appears to be a good alibi, but it also afforded you the perfect opportunity to dally with Duke's car today, as he dallied with your true love last evening. Be open-minded, son. Surely you can see why these good folks tend toward suspicion."

"Yes, I can see why they'd be suspicious," Jude retorted. "And I admit to being mad as a hornet at Duke for what he did last evening, but I'd never do anything dumb like this. Cory and I are trying to put last evening's little incident behind us. I'd never hurt Duke's snazzy car." *Do I have any sympathetic hearers here? Are they with me or not? How all occasions do inform against me!* "What I'm saying about Cory is true. She took a horrible blow to the head at Beatty's Mill, and her headache is so severe that the doctor is very concerned. I brought her here just so she could get her Bible and sketch pad, but I've got to get her home immediately. Why is that so hard to understand?"

At this point, Jude looked over at the building and at last saw Cory, standing to the right of where he thought she would exit. *Has she been standing there the whole time and watching this mad alterca-*

tion? Reenergized by her presence, Jude attempted a more assertive stance. "Look, people, I don't know a thing about this, and I feel terrible for Duke. I hope the culprit is caught immediately and brought to justice, but I didn't do it. Surely you can see that I must get Cory home. We can't stand by and allow her to have another irrational episode." *Maybe I can appeal to their emotions.* "Look at her standing there. Don't her haunted eyes show the stress she's enduring?" Jude decided to go on the offensive. "Why are you subjecting a fellow employee, one who's performed award-winning work here for years, to this kind of inhumane treatment?"

Another of Cory's good friends, Cindy Atkinson, quickly allied with Jude. "I believe what Jude's saying. My niece was one of the nurses in on Cory's case, and she said that Cory was babbling nonsense. We owe it to Cory to give her a fair shake. She's one of the top pickers in the mine and would never hurt a flea."

Izzy came to Cindy's aid. "Look at Cory, standing there scared to death. I've never seen such haunted, red eyes. You can tell she's been crying her head off!" Not at all threatened by the men, Izzy looked at them fiercely. "I can't believe you guys are doing this to her!"

The entire group turned to face Cory, who had walked from the entrance toward Jude's car. Jude managed to get her attention and yelled across the parking lot. "Hi, Cory! I'll be right there. There's nothing to worry about!" *Then we'll flee these tragedians of the city!* Turning his attention to the group, he spoke again, a tear in his eye. "Guys, I see the seriousness of the problem here, and I completely agree that we need to get to the bottom of it. I'll gladly help, but right now I need to take Cory home. Let me do that, and if you want, I'll come right back."

Jude started working his way through the murmuring crowd. Some of the men and women, assuming his innocence, stepped aside to let him pass. Others, imputing guilt, stood their ground and forced Jude to shove by them, a couple of the stalwart men even elbowing and shouldering him as he passed.

Nearly frantic by now, Jude pushed his remaining way to the periphery. Free of the crowd, he quickly ran across the parking lot to Cory, who by now stood near the passenger door of his car. *Even at this distance, I can tell that she's terribly upset—a document in madness! Oh no, she has that awful, blank, death-in-life look on her face! "O heavens, is it possible a young maid's wits should be as mortal as an old man's life?"* Fighting panic for his beloved Cory, Jude sprinted the final yards to his car, just as Duke, informed about the damage to his car, exited the building and raced in the direction of the crowd.

"What the hell is going on?" Duke bellowed, his face red with fury. Focused on his '57 and the people around it, he did not see Jude, at his right periphery, getting into his car.

"Duke!" Huddy screamed. "Nab Jude before he gets away. We think he knows something about your damaged car. Grab him!"

Duke stopped midstep and whirled around. "Hey, Hepler," he screeched. "Is that true? Tell me now—I'll not be juggled with! What's going on?" Duke watched Jude moved toward his car. "Don't dare get in that car before I talk to you!" He started toward Jude, who was now at the driver's door.

"Jude, let's get out of here. I'm going crazy!" Cory yelled from inside the car. "I'm not feeling well, and I want to go home and see Mom. Mommy, mommy! Want mommy!"

"I have to get my Cory home. She's very sick!" Jude screamed at Duke. His legs and torso were already inside the car, his head awkwardly craned backward toward Duke. He slammed the door shut and sped away as Duke ran toward his car.

"You bastard, come back here! Stop or I'll kill you!"

Jude raced out of the parking lot.

CHAPTER 24

His face contorted in fury, Duke sped in the direction of his car. Venom shot from his mouth. "I'll kill that SOB! I swear I will! Why didn't someone stop him?" Arriving at his '57, he angrily pushed several people out of the way, shoving one of the women into another car.

Huddy spoke first, "Jude Hepler was acting awful suspicious when he was here a second ago. You saw him make a fast getaway even when you told him to stop. If you want my opinion, you just let the culprit get away." Never one to recoil from any intimidating scene, even the furious Duke, Huddy looked him square in the face. "You had your chance to nail him and you blew it, big guy. Don't pin this sabotage on us. He slipped out of your hands like a squealing greased pig!"

"What the hell are you guys talking about, and what's this about my car being banged up? If that's true, someone's gonna die!" Pushing people aside as though they were mannequins in Montgomery Ward, Duke cut a path to the back of his car where several people were pointing at the damage. "Who did this, and what's Jude got to do with it?"

"Calm down!" Abe said to Duke. Giving Duke this gentle admonition was a gutsy move on Abe's part since he had not seen Duke so enraged for years. *I meant for that little calculated reprimand to be firm because I haven't seen Duke this out of control for a long time, but that two-word directive, though intended as loving fatherly advice, was pretty abrasive. Yikes! The last thing I want to do is turn Duke's ferocious wrath toward me. Yet if the next part of my plan is to succeed, it's important for Cory and Jude to regard me as their just and fair ally, who would even stoop to the stupid, if dangerous, level of admonishing Duke.*

To save his own skin, Abe redirected Duke's attention to the matter at hand. "Yes, someone damaged your car this afternoon. We have no idea who, though some are pointing the finger at Jude." Abe gestured toward the taillight and mag wheel. "You see how bad it is."

As Duke ran his fingers over the taillight and the mag wheel, his temper was kindled to white-hot anger. "Somebody is gonna die, and I mean it! I ask again, who did this?" Screaming in rage, he violently kicked the damaged taillight, smashing it to bits.

No one had the nerve to speak, but after a short while, Huddy responded, "The problem is, we don't actually know. Jude Hepler looked like Carl Lewis in the hundred-meter dash when he ran across the lot, and then he drove out of here like he was at the Lernerville Speedway. He made up this flimsy excuse about Cory being wacko and hightailed it out of here. He was antsy to leave before you showed up. In fact, he kept looking across the lot toward the door to see if you were coming, as if he didn't want to face you. Well, when he saw your butt, he took off in a run." Huddy turned and looked at some of the assembled people. "It doesn't look good for the professor. Am I right, guys?"

"Yep, I agree," several others joined in.

Abe felt that his mission, to this point, was accomplished. *Duke and several of his close friends are very upset about the damaged car, but much more importantly, they point their fingers toward Jude. So far, so good. Well done, counselor! My next objective is to leverage Duke to retaliate, but before that, I must prove that Jude is culpable. If that is not done to the satisfaction of the mine workers, there will always be those who feel that Jude and Cory were railroaded out of the mine unfairly. Unanimous consensus, dependent on incontestable proof, is necessary. Revenge should have no bounds, true, but it can't appear to be the reckless work of inebriated thugs!*

All of this flashed through Abe's brilliant mind in seconds. *This jelly mass is starting to mirror Duke and Huddy's increasing irrationality. That is not good, and if I'm not careful, I could have lynch-mob justice on my hands! Boys and girls, it's time for me to act. One needs a good exit plan in case of emergency—my motto always—and this is the perfect time to reestablish decorum and control.*

"Look, folks," Abe calmly began. "No, we're not chasing after Jude, and nobody's going to Grannie Rosetta's farm to get him. We're too civilized to stoop to lynch-mob vigilante justice. We had one whiskey rebellion around here, and we'll not have another one!" *How am I doing? You suckers taking this in?* "All of you go home. Duke and I will talk this thing through and strategically plot our course of action. Don't you agree that this is the thing to do?" *Animal-man Duke is still fuming and standing there like an armed savage!* "What we don't need is a lot of infighting since there are many intelligent ways of proving Jude's guilt or innocence. Duke and I will calmly plan our strategy. Right, Duke?" *I'm crossing my fingers that he'll comply so I can break up this tense scene! Agree with me, you stooge! Everything's on the line!*

"Well, I guess so."

During this speech, Abe appeared to be the picture of calm, his one hand on his hip in his characteristic posture and his index and center fingers stretched across the chin and lips, sporadically tapping them. He feigned tranquility, but this was one instance when even he was rattled. *I've seen mob mentality in the past among workers in various plants and don't want it to happen here!*

"Please go to your cars," he again urged. Mainly out of respect for Abe, people started walking away. "Duke, I think you should stay here so we can talk for a moment."

"This better be good since talking's the last thing I want to do! You saw Hepler run from me when I showed my face. What more proof do we want?" Inches away from Abe's face, he again spoke loudly, "You're delaying the inevitable. Don't piss with me, old man! I'll be revenged!"

"Slow down." *Your rebellion looks so giantlike!* "What if Jude is telling the truth? Besides, if anyone knows why Cory's upset, it's you. Her face is still puffy and swollen. Cindy's niece saw Cory at the hospital and said Cory was speaking irrationally and even hallucinating. We need proof before we act. Do I think Jude did it? Probably so. But we need proof. Will you be ruled by me?"

"Abe, talk to me. How are we ever going to prove it?" Duke was beginning to calm down, but his face was still flushed in anger. He rapidly flicked his index and middle finger back and forth, one of his mannerisms when nervous.

"Easily. Have you ever heard of fingerprints? All we need to do is dust the car to see if there are prints. Then we compare those to Jude's, and that too is easily done. We can dust his helmet, steering wheel on the shop mule, or anything he's touched. Anything."

Duke pulled his work boot off and massaged his toes. "I kicked that ole taillight harder than I meant!" Putting his shoe back on, he answered, "Maybe you're right, after all. This damage isn't all that much to fix." Duke was already mentally calculating the short time to replace the taillight.

"I agree." *His spirit has settled down, but how much I had to do to calm his rage!*

"What you say about Cory is true. I don't want to see her hurt." He paced back and forth, still flicking his fingers. "What I did last night was awful, but it happened because I was drinking." He angrily spat on the ground. "Tina drags me down because she's so sexy and turns me on in a second!"

Abe resumed his jovial, easy manner. "Well, I make no comment about you and Tina, but I do know that checking fingerprints is the one sure way to ascertain innocence or guilt." *I've regained my composure now that Duke's wrath has dissipated. At last!* "Drive your car over to my house, and we'll dust it right now for prints. Don't touch the car."

"Why would you have fingerprinting equipment? Who has that kind of stuff at their house? Do you moonlight as a freaking detective?"

"A good friend of mine from Glen Burnie, Maryland, was a Secret Service agent who used to do detective work on the side. When he retired, he wanted rid of all the reminders of his tough law-enforcement days. Instead of throwing out this kit, I told Bill I'd take it. I've never used it, but it can't be that hard for the two of us to figure it out." *What a lie—I'm a pro at using it!*

Duke immediately drove to Abe's house. Once there, Abe pretended to look in several places for his fingerprinting set, but it was not to be found. Finally, he located it in a lower desk drawer. *I'll pretend to read the instructions as though fingerprinting for the first time.* With Duke's advice and assistance, he began to dust the car. "Here, you do it, Duke. My hands aren't as nimble as yours, and my knees are acting up again."

Duke started to dust the car. "Is this how you do it?" He went over the car, especially dusting the area of the taillight and dented mag wheel. "There aren't any prints around the taillight. I guess I'm not doing it right."

"Some clever chap," Abe indifferently commented, "was wearing gloves when doing the dastardly deed."

"I think you're right."

After a while, Abe walked away as though they had completed their task but then glanced over his shoulder to an area neither of them had dusted. *Duke's almost finished, so it's time to stop playing games and dust the area in the center of the trunk where Jude's hand touched.* "What about the trunk, Duke?" Abe said, pointing. "You didn't take any prints there, did you?"

"No, I didn't."

Allowing Duke to take the lead, Abe stood back. "This work never ends. The grass needs mowed again, and the strawberries need picked." He moved his head as though looking at the lawn and feigned indifference to the fingerprinting task at end, but his eyes were riveted to Duke's work the entire time. *Soon he'll be at the place where I pressed my hand on Jude's!*

"Look at this," Duke said in a moment. "Most of the prints are kind of blurred, and the ones that are clear are probably mine—they're everywhere. But look at this. Here's a vivid print of an entire hand!"

"Lovely," Abe said. "Good work!" *You stooge!*

CHAPTER 25

Duke continued to look at the fingerprints which he had dusted from his car. "These prints from the trunk are definitely different from my fingerprints, so what do we do now—somehow get Jude's prints and compare them?"

"Do you think we should? How would you do that?"

"Like you said before. Get them off his helmet or steering wheel or anything we know he's touched! I can't believe it—the lousy SOB!"

The next morning at work, Duke, with Abe's assistance, managed to pull Jude's fingerprints from his locker, lunch box, helmet, and even the steering wheel of his shop mule. As previously arranged, the two men met a while later outside room 8 to compare the fingerprints with those they had lifted from Duke's Chevy.

"Well, I'll be!" Abe said, noting the similarity.

"These are Jude's prints, no doubt about it. That liar acted like he knew nothing about the damage to my car!" Duke leaned back against his mule, looking at the two sets of prints. "Now we have proof that he smashed my car! Abe, I swear I'll kill him!"

"Slow down, Duke. Remember what we said last night. The guys will tar and feather Jude over this because they'll hate him for damaging your classic car. Let them be the ones to take the lead in punishing Jude. Your hands can be as lily white as a mafia boss who uses underling soldiers to do the dirty work."

"Yeah, I suppose you're right, but it kills me not to get my own sweet revenge."

"Look at it this way. You don't want Cory crying over him after he's gone. In time she'll slowly come around, and if you play your cards right, you'll soon be back with her as you were before."

"I'm not so sure. I really blew it with her."

"I told you the way to do it. Help her dad and Joey on the farm as you did before and express interest in the kind of things she enjoys. I'm planning to go to Pittsburgh to see a production of Shakespeare's play *Hamlet*. If you went with me, you'd make up a lot of lost ground."

Duke held the fingerprints side by side in his hand and closely examined them. "I don't know. I can handle farmwork but not a loser Shakespeare play!"

"In a short time, Cory will slowly start to come around. If you'd get your head on straight, you'd go with me to see the play this Saturday. Yes, it'd be a sacrifice on your part, but it's the kind of sacrifice you have to make to compensate for your jackass deeds. You aren't forgetting how worthwhile the prize is, are you?" Abe pulled out the wallet picture of the nude Cory. "This is why you proceed cautiously and why getting rid of Jude is half the battle. As they say back in the shop, you need to cool your tool, fool."

"Maybe you're right."

"Of course, I'm right." Abe returned the photo to his wallet. "As I said, we need to come up with a plan that will turn Cory against Jude. Once Jude is out of here, she'll get over him in time and be ripe for picking. And what a luscious dessert she'll be!"

"She'll never turn against Jude."

"Just hear me out. There are ways to a woman's heart. Besides, it won't take much to remind her that Jude walked out on her for five long years. That's her very vulnerable spot, and she no doubt lives in fear that he might do it again."

"I'm not so sure. After Beatty's Mill, I can't imagine Cory ever dumping Jude for me."

"Not so fast. Remember how Cory lit up when she talked to you last spring about the Bible and art and Shakespeare? That's the way to her heart. Tell her you're interested in speaking about her favorite artists. Say you miss their discussions, that you want to go to church again, that you need help in understanding the Bible. That's a huge one, very big. Yes, tell her you're reading the Bible again."

"I don't think even that will work since I've reached the point of no return."

"No, you haven't! Stop saying that! Cory talks incessantly about forgiveness. You know she'll forgive you since her religion requires it. You want to score big? I'll say it again." *I can't believe it, big as an ox, but you're starting to melt already!* "Go with me to Pittsburgh to see the play. Cory will be there and will love you for going. The woman is wild over Shakespeare."

"Will you listen to yourself! You keep telling me to go to a freaking Shakespeare play! You're nuts if you think I'd ever show my face at a place like that. What would the guys say? I can just hear Bull, Blassie, Hank, and the rest. Next thing I know, Huddy will be giving me a skirt and a voucher for ballet classes! The guy's as tough as Jack Lambert and even built like him."

"Think again, Duke. Cory is definitely worth the sacrifice. Sacrifice is the name of the game, and it's what you have to do. I'm going to the play, and you ought to be seated beside me. Keep this in mind. If you get the prize in the end, who cares about the cost?" *This will get him!* "When you're with Cory—in all the ways you want—you won't be thinking about your buddies' wisecracks. Your sacrifice will be worth it, and you'll be thanking me, and Shakespeare too, a thousand times over!"

"But isn't there some other way? This is an awful plan."

"'Love bears, believes, hopes, and endures all things.' Remember how Cory used to quote you that verse? Love bears and endures lots of things, and that includes doing things you don't like. It's your call, Duke. I'm not about to tell anyone what to do, but I wouldn't take the prize too lightly." He patted his wallet to remind Duke of the photo. "The belle of the ball and the tigress of the tunnels can be yours and yours alone *if* you play your cards right."

"Abe, let me set you straight on one thing. I'm not about to deny that I'd like to get it together with Cory, but I'm changing and changing fast since I've started to have deep feelings for her. I can't say that I love her, but I do know it just ain't about wanting sex like it used to be." Duke looked wistfully down the darkened corridor. "I'm telling you, man, I care a lot for her." He paused talking while one of the noisy personnel carriers passed.

"I know you do."

This will sound strange to you, old man! "What I'm saying is that I'm feeling the need to settle down and get married, and I'd even love to have kids. At some point, I have to grow up and stop acting like a freaking adolescent." He paused and looked at Abe. "But if you tell Huddy and the guys I'm thinking about going to a Shakespeare play, you're dead meat."

"Don't be so concerned about the reaction of your friends. You can't have any more missteps with Cory. Even across the parking lot I could see her swollen face. That was idiotic, Duke. Just where was your head?"

"I know. That was really dumb, but consider the source. I'm stupid—period!"

Abe returned the two sets of fingerprints to Duke, who, prints in his hand, departed into the dimly lit corridor. As Abe watched him walk into the darkness, a mental image flashed in his mind of an incident that occurred during Christ's passion. *He reminds me of Judas's farewell to Jesus Christ in the Upper Room when, departing to sell Jesus for thirty pieces of silver, Judas walked away from his only source of redemption, peace, hope, and sanity. The Gospel writer John symbolically captures that hideous moment: "He then went out immediately. And it was night." Well, it was night for Judas, as it's night for you, Duke. I just have to keep it that way. Yes, keep him in the dark. What's the proverb? "For by means of a whorish woman a man is brought to a piece of bread." May that be the case with Duke. I merely have to convince him that Cory's a whorish woman and his for the taking. So what will my next move be? Swill that brain, then suck it dry. Won't be in vain, Jude's gonna die!"*

That evening in his study, Abe was apparently satisfied that, with the success of the fingerprinting, he had planted the revenge seed, as his journal entry made clear. "I can't believe I had the audacity to do it, but I actually urged Duke to join me at the Three Rivers Festival production of *Hamlet.* In fact, I referred to it a couple times. At first, he snickered in the way I knew he would, but I can tell he's giving it serious thought. Ah, *Hamlet* in Pittsburgh—what a clever mousetrap that will be!"

CHAPTER 26

After the debacle surrounding Duke's Chevy, Jude blasted out of the parking lot, the whole time trying to divert Cory's attention from the jostling crowd, especially madman Duke.

Cory, unfortunately, had turned around and saw the hysterical Duke running after them in mad pursuit. "Hurry, Jude! He'll rape me. This time, he'll do it! Go faster!"

Her headache more intense, she clutched her head with both fists as though it would explode. On their way out the long entrance road to the mine, Cory rested her head on the back of the seat. "I keep seeing Duke come at me!" She vigorously rubbed her head. "I can't take this pain!"

Jude did his best to calm her as they drove home. "Honey, it's going to be all right. Duke won't get you now that you're with me. Soon you'll be home, and we'll get you a pain pill right away."

At Cory's farmhouse a short while later, Jude walked her to the porch, his arm around her, and offered to make her a cup of tea.

"Thanks, but no thanks. I need to rest, but I do want to talk to you since that's the only thing that seems to calm the voices in my head. You wouldn't believe the weird thoughts that keep shooting through my brain, especially flashbacks of the bad days."

"That's probably natural."

"The voices are crazy and say things like this: 'You'll never amount to anything. You've gotten in life what you deserve. Jude doesn't truly love an emotional wreck like you. There's no way out!' On and on, the garbage never stops." She looked at him forlornly. "I agree that a nap is what I need right now, but promise me we'll talk this evening."

"Yes, we'll talk, but not now since you need to rest. If you feel up to it, you can work on your latest sketch or read the Bible once you awake from your nap."

"Sounds good."

"We could sit on the porch or ride up on Vinlindeer this evening if that isn't too taxing. What do you think?" He brushed the stray hairs from her cheek and kissed her gently. *Sometimes when you speak, you have that faraway, disconnected look! Do you see this, O God?*

"It all sounds good. We'll decide once you come over."

"It's a deal." *But what a relief that she's at least talking rationally!*

Back in his room at grandma's house, Jude collapsed on his bed in anguish. He was appalled at the number of events that conspired against him in recent days. *Earlier, Cory was so wildly distraught that she was hallucinating, a full-blown conspiracy against the two of us is brewing at the mine, Duke has vowed vengeance against me, and through the whole ordeal, Abe becomes ever more mysterious.* Jude cried out to God as he gave full vent to these horrible developments. *These men, though typically fun, good, and even honorable, can be dangerous when riled. Though that's a real problem, it's but a trifle when I think of my ultimate worry—what's going on with my beloved Cory? Why such violent headaches and periodic delusions? What should be my course of action?*

While kneeling in fervent prayer, an idea came to him. *I can't talk to Dr. Buck until morning, but I could call Chuck Claypoole on the telephone!* After a few pleasantries, Jude explained to Charles that Cory was doing poorly and "was divided from herself and her fair judgment."

"Very good, Jude. I like your *Hamlet* quote," Charles responded. "Though, of course, I'm very upset to hear this. You're saying she has been 'troubled with thick-coming fancies that keep her from her rest.'"

"*Macbeth*, act 5, scene 3. Exactly. Her hallucinations are like Lady Macbeth's thick-coming fancies. Chuck, I'm worried sick about my dear Cory. She's been a mess ever since the trauma at Beatty's Mill."

"How sad!"

Overcome by the gravity of the whole mad affair, Jude hesitated for a moment. "I'm at my wit's end and don't know what to do. We're in the middle of an imbroglio at the mines that worsens by the hour, and even more awful than that, Cory was crazy delusional today. Fortunately, she's now resting comfortably and seems to be herself again." He paused. "At least for the time being."

"Here's an idea. Take her mind off Duke and the situation at the mines by getting her away from this immediate environment, somewhere far removed from the distressing things that plague her here." Charles paused to reflect for a moment. "Maybe you could take her to Pittsburgh. Everybody likes Oakland—Heinz Chapel, the Carnegie Museum, Phipps Conservatory, the Frick Fine Arts Building. She'd love some time in Oakland, and the change of scenery would do her a world of good."

"Great idea!" Jude said excitedly.

"You could even stop by Stephen Foster theater to watch some of the afternoon *Hamlet* rehearsal. Surely she'd like that."

"Fabulous, Charles. You don't think the director would mind?"

"I'm positive. I know the codirector would be delighted, and I'm sure I speak for Winnie Armrose too."

"This really is a good idea, and maybe just what the doctor ordered."

After Cory's refreshing nap, Jude told her of his plan later that evening.

"What a great idea! I'd like that a lot, and seeing the rehearsal of *Hamlet* would be thrilling."

"Good!" *It's been a while since I saw a spark like that in her eyes! I can't help but wonder, what will the morrow hold?*

As they sat on the porch that evening, Zoe beside them, Jude was greatly relieved to see that Cory's tranquility continued. *She's made perfect sense the entire hour we've been together, and she's spoken of the things that typically interest her—working on her sketches, reading* Hamlet *and the book of Esther, and talking to Old Mary again.*

"Old Mary talked about the rose story today, and though I remember a lot of it, some of the details are foggy because I had such a headache while she was talking. I wasn't focusing properly and couldn't grasp all the relevant details."

"There will be time for that." *She's yawned a couple times and appears to be getting tired again. I think I should call it quits.*

As Jude got up to leave, Cory took his hands in hers. "I hope we can chat with Old Mary soon. She was on the verge of telling me something important when I had to leave her room at the hospital. There's something crazy about her recurring dream."

"Yes, there is."

"She says it relates to us. That's the part she was coming to when I had to leave. Now there's a strange thought! I hope we talk to her soon."

Moments later, Jude held her tightly and kissed her passionately. *How I love this woman!* He tore himself away with the greatest difficulty.

He ended his journal entry for that day. "Pittsburgh is our tune! *Hamlet*, see you soon!"

CHAPTER 27

Jude and Cory had planned their outing to Pittsburgh for the next Saturday. During their phone chat early that morning, Cory did not tell Jude that her headache had returned with a vengeance through the night. Because the bedtime pill eased the pain only slightly, she took another at 3:00 a.m. Though this middle-of-the-night medication gave her temporary relief and induced fitful sleep, the headache and general feeling of disorientation lessened only minimally. *Maybe I ought to cancel, but I don't want to since a day in Pittsburgh will be very exciting. I just don't want to miss it!* She leafed through a tour guide of Pittsburgh. *These cultural gems rival the very best in the nation, and sitting in on a rehearsal of* Hamlet *for a while would be great.* She picked up a leaflet on Heinz Chapel. *The stained-glass windows in the chapel are beautiful! Best of all, I'll be spending the day with my beloved, away from the lunacy of the mine. I want to do this. I really need to do this!*

On the one hand, she was encouraged that she continued to think rationally; but on the other hand, her headache worsened by morning and was nearly as intense as it had been after the initial assault. *Here I am again, wondering if I should postpone, but the exciting stimulation of the city would compensate for my duress, so I think it's best not to tell Jude about my headache. He'd just worry and, as always, be completely sensible and try to talk me out of going. I don't want that to happen.* She again rubbed her temples. *But this pain is so intense!*

She picked up the phone and called Jude. "Honey, I'm not at my prime—far from it, as you'll see—but I still think we can go. In fact, I think it's what I need to get my mind off things. I really feel I should get away for the day."

"We can cancel since the last thing I want to do is take you into Pittsburgh if you're not up to it. It's all right with me if we go some other time. Besides, we've got all summer, so maybe it's better if we delay? Think about it. A quiet day of rest here is a pretty inviting alternative."

"But I really want to go. I was so looking forward...to our day together. I think...I'll be okay. At least I'm not nauseous now, and those horrible thoughts in my brain have stopped." She paused and neither said anything for a moment as she sipped her Earl Grey tea. "Yes, I've made up my mind. I want to go. If I start feeling really bad through the day, we'll just come home and save part two for later."

"If that's what you want, but there's no need to force this."

"I'll be fine." She hung up the phone and took her third pill in eight hours.

A short while later, Jude was shocked when he picked up Cory. *She looks unwell and has a haggard look from her poor night's rest.* He was so astounded that he wrote of it in his journal:

> She had black rings under her eyes, the first time I had seen anything close to this. For a moment, I thought that she applied mascara or sloppy eyeliner! She seemed unusually nervous and fidgeted with her hands—a constant drumming and tapping of her fingertips—which I'd never seen before. I again proposed postponement, but Cory was adamant. "I want to go!" Since she had not spoken irrationally and was not hallucinating, I attributed her distressed look and unkempt appearance to her bad night's sleep and her headache, which I hoped would pass as the day wore on.

Nevertheless, how strange it was for Jude to see her this way. *Normally, she's a fanatic about her neat appearance—every strand of hair in place, clothes neat and perfectly ironed. But today her hair is awry, her jeans and blouse rumpled, and she's wearing an old pair of shoes, which she wears only for outdoor work. I wish I could gently override her strong desire to go and cancel. I just don't know what to do!*

Nevertheless, they drove to Pittsburgh and started their day with a leisurely tour of the Phipps Conservatory Summer Flower Show. It was a huge hit for Cory. "I have so many favorites rooms that I can't decide which one I like best. Which is your favorite?"

"That's a tough call," Jude replied. "I love the stateliness of the Palm Court. It really is magnificent, but I guess the Broderie Room is my favorite. At least for today."

"Why?"

"The manicured boxwood and the symmetrical layout of that room remind me of the Italian Renaissance gardens of Europe. It makes me think of the gardens at Hampton Court or the Knott Garden at Stratford-upon-Avon. In case you didn't know, Knott Garden is behind the ruins of New Place where Shakespeare used to live. What's your favorite?" *I've caught her rubbing her temples as we've strolled from room to room, but since she hasn't complained about her headache, I won't mention it.*

She thought for a moment. "I really like the water display, the cute bridge and so on in the East Room, but the Orchid Room is truly magnificent. I saw that room as a child and remember that it was Mom's favorite. That's partly why I like it so much—it makes me think of Mom. In fact, I purchased the Milton Orchid in the den for her."

"I didn't know that."

"I bet you didn't know this either. I like orchids almost as much as roses."

"No, I didn't, but I see why. They are exquisite." They continued their stroll hand in hand through the various galleries. "Name one more favorite room, and then I'll give you my other favorite."

"Okay." She thought for a moment and looked again at the brochure to remind herself. She pointed to the map. "The Victoria Room is amazing to me, so I guess I'd pick that, but the Sunken Garden is truly special too. I guess I'd go with the Sunken Garden as my other favorite. And you?"

"If you can pick two, so can I!" Jude laughed, and so did Cory. *That was a pretty subdued laugh and not the full-throated one that normally wells up from deep inside her.* "I'd say either the Desert Room because of the way it reminds me of the great American West, or maybe the Serpentine Room. But I'd better not pick the Serpentine Room because that makes me think of a certain other serpent, and goodness knows we came here to escape thoughts of him today! Right?"

"You're right!" She again glanced at the brochure. "The fact is, I enjoy all the award-winning flower arrangements, the festive color, and the artful arrangements. That's why I shouldn't pick favorites. I love all of them. It takes a really skilled staff of floral artists to arrange all these exhibits." She gazed at the plethora of flowers surrounding her. "I'd love to do some still-life paintings of the flowers. I'd start with that bird of paradise over there, and there's a daisy. I would give you some violets, but they withered all. But this bird of paradise hasn't withered. It is gorgeous!"

What of rosemary? "That's for remembrance. Pray you, love, remember." Remember, Cory, remember what you are! My love, don't ever again be divided from yourself and your fair judgment!

As they neared the exit and looked back on the flower exhibits, Cory continued to feel well and spoke with genuine excitement. "Jude, look at these marvelous flower arrangements. The mix of colors is…brilliant." She lifted her eyes from the flowers to the architecture of the building. "Here's something else. I didn't know that Phipps was the last…Victorian-style conservatory in the nation. At least I think it is. There's another credit to our great city."

"It is indeed, and speaking of great architecture, it's now time for stop two, Heinz Chapel!"

Although the second stop at Heinz Chapel a short while later started well, Jude suggested that they cut their day short. *She's showing signs of exhaustion. I've caught her rubbing her temples several times, and she keeps rolling her neck. Her headache has intensified too, and there's something going on with her speech. She's speaking less and hesitating more and even started a sentence or two which she didn't complete, almost as if she lost her train of thought. That is pretty disturbing!*

Out of fear that another attack was impending and might cut short their enjoyable sightseeing, Cory went to the restroom, where she took yet another pill. *I won't tell Jude I took this. He'll want to go home right away, but I think this headache will pass once the pill kicks in.*

"I don't want to leave just yet," Cory protested upon her return from the restroom. "These stained-glass windows are magnificent." They were marveling at the famous Heinz Chapel windows by Charles J. Connick. "Let's stay just a little bit longer, okay?"

"It's been a great morning. I say we postpone part two."

"If I get tired, we'll leave. Pretty please!"

Jude reluctantly agreed. *Maybe I'll try a diversion to distract her from her anxiety.* "For openers, tell me something about Connick. Wasn't he one of the top stained-glass artists in the nation? Give me a few facts out of that encyclopedic brain of yours."

"You're hitting me at a weak spot. I don't know that much really, but I do know that he produced some of the best stained-glass windows—in the Gothic Revival style, that is—in the USA."

Jude stopped and ran his eyes over the windows of Heinz Chapel. "His stained glass is truly superb. I heard Old Mary once say that his windows can be found in Pittsburgh-area churches. Is that true?"

"Yes, like Cram's Calvary Church, some of the churches in East Liberty, and Goodhue's First Baptist Church. Those are the ones I remember from the brochure."

"Look at these amazing windows! I know this is great art, but tell me what makes it great. I don't have the artistic sensibility to fully appreciate it, nor do I have the vocabulary to express it. To its high requiem I am a sod!"

"What line of poetry did you adapt there?"

"Keats's 'Ode to a Nightingale.'"

Cory again massaged her temples and forehead and hesitated before speaking. "I wish I felt better to tackle such a good and pertinent question. This will be off the top of my head because I know little about this art form and never studied stained glass." She drew closer to the window to examine it more closely. "But just by looking at it, I'd say his sense and appreciation of color are brilliant. Not all artists blend such a rich array of hues so exquisitely." She stopped speaking, tilted her head to the side, and looked again. "There's a lot going on here in terms of the vast array of subjects. Connick's range and reach astound me. Look how he's all over the world of culture and history." She paused and studied the windows. "But there's something else here, which I'm having trouble grasping."

"What? What are you seeing?"

She stopped speaking and looked again more deeply. "Something about the way in which these particular subjects are good for—I mean perfectly suited to—the stained-glass medium." She massaged the back of her neck. "I'm in over my head here, so I'll stop at that, but who but Connick could adapt such a magnitude of varied subjects for stained-glass windows? That's the point I'm feebly making."

As soon as Cory finished her minidiscourse on Connick's art, she stumbled slightly and sat down as though exhausted. *I'm surprised to see her sit down like that, though I've seen her do this sort of thing when she's overcome by art and left virtually speechless by its beauty. But that was different and smacked of extreme weariness.* Jude sat down beside her. *My guess is that she isn't feeling as good as she's letting on!*

A short while later, Cory rose and ambled to the center of the chapel, touching the pews as she walked. Side by side, they strolled toward the impressive stained-glass windows in the north transept where they gazed in awe.

From the moment she rose out of that pew, she's been different. I can't explain it, but her behavior has definitely altered. He peered into her eyes. *She isn't focusing, her walk is less brisk, and she's not even looking at these stunning windows! Up there's Marcus Aurelius, Massasoit, Pocahontas, and Florence Nightingale. She loves these historic figures so ingeniously rendered in stained glass, but she's barely given them a passing glance! How could she not be aghast at this overwhelming art? She's definitely not herself. Is it possible a young maid's wit should be so mortal?*

Jude pointed to the William Penn window in the north transept. *Maybe this will snap her out of her lethargy. She loves Penn, and his classic* No Cross, No Crown *is a favorite to which she often refers.*

"For obvious reasons, this Penn window has always been a particular favorite for us Pennsylvanians. You agree?"

Cory responded, "It is lovely." She studied the detail in the Penn window. "What would Ohio be without its founder, Penn?"

Jude made no response, though he stole a sideways glance. *Uh-oh! Is this another onset of irrationality starting? What do you mean that Penn founded Ohio?* He clenched his clammy hands as he looked at Cory, who nervously drummed her fingertips on the top of a pew and vigorously rolled her head to massage her neck.

How could she confuse Ohio with Pennsylvania? Jude was aghast. *Lord, help!*

CHAPTER 28

Moments later, Jude and Cory strolled over to the south transept of Heinz Chapel, where he pointed to the depiction of Leonardo da Vinci halfway up the left panel of the right window. *I'll offer some biographical highlights on the great Leonardo. If I babble for a while, I'll give my subconscious time to think and, simultaneously, maybe spark her interest in her very favorite subject—art. Maybe that will help reground her.* "Were you aware that Leonardo didn't put a halo around the Virgin Mary in the *Virgin of the Rocks* because he felt such an accessory was superfluous? Scholars think he was striving for greater realism." *Is she mentally engaged? Not sure, but I'll keep going.* "That was a key component of Italian Renaissance painting. If anyone knows about that, it's you. Sorry to invade your domain of expertise. You should be educating me!"

"No, I wasn't aware of that…but the Sistine Chapel is still my favorite Leonardo painting."

When Jude looked at Cory, he saw the same emotional blankness that had so alarmed him immediately after the injury. *People who are completely ignorant of the world of art might attribute one of Michelangelo's masterpieces to Leonardo, but Cory Mohney would never ever be one of them! Cory's severe headache and exhaustion may, at a stretch, account for such mental slips, but I just can't discount the severity of the blow to the head or minimize the frequency of these cognitive lapses.* He tightly clenched the top of a pew. *We should be visiting a doctor instead of cultural showpieces! What do I do? Maybe I ought to encourage her to step outside for some fresh air. The bright sunlight could be a real balm.*

A few moments later, they departed Heinz Chapel and meandered toward the Cathedral of Learning. Jude was seeking for a viable excuse to return home when Cory, again rational and smiling, said that she eagerly awaited the rehearsal of *Hamlet.* "Seeing the *Hamlet* rehearsal will settle me down. I'm really excited about that. Do you believe I confused Leonardo da Vinci and Michelangelo back there in the chapel? That was surely a first for this old gal! Maybe this pain med is playing with my head!" Smiling warmly, she put her arm through Jude's and leaned her head against his shoulder as they walked toward the Cathedral of Learning. "Thanks for being patient with me, Jude. I don't know what came over me, but I'm feeling great now." She looked up at the sky. "What a beautiful day. Look at those towering thunderheads. I've never seen taller cumulous clouds. Give me an easel and a brush to paint that Empire State Building of clouds in the sky!"

That, my dear, was an impressive metaphor. Well done, Cory! I'm happy to see you gush so animatedly, but I can't forget the distressing mental disconnect back there in the chapel! "Are you sure you want to do this, Cory? There's always tomorrow."

"Yes, I really do. I want to watch at least some of the rehearsal. I'm so proud that Center Hill's Chuck is a big city director, especially for Shakespeare's immortal masterpiece. I want to see the results of his hard work."

"We can come later for the dress rehearsal or even the main production someday next week."

"You gave Chuck some important insights into the main characters, and I want to see if those will creep into their dramatic portrayals. We won't know till we see!" Again she smiled in her girlish manner, crinkling her nose into that half-smile, half-snoot look. "Pretty please? I promise to be a good girl...and sane too!"

With a feeling of trepidation, Jude, a short while later, seated himself beside Cory in the third row of the Stephen Foster Memorial theater. Charles Claypoole, standing in the front of the auditorium next to the stage, saw Jude and Cory enter and walked down to them. More than a little shocked, he stole a sideways glance at Cory. "Glad you could make it. I realize I'm speaking to two Shakespeare aficionados, so do please give me your opinion after the rehearsal, all right? I'd love to have your reaction."

"Promise," Jude said.

Charles's detailed journal entry described the scene:

> I knew something was going on with Cory as soon as I saw her. She just wasn't herself. The joy and the sheer effervescence that have consistently been her hallmark since her reconciliation with Jude were completely absent. More telling than that, she was sloppy in appearance. That I don't ever remember seeing, not in Cory. She barely spoke to me and slouched in her seat in a most slovenly way. Because she was standing directly beside him, Jude wasn't able to speak to me about Cory's comportment, but his eyes spoke volumes. At one point, when Cory was preoccupied with the stage proceedings and on the verge of commenting about it, he looked at me almost in helpless appeal, and I thought he was on the verge of speaking, but then, for whatever reason, chose silence.
>
> Upon their first entering the theater, Cory, though unkempt, made sense, even if her crisp witty retorts and normal mental acuity were noticeably absent. But shortly into the rehearsal, Jude knew they had made a mistake in coming to the rehearsal, though I was slow to come to that realization, preoccupied as I was with the rehearsal. After their short break, the actors started into scene 4 of act 1, the scene during which King Claudius's counselor, Polonius, tells his daughter, Ophelia, to reject Hamlet's overtures of love. We were at the line when Polonius tells Ophelia that he doesn't want her "to give words or talk with the Lord Hamlet."

Before speaking of what happened at this juncture, I offer a side-bar observation. The character of Ophelia, whether on the page or stage, has always fascinated me. Such was the case in this instance. I was more interested in Shakespeare's fantasy character than in Jan Neale's solid, flesh-and-blood depiction of it on stage. But the truth is, whether in the theater of my mind or the theater of the stage, I find Ophelia's painful demise terribly sad and am brought to the brink of horror every time I see her undoing. As I walked to my place offstage right to watch the scene, I recalled Eugene O'Neill's line from *Long Day's Journey into Night*: "The mad scene. Enter Ophelia." How ironic that this particular line came to mind at this precise moment of our afternoon rehearsal!

We were not far into the scene when I stole a glance at Cory and noted a change in her behavior—a profound change. Despite her appearance and lethargy, she had been emotionally calm upon entering the theater, but now she was nervously squirming in her seat. She spoke so loudly to Jude—"Poor girl. What a head case Ophelia is!"—that it caught my attention and that of the downstage actors, who stole a quick glance in her direction. As the scene unfolded, I found myself watching Cory as much as the actors on stage!

A moment later, when Ophelia said to Polonius, "I do not know, my lord, what I should think," Cory turned and spoke loudly to Jude, "I know exactly how she feels. I too don't know what I should think at times. What a scary feeling!" Fidgeting in her seat, she kept her eyes glued to Ophelia the entire time. I could only imagine what was going through Jude's mind. "Please be

> quiet!" was the only thing he frantically whispered. By now all of the actors alternated their gaze between fellow actors on stage and Cory in the audience.

Charles continued to watch Cory as Jude picked nervously at his fingernails. Charles managed to establish eye contact with Jude and even gestured covertly, a shrugging-shoulders motion, as if to ask, what's going on? Jude only rolled his eyes and inconspicuously shrugged his shoulders too.

During the subsequent exchanges when Polonius offers Ophelia a series of reasons why she should reject Hamlet's advances, Cory became increasingly more distraught. Jude was preparing to usher her out when Polonius delivered the line, "Do not believe his vows." Cory immediately blurted, "I can't believe this! That is a ridiculous thing to say!" She stood up and yelled in Ophelia's direction, "Honey, don't listen to the old fool!"

The production stopped immediately, the cast members transfixed as they stared at Cory. Jude immediately tried to calm her and again lead her out of the theater, but she protested. From his stage-right position, Charles had a commanding view of the entire scene and wrote at length of it:

> It transpired so quickly, but herewith, for my own satisfaction, I offer a brief overview of what happened next. After Cory yelled out, I stopped the production. I had no choice since every person on and off stage was looking at Cory. I covered for Jude as best I could by making some silly offhand comment: "Jan, you see how effective you are as Ophelia. Look at the reaction you're getting from your audience!"
>
> Everybody laughed nervously. Cory was back in her seat by this time and forcefully rejected Jude's repeated appeal to leave. "I want to stay," she loudly insisted. I was shocked to see

her give Jude a slight push. No wonder, when he almost lost his balance, that he was fast approaching panic mode. Because she settled down right away, Jude apparently concluded that staying for the rehearsal, foreboding as the prospect was, seemed a better alternative than forcibly carting her away kicking and screaming. Initially, I thought that Jude had made the right decision. Sitting upright and appropriately attentive, Cory again calmed down and seemed to enjoy the rehearsal. She even stopped that incessant drumming of her fingers on the seat and arranged her disheveled hair as if concerned, at last, about her disorderly appearance.

Then we came to Ophelia's concluding line of this scene: "I shall obey, my lord." At this point, Cory stood up as though to speak, but Jude pulled her back to her seat and tried to hush her. She sat back down and spoke to Jude in a voice that was quieter but still loud enough for me to hear. "Ophelia is making a huge mistake in rejecting her true love. Why is she doing this? It doesn't make sense to me!"

After these outbursts, Cory remained silent and again seemed to settle. I thought the worst had past, and the look of panic on Jude's face even started to vanish. Nevertheless, the whole incident was unnerving to me since the drama in the third row was real life, the one on stage mere fiction. Though we were nearing opening night and I should have been preoccupied with performance details, I couldn't take my eyes off Jude and Cory. It looked as though Jude had weathered the worst of the storm by this point; and I, with him, breathed a sigh of relief.

How wrong we were!

Chapter 29

Charles's journal (continued)

In keeping with the announced rehearsal schedule which I had posted earlier, we then switched to the first scene of act 3, when Polonius and Claudius tell Ophelia to engage the seemingly deranged Hamlet in conversation, as they spy from behind the arras. From the very start of this scene Cory, who had settled completely after her earlier outburst, became progressively more agitated. This heightened anxiety really bothered me—*discouraged* is probably the better word—since I thought Cory had worked through the tension of the previous scene, but now she was regressing again.

It dawned on me later that she was agitated because she knew what Ophelia was about to do. The further we moved into the scene, the more Cory's anxiety increased. Again, I saw Jude whispering to her, apparently urging departure and pointing toward the exit. He even stood up at one point and tugged on her arm. "Come on, Cory, it's time to leave!" As Jude explained to me later, "She would have no part of it and kept saying, 'That dear girl needs help desperately. And

I'm going to give it to her!'" Jude was clearly beside himself.

When Polonius and Claudius took their place behind the tapestry to spy on Hamlet, Ophelia pretended to be reading a book as Hamlet entered. At this point, Cory immediately stood up. At first, Jude was relieved, thinking Cory had at last agreed to depart; but before he had time to react, Cory dashed up the stairs and on to the stage, shouting to Ophelia as she ran, "Honey, you need to think this through!" In front of all the stupefied actors, Cory crossed the stage directly to Ophelia, speaking the whole time. "Hamlet is a prince! Turning your back on him is most unwise." Cory put her arm around Jan—perhaps I should say Ophelia—and started walking together across the stage like long-lost friends!

Nearly traumatized by the whole ordeal, Jude followed her to the stage but stood at the edge, frozen in his tracks. His gesture of helplessness was absolutely pitiful. Temporarily shocked into stunned silence, the actors, through my example and urging, eventually regained composure and hit the height of their excellent acting for the day. Pretending all was fine, they "acted" as though such audience interruptions—and interactive interpolations, as it turned out—were normal. I thought again of my reaction at the start of the scene: "The mad scene. Enter Ophelia." How right I was! Or as Hamlet would say, "O my prophetic soul!"

As director of this scene in the play, I had a choice: let the mad scene unfold or stop it then and there, smoothing over the interruption as best I could and helping Jude and Cory depart the theater with a modicum of dignity. After a moment of tense thought and quick prayer, I chose the former because I thought that something good just might result. A "glooming peace" (as Shakespeare's prince says at the end of *Romeo and Juliet*) came over me and enabled me to assume a hint of leadership while I sat on the hot seat.

Here's how it unfolded. I motioned for Jude to stay where he was and told the cast to remain silent and courteous. Unobtrusively, I tapped my index finger on my temple to explain that the woman, a very close friend, periodically suffered such brief bouts of delusion. "We need to be kind and humane," I whispered to those actors nearest me, who spread the word to the cast members on stage. What could we do but stand back and watch Cory interact with Jan Neale, our Ophelia for this production, and Rick Olzewski and Keith Boyer, our Claudius and Polonius respectively? I motioned for the three actors to adjust their earpieces and take their cues and lines from me. The actor nearest to me passed along my instruction.

Cory continued speaking to Ophelia, "My dear, I have something to say to you. I hope you will listen carefully to me because I feel very strongly about this." Reaching out, Cory took Jan's hand and peered deeply into her eyes. As Cory paused, I could tell that tears were starting to form. "Turning your back on your true love is something you'll regret the rest of your life. Don't do this to your beloved. Don't run from him no matter the circumstance, no matter how bleak your future looks." Turning to Claudius and Polonius, Cory virtually screamed at them. "You ought to be ashamed of yourself! Why are you trying to break up this dear couple who are so madly in love, and why are you hiding behind that curtain? Hiding is the worst thing you can do. Hiders never win!" She wiped a tear from her eye and spoke again after a short pause, "Hiders pay a heavy price." She turned to Jan. "Don't ever hide, Ophelia—ever!"

I spoke to Jan through the earpiece and gave her the following lines. The conversation that follows is a word-for-word extract because I lifted it from the tape which Paulette, our sound technician and videographer, recorded during this scene. Upon my request, she subsequently presented me with this transcription, which became the object of endless discussion for Gabe Wyant and me.

Jan and Cory's lines, as transcribed by Paulette:

JAN. I hid once and later regretted it.

CORY. Why did you hide? I mean, what did you hide from?

JAN, *an awkward pause as she adjusted her earpiece and struggled to hear my prompt.* Oh, I've hidden lots of times. In fact, I've sort of gone through life hiding. Some people hide so much that it becomes a way of life.

CORY. Yes, I do understand. Hiding is awful since it's like living in an underground cave where you watch life pass you by.

JAN. You sound as if you, like me, have had some experience hiding. Did you ever hide?

CORY. Oh yes, many times, but one time in particular stands out. It was awful. (*Cory bodily shuddered here, turned away from Jan, and then faced her again but with her head down.*) I guess you could say that hiding's my number one avoidance strategy. I don't know what I'd do without it because it protects me, sort of keeps me safe. I like hiding.

JAN. Can you tell me about the one time that bothers you the most? Maybe I could deal with my pain better if you showed me how you've handled yours. (*Jude had never been a nail-biter, but during these frantic moments when I was feeding lines to Jan and trying to direct the whole mad scene, I caught a glimpse of him gnawing at his nails like a bewitched lunatic. On the other side of the stage, he was pacing like a first-time father waiting to receive word from the delivery room!*)

CORY. That horrible event is too painful to talk about, and besides, I've always been more of a drama person than a poet. You see, I'm an artist, and we artists are visual people. If I can paint things—that's my favorite medium, by the way—or if I can see them, then I understand them better than if I just talk about them. That helps me understand them." (*Cory stopped speaking momentarily and looked overhead. I wasn't sure why. Perhaps she was just collecting her thoughts. Then she started to speak again.*) Reality is better if experienced obliquely. My friend Emily Dickinson says in a poem, "Tell all the truth but tell it slant." She means that slanted truth softens the blows since direct and unfiltered reality hurts too much. I can handle reality and truth if it's cushioned since, that way, I can hide from the blow of awful truth that crashes down all at once. This strategy enables me to choose life on my terms and process it in the small doses I can manage. This is the life we hiders and cave dwellers prefer.

JAN. That's interesting. I'm a drama person too and tend to keep things to myself. Here's an idea. (*Jan paused awkwardly at this point since she had trouble absorbing my complicated cue.*) Let's act out each other's stories here on this stage. You do yours, and then I'll do mine. That's what we do on this stage—we act out stories. That's why my friends are here, in fact. Since you're our visitor, we'll let you take your turn first if you want. (*Another pause when Jan asked me to repeat my cue.*) You can be the director and direct a scene. It's simple. You cast the characters you want, give them their lines, and then we role-play it. Improvised skits are great fun. I'm sure you'll enjoy it. Do you want to do one?

CORY. Yes, this is a great idea. I've always wanted to be an actor.

> Completely beside himself, Jude, early in this exchange, had slunk, burglar-style, across the back of the stage behind the curtain to join me at stage right. It took me a while to settle him, but at last I succeeded. "I see what you're doing here, Chuck. The impromptu play within the play might have a meritorious end since it could help Cory unearth some deeply buried experiences in her past." He tightly squeezed his arms around himself. "But divided from herself and her fair judgment as she is—it's killing me to watch!" We spoke softly through these exchanges, but after a while, Jude actually whispered a number of Jan's cues to me, sensing by this time a possible positive outcome of the improvisation. "I have a glimmer of hope, but only a slight glimmer, that something good might result from the document in madness before us!"

JAN, *speaking to cast.* Ladies and gentlemen, we have another guest director today in our ongoing improvisation series, and like previous guests, she is going to help us enact the first of our afternoon skits. Others of you will have your turn too, so please be thinking of your improvisations. As is our custom, the guest director will handle casting and line assignments for our first skit. (*She turned to Cory.*) Thank you for your excellent help, Madam Director, and welcome to our theater. The stage is yours, and we await your details and directions about your skit.

(Jude, at this point, whispered to me, "This is mere madness.")

Cory. Thank you for your good counsel. In this scene, we will continue to work with the hiding motif. Imagine, cast, that we are in a large structure—a big building, like a barn. I'll need just three actors for this scene. Could you (*she pointed to Polonius*) please be the older gentleman? What is your name? (*A pause.*) Thank you, Keith Boyer. We appreciate your fine help. And could you, my dearest friend (*motioning toward Ophelia*), play the little girl? Thank you so much. That's very kind of you, and I am deeply grateful to you as well. Remember, Jan, you're a little girl, say, seven years old. Would you agree (*she motioned toward the actor playing Hamlet*) to be our little seven-year-old boy? Good. And may I have your name? Thank you, Carley Metz. Remember, Carley, you're not a youthful and refined university student/prince. (*In a kind of reverie, she here lapsed into a monologue.*) You're a little boy, a very scared and overwhelmed and very dear little boy alone in a big barn, and you're very afraid, and you don't know what to do, and he was all alone and he was so frightened. It breaks my heart to think on it!

(*The faraway look in her eye then ceased, and she was once again with us on the stage as she turned to Keith Boyer.*) In this scene, Polonius, you walk up the stairs to the catwalk. (*She pointed to the center of the catwalk, and Keith acknowledged that he understood.*) Yes, up there, and take your place in the middle of it. You're an old man, and you must put on a white beard, for his beard was as white as snow. You may take your place there now. (*She again pointed to the catwalk center.*) Yes, please go as soon as you don your beard. That's it. Good." (*I was proud of Keith who, with the regal stateliness of a king, took his place on the catwalk.*)

I need a tall ladder (*Cory continued*) which should lean against the catwalk. Yes, that will do (*I pointed toward an extension ladder and directed a stagehand to retrieve it from backstage and position it against the catwalk.*) Thank you very much indeed. Do we have a dummy around, especially a dummy of an older man? We'll pretend that he looks like Polonius. We need a dummy or something which can be dropped from the catwalk to simulate the fall of the old man in the barn. The scene also requires a loud banging sound when the dummy hits the floor, for it was an awful noise, a very loud thunderous crash. (*Cory shuddered at this point, turned to Jan, and said with tears in her eyes.*) He is dead and gone, lady; he is dead and gone. We must be patient, but I cannot but choose to weep to think they lay him in the cold ground. (*Cory and the cast members started looking about for an object that would simulate the thudding sound of the fallen body.*)

Charles's journal (continued)

During this short lull on the stage, Jude nudged me. "Chuck, when are we going to end this madness?" When I turned away from the proceedings and looked at Jude—really looked for the first time to see how he was reacting to the improvisation—I saw a face as pale as the glistening white bark on my backyard birch tree. He was trembling and breathing so hard that he was close to panting. Only later did I put all this together and understand why he was experiencing such emotional upheaval. Perhaps it was the peace of God which Gabriel so often speaks about that came over me at that moment. To be honest, that is something I've never understood, but what I am sure about is that I began, even in that tight place, to feel a pervasive calm as I watched the play unfold on stage, sensing, I suppose, that some larger good may indeed come out of it. I turned to Jude and said, "Though this be madness, yet there is method in it."

"You're suggesting," Jude replied, "that she's essentially not in madness?"

I didn't respond but instead turned to Cory. "Will this work?" I asked. I gave her an old backpack, in which I keep my prompt book, Shakespeare text, and so forth. I wrapped it in a large sheet and directed a stagehand to carry it to Ophelia. "This will make quite a loud sound when it hits the floor. We can pretend this is the dummy of an older man falling from the barn loft." Jude nearly collapsed into the back wall when I referred to the fall of the old man!

"Perfect," Cory said. "But I forgot something. We'll need a step stool which the little boy drapes across his back when he climbs the ladder." Here she stole a fast peek at Jude, a knowing look.

"Will this collapsible stool suffice?" I asked. I gave her the director's stool on which I was sitting.

"Perfect. I thank you all. I thank you for your good counsel." She turned to Jan. "They say the owl was a baker's daughter." Then she addressed the cast. "This scene, dear friends, is brief." She pointed to Hamlet and said, "Start climbing up the ladder with the stool slung across your back."

Hamlet, at this point, began to climb the stairs. For Jude and Cory's sake—and my own, I admit—I remain very grateful to Carley Metz and to all the actors for playing along with our improvisation so patiently. Carley as our Hamlet was completely poised and acted as though he had come to the theater today for the sole purpose of participating in Cory's improvised skit. I couldn't help but marvel at both his acting and humility. He had scored big in the Broadway production of *42nd Street* at St. James Theatre last year—the reviews were marvelous for him—and here he was in the middle of this Pittsburgh craziness. I kept wondering to myself, Carley, what is going on in your mind? I couldn't help but be thankful for his good heart in helping this distraught woman!

At this point in the mad proceedings, when Cory was giving Carley instructions, I again turned my attention to Jude, who used the occasion to vent. "The whole thing is totally mad, but calling 911 and having an ambulance come to carry her away, violently kicking and screaming against her will, is an even worse alternative. Besides, Cory in her madness is deep inside her own head and is probably, for the first time ever, exploring that uncharted mental terrain." Yes, I thought to myself, that uncharted mental terrain, the exploration of which inertia often impedes, sanity forbids, and fear prevents. Why fear? I reflected to myself. I thought of T. S. Eliot's simple but profound pronouncement in "Burnt Norton," the first of the *Four Quartets*: "Humankind cannot bear very much reality." Eliot is exactly right; people are fearful of, or totally shun, unpleasant realities of life that overwhelm us so completely.

When Hamlet started climbing the ladder, Jude went straight into a full-blown anxiety attack. He began pacing; and I could hear him, positioned slightly behind me and to my right, gasping for breath. When I turned around to look at him, I could see, even in that dimly lit offstage area, his pale face, trembling hands, and fear-glazed eyes. Part of me anticipated this reaction because of the direction the scene was taking. After all, Jude's worst nightmare—the death of his grandfather—was about to be reenacted before his very eyes.

But one overwhelming question remained: How could Cory direct this scene, complete with positioning the people and props so perfectly and offering lines to the actors, when she had not been present in the barn at the time of the accident? How could she get all these details exactly right, for only Jude and his grandpa were in the barn that fateful day? The difficult questions were clearly answered moments later, but at this juncture, while still in the dark, I alternated my view between the madwoman on stage and the distraught lover beside me.

"Jude, are you all right?" I whispered between Cory's comments. I thought he was going to collapse on the floor!

"I can't take this! I can't take this! *I'm* the document in madness!" He held his head in both hands. "Memory barely holds a seat in this distracted globe!"

Chapter 30

Charles' journal (continued)

During a lull in the stage proceedings, Jude turned to face me. "This whole thing is driving me crazy! How much more do we have to endure? I want my Cory back, and I want this pain to end!" He crossed his arms, took a few steps away from me, and then stomped back. "Why is she choosing this ridiculous skit? It's a bunch of nothing—words, words, words!"

"Wild and whirling words?"

"Definitely!" Jude knew he was stammering madly as a way of avoiding the big question, which *finally* he mustered the courage to ask. "How is she able to direct this so precisely?" I could see the look of sheer horror on his face as he desperately craved the answer to that all-important question and simultaneously feared it. "It's as though she was in the barn that awful day! Chuck, she must have been there, but she couldn't have been! She was not there! Another person may have left me there alone and crying and abandoned, but not my dear childhood friend!" He was nearly screaming by now.

"How is she able to direct this so precisely?" What a tough question! I think I'll soften my

response by couching it in Shakespearean language! "Well, what she spake," I responded with a fixed eye on Jude, "though it lacked form a little, was not like madness. I suggest that we watch to see where she takes this since, during her hallucinatory state, she's outside of herself completely."

"You surely have that right!"

I paused before I asked an equally tough question. "Don't you think the terminus to which she's headed more than compensates for her separation from self and your temporary discomfort?" *That was a pretty direct shot between the eyes. Wonder how he'll take it!* "Look at it this way. There's a sense in which this drama skit is a welcome break from the craziness at the mine. Don't you agree? More than that, she's working through the pain via this long-delayed visitation to her deeply buried past and enjoying the journey in the process. Better to have her plummet the depths of her soul here in a safe environment than with the thugs in the mine. See my point?"

"I still don't like it," Jude grumpily responded. "If you can quote *Hamlet*, so can I. You ask how I feel? Here's the answer. 'I have of late—but wherefore I know not—lost all my mirth.' Get my point? Lost all my mirth, professor, *all my mirth!*"

During my exchange with Jude, Cory completed the blocking assignments, but then a final idea came to her involving the stage manager. "Could you please retrieve that tarp lying over there? Thank you. Please crumple it and place it outside a makeshift door. The door will be right here." She moved her hands up and down in a vertical motion to create the make-believe door. By now she had completed her stage directions and was ready to begin her skit. "All right, we're all set. Hamlet, are you ready? Good." Then for a brief moment, a faraway look in her eye, she became pensive and dreamy. "It broke my heart to see him cry that way, for he cried so much." Then remembering her place as director, she instructed Carley, "As you take a few slow steps up the ladder, remember you're a little boy, so it's all right to sniffle and cry." Again, far away: "For he cried so much, and it broke my heart to see him cry that way!"

When Carley came forward to act his brief part, Jude palpitated and paced so wildly that I actually thought he was going to faint. At one point, he even clutched his heart and said, "Angels and ministers of grace defend us." Cory told Carley to approach the steps a second time. "Do this again please, but this time, come to the steps with more trepidation and fear. You're afraid because you're scared silly and don't want to do this. You're a little scared boy who hates the idea of climbing up the barn beam to such a high place. With a stool on your back, no less."

Suddenly Cory, looking into space, was far away from a Pittsburgh stage. "It was so very high. The stool was awkward and kept sliding on his back and wouldn't stay in place. The pressure was awful for the dear little boy, just awful, for the rope was slipping, and Grandpa could no longer hold on." During these moments, she repositioned the imaginary stool on her own back and then, just as suddenly, was again the director of a skit on a Pittsburgh stage. Again, to Carley: "You know your Grandpa is in trouble, and you have to hurry to the get the stool up to him. Show lots of dread and agony as you make this terrible climb."

During her comments with the actors, I tried to maintain my conversation with Jude. I pretended to know nothing about Jeremiah's fall to his death in the barn. "What's the basis of your panic attack? Why is this unnerving you?" I knew my questions were too direct, too near the raw nerve, but I had no time to dally with language or tiptoe around exposed emotions.

"What's the cause of my attack? Seeing Cory this way! 'Is it possible a young maid's wits Should be as mortal as an old man's life?'"

"Nice quotation from *Hamlet.* I recognize Laertes's description of his crazed sister." Again, my language was too direct, but I couldn't think of a way to soften it! "But your anxiety intensified just now when Carley started up the ladder. It's not just Cory's mad paroxysms that set you off. What is it, Jude? What are *you* processing?" Emphasizing *you* quite intensely, I was again too blunt and not at all adept in this tight place at playing the gentle-counselor role who by indirections finds directions out. "You can layer the pain or lance it. You can coat over whatever's been eating at you with yet more dazzling escape artistry or cure it once and for all. How many years has this been going on? How many more years will you allow a childhood tragedy control you? 'Madness in great ones must not unwatched go.'"

He looked at me as though hit with a thunderbolt. "I get it. While you're watching Cory, you're also watching me endure my pain—my old childhood pain." He observed Cory in total exasperation and then slowly turned to look me full in the eye. "How can I work through it, you asked? It's impossible. I killed Grandpa. I think you know that. You want me to work through that?" He stopped momentarily and shook his head back and forth.

"That's an unfair and wild exaggeration!"

"No, it isn't! Then there's also the vow I made to Grandma when I was a little boy that I would never write. She made me promise never to pick up a pen, and I made that promise. You want me to work through that? Besides Cory, writing's the one thing in life I've ever wanted."

"I don't understand."

"Grandma always thought writing caused Grandpa's death. In her mind, writers come to bad ends. 'Promise me you won't write, little Jude.' She said that to me constantly. In front of God, I made that solemn vow!"

He stopped speaking and watched Cory talk to the players. Although we both wanted to observe the spectacle on stage, he turned to me to say one more thing. "Well, through it all, I've become a galloping maverick who runs from one illusory mountain getaway of the mind to the next. If that's not enough, feast your eyes on this 'document in madness.'" He continued to watch Cory. "I can't believe we're allowing this charade to happen. Surely you know I'm the centerpiece of her play. I'm the invisible white elephant on this stage." He grabbed my shirt collar and pulled me toward him. I was inches from his face. "This mad spectacle is about *me*!"

I hated missing Cory's instructions to the players during this exchange with Jude, but I knew my conversation with him was as potentially revealing as any psychological breakthrough which Cory might experience through her skit.

My comments with Jude settled him a bit, at least enough that I didn't have to usher him out. He was breathing more evenly, and color returned to his face. We turned our attention to Cory, who was wrapping up her revised stage directions.

"Let's go over the next part," Cory resumed. "After Hamlet takes a few steps up the ladder with the stool on his back, you, Polonius, gently tell him to come to you up there. From there in the middle of the barn loft, you extend your hand downward to assist him, encouraging him as much as you can. Your line is, 'Take it easy, little Ju—' Forget that, I made a mistake. It's Carley. You say, 'Take it easy, little Carley.' When he starts to fall, you reach down to grab him, but that causes you to lose your balance, and he fell. Of course, you don't actually fall"—she laughed—"as he did! Just pretend to do so." When she chuckled at her attempt at humor, the entire cast nervously laughed with her. How that helped me understand the function of comic relief!

She then spoke to Jan, "Through this whole scene, Ophelia, you are standing outside the barn looking in. You are not in the barn. You wish you weren't there seeing it all, but I was—*you* were, you are. You see it all. Do you understand?" She spoke this last line loudly and with deep passion. "You are scared to death when you hear Polonius hit the floor with that thud, that awful noise that rings in the ears forever. Nothing will ever take it away. I keep hearing it. Polonius, when you pretend to fall, drop the backpack to simulate the terrible thud." When she said this, she held her hands to her ears to block out the sound and yelled as though in pain. She then spoke, "Got it, everyone? Great. Lights, camera, action!"

At this point, Cory walked over to Ophelia and whispered something in her ear. I didn't hear this but surmise it dealt with an additional stage direction. When Hamlet started moving toward the ladder, Ophelia/Jan, now a little girl, peeked through the fake door and then, as instructed, started to run offstage and out of sight. This is where the improvised skit turned really crazy. Cory had been standing slightly behind Jan and was also watching through the pretend door. They both had leaned far to the left as though sneaking a peak from behind the doorframe. The acting was superb. After watching Hamlet/Carley intently, Cory started to run for the left rear corner backstage ahead of Jan. With no recourse but to do as Cory did, Jan followed her backstage and mimicked her actions. According to Isaac, one of the managers at stage rear, "Cory was crouched in the corner with her face tightly buried in her hands, her back to the stage. Jan copied her actions."

Through the earpiece (Isaac was also wearing one), I told him to tell Cory and Jan to return to the stage. He explained to them that the "coast was clear" and that, because we were moving to the next improvisation, we needed Cory's help again. The two women reentered the stage, but Cory carried a bunch of plastic flowers, which she had picked up from a pile of old props backstage.

At this point, the improvised skit hit its mad height. Cory came over to Carley, our Hamlet, and, as she gave him the flowers, said, "There's rosemary, that's for remembrance; pray you, love, remember. Remember as I remember and have never forgotten." But as she said the line—"pray you, love, remember"—she turned to face Jude and spoke the words in *his* direction! After Jude dropped to his knees in agony, Cory pivoted around and resumed her role as director.

With my mind working at a fever pitch, I thought I'd try one last thing before I terminated the mad scene. I spoke to the cast, "Before we move on to the next improvisation skit, we're going to do this hiding scene again, but this time, Jan and Cory will change places." Jan, understanding, nodded in agreement. Cory too—this was the risky part—agreed to take Jan's part and play the little girl outside the fake doorway.

The scene commenced the same way. Carley climbed the ladder, but when he pretended to fall down and Keith simultaneously dropped the backpack, Cory, instead of running backstage, peeked around the doorframe and watched the entire episode! Only when Carley got up and pretended to look at the fallen old man did Cory move away, but instead of running to the back of the theater as she did the first time, she now slid under the crumpled tarp by the imaginary barn door!

Standing directly beside me, Jude gasped in astonishment. "No!" he cried. "Surely not! She couldn't have been there! She never saw it! My friend wasn't there, and she didn't forsake me! This is madness, and it must cease!"

I paused for an awkward moment, during which time nothing happened. Time stopped. While the actors stood nervously in place, awaiting my directive, Jude was collapsed on his knees at the side of the stage. Cory remained under the tarp. After a few moments, I motioned to the cast to just relax for a moment and hold their positions. "At ease!"

I walked the whole way across the stage to Cory, picked up the edge of the tarp, and with my head under it, whispered, "Cory, are you all right?"

"Who would have thought the old man to have had so much blood in him?"

"What old man?" I asked.

"You know. Don't play dumb."

"No, I really don't know."

"They say he made a good end."

"Cory, you're talking in riddles. We have to go and get to the next scene. Who made a good end? Please tell me who you're talking about." She didn't respond, but I still felt the need, despite the pressure to get back to our rehearsal, to try again. "Tell me what's going on." A pause, but again she said nothing. "At least tell me where you are."

"Under the pile of hay. I've never left it. I've lived my whole life here. This is my home—always hiding, always watching Jude's grandpa fall to his death. Running from Jude. Always running from dear little Jude." She looked into space with those pitiful eyes and then grabbed my shirt. "I did nothing to help him. That poor little boy! I ran out on little Jude when he needed me most." She shook her head in utter despair and brushed a tear from her eye. "I should have said, 'Jude, I'm here to help. You can always count on me,' but I just stayed under the haymow and did nothing. Absolutely nothing." She wiped the tears from her eyes. "I'm a wretch of a human being." She looked me eye to eye for the first time. "I'm not worthy of love! Sick, O, sick!"

CHAPTER 31

Charles's journal (continued)

I continued speaking to Cory under the crumpled tarp. "What did you see that awful day? Tell me." She fiddled with the tarp and said nothing, yet I could tell by the intense focus of her eyes that she was completely lucid. "You can trust me."

"Everything. I saw everything—Jude screaming his head off, Grandpa falling to his death, lying there inert, little Jude panicked out of his mind. There's not a day when that scene doesn't blast in screaming color on the screen of my mind. Poor little Jude. I ran away and just left him bawl his lungs out. Walked out on dear little Judah Jedidiah! Grandpa Jeremiah called him Jedidiah because *Jedidiah* mean's 'beloved of the Lord,' and he said that's the right name for Jude, the perfect name because he's so beloved by God and everyone, but not by me, not when he needed to be loved, not when it really counted, because I was a traitor, because I am a traitor, and I kill friendships and betray people far worse than Benedict Arnold ever did, and I am the destroying betrayer, and I am worth nothing because I destroy the thing I love."

Completely out of the breath, she ceased her stream-of-consciousness venting and quietly sat there looking into space. She had uttered these sentences rationally and calmly with no hint of mental derangement, but she made the blood stop in my veins. Impulsively—reflexively, I guess I should say—I drew back in shock. Jude was still across stage and didn't hear, though he wildly gestured for me to explain. No longer collapsed on the floor in a fetal position, he slowly struggled to his feet as I walked toward downstage center. The cast withdrew and assembled at the back of the stage, sensing the gravity of the situation. I met him at center stage, relieved to stay out of earshot of Cory at least for a moment.

Jude was beside himself but nevertheless hushed his voice. "What did she say? Tell me what she said!"

"Words, words, words. It was a bunch of nothing. I'd say we need grounds more relative than this." (A Shakespeare scholar, he knew I was alluding to *Hamlet* and using the word that meant "proof" in Shakespeare's day.) "We need proof."

"Proof of what?" He asked this rhetorically and didn't wait for an answer, impatient as he was to get to his second question. "How can we catch her meaning?" His eyes were blinded with tears.

"The play's the thing Wherein I'll catch the conscience of the king."

"Catching the conscience of a king is good, but exploring Cory's conscience is scary business. In her condition, that's like exploring the back side of the moon!" Jude slowly walked toward Cory, who, by now out from in under the tarp, made no resistance when Jude escorted her to the door.

Cory turned as she neared the door and spoke to me, "Thank you for your counsel." Then they quietly departed, and sanity was restored as quickly as it had vanished.

A short while later, the cast, as best they could after the mad interlude, resumed their rehearsal. The actors performed well—at least I think they did—but I'm not sure, to tell the truth, because my head was more engrossed with the reenactment of a childhood trauma than the production of a Shakespeare masterpiece.

Once the rehearsal, which I cut short, was finished for the day, I sped to Jude's grandma's house since an idea had come to me during my return trip to Center Hill. It excited me so much, in fact, that I started driving faster than I realized. When I drove by a state trooper pulled off behind an overpass at the Slate Lick interchange, I slowed just in time to avoid being ticketed. That was a close call, and I had learned my lesson!

The idea that led to my speeding was a good one. The photographs of Jeremiah Wakefield's farm had been taken, in an irony so great that it could be condemned as one of life's improbable fictions, on the very day of his grandpa's death. According to what his wife, Rosetta, said many years before, Jeremiah must have sensed his end was drawing nigh, even though, for a man his age, he was in remarkable health.

He was prescient that way quite often across his life. In the days before his death, he had family portraits taken, arranged his papers, made some interesting diary entries, mysteriously hid the manuscript of his novel, and even hired a professional photographer to take exterior pictures of the farm. Why had he wrapped up so many loose ends near the end? Many believed in those years that he somehow sensed it was his time to shuffle off life's mortal coil.

It was the pictures of the house and especially the barn that fired my imagination as I drove home. I knew it was a long shot, but remembering the strange incident of the photographer's taking pictures on the day Jeremiah died, I dimly recalled that one of the photographs on Jeremiah's desk featured the exterior of the barn with a large haymow in the right foreground. It was this thought that was boiling in the cauldron of my mind when I sped by the state trooper. Seeing Cory under the crumpled tarp and hearing her comment that she was under the mow on the day of his death made me think anew of this photo.

I headed to the Wakefield farm as I motored northeast through the lovely farm lands of Armstrong County. Rosetta greeted me in her characteristically warm fashion. After a quick hello, she offered me a cup of tea. We in the Kittanning and Center Hill area thought she could have English blood in her for the way she loved her tea. As was always the case with Rosetta, it was the full deal—matching pot, cups, sugar and milk pitcher, served on a lovely tray "with a spoon which Jude picked up for me in the Cotwolds, either Moreton-in-Marsh or Bourton-on-the-Water. I'm not sure which! Goodness, this ole brain! How can I forget *that*?"

"Of course, you can look at the photographs, Charles," she had begun. "But surely you can sit down and enjoy this cup of tea first. I'd like your opinion on this brand of tea. Jude picked up a fancy-dancy tea when he was down at the Strip in Pittsburgh recently. Let me get the box." She walked to the pantry to retrieve the tea. "I can't even remember its strange name. Ah yes, look at this—Caramel Cocoa with Golden Monkey Tea. Can you imagine a tea like that? Not very English if you asked me!"

"Are you serious? I never heard of such a tea!"

"Yes, that's its name. Jude says that it's called golden monkey tea because of the way the monks used to train monkeys to climb to the tops of trees. The monkeys were trained to pick the higher-quality tea leaves and buds that grow at high altitudes. Do you think that's true? I have no idea, but I'll ask Jude! He'll know." She sipped the tea. "I must say, it's very soothing, but the cocoa flavor would suit the winter season more, don't you think?"

"Yes, I think so, but it's nice for a change." He took another sip. "Yes, quite tasty and full-bodied! Thank you very much."

Shortly after tea and pleasantries, I proceeded to Jeremiah's study and hurried directly to the wall by his desk where the photo collage hung. I took the framed pictures off the wall, walked to the window, and carefully examined the photos. I paid special attention to the photo with the haymow, of which there was only one.

That was the disappointment. I had hoped for a couple photos in the collage and for a distinct clue that might suggest whether or not Cory had actually been present the day of Jeremiah's death. I guess I was hoping to see if she had concealed herself in this haymow. Jude always maintained that he and Cory had been together all that morning and that they had paused only long enough for the family portrait. He further insisted that Cory departed shortly after the photographer had finished and that he and Jeremiah had gone to the barn alone, a point he always emphasized. She was not on the premises at the time of the accident, so he thought, and so she had always allowed him to think. After all, wasn't it better to keep that horrible day a secret? Would I unearth something different in looking at the photo? The granddaddy of all questions was never out of my mind: did Cory's reenactment depict an actual past event or dramatize an imagined fantasy? That is the question!

While returning the collage to the nail on the wall, I looked at the back to grab hold of the string to rehang it. When I did so, I noticed that several of the photos had been fastened with tape to keep them in place in their collage window cutouts. A closer look revealed that some of the windows did not have single photos. When I loosened the tape to examine the duplicate pictures, I saw that most of them were similar and revealed nothing new, but then I examined again the duplicate of the haymow photo.

With the aid of the sunlight, I looked at the photo—I had by that time gone over to the window to catch the light of the evening sun—and saw something that caught my attention. A very small black object, an unimportant-looking dot, was present in this duplicate photo, which was not present in the window one. Did it contain a clue? As I examined the side-by-side photos more closely, I noticed a second slight and potentially even more important difference. The haymow in the duplicate copy appeared to be slightly higher than the other. Might that be the case and, if so, possibly relevant?

I was so excited by this find that I had trouble sleeping through the night. Early the next morning, Luci, the church secretary, scanned the duplicate photo into her computer and, at my request, greatly magnified the corner section with the haymow. With the aid of a magnifying glass, I could clearly see both the sole and part of the patent leather side of a small child's shoe protruding from the haymow! In my excitement, I blurted to Luci, "It's not a dot. It's a shoe!"

I noted as well a very small discoloration nearer the top of the slightly higher haymow. When I looked at the greatly magnified copy, I could clearly see a couple fingers which were grasping hay! Cory had apparently hidden under the haymow and, as I surmised, frantically attempted to strew handfuls of hay over her head to cover herself completely. Although my mind was racing to conclusions, I knew I had to proceed cautiously and methodically. Had she actually been present to witness the accident? How was I to know if this shot was taken before or after the accident? That led to an even tougher question: how could one prove that this was indeed Cory? I knew I had stumbled onto a potentially useful find, but difficult questions remained, and my detective work was far from over.

* * * * *

Through it all, the big concern for all of them, of course, was Cory. Why was she hallucinating, and why did the hallucination hit its height in the Stephen Foster Memorial Theater? Had the doctors underestimated possible head trauma? That was the subject Charles took up with Pastor Gabriel Wyant later that evening in the pastor's study.

During their conversation, Pastor Gabriel said that he planned to attend the Saturday-afternoon dress rehearsal. "I wouldn't miss it, Charles. The play itself is a drawing card, but this new relevance to Jude and Cory's lives makes it doubly important. I'll be there. Yes, I'll definitely be there!"

CHAPTER 32

After the improvisation during the *Hamlet* rehearsal, Jude and Cory walked out the door, faced Forbes Avenue and the Carnegie Museum, and then aimlessly walked around the corner to the spacious lawn between the Cathedral of Learning and Heinz Chapel. Trembling all over, Jude tried to steal a quick glance at her without being observed. *Is she still hallucinating? What just happened in the theater? This is crazy but true—I'm afraid to look at Cory! What will I see, a delusional woman? What in the world must be going on in her head, and how do I determine my best course of action? There are superb hospitals a mere two blocks away. Should I take her to an ER?*

Jude had just witnessed the traumatic reenactment of his grandpa's death and, even worse, endured the shocking revelation that Cory had most likely been present during it. Listlessly walking along, his ruminations continued. *Barely staving off my own anxiety attacks, how can I offer any sort of help to the love of my life?* He tightly held Cory's hand as they ambled to Heinz Chapel but let go long enough to take his pulse. *It's got to be over one hundred beats per minute. I have to get myself settled down!*

Despite his emotional turmoil, his sole mission was to help Cory. She gradually grew calmer in her spirit now that she was outside and had the strange experience behind her. Nevertheless, they walked in silence. Jude again stole a glance at her. *I want to talk to her, but I think silence is best for the time being.* Jude's journal entry recorded the moments after the mad improvisation.

Jude's journal

Once outside in the fresh air, I calmed down considerably and even stopped trembling. Up to that point, I was, sadly, in no shape to tend to Cory, so intense had been my own anxiety inside the theater. On one level, I was shaken because the improvisation scene reenacted my childhood trauma, the horror that never goes out of my head—Grandpa's death. I had learned over the years that the slightest provocation sparked such attacks, but all those anxious moments paled into insignificance when compared to the full-blown anxiety attack which I experienced during the reenactment. This was a first. I had often imagined it, even dreamed about it, but I had never seen the actual event recreated, and I certainly never had the experience of reliving it as I just had.

That the scene had been scripted by Cory shook me even more deeply because it meant, apparently but not obviously, that she had been present during the accident. That was a major revelation to me, but how could she have been present? Did the reenactment, to take this to a deeper level, dramatize something she merely imagined but hadn't actually experienced? Or here's another way to state the huge question: Was the scripted improvisation based on something she had witnessed, or was it an imaginative dramatization—a cleverly pieced-together patchwork of the various accounts I had shared with her over the years?

On the morning of the fall, she had disappeared shortly after the photographer finished the family photographs and miscellaneous exterior shots. When Grandpa and I started for the barn, I looked for Cory to accompany us since playing in the barn was something we always enjoyed. After all, there was no place like the barn for hide-and-seek and playing with the kitties; but on this occasion, she was nowhere to be found, or so I thought. I've always thought she had gone home.

I screamed and screamed that horrible morning, crying for her help as Grandpa lay dying on the barn floor. How desperately I wanted her by my side in those awful moments! That had been a real part of my panic that day: stay and do something for my dying grandpa or run to get the help of older, more experienced people who would know how to handle the crisis? Even as a seven-year-old, I knew that my actions during those vital moments would determine his fate, knew that I held his life in my little hands. How I needed Cory who could have run for help as I stayed with Grandpa for those precious dying moments! But she was nowhere to be found, nor did she ever come despite my constant screaming. That's how I knew she had gone home. She would never have allowed me to handle this trauma alone if she had been in the area. Not Cory, because even as a child, she was my true and good friend, a loyal friend who would never leave me.

I glanced at Cory as we walked along the walkway of former University of Pittsburgh star athletes and was again about to speak, but in looking at her, I could see that she was still deeply inside her head, most likely reenacting the drama of those bygone years. What was she thinking, and what was I to make of her hallucination? Was this total split from reality, which I had just painfully witnessed in the theater, temporary? And would a reversion to normality shortly ensue? Or had she experienced a more permanent injury that would make splits from reality more frequent and more intense? But if there was serious head trauma, why hadn't the doctors discovered it? Should she be taken to one of the world-class Pittsburgh specialists for observation and further testing? Again, I contemplated driving her to one of the nearby hospitals.

By this time, we were at the steps of Heinz Chapel. Seeing the doors open and no one around, for which I was most grateful, we started up the stairs. She let go of my hand and proceeded through the narthex ahead of me. Allowing her to take the lead, I was happy to see that she walked with a kind of vitality which contrasted to her previous ennui. Was it the prospect of seeing the beauty of the sanctuary inside that had emboldened her step, or was the sacred atmosphere resuscitating her? While not certain, I detected a faint glimmer in her eye. Was she becoming Cory again?

I followed her as she went directly to the windows on the left immediately inside the main sanctuary of Heinz Chapel. As she approached the left-most window, she read the bottom verse embossed in the stained glass:

O, Lord, in thee I have trusted; never let me be confounded.

O, that men would praise the Lord for His goodness

And for His wonderful works of the children of men.

As her hand glided over each of these stained-glass words, I noted that the trembling of her fingers decreased. The verses clearly had a calming effect on her. She traced again the words of the first line, "Never let me be confounded." Back and forth she ran her finger under the word *confounded* and then bowed her head in prayer. She took a step to her right and looked at the text in the next window: "O, Lord, have mercy on us." Cory lowered her face to the window and reverently kissed this verse. Speaking the words softly—"O, Lord, have mercy on us"—she then placed the palm of her hand against the window and again bowed in prayer, her forehead touching the word *Lord.*

The large central windows in the north and south Transepts, at which she marveled by the hour in a happier day, were of course magnificent, but today it was the profundity of these scriptural truths in the less ornate, smaller windows that deeply affected her. On this occasion, she was drawn to the power of the biblical language more than the stained-glass artist's oh-so-potent art.

Eventually, she turned to look at me and took hold of my hand, held it to the side of her face, and caressed it. In that simple gesture, I could tell that she was herself again. I looked deeply into her beautiful eyes, now glimmering with life. "Jude, how can you ever forgive me?" We walked to the center aisle, where she stopped long enough to hug and kiss me. "I've run from this moment my whole life. Now you know." She hugged me again. "Now you know that awful, awful truth."

She stopped speaking and looked at the window again and then me. "At least that's one good thing. It's out in the open at last, and I no longer will have to hide or live in fear of being discovered. Yes, Jude, I was there when your grandpa fell." She squeezed me tightly at this point. "I saw it all. Though you were a scared little boy who needed help, I ran and hid. You cried and screamed and sobbed like a baby, but I was too frightened to move. I hid under the haymow and held rock still while you screamed your head off. You kept screaming and screaming and wouldn't stop. You came outside to look for me, yelling hysterically. You were feet away from me, but still I didn't move. I didn't know what to do. Please stop that terrible screaming! I thought to myself. My head was pounding. Jude, I was so very afraid!"

"Of course, you were."

She stopped talking and again peered deeply into my eyes. "How could I have done that to you? Jude, forgive me. I was so afraid at the time of the accident that I didn't know what to do." She gazed at the Cross in the chancel. "I never told you because I was afraid you wouldn't forgive me."

Seemingly unable to go on, she paused but then continued a moment later, "You're not saying anything. Are you taking this in? I watched your grandpa fall, Jude. I saw the whole thing. I betrayed you. I hid from you. I had come to the barn when you yelled at me to join you for hide-and-seek, or maybe it was to hunt for the kittens." Cory found her stride and, after years of silence, opened the floodgates. "I arrived at the door just as you were climbing the last steps to the hayloft and were handing your grandpa the ladder. I remember seeing him way up there on the loft—so high up, so far away. He looked right at me and winked with that huge grandpa smile that always made me feel good all over. You didn't see his smile or wink because you were looking down as you climbed the last couple rungs of the ladder. He smiled and winked at me right before he fell! That has always made his death extra difficult for me because I felt that I distracted him by being there and made him lose his concentration."

Cory stopped talking for a moment, seemingly too overwhelmed to continue. "I watched you lose your balance on the ladder near the top, saw him reach out to grab you, and watched you harmlessly fall into the giant pile of hay." She wiped another tear from her eye. "That huge haymow we used to jump into by the hour." Cory stopped talking and stared into nothing. "But he didn't fall into a soft pile of hay." She glanced at the chapel ceiling as if to note its height. "He crashed with a thud onto the hard barn floor. I saw it all. I watched him sacrifice his own life to save you, but like a criminal, I ran from the scene." She bit her lip and allowed the tears to course down her cheeks. "He did everything to save you. I did nothing. He gave his life. I hid mine." She put her hands on my cheeks and turned my face directly toward her. "You should hate me. Oh, my lover, how can you ever forgive a sin like that?"

After we sat down in a center pew of Heinz Chapel near the large central stained-glass windows, I put my arm around her and held her tightly. Her body shook all over as she cried hot tears of penitence and remorse. I wiped her cheeks with my handkerchief. That was the first time I ever noted the temperature of tears—hot, like water warmed in a pan. I continued to hold her and stroked her face and arm until she calmed down.

"Cory, I forgive you. I forgive you, my love! I totally forgive you. You could have done nothing even if you had come back in the barn. We couldn't have saved his life. He died from massive internal injuries."

After incessant assurances that I loved her still, that I forgave her completely, and that she should forgive herself as much as God and I both did, she eventually stopped crying. I even detected a faint smile! I recited the verses she read in the window upon our entering the chapel: "O Lord, in thee I have trusted; never let me be confounded." When we contemplated the profound scriptural truths of those beautiful windows, I began to see a fragile green shoot of joy arise in her—just a hair root of hope—but it promised a new beginning.

I then quoted the second verse: "Lord, have mercy on us." I peered deeply into Cory's eyes. They were flaming candles that shone into the lonely corridors of my heart, that dark desolate labyrinth of nothingness. Sitting there, my arm around Cory, a thought flashed in my brain. *Did I like the mushroom mine corridors, that underground world of darkened tunnels, simply because they mirrored so perfectly the darkened pathways of my own soul? Were the mines an objective correlative or a kind of external representation of my own soul?* I knew it was crazy, but I nevertheless made a mental note to check to see what T. S. Eliot meant by that famous phrase: *objective correlative.* Had I just given an example, albeit a pretty dumb one, of that phenomena?

We stood up again to look at the windows to get a closer look, my arm around her tightly. I kept massaging her shoulders and lower back. As we did so, the words of David in Psalm 119 flashed in my brain: "The entrance of Your words gives light." I thought how very true that was. Cory had been in the throes of deep depression, yet the torrent of her gushing confession had purged her being of the toxic emotions that had poisoned her for years. The negative emotions and the self-laceration that accompanied them were gone, the burden of years lifted. That was the result of the purging which occurred both during the improvisation and the confession here in the chapel, when she cried out to God and, unnecessarily, begged me for forgiveness.

Standing there in the chapel, I couldn't help but continue my reflection. *Until she looked at the windows, there was nothing positive to take the place of that happily voided negativity. True, the harmful imagery was gone from her brain, and the debilitating negative self-talk had ended—and how joyous to be rid of that!—but it was the entrance of these bedrock biblical truths that breathed new life into her mind and that gave her hope. She feasted on those sacred words, ran her fingers across them, and wouldn't stop looking at them. Hungering and thirsting for righteousness—that's what she's doing! Cory Mohney, how we both, like the beleaguered deer that pants for water, crave that light of truth!*

It is now late evening, and I sit here at my desk in Grandma's farmhouse, the whole crazy experience behind me. I turn my head and look out the window across the enchanting moonlit fields of Cory's farm. In the distance, I see her farmhouse. She sits there in her house—possibly in the kitchen, the den, or up in her bedroom. I feel the balmy night air blow in through the window. A strong gusty breeze just blew my Jerusalem bookmarker on the floor, the one Pastor Gabe had given me. I open my Bible to the verse in one of David's psalms which Cory had marked a week or so ago: "He who continually goes forth weeping, bearing seed for sowing, shall doubtless come again with rejoicing, bringing his sheaves with him" (Psalm 126:5–6). How I pray that this is true for us! Will we ever rejoice? Will we ever bear arms full of ripened sheaves in amber fields of gold?

As I compose that question, I think of the song Cory and I used to play when we listened to Grandpa and Grandma's '50s-era music. Possibly the song was called "Green Fields." I'm not sure of that, but I can paraphrase the line: "Once there were green fields kissed by the sun. Once there were valleys where rivers used to run."

How I long for green, sun-drenched fields where larks sing, rivers run, and lovers stroll. I tire of these scorched meadows where brooks are dried, trees wasted, everything thirsts, and madness reigns. Is there a river? There must be. There has to be! And how we need it now!

CHAPTER 33

On the return trip from Pittsburgh that afternoon, Jude thought of the activities that might sustain Cory's emotional equilibrium. *It's a relief to have her back to normal or at least settled for the time being. At all cost, I must avoid anything that might excite her again.* As he was passing the Freeport exit on Route 28, he made the connection for the first time between Cory's hallucinations and her pain medication. *That's it! The hallucinations correlate to her ingestion of pills. The more medication in her body, the more virulent the hallucination! Why didn't I think of that before? That's so obvious!*

"Up to this point, I thought your bouts of irrationality were injury-related, but maybe they've been caused by your meds. I just now thought of that. What do you think?"

"Very interesting possibility. You might be right. My total breaks from reality have all occurred shortly after I've taken the pills, especially today when I was completely wacko because I had taken so many. Why didn't we think of this sooner? This morning is a case in point. I'd taken several pills back to back because my headache was so intense."

"I didn't realize your headache was so bad this morning. Had I known, I would have insisted that we not go to Pittsburgh." Looking across the valley in the direction of the mushroom mine, he spoke a moment later, "Cory, I have an idea. Would it upset you if we went to Little Gidding for a while? You could sketch, and I could write poetry. What do you think? Or maybe we could just sit on the couch and blissfully love each other to death!"

She kissed his hand and said, "That's a great idea. Our bower of bliss would be a beautiful balm."

"Ha! And you make fun of my alliteration! You're sure that returning to the mine parking lot wouldn't upset you? If I remember correctly, we were in a bit of a fracas there recently."

"A scratch! A scratch!"

"That one's easy—*Romeo and Juliet.*"

"Right you are. No, going to the mine wouldn't upset me, and even if it temporarily did, being with you in our wonderful hideout would more than compensate for the momentary discomfort in getting to it. What better place to process the events of this momentous day?"

"I couldn't agree more!"

Jude took the Slate Lick exit off Route 28 onto Freeport Road and then turned left at the cutoff to West Winfield by Colton's Service Station. A short while later, Cory and Jude nestled themselves in Little Gidding. Slouched back on the couch, his legs stretched out on the coffee table, Jude resumed his reflection later in the afternoon. *After the debacle at the rehearsal of* Hamlet *in Foster Theater, our retreat is especially welcome today—our green world where everything makes sense again.* He glanced over at Cory, who was painting at her easel. *Her equilibrium has been completely restored during these magical moments, further substantiating our theory that her hallucinations are medication-induced. Now that she's been off the pills a while, all side effects are completely gone.*

As a result of the calm that came over her—or perhaps because of the crisis that preceded it—her creative impulse was so powerfully stirred that she finished the broad strokes of her sketch, *New Every Morning,* that afternoon in Little Gidding.

Jude spoke of this in his journal:

> It was fun to watch her paint. Completely back to normal, she painted with a speed and confidence I had never witnessed before. I actually stood behind her for a while to watch her paint. Every stroke was perfect, every touch of that

> brush faultless. Watching those adroit strokes, I was reminded of Michelangelo's passing reference to his contemporary Andrea del Sarto as the "faultless painter."

Cory's as faultless as del Sarto today! I thought. *I have my Cory back again. What a creative surge she's experiencing after the bizarre afternoon on a Pittsburgh stage!*

The more intensely she was absorbed in her art, the more profound the emotional calm that came over her. After working for a while on her sketch, she began to talk. "Jude, I think I know why I like painting so much. I'm developing a theory."

"What is it? I'm all ears!"

"Because in my art, I can make the world as beautiful as I imagine it to be instead of the sick way it actually is. Think about it. An artist often depicts the perfect, idealized world—the world soothed over, softened, made right, and feather-brushed by the artist's loving caress." She made a couple deft touches on her canvas as she further formulated her thought. "In one view—and I know there are many alternative opinions—but in one view, the artist's perspective is reality perfected." She backed away from her easel to appraise her artistic effort. "What do you think of my theory, Professor?"

Jude placed his hands on her shoulders. "I think it's brilliant, Mary Cassatt."

"Mary Cassatt. Now that's a real compliment!" Cory dabbed more paint on her canvas. "Did you know that she was born in Allegheny City? That's one of Pittsburgh's suburbs, so we definitely claim Cassatt as one of our acclaimed Pennsylvania artists."

"No, I didn't know she was a Pittsburgh artist. When was she born?"

"May 1844. I think it was May. I know I have the year right."

"You're a walking art encyclopedia."

"I don't think so, but thanks anyway for the compliment. I just wish I knew art the way you know literature."

By the time they departed their hideout in the early part of the evening, Cory was completely fine—"back to her normal self," as

Jude noted in his journal. Because Cory was feeling tired once they arrived at Cory's house, they declined the walk on Vinlindeer during the evening and chose instead the less-taxing stroll on the lane leading to Cory's home.

"Have we talked through all the issues?" Jude asked as he rested his hand on the fence post and looked across the fields.

"Yes, I think so. Actually, there's little to talk through. I'm completely convinced that my hallucinations were brought on by the medication. Now that I'm off the pills, I feel great. Well, maybe a bit wiped out, but mentally I'm back on terra firma. Hallelujah!"

CHAPTER 34

As soon as Jude stopped by Cory's house on Sunday morning to pick her up for church service, he realized she was totally beyond the effects of the medication. *The good night's rest makes her look positively radiant!* "Cory, you look fantastic!" he said, meeting her at the kitchen door. Her hair, just shampooed, hung in long waves and bounced as she walked. "You look so rested, and your hair shimmers in the sunlight."

"Sleep is the best physician of all. 'O sleep, O gentle sleep, Nature's soft nurse.'"

"That's Shakespeare, right? What play? I can't remember."

"*Henry IV, Part 2.* I looked it up so I'd get it right. Sleep has sure been a soft nurse for this emotional wreck! What would we be without it? I feel great!"

At the end of a fine church service that morning, Pastor Gabriel announced that, because of the heightened interest in the Esther Bible study, he was going to hold an informal discussion in the parsonage during the afternoon. "Anyone who wants to participate should feel free to stop by for Esther, tea, and scones. In that order!"

Cory whispered to Jude, "I know where we ought to be this afternoon!"

"Front row, pilgrim!"

Coming as it did shortly before the production of *Hamlet*, the afternoon discussion in the parsonage proved to be one of the most providentially orchestrated events of the entire summer. Pastor Gabriel began the afternoon session by quickly rehashing the pertinent background on the book of Esther, which he had presented at the Wednesday-evening Bible study. While this topic is heavy sledding for non-historically-minded folks, Gabriel's audience at the Center Hill church, having explored this historical terrain in some depth in the past, were surprisingly cognizant.

After a quick recap of the Wednesday discussion, Pastor Gabriel launched into the topic at hand. He reminded the eighteen people who had stopped by the parsonage that the Jews who comprised the northern kingdom had been transported from their home in Israel to Assyria in 722 BC, whereas Judah, the southern kingdom, had been exiled to Babylon, which had by then succeeded Assyria as the dominant world power, in several different waves between 605 BC and 586 BC. "The book of Esther," Pastor Gabriel explained, "covers events from 483 to 473 BC when the Persian king Ahasuerus was ruling in Persia. The book, thus, is set during what is called the Persian period when Ahasueras was king. Xerses, by the way, is the Greek word for his name. The king was assassinated in 465 BC, but the events in the book of Esther end in 473 BC."

"This stuff is great," Jude whispered to Cory. "I can't believe how erudite Gabe is among these country folks. Even history majors don't get such detailed information."

"I agree!"

"Seriously, he rivals the best lecturers I hear on campus!"

"During the years in which the book of Esther is set," Pastor Gabriel continued, "Persia had risen to supremacy and defeated Babylon. A key official under King Ahasueras, Haman, bore a hateful and historic revenge against the Jews, dating back to an incident, which had occurred some 550 years earlier when the Jewish prophet Samuel had killed Haman's ancestor Agag. The Agagites, as Haman's lineage was called, continued to despise the Jews throughout history. So when Esther's older cousin Mordecai, an intelligent Jew who acted as surrogate father to the young and beautiful Esther, would not bow in deference to Haman, Haman was reminded of and again irritated by the age-old enmity. "Using his smoothest and most Machiavellian machinations," Pastor Gabriel explained, "Haman sought revenge by inducing the king to sign a decree that would exterminate the entire Jewish race. Learning of this plot, Mordecai told Esther of the genocidal madness and urged her immediate involvement."

"Go for it, Pastor!" Jude whispered to Cory when Pastor Gabriel paused to take a sip of water. "I can't write fast enough in my notebook!"

Pastor Gabriel then came to his primary text from Esther chapter 4 when Mordecai relates to Esther the sordid details of the genocidal plot. "This, good folks, brings us to the main text for this afternoon's discussion." He read from the book of Esther when Mordecai speaks to his beautiful young cousin. "Do not think in your heart that you will escape in the king's palace any more than all the other Jews. For if you remain completely silent at this time, relief and deliverance will arise for the Jews from another place, but you and your father's house will perish. Yet who knows whether you have come to the kingdom for such a time as this? [Esther 4:13–14]." He repeated the last verse, "Who knows whether *you* have come to the kingdom for such a time as this?"

Pastor Gabriel's climactic question, the centerpiece of the afternoon session to which he had been leading, relentlessly hammered at Cory's brain. In large measure, she later asserted, that question—have you come to the kingdom for this time?—was the impetus for the bizarre but brilliant interlude which occurred during the play the following Saturday afternoon. *I was so emboldened by Esther's heroism that it instantly spawned in my mind the improvised Hamlet scene.* She later shared with Pastor Gabriel, "The catalyst was your Bible study, especially your concluding comments." Learning from the pastor that the terminating points of the afternoon discussion provided the impetus for Cory's fascinating improvisation—later dubbed the "Pittsburgh Hamlet" by the Pittsburgh media—Charles requested a copy of the taped Sunday-afternoon discussion, which he painstakingly transcribed.

Transcript of the conclusion of Pastor Gabriel Wyant's Sunday-afternoon session

Esther, we see then, was placed in a very difficult set of circumstances and given a task so challenging that it became the defining moment of her entire life. Without realizing it, she had arrived at this momentous crossroads. I want to emphasize that her response to this once-in-a-lifetime opportunity set the tone for and determined the nature of her entire future existence. What would have happened if she had missed that opportunity in Persia, or as we say today, blew her chance? Do you think there would ever have been a comparable second chance? [*A pause and then indistinguishable sounds in the background*]. I doubt it too.

Here are the predictable questions I put to you good folks this afternoon before we drink some tea and eat some of Martha's delicious scones. Remember, I said these three things would be in this order! [*Everybody laughed at the pastor's wit*]. Is the challenge, which God has currently placed in your path, *your* ultimately defining moment? To dig deeper, have you accepted this challenge the way Esther did, or have you, in a manner of speaking, run from it? Have you mustered the bravery and courage to slay this formidable lion? Lions come in many different forms. Yours may be a major life decision you're facing. Do you see the relevance of this text to our lives? Good people, please grasp this all-important point: God's kingdom will be established, and His larger will accomplished; there can never be any doubt about that. The real question then is this: Are you going to facilitate or impede that

> kingdom work, or as we colloquially say today, be part of the solution or part of the problem?
>
> All these questions are more or less subsumed within one overarching question. Are you aware of God's master plan for your life? Have you accepted that role, and are you radically bent on accomplishing it? The choice is yours as surely as it was Esther's. My concluding suggestion to you this lovely Sunday afternoon is to be on the lookout for those providentially orchestrated opportunities in life, which, if responded to properly, lead both to higher planes of self-illumination and, very possibly, sanctified participation in the divine plan. Few occasions in life offer such clear, ready-made opportunities to become a hallowed instrument in the hands of Almighty God. No one ever experiences a higher calling in life than this, and nothing will give you the fulfillment and satisfaction of serving Him so sacrificially. You may well be more like Esther than you realize. Have *you* come to the kingdom for such a time as this? Amen.

During the pastor's concluding comments, the transfixed Jude and Cory hung on every word. Shaken to the roots of her being, Cory, especially, identified with heroic Esther, who in that singular moment of crisis, made a brave decision that affected the history of the entire Jewish race. Pastor Gabriel well understood the impact of the session as his journal attests:

Pastor Gabriel's journal

> I was going along just fine in our Bible study. Some eighteen of us had assembled in the living-

room parsonage. These good folks had warmed to my subject very nicely, reminding me anew of why I chose this profession or, more accurately, why I'm so pleased that God called me to it. Because I, like most seasoned speakers, read my audience fairly well and know when they are engaged and when they're not, I was automatically attuned to their interest level throughout the session. Upon scanning our oval-shape group at one point, I laid my eyes on Cory and Jude. Yes, I had observed them earlier and knew they were attentive, but I thought nothing of it since they always listen intently.

At this juncture, when discussing Esther's sheer bravery in laying the trap for evil Haman, I emphasized a point that is too often blithely glossed over in the discussion of her courage—namely, her intelligence. "Her cleverness," I asserted, "equaled her courage. She was dealing with a ruthless despot, King Ahasueras, who could cut her head off in a whim, and a comparably evil second-in-command, Haman, who was intent on exterminating every single Jew in the land. Standing up to both, Esther nevertheless concocted a plan so superb that even the devilish Haman was duped, his scheme thwarted, and his life destroyed in his self-made trap. Good folks, don't underestimate the sheer brain power it requires to come up with a plan that mentally astute. You see my point: Esther's intelligence must have been astounding!"

During our consideration of these chapters, we waded into a good discussion, as we often do in these sessions; and during today's give-and-take, several of our people made some astute observations. Of these, it was Cory's comment which, for me, was most telling. I cannot quote her directly, but Cory said she wanted to consider again Esther's comment to cousin Mordecai when, having decided to pursue her daring plan, she boldly stated, "If I perish, I perish." Cory quoted Esther's phrase and said, "Can you imagine that kind of bravery?" Deep in thought, she looked across at Charles's house and then continued, "I know it's a philosophic question of sorts, but I do wonder if such extraordinary service to God always requires this kind of sacrifice." Pondering deeply, almost as though thinking out loud in a private setting, she followed with a second probing question: "Does true service to God always require such a deep sacrifice?"

Though she again paused, we remained silent, sensing that she had not yet fully articulated her thought. "This is tough," she began. "I'm trying to figure out how to say what's on my mind." As she sat in silence, the room grew very quiet.

"That's very biblical," I said at last, filling the awkward silence as she struggled to formulate her thoughts. "I give you Proverbs 15:28: 'The heart of the righteous studies how to answer.'" I looked at the group. "That's what Cory is doing, studying how to answer! Take your time, Cory. You're on to something wonderfully profound."

After Cory nodded in agreement to my citation of this text, her eyes went to the large Warner Sallman *Head of Christ*, which hangs on our living-room wall. She then commenced speaking, "That's exactly right, but before I continue, look at the Cross under the right eye in Warner Sallman's *Head of Christ*. See it?"

We all turned and looked on the wall at the painting, which was given to Martha and me on our twenty-fifth wedding anniversary.

"Sorry to divert from the subject," she continued, "but I just now noticed the perfect Cross underneath the right eye in Sallman's famous painting. Sorry, that's the artist coming out in me! I always heard that Sallman introduced a lot of Christian imagery into his famous painting but never realized that this one is so very obvious!"

We all looked in a kind of amazement at what we'd never seen. Someone said, "Well, can you beat that!"

Then Cory continued, "Here's what I want to ask. Can a person be God's earthly agent without dying to self? I guess lying down on the altar and presenting ourselves a living sacrifice means that we have to get to the point where we say with Christ, 'Not my will but thine be done.' That means that the cross which we daily carry has to be as visible as the one on Sallman's Christ!" She again pointed at the painting.

Her comment stirred quite a discussion which I will not summarize here, but I recall Jude's patting her on the back and vigorously nodding in agreement. "What a challenging observation!" Because Cory had offered these comments in her typically passionate fashion, it was obvious to all of us that she identified with Esther completely.

I did not realize the significance of her question until we adjourned and noted that several people—Jude, Cory, Zane, Barry, Jim, Cindy, Lori, and Dave—had congregated on the porch to continue the discussion a moment before saying goodbye. It was one of those lovely summer afternoons when the cumulus clouds were dazzling white, colossal, and other-worldly. The edges of the clouds were so rigidly defined that they looked as though cut from a magazine and pasted on an artificially Persian-blue background. In the distance, we could hear an occasional car over on Route 28. As I walked toward the group on the porch a moment earlier, I thought to myself, *How I love this place! No wonder I left the big city church and all its prestige for these beautiful people in this beautiful country setting.*

This handful of folks continued their discussion of Esther and her plan to set a mousetrap for Haman. "Not unlike Hamlet's improvising a play for Claudius in Shakespeare's *Hamlet*," I said in passing. I spoke this for Jude and Cory's benefit, knowing that the allusion would have been over the heads of most who aren't up on their Shakespeare. Up to this point, Cory—and Jude as well—marveled at Esther's strength, but Esther's bravery had been that of another person in another place in another day. My mousetrap comment broke in on them like the shooting rays of sunlight that beamed through those vast clouds sailing blithely along in their ocean of blue.

"That's right," Jude said, looking at Cory. "Hamlet stands up to evil just as Esther does."

Then Cory gave voice to the thought that she had been working toward the entire time. "I think we're being called to stand up to Abe Badoane and confront him as surely as Hamlet stood up to Claudius and Esther stood up to Haman."

I could tell the comment rattled Jude, who, after a somewhat lengthy silence, finally retorted, "Ah, there's the rub."

During the next few minutes, I noted Cory's relative silence. The connection with *Hamlet* prompted my response: "God calls us to be proactive. Recognizing evil and abstaining from it is not enough. Evil prevails when good people stand idly by and do nothing. We must pull down evil strongholds and wage war against the forces of darkness." I paused and looked directly at Cory. "Sometimes—Cory, you are right—sometimes that means laying a mousetrap." I was merely piggybacking on what the others said, but that comment (or maybe it was the mousetrap image) must have unleashed a whirlwind in Cory's mind. She offered no response but wildly stared toward the Bonner Cemetery across the road. What was racing in that mind of hers? All I heard her say, almost to herself, was one isolated mysterious comment: "Sometimes mousetraps are needed… and justified too!"

CHAPTER 35

Jude's journal

After the Sunday afternoon discussion on Esther, I drove Cory home and told her that I needed to spend some time with Grandma, whom I had been "neglecting" lately. While essentially true, I had the ulterior motive of opening up free time for Cory's much-needed afternoon nap. Her recent days had witnessed a succession of crammed activities, each tightly wedged in next to the other like the kernels in Grandma's bird feeder. She agreed but said she wanted to do the one thing that helped her relax the most—walk up on Vinlindeer, watch the late-evening sky, and dream across the vale "in the arms of my true love." I proposed a stipulation. We would do this but only after some rest. She happily, if a bit reluctantly, agreed.

Later that evening we rode the horses up to the ridge where we tried to process the kaleidoscopic events of recent days, several of which had crashed over us with the force of a tsunami. The more I reflect on this, the more I see that the creative surge bursting forth in Cory this evening had actually started in *Little Gidding* with her work on her painting, *New Every Morning*, and continued through the Sunday-afternoon Bible discussion. The creative streak hit a kind of climax during Cory's random comments on the parsonage porch afterword when she realized that, like Esther, she had arrived at a major challenge that had to be confronted. In my humble opinion, it's one thing to spawn forth ingenious thoughts during a spurt of creativity; but in my book, it's something else altogether to imagine yourself an actual part of that plan. That, nevertheless, is what happened on the porch. Cory, in those moments, was scripting the germ of a play—her own mousetrap—in which we, she especially, would be the principal players!

But my love faced a huge dilemma. The die was cast when she, as a young girl, hid from me in the barn the day Grandpa died. I gradually came to see that her hiding instinct, that predilection to run from pain and difficult choices, had more or less characterized her approach to life right to the present time. That's why she has always been such a private person—"emotionally unavailable," as I suggested to her one day—and frequently lapses into an incommunicado mode with mushroom mine and even church friends to some extent. She had started hiding from troubling events and threatening circumstances when she was a young girl. Now though a lovely mature woman, she was powerless to stop the tendency. "Hiding's a rut in my mind like the Oregon Trail," she once quipped. "Like a hardened old wagon-wheel rut, I can't get out of it!"

Is that why she ran and hid from me all those years ago when we were so much in love? Was she afraid of commitment? During our high school years, she would no doubt have periodically flashed back to the day in her childhood when she hid from me at the time Grandpa died—that awful error, that nagging thorn in her side, which she constantly fought to repress. The business of the doctored nude photos of me, the ostensible cause for our breakup, was simply a convenient excuse to break up with me. Our deep love for each other had lured her out of her cell—that was definitely true—but that life of exciting freedom and love simultaneously entailed risk. Thus, her inner soul, despite her best intention, sought the comfort of darkness again. No wonder she often used to sing Paul Simon's lyric, "Hello, darkness, my old friend." Darkness really was her constant and abiding friend in those days.

As I lay there with Cory in my arms this evening on Vinlindeer, a related thought flashed in my mind. Her relationship with Duke, brief and stormy though it was, was immensely exciting for her because throughout its duration, she had authored her own actions. She willed to do something, actually followed through, and did it. Charting her own course out of the darkness and ceasing at last the cycle of inaction—maybe *inertia* is the better word—she had temporarily peeked out from her subterranean existence. Like a nocturnal creature of the night, she had emerged from her mental cave in the happy morning dawn to see reality in all its refulgent glory. I now understand why she cited Thoreau's quotation from *Walden* out of the blue that one evening in Little Gidding: 'Only that day dawns to which we are awake."

How refreshing it must have been for her to stop hiding, face the dawn vibrantly alive, and indulge in this brazen act of self-determination, even if some of those actions—like her involvement with Duke Manningham—were ill-made and ill-timed. Still it was her action. She owned it, and she delighted in doing something for a season, even if that something was foolish and ultimately injurious. How glorious that unrestrained, that unbridled spontaneity, must have felt after years of her death-in-life incarceration!

Another small detail fell into place as I reclined there on the hill. When I first came to Armstrong County in early May and Cory had been seeing Duke, she often sang the refrain of Elvis's "My Way": "I did it my way." As I held her in my arms this evening and felt the warmth of her head on my shoulder and allowed her hair to blow across my face, I connected these dots for the first time. The song gave voice to her life in those days when she had stopped hiding, run into Duke's arms, and enjoyed the thrilling freedom of self-authored action. How novel, at last, to be the ordering center of her little universe! She had at last done something her way. She used to sing it over and over, "I did it my way." No wonder it was her theme song!

"It's been a long time since you've sung or hummed, 'I did it my way.'" That was all I said and then resumed my cogitation. Why did she have difficulty transitioning to me in the intervening quiet years? More to the point, why wasn't she as attracted to me as she had been to Duke back in the late winter and early spring? What held her back? Why the temporary resistance? Come to think of it, why had she limped back into the cave during my periodic visits to Armstrong County in the five silent years? The answer, as I lay there this evening, hit me with a thud like the apple that fell from the wild apple tree and smacked me on the shoulder. How we laughed when that happened. I jumped like a sissy! "What the heck was that!"

Here's the point. I was a walking reminder to Cory of the old hiding days! She had run from me as a little girl and maintained that running pattern through the years. Running was her comforting, reflexive action, which continued her entrenched pattern of dealing—or, technically, not dealing—with me. She saw me and, like Pavlov's dogs, ran to her cave. She saw Duke and, enthralled with the freedom he offered, greedily (if ill-advisedly) ran to it, desperately desiring to emulate it.

That glimpse of her mental terrain on Vinlindeer this evening was invaluable for the way it helped me appreciate her impressive journey. A frightened young woman, she had shirked from a hostile world where moms die young, dads quit work owing to injury and clinical depression, and high school sweethearts slam the door in your face. Since my return in May, she had pushed Duke to the periphery, dared to fall in love with me again, and even allowed the world to see her affection. If that were not enough, she had transitioned from survival mode to creative mode. Her heart cry had always been, What can I do to get through the day, and how can I best preserve myself and survive the moment? But as a result of her recent transformation, she had connected to her beautiful inner soul, possibly for the first time in her life, and was reveling in its rapturous expression. *New Every Morning* flowed with gushing force directly from the fountain-head of her utmost being. That's where things stood when we came to the hill this evening.

After we lay in each other's arms awhile, our peace deepened into a supernatural calm. In that paradisiacal serenity, the spurt of meteoric creativity, which we had experienced the previous evening in Little Gidding and again during the post-Esther porch discussion, opened up a world where we saw with halcyon-clear, rationally astute eyes. There on the hill, we channeled that stream of creativity to the problem of the day—namely, the situation with Abe Badoane—and began to think of the upcoming production of *Hamlet* in Pittsburgh.

These two forces, surging creativity and heightened rational clarity, blended together and culminated in a kind of thunderous crescendo of imaginative thought. I know that must sound crazy, but that's exactly what it was. The creativity culminated like a blasting rocket this evening. It was liked being touched by the divine as the idea of the theatrical interlude in the middle of *Hamlet* crashed into our brains.

The notion of superimposing our crisis with Abe onto the most brilliant scene in all of Shakespeare, the *Hamlet* playlet, *The Murder of Gonzago*, was a flash of lightning in our heated brains. I couldn't believe it. I simply couldn't believe it!

CHAPTER 36

Jude's journal (continued)

It happened this way. Cory and I had picked up our reading of *Hamlet* at the point when a troupe of traveling actors visits the Danish castle and, at Hamlet's suggestion, stage a play called *The Murder of Gonzago* for King Claudius and Queen Gertrude. Cory knew the scene well and, like me, marveled at its ingenuity. During this reading, a few thoughts which hearkened back to her "directing" a skit in Pittsburgh the day before imaginatively coalesced in our minds.

Up to this point, I felt that her brief hallucinatory-induced foray at being a stage director in a famous theater—surrounded, no less, by a couple of renowned equity actors who had scored big on Broadway—had been a worthless exercise in futility, "an embarrassingly mad episode" (as I said to Charles), which I had to endure and couldn't forget soon enough! That had been my reaction before talking to Charles, who in responding to my sarcastic allusion to the mad interlude, said, "We need to see this through Gabriel's eyes of faith. I know you're surprised to hear that coming from me, but we both know that Gabe would remind us that whatsoever things you ask, believing, you will receive." I thought Charles, as is sometimes his wont, was being dismissively glib. In this case, he wasn't.

My response was pointed. "Do you actually think something good might come out of that bizarre interlude that nearly sunk your rehearsal and put the two of us in the psych unit?"

"Don't sell God short. Gabe is starting to show me that those who call upon God must believe that He is and that He rewards those who call upon Him."

That was all Charles said, but I could tell he meant it. In that brief exchange, I had proof yet again of how this intelligent man, though awash in the cynicism of modern academia, was growing in a faith that was light-years beyond mine.

I certainly had my doubts about any good that could result from Cory's insane moments on the stage. I had doubts, that is, until this evening on Vinlindeer when we saw with razor-sharp clarity how brilliant Shakespeare's *The Murder of Gonzago* playlet really is. Cory and I paused after we finished reading this part of the play and said nothing for a while. I bided my time to see if any of the whirling thoughts, locked in a holding pattern in my brain, would eventually circle around and find the landing strip.

Meanwhile, I waited and watched a red-winged blackbird dive at a crow who had threatened the blackbird's fledglings, which were nesting on the ground. "Is it true," I said to Cory to stall for time while my subconscious hammered through these thoughts, "that blackbirds try to retaliate when crows attack their young by plucking the bottom center feathers of the crow's wing?"

"I'm not sure. Why those feathers?"

"Something about those being the guiding feathers, the ones that enable the bird to direct flight. If those are plucked out, the crow's ability to fly is greatly compromised. Do you think that's true? I have no idea if it is, but one of the guys told me that once up at Scott's camp. I guess I'll have to ask Pastor Gabe. I understand he's quite the ornithologist."

Cory resumed silence. She too was ruminating on *Hamlet* and the events of the day. "Isn't it something, Jude?" she said a few moments later.

"What is?"

"I can't stop thinking about what we said after church this afternoon. Hamlet opposes great evil when he stands up to Claudius in Denmark, just as Esther does when she faces Haman. Think about it. Esther, in a real sense, stages a play as surely as Hamlet does. I find the parallels absolutely amazing. That's why I went crazy when Gabe made his mousetrap comment."

"Your connection today was marvelous." It was obvious to me that her creative juices were again starting to kick in. "Keep going. I think you're back on the fast lane of creativity!"

"There's an even more important connection, an even more important play, that concerns us."

"What are you talking about, mystery woman? To absorb what you're about to say, I think I should first drink a giant glass of cold water!"

"I'm talking about us. I'm thinking of the dress rehearsal next Saturday."

"What about it? I'm not following you."

"Hamlet stages a play to catch the conscience of the king, to expose the king and unmask his chicanery."

"Right. I know *Hamlet* well, but what does that have to do with us—little ole innocent viewers in the audience?"

"I'm thinking that we can catch Abe in a mousetrap as surely as Hamlet and Esther catch their foes."

I looked at her in silence and then realized she was serious. "Have you been popping pills again?" I watched the blackbirds again swoop at the large crow. "I think he got the feathers that time! I wish I had my binoculars. I swear that blackbird succeeded in plucking the feathers from the crow's wing. Yeah, the little guy beats the giant!"

"I think you're right."

After stalling, I was ready to hear Cory's idea. "I understand that Abe most likely will eventually be enmeshed in a trap of his own making. That's a big theme in *Hamlet*—all things will be brought to their destined end—but what's that have to do with the coming stage production in Pittsburgh or us?"

"I'm thinking of a way of staging a play within *The Murder of Gonzago* playlet—a play within the play within the play."

I flashed a look of utter astonishment. "You're thinking of what!"

"Hear me out. By inserting a few lines, we could adapt the scene to our situation. During this improvised enactment, we'll watch Abe's reaction. If we can expose his guilt, as Hamlet exposes Claudius's guilt, then we would bring Duke to enlightenment, Abe to justice, and us to safety. Seeing Duke witness Abe's undoing would be the sweet part. Tell me what thought is sweeter than Duke's coming to see the extreme evil of the serpent who plays on him like a flute. Seriously, Jude, I think the idea is brilliant even if off-the-chart dangerous."

"You mean you want to do this *during* the production itself? You plan on interrupting a live performance in front of real people and highly paid equity actors? Take no offense, but I thought the insanity bit was history, and you were back to normal." I laughed to let her know I was partly, but only partly, kidding.

"Let me finish. I have the perfect alibi—my hallucinations and craziness. As far as we know, Duke and Abe plan to be at the theater."

"Tell me again how you know that. I find it very hard to imagine Duke Manningham within a ten-mile radius of a theater, and if it's a Shakespeare play, make it a hundred-mile radius!"

"Tina told Brenda, and Brenda called to tell me right before I lay down for my nap. I thought I had told you that when you picked me up. Well, Brenda said Tina's dead certain Abe's going, and Duke says he'll be with him. Let's assume for now that's true."

"You didn't tell me that Brenda called."

"Sorry, too much on my mind. Well, she called and filled me in on some other things too." Cory paused, intent as she was to flesh out her brainstorm, but then she realized that she had forgotten to clue me in on a very important conversation with a good friend. Cory came back to the phone conversation. "Let me say this before I finish my *Hamlet* idea since this is important. Brenda says that Tina wants to settle down, get married, and have a dad for her son, Tony."

I looked in amazement.

"It doesn't end there. Tina's convinced that Duke is Tony's father, so she wants to marry Duke! Brenda quoted Tina: 'I want my adorable son to have a dad like other boys.' Tina stopped at that and then added, 'The added cash wouldn't hurt either.' Doesn't that sound like Tina?" Cory laughed.

"Okay, thanks for filling me in, but get back to the 'ultimate plan crazy.' Believe me, I want to hear what you're hatching, yet I can see why you stop to give me this great news about Tina wanting to settle down. That would be amazing if Duke really is the father of Tina's boy and wants to marry her. Okay, good news. Now back to your mad plot. Should I say, 'more matter with less art'?"

I remembered something else before Cory resumed talk about her plan, and I figured this was the time to mention it, even though I regretted breaking Cory's train of thought. "Oh, sorry to interrupt, but I too remembered something I need to share with you. I forgot to tell you a fact that's important to the little drama you're spawning. Duke let it slip that Abe has fingerprinted me and thinks for certain that my fingerprints are on Duke's car. He surmises that I'm guilty. Well, Duke more than surmises—he's totally convinced!" Cory was obviously shocked by this revelation, but instead of talking through its nuances, I encouraged her to return to her plan.

"That's major news. Really major. Okay, back to *Hamlet.* During the production, I'll assume my antic disposition—you know, act crazy again—and go up on stage to direct a slightly different mousetrap." She could tell from my reaction that I thought the whole thing was

> more than a little bizarre. "Look. It's only a dress rehearsal. Charles says that few audience members typically attend dress rehearsals, just some family members and a few friends of the cast. It won't be that much different from what I did during the afternoon rehearsal when I directed my own little barn skit. I'll be doing essentially the same thing, but this time around, I will have had experience. Hey, I'll be a pro and nominated for best director!" We both laughed hard.

Jude's journal entry for that evening goes on for pages as he recounts their Vinlindeer discussion and the actual interlude plan in detail. At first, he was dismissive, thinking Cory was kidding, but when he learned she was dead serious, his jocular response gave way to shock. "You're serious about this, aren't you? Do you realize how nuts this is? You actually want our play to be subsumed into the playlet *The Murder of Gonzago*, which occurs inside the play *Hamlet*? That certainly is a lot of layers of playing! And another small thing: there are only a few hundred variables to handle."

Realizing how intensely impassioned she was, Jude nevertheless seriously contemplated her plan. He saw the whole thing as one audacious act of "brazen gutsiness" but praised its brilliance too. He did not sleep well that night and wrote in his journal instead. In that prolonged journal entry, which synopsized the discussion on the ridge, he came to see in the parlance of the Center Hill folks that "the Vinlindeer plan" was "anointed by God."

As Jude lay in bed after composing his journal entry, his teeming brain replayed the events of the last days over and over again in an attempt to impose order on them. *First and foremost, we have learned from Tina Reynolds one staggering bit of information: Abe and Duke plan to go to the theater to watch the play on Saturday. Abe will be in his element in the theater and could easily be taken for a drama critic, but can you imagine Duke Manningham in the theater? Also, I've been fingerprinted and in Duke's eyes am 100 percent guilty for damaging his car. The fingerprints offer incontestable proof to them that I'm guilty. Because of the damage, Duke will definitely seek retaliation, though I can't imagine what kind, but I do know that caution is the name of the game since the metaphor commonly used among mine employees to describe him is "loose cannon."*

If Abe was to be caught in the trap which they were laying for him during *Hamlet*, he would have to be convinced that Cory was on the outs with Jude and desired reconciliation with Duke. That was one of the main points of their discussion on Vinlindeer. *In such a short time, how can we rekindle Duke's love for Cory and simultaneously convince both Abe and Duke that she was serious about wanting to drop me? How can we convincingly intimate to others that we're having "trouble"?*

Even more important, Jude and Cory were brought face-to-face with the biggest problem of all. What sort of a mousetrap could be laid for Abe that would absolve Jude of all wrongdoing and simultaneously implicate intelligent Abe for masterminding the sabotage of Duke's car? Such a plan would require a great deal of stealthy—and incredibly courageous—cunning. *Given the powerful personalities with whom we're dealing, one wrong step could spell disaster!* These points, dissected from every possible angle on Vinlindeer, hammered through Jude's mind as he struggled to sleep.

Yet one point boldly foregrounded itself in front of all others. *Against all odds, we have conceived a potentially workable if utterly dangerous plan! Cory, my love, you are something else!*

CHAPTER 37

While manicuring his strawberry plants after work one afternoon, Abe Badoane reflected on his plan of revenge. *Revenge should have no bounds! Well, so far so good. I have Duke Manningham exactly where I want him.* As often his custom, Abe spontaneously composed a little ditty as he shuffled up and down the rows:

> Yes, I'm the ugly serpent,
> Obsessed with Jude's undoing,
> 'Cause the wily cobra's bent,
> On his very speedy going!

It matters not to me how I get Jude out of my life, but duping Duke the dolt to do the deadly deed will work just fine!

Abe picked off dead leaves from the plants, plucked a few miscellaneous weeds, and examined the berries. *Okay, you darling berries, now for verse two:*

> I'll be the sneaky snake,
> Smiling all the while.
> Destroying foes is cake—
> They're no match for my guile!

I like that! Good job, poet laureate of the strawberry patch!

He stood up to work out the kink in his knee and then knelt again. *Another thing is in my favor: Duke's convinced that Jude sabotaged his car. Like a coward, Jude ran away in the parking lot, and best of all, his prints are the only suspicious ones visible on that beautiful '57 Chevy.* He bit off the tip of a strawberry but, finding it bitter, tossed it into the weeds. *While I'm pleased that Duke is bent on retaliation, I perceive a potential problem. Duke's act of revenge, whatever it is, could elicit sympathy from Cory and make her love Jude even more than before. We can't have that—the forlorn damsel pining for her departed knight in shining armor!* Playing the damsel in distress, he mockingly spoke out loud, "That wily serpent Abe has forced my true love out of the castle. Oh, my true love, come back! Come back to me, my Jude, so we can happy-ever-after in our Camelot!"

Sampling a luscious berry, Abe continued to reason. *If I don't turn Cory against Jude, then I can just imagine them happily ensconced in their bower of bliss in southern Miss. Now there's a thought that fills me with rage! It is not enough to have Jude furiously storm out of the mine because of Duke's act of vengeance. Component two of the plan, splitting up the lovers, is even more important to me, but how can I accomplish both objectives in one fell swoop?*

Abe's dilemma required a mind as scheming as Shakespeare's Claudius. *The best way to achieve this end*, Abe decided over the weekend, *is to rekindle Duke's love for Cory. The Cory-as-sex-bait plan was coming along very nicely until Duke tried to hump her at Beatty's Mill. What a jackass! Well, he says it over and over again, "I hurt her, Abe. I'm telling you, I really hurt Cory!" That being the case, it's now time for a gentler strategy that capitalizes on Duke's remorse.*

In the parking lot on Monday morning before the workday began, Abe launched his plan, again urging Duke to attend the upcoming production of *Hamlet* in Pittsburgh. Before speaking, he made sure no one was around. "Hey, Duke, did you make up your mind yet?"

"About what?"

"For crying out loud, about going with me to see *Hamlet* next Saturday!"

"I can't believe you're pushing this on me, man. Yes, I'm interested in Cory, but I hurt her bad and really regret what I did." He kicked the tire of his car. "I blew that forever, so I'm moving on. After all, you're the one that said that since a relationship is like glass, it's sometimes better to leave it broken rather than hurt yourself by putting it back together. So I'm done with broken glass and have made up my mind to settle with Tina." Using his shirttail, he buffed out a smudge on the fender of his car. "You know, maybe even marry Tina and be a dad to Tony. In Cory's eyes, I'm the enemy."

"Not so fast. Remember Martin Luther King's pronouncement, 'Love is the only force capable of transforming an enemy into a friend.' She doesn't have to keep seeing you as the enemy. Love can change her heart."

"You're being naive. When I dropped a hint to the women about marrying Tina, they grabbed hold of it like we'd be standing at the altar at sundown!"

"Slow down, Duke. You're moving too fast." Abe put his arm around Duke, and together they moved to the rear of the '57. *Hmm, Duke's a tough case, but the right dosage of poison will swill any brain!* "What interests you in Tina? Think about it." He paused and allowed his words to sink in. *Come on, poison, do your work!* "Yeah, I know, lots of good times in bed, but be reasonable. There's more to life than sex."

He paused to give Duke time to respond. "Well, I haven't seen its equal yet."

"You need a woman who'd be happy by your side, a woman you'd be proud to call your beautiful wife, and not a woman who's been overly familiar with battalions of men and is on the prowl half the time." *That was a devastating hit, a dagger to the heart. Look at him fold! Duke's actually shaking his head, a little sign, but I saw it! I'll keeping jabbing that vulnerable spot.* "How many have had her, Duke? You want that sort of woman to be your wife? Once married, how long would it be before she tires of you and will start her infernal two-timing?" *Another snakebite to the heart!* "It's the only life she knows. You actually think she'll change?"

"Yeah, I know what you're saying. There's no comparison between the two women." Duke shuffled his feet nervously. *Going one-on-one with the serpent and pitting myself against his brain is something I can never do, but I have to try.* "There's something else. I'm a loser compared to Jude Hepler, and like I said, Cory would never forgive me. Never be satisfied with me." He spat angrily on the ground. "Much as I hate to say it, Hepler's a class act compared to me."

"But there are other ways to win her over. You can do it if you set your mind to it and stop the flow of negative thoughts that are pouring out of you right now. You have to curtail this mental bleeding."

"How? My head's a dungeon and I'm trapped inside!"

You sound like Macbeth—"O full of scorpions is my mind, dear wife!" "There are plenty of ways to win her, but they won't help you make up lost ground near as quickly as going to see *Hamlet. The big ape is folding. I can't believe it!* "And don't kid yourself. You lost a lot of ground."

"How long will this freaking play last, and can we get a beer afterward? I can't believe I'm even thinking about this!"

"We'll be in and out of the theater before you know it. It's an afternoon dress rehearsal, and not the big-deal evening production when all the fat cats are there with their fancy cars and flashy clothes. The audience will be small and the play fast." *He'll love this!* "Your evening will be free, so you can carouse with the cows...then house with the sows!"

"You're ridiculous!" Duke watched some of his buddies park their cars and walk toward the mine entrance. He lowered his voice. "Don't you dare tell the guys. They'd think I'm as nuts as Cory on meds." He spotted Meg Barley getting out of her car in the next row. "Or Meg the keg on booze."

"You think I'm ridiculous? Well, you're hilarious!"

"I swear Meg drinks a whole bottle of bourbon by herself in a day! You should have seen her at The Inn the other evening."

Abe flashed his big smile. "Forget Meg and stay focused. I promise I won't tell anyone you're going to the play. No one will ever find out." They took a few paces toward the entrance. *I'll be the sneaky snake, smiling all the while. You eat the sweet cake, not knowing that it's bile!* "Trust me, you'll be very grateful that I talked you into seeing the play."

Duke and Abe entered the mine, Abe stopping in the lounge as usual and Duke at the vending machine for his morning coffee. Cory saw Duke there and instantly set Jude's and her plan in motion. "I'll try to talk to him right now if no one's around," Cory whispered to Jude. "You hold back and talk to the others. What do you think?"

"Perfect. Good time to chat with Duke since he's alone right now."

This is an answer to prayer, she thought as she approached Duke. *I wanted to talk to him first thing without a cluster of men around.* Cory motioned him to the side of the vending machine, her back turned to the group. "Duke, I just want you to know that I forgive you for the other evening."

"I find that hard to believe!"

She touched her face gently to show that it was less sensitive. "My face is pretty well healed, just a bit of swelling right here. I don't hold the incident against you." She spoke softly and looked down as if the right words wouldn't come. *Praise God that what I'm saying here is absolutely true!* "I just can't go on with hate in my heart."

"You're the best and kindest person I know."

"I have to admit that my feelings for you morphed to hate because of what you did at Beatty's Mill." Overcome with emotion, she bit her lip. "My spirit won't tolerate unforgiveness. Surely you know that about me. Yes, you hurt me and made me mad, but I know that I have to forgive you. I try to blame the whole thing on your drinking." *I'm being truthful when I say this!* "Please tell me it was the beer that made you do it."

"It was! I was drunk!"

"I just can't believe you tried to do that horrible thing to me!"

"It was the booze. Cory, I swear it was. You know I'd never hurt you! Look how nice I've always been to you."

Cory rolled that thought around in her mind. *This has a biblical ring to it.* "I'm relieved to hear that! Somehow it sounded biblical."

"Biblical? You've got the wrong dude. You're talking to Duke the loser, not Jude the winner. What happened the other night wasn't very biblical! Abe referred to the mad thing with one of his silly rhymes. He said you were almost the maid who was made, the lass who was laid! Doesn't that sound like Abe?"

"Definitely! Have you completely forgotten our talks at my house? Remember we spoke of Romans 7 once. Remember?"

"Remind me."

"The apostle Paul says in that famous chapter that it was the sin in him that caused him to do bad things. Yes, Paul too faced the sins of the flesh. Well, that, in some ways, is the story of your life. When sin drags you down, you become Duke the animal. The Spirit tries to lift you up to become a good and decent man, but the flesh always pulls you back to the gutter." She looked at him with a slight smile; the pain in her cheek lessened. "I know who won the ongoing contest that night at Beatty's Mill!" Cory managed a slight laugh.

Sipping his hot coffee, Duke looked at Cory in disbelief. "Do you really mean what you're saying? I can't imagine that you'd ever forgive me for what I did. Cory, I tried to rape you. I even pulled your panties down." Duke massaged his swollen hand. "Well, I tried to. Jude got there in the nick of time. I hate his guts but am glad he stopped me and protected you. I was a monster that night, and I hate myself!"

"Remember what we said about love. It forgives all wrongs, renounces all revenge, and bears no grudges. I'm not there yet because I can't honestly say that I bear no grudges, but I'm definitely gaining on it. I have to start by forgiving you for what you did."

"You're unreal. Nobody's that much of a saint!"

"But we must try! That's why I'm saying this right now. It's my first step in trying to act as Christ calls us to act." She again bit her lip and shook her head slightly. "I do that right here right now. I forgive you, Duke."

"Nice words, but I've never met anyone who actually practiced them. Except maybe you. And by the way, don't expect me to forgive Jude for what he did to my car." Duke looked over to where Jude was surrounded with several workers. *The loser!* "You and I were doing fine till he came on the scene."

Forget the revenge, Duke! I must get him to refocus on my comments. She touched his arm to get him to look at her again instead of Jude. "Look, I'm not the saint you say I am, and I sin daily, but I can choose to forgive you as Christ forgives me. That's what we're supposed to do. Don't put me on a pedestal. You're forgetting how deeply human and flawed I am. I'm just another woman trying to make it in a mad and sinful world."

He looked at her incredulously. "Are you saying you want to forget what I did and restore our friendship? I mean, get it back to where it was before?"

"What I am saying is that I forgive you and that I want to be your friend." *I can tell he's a good man at heart, but he remains deeply conflicted.* "You're a man of tremendous potential, Duke, but up to now you've realized a very small part of that potential."

"You've got that right!"

"Stir up the gift that is within you. That's something the apostle Paul said to young Timothy. He told him it was high time to do something with his life as I'm telling you."

"When your life's as badly wrecked as mine, it's tough to make it right again."

She lightly touched his swollen hand with the tip of her finger. "Duke, I want us to be friends. Will we get back together in the way you mean? I'm not here to talk about that, but we can forgive each other and mend our friendship."

Duke gently took a sip of the steaming coffee. *I need to convince her that I really want to change.* "Did you know I'm going to the theater Saturday afternoon to see a play? I forget what it's called…*Romeo and Juliet*, *The Three Musketeers*, or some dumbass thing!"

"Yes, I heard. You're going to see *Hamlet.* I think that's wonderful."

"Yes, that's it!" *I'm doing it for you!* "Abe conned me into it. He thinks it would help me win you back. Nobody ever knows what's up that guy's sleeve." Duke looked around at a couple of his buddies loitering in the area. "Don't tell anyone I'm going to Picksburgh to see a freaking play!"

"Who knows? You might like it!"

"Never! I wish it was a Pirates baseball game instead. I'm dying to see Barry Bonds, Andy Van Slyke and Bobby Bonilla play. Slyke's been red hot the last couple games. Have you seen any of the recent games? I can't take my eyes off the TV!"

While they talked, Cory smiled in her typically friendly fashion. *This kindness is not hypocritical, nor is it difficult for me to forgive him. I'm called to do that, but I have to admit, my pleasant demeanor won't hurt in furthering along our plan.* "You guys and your baseball!"

Upon exiting the lounge, Jude "accidentally" saw Cory and Duke during their lengthy exchange. *Time to feign some hot-collared jealousy, which I'll boisterously voice to these people around me.* "What gives with Cory? Why's she talking to Duke so much? I swear she's been talking to him for ten minutes. Look at her smile. She's been cool toward me the last couple days, and now she's talking to Duke like he's her long-lost love!"

Several of the women near Jude looked at him in amazement.

Cindy, in shock, dropped her helmet. *What did that mean? What's going on with Jude and Cory?* She whispered to a nearby friend, "Did you hear *that*?"

CHAPTER 38

Jude continued his diatribe in front of the flabbergasted women. "Cory actually dragged her feet when I asked her to go to Pittsburgh to see a Shakespeare play." *Here's my most sarcastic voice!* "I can imagine how much fun that afternoon will be!" He looked at Cory and saw her smile at Duke. "Look at that! She's smiling like a Cheshire cat!"

A number of the women peered toward Duke and Cory. "I'd say she's forgiven him!" one of them quipped.

That's the kind of reaction I wanted! "Can someone please tell me what's going on? She's been acting very haughty lately. You'd think she'd hate Duke because of what he did to her at Beatty's Mill, yet she's showing more interest in him than ever!" Jude flashed a look of disgust at Cory and Duke and turned his back on them. "I think it's high time I gave her a piece of my mind!" He donned his helmet. "I, for one, won't be played for an idiot!"

The men and women standing with Jude were astounded. "I don't believe this!" one whispered to another. A calculated part of Jude and Cory's plan, the strategy worked perfectly. The "trouble" between Jude and Cory traveled like lightning as the workers moved toward the locker rooms.

"Sounds to me like Cory and Jude are fighting!"

"Can you believe it?"

"The perfect lovers are on the outs with each other!"

"I swear I've never been so shocked!"

With a few nonchalant words, Cory deftly fueled the fire in the women's locker room moments later. "Making up with Jude is a lot harder than I thought it would be. I didn't realize we had grown so apart, but the truth is, we've become very different people over the years." She slammed her jacket onto the hook in her locker.

"Sounds like you're describing my marriage!" Freda joked.

"In many ways, he's just not one of us. He keeps playing the part of this brainy intellectual. Sometimes I feel like throwing in the towel." She pulled her hair back as she put on her miner's hat. "I hate to admit it, but I'm starting to learn that you can't go back and love as you did when you were young." *I can tell they're falling for it!* "When we were high school sweethearts, it was so easy, but now it's so self-conscious and difficult. Does this make sense to any of you?"

"I, for one, completely understand," Lena commented. "People change."

A number of the nearby women looked at one another in disbelief. Standing by Lena on the other side of the lockers, Freda whispered to Lena, "Can you believe that Jude and Cory are having trouble?"

"I'm amazed! This is the juiciest development I've seen in this place in a long time!"

Cory's passing comments were later replayed in detail to both Abe and Duke, both of whom seized on them with ravenous delight. After a brief spell of idly teasing out the nuances of this development, Abe carefully implemented the next phase of his plan. *Good! This quarrel will make it easier for me to talk Duke into taking a very necessary step: confronting Jude about the damaged car.* Abe tapped his lip with his index finger. *But his run-in shouldn't occur here in the mine since a mild altercation could easily ignite a huge fire, and even the cunning serpent might not be able to extinguish that conflagration! I can't allow that to happen and must maintain control at all times. As I constantly tell the workers, "Don't ever allow yourself to get in a position where you lose control. It can wreck your life forever." That's my credo—"Always keep control!"—and that must be the case now.*

As the day wore on, Abe continued to ruminate on his plan. *Here's something else. If Duke's confrontation with Jude were to be the opening salvo in a major brouhaha here in the mine, then the workers would, as in the past, divide into two warring factions. That's a real problem because which camp would be larger, Jude's or Duke's? The solution? I must bring the matter to a head in a safer, more cultured setting. The journey to Pittsburgh to see the play then must be used to accomplish two major objectives. First, I'll get Duke to commence building a bridge over the ravine to Cory and, second, simultaneously detonate the one to Jude forever. Clever, clever, even if I do say so myself! Yes, it will be* The Bridge on the River Kwai *all over again, and this part 2, like some other sequels, will be excellent.* He dug his whitened fingers into the steering wheel of the mule as he sped down the mine corridor. *But how to go about accomplishing both ends in one adroit move? Thinking, thinking—what's my play? Time to sculpt this stooge of clay!*

Content a short while later with a plan which hit him with the speed of a cobra bite, Abe caught up with Duke in a rear section of the mine to give him additional details about their forthcoming trip to Pittsburgh. "So the plan is airtight," he concluded after sharing the plan with Duke. He jumped up on his shop mule. "I'm completely convinced it will work. We just need to have the proof, and as I say, we have that in the fingerprints. Be sure to bring them with you since they're the key to the whole plan. That's your small responsibility."

"You have them!" Duke responded, a quizzical look on his face.

"I do? Really?" *That little memory lapse will make Duke perceive me as, on the whole, indifferent to our plan. It's important that he scripts himself as the mastermind.* "I forgot. Okay, I'll remember to bring them. You'll see why they're so important."

Abe Badoane was not the only one inching a scheme toward fruition that morning. Cory sought an opportunity to talk to Abe, but no matter how hard she tried to meet him, something always intervened. *I keep missing him! I'm trying to keep myself calm by repeating a favorite verse which Pastor Gabe taught me. "Let patience have its perfect work in you so that you may be perfect and entire, lacking nothing" (James 1:4). Patience, patience—I must be patient. But this is so hard!*

Finally, her chance came when Abe, returning from the packhouse, dismounted the shop mule near where Cory was picking. "Abe, if you can grab a minute later, I'd really like to talk to you."

"No problem, darling. How about during lunch? Let's talk then."

"That will work fine." *This is perfect—another answer to prayer—since that's exactly what I was hoping for!*

Cory knew that she had hit a vein when she spoke to women earlier about Jude's being so different from the other folks in the mine. *That resonated because Jude is indeed utterly different from them. They could easily empathize with the difficulty I face in maintaining a close relationship with someone who, to them, is a fish out of water. The gossip among the women is now nonstop. Since that approach worked so well, I'll use it when I talk to Abe during lunch, but this conversation will be fraught with danger because he's so discerning and sees through any subterfuge. Lord, help!*

Chuck Berry's "You Never Can Tell" played in the background during lunch.

> It was a teenage wedding and the old folks wished them well
> You could see that Pierre did truly love the Mademoiselle
> And now the young Monsieur and Madame have rung the chapel bell
> "C'est la vie," say the old folks, it goes to show, you never can tell

Jude's eating lunch in a different lunchroom, so I'll have this chance to go one-on-one with Abe. "Abe, I want to begin with a question. Do you think two people"—Cory paused for a moment—"can become so different that it's"—another pause—"impossible to keep their love relationship going?" *The hesitation in my voice will make him think I'm having trouble articulating this. Well, I hope so!*

Abe looked at her intently. "Whatever do you mean?"

"I mean this. I used to be very close to Jude and got along with him superbly. You know that as well as anyone. The relationship was easy in those days because we were so similar. We were so close that we could nearly read each other's thoughts, and conversation flowed between us like the paint on a Titian canvas." She looked down as she talked and then, as though mustering courage, looked at Abe in the eye. "But now he's become this person I don't even know. I keep thinking he's bored with me." *I wish you'd react, Abe. Your stone face tells me nothing!* "Sometimes he's condescending too. Does that make sense?"

Abe nodded vigorously. "Yes, of course."

"He talks about his teaching and his dissertation constantly. That stuff bores me, and it's as though we have nothing in common anymore."

Abe looked piercingly at Cory but spoke only after a prolonged silence. "I can understand that."

Cory nibbled on a chip and waited for a moment as if deciding what to say. *This is so dangerous!* "Here's something else. I'm self-conscious around him in a way I didn't used to be. I always wonder if he thinks I'm a dunce or if he's comparing me to the sharp women in his graduate classes. He talks about his classes constantly."

"He loves to learn as I do. We're very similar that way."

"Well, I'm tired of trying to impress him or conform to his inflated expectation of what I should be or should become." She ate another chip. "I didn't have to worry about this around Duke. I could just be myself. In fact, Duke looked up to me and put me on a pedestal. Jude doesn't look up to me—ever! In fact, he looks down. *Way* down!"

This is playing right into my hand! "This makes sense to me. Go on."

Cory watched Abe to gauge his response but saw a completely expressionless face. *I'm losing heart! This plan is too daring, and he's so smart that I fear he's on to me!* Cory looked down, bowed her head, and breathed a prayer. *Well, I'm resolved to step even further into the muddy river.* "Should I continue?"

"Please do."

She glanced around her to see who was listening but didn't seem to be especially concerned. "Things used to be easy with Jude, but not anymore. Maybe I expected our love to pick up where it used to be. Well, I'm learning you can't do that." She pushed the food around on her plate with a fork but ate little. "Abe, I'm worried. Here's the real kicker. On bad days, I wonder if I should have given Duke more of a chance."

This is wonderful! What a joy to hear this! Seeing that Cory wasn't muffling her voice nor seemingly minded that nearby pickers were eavesdropping, Abe followed suit and spoke in a normal conversational level. "Keep going."

I can tell the neb-noses are listening to every word. They're even craning their necks! That too was Cory's intent since the more people who were aware of the supposed tension between Jude and Cory, the better, yet she well knew the danger of what she was doing for one simple reason. Given Abe's intelligence, he was capable of seeing through her ruse in a heartbeat and exposing her in the presence of everyone. *Am I fooling him, or is he merely playing along and, in a classic and not uncommon irony, duping me instead? How can I tell? How does one ever know anything for certain about the cunning copperhead of the corridors? I mustn't push my luck, but if the Pittsburgh plan is to succeed, I have to push further and risk more. But how frightening this is! Is he taken in by my subterfuge?* "Abe, this is a really challenging thing to talk about!"

"I know it is, but as General George Patton once said, 'Accept the challenge so you can feel the exhilaration of victory.'"

Or as the apostle Paul said, "But thanks be to God! He gives us the victory in our Lord Jesus Christ" (1 Corinthians 15:57). She steeled herself with another consoling thought: *Without faith, it is impossible to please Him.* Impelled by the added confidence the verse gave her, she waded deeper into the murky waters. "I have more to say, but this is so difficult!"

CHAPTER 39

"Abe, do you have to go, or can you stay a little bit longer?" *I'm afraid if I don't continue our talk now, I won't have the courage later!*

"I have lots of time for you, darling." He looked at his watch. "We don't need to return to work for at least ten minutes."

"Good, since there's something else I need to talk about." She looked behind her at an empty table at the back of the lunchroom. "Can we sit back there? I don't want any busybodies to hear! You can tell they're hanging on every word. We'll be out of earshot at the rear table."

When they took their place in the corner, many of the nearby employees, following the discussion word for word, watched them relocate, their heads slowly turning in whispered unison. Alice spoke for the group, "Princess is picking Abe's brain!"

"It's not just my awareness of our incredible differences," Cory continued, "that's making it tough for me to get back with Jude. There's something deeper than that." She tapped her fingers nervously. "It's a matter so personal that I can't talk to anyone about it." She mustered the courage to look Abe in the eye. "I haven't mentioned this to my pastor or even Joey's girlfriend, Laura, who's like a sister to me." Cory hesitated, as if unable to continue. "I'd die of embarrassment if I talked to anyone else about it."

"What is it?" Abe reached across the table and put a consoling hand on Cory's arm. "You know you can trust me, and 'to be trusted is a greater compliment than being loved,' according to George MacDonald."

"You and your quotations!" She paused for a while before responding. "Abe, this is so hard for me." Her eyes were downcast as she looked at the napkin on her lap and frayed its edges. *Does my nervousness look real or faky?* She paused another moment and then, scoping the room to make sure no eyes were on them, leaned closer toward Abe and whispered, "I don't think Jude loves me as he used to." Another pause as she waited for Abe's reaction, during which time she tore part of her napkin into little pieces. "There's something else. I'm beating around the bush because I'm afraid to say it. That's because I denied or cut myself off from my real feelings for so long that I'm not used to expressing them as I am now." She crumpled the corner of her napkin and stabbed it with a fork. "I'm not going to say it."

"Say it. Amy Tan said something similar to this in *Saving Fish from Drowning*: 'I hid my deepest feelings so well I forgot where I placed them.' That's what you've done, but you know you have a friend in me." He squeezed her arm. "Tell me!"

On the verge of tears, Cory pathetically looked up at him. *This is difficult because I can well imagine the pain, as I once did, if what I'm saying were true!* "Okay, here goes. Don't breathe a word of this to anyone. I can't believe I'm going to say this!" She paused, waiting for Abe's assurance, and whispered softly, "Do you promise to tell *no one*?"

"Promise."

"Here goes! I don't think Jude's sexually attracted to me. It kills me to talk about this, and I definitely don't know how to say it, but let me try, and maybe you can help me say this the way I want or at least understand. He knows I'm a moral person and that I'm saving myself for marriage, and I actually respect him for that, but does that give him reason not to at least show some interest?" Cory wiped a tear from her eye. "Okay, here it is. It's as though he doesn't see me as physically desirable." Another pause as she picked up the largest part of her torn napkin and dabbed her eye. "Do you know how that makes a woman feel?"

"Of course, I do."

"A lot of the men around here think I'm pretty shapely since they don't go out of their way to hide their feelings. I don't need to tell you how they gawk and gaze, and we women are well attuned to men's not-so-subtle stares and asides!" Cory spoke with urgency here, almost hissing the words. "But not Jude! He doesn't show even a hint of interest. Nothing. *Le rien. Le zero.* Can you understand what I mean? Do you have any idea how that makes me feel?"

"Completely. I too get the feeling that he looks on you as a goody-goody saint—so heavenly-minded that you're no earthly good. That's what a pastor once said back in the days when I used to attend church. Yes, that would hurt a beautiful woman's femininity. This makes perfect sense. Go on."

"There's something else. Again, I need you to promise to keep this to yourself and not tell a single soul." To maintain the ruse, Cory hurriedly glanced around to make sure the gossips weren't tuned in, though she secretly hoped they would catch at least a random phrase.

"You know you can trust me." He put his hand on top of hers.

"This is a confession. Here goes. I'm not so physically attracted to Jude either." Cory wagged her head back and forth as if struggling mightily to finish her point. "What I mean is, not like I should be. Jude's a hunk of a guy—don't get me wrong—but his not appreciating me physically makes me do the same to him, even though I've tried to keep that from happening. I know I should be attracted to everything about him, but it's as though we're so different, or I've been hurt so much that I just don't have those feelings for him anymore. I just don't desire him the way a woman should desire her man." She played with the torn pieces of napkin. *This next big comment could make or break me!* "Here's the kicker—I do see Duke as supersexy and have feelings toward him I shouldn't. I know these feelings are terribly wrong." *Glad these tears are real and not fake!* "Abe, do you see how confused I am?"

"You're not alone. We all get confused. The famous writer Jack Kerouac once said, 'I had nothing to offer anybody but my own confusion.'"

"That's pretty pessimistic!"

"It really is, so let me cite something more upbeat." Abe looked down at his plate of food and thought for a moment. "This famous Anne Frank quotation will be more to your liking: 'I simply can't build my hopes on a foundation of confusion, misery and death.' Listen to this next part: 'I think peace and tranquility will return again.' For me, that's beautiful."

Cory paused and looked at the ceiling, shaking her head back and forth as another tear formed in her eye. "When will I know tranquility again? This whole thing is so sick. I'm sick, so very sick. Why do I say that? Because Duke *does* turn me on. Imagine this." She leaned over the table so she was inches from Abe's head. "Here I am trying hard to reform Duke, but even as I speak of the moral life to him, I'm simultaneously fantasizing something immoral! How awful is that? Did you hear what I said?"

"Every syllable."

"I fantasize togetherness with Duke and not Jude! I am one messed-up woman!"

Back in her seat, Cory spoke in such a low whisper that Abe, though leaning forward, couldn't hear her. "Sorry, darling, I missed that."

"I saw Duke's body when he pulled down his jeans the other night. He wasn't naked. I mean he still had his underwear on, but I saw him." *I actually didn't, averting my glance just in time!* "He was ready for, you know, action. What a body!"

"I missed what you said. Sorry, the hearing isn't what it used to be."

"I said he has an amazing body—really sexy!"

"Yes, of course."

"I preach to Duke on the farm but want him"—Cory looked around to make sure no one was listening—"in ways I shouldn't! I keep seeing his nearly nude body at Beatty's Mill, and that really turns me on. How crazy is that?" She sat in silence and shook her head back and forth. "Hamlet had it right. 'Frailty, thy name is woman.' Right now, I feel as though I'm the walking embodiment of frailty. Or sickness. Or a mental case! Something's rotten in Denmark, and you're looking at her!"

"You're also human. Why wouldn't a lovely and well-endowed woman have such thoughts? Physicality is in many ways the centerpiece of the way God made us. We are sexual beings as He designed us. 'C'est la vie,' as Chuck Berry sings. Remember the words of the song we just heard. 'You could see that Pierre did truly love the mademoiselle.' And what was the next line in the song? 'But when the sun went down, the rapid tempo of the music fell.' Why? Because the newlyweds were moving toward intimacy. We're made to express ourselves physically."

Cory nodded in agreement and then resumed. "Abe, I can't thank you enough for listening to me and understanding. I lived in fear that you would somehow belittle me."

"I would never belittle you, Cory. Never!"

"Let me tell you how serious my problem really is." She stopped and looked at her watch. "Do we have to go, or can we talk another minute?"

"We have a few minutes."

"The other night when Duke attacked me at Beatty's Mill, I recoiled in fear because he was a drunken monster. He scared me silly, and I kicked him hard in the groin. That was a reflexive act that I later regretted."

"You were protecting yourself."

"I really didn't mean to hurt him, but here's my point. If he would have been gentle and loving and moved things along slowly in that beautiful and secluded place and then tried something, well, I don't know if I could have resisted. I keep picturing a much different end at Beatty's Mill. It's as though deep down I wanted it to be different."

"I see." *This is wonderful to hear. I can't wait to tell Duke!*

Appearing wan and hopeless, she played the distressed woman at the end of her rope. "I know that is so wrong, but how long can I withstand this temptation when I have this crystal-clear image of his body in my mind? I think a lot of that kind of love—I'm talking about the physical part—as many women do."

"The apostle Paul said it somewhere, 'We are of the earth earthy.'"

"First Corinthians 15:47. I suppose that's natural for one who's waited so long to have these 'earthy' experiences, but when I think...

of doing things, it's not always with Jude." She wrinkled her brow and vigorously shook her head back and forth. "There, I've said it all, and I know you think I'm nuts. I give you permission to think I'm totally crazy. You can quote O'Neill's *Long Day's Journey into Night*—'The mad scene. Enter Ophelia'—and apply it to me since I'm the Ophelia of the mad scene!" She laughed nervously.

"No, I don't think you're nuts. You've made my respect for you, and your honesty grow by leaps and bounds."

Staring at him in disbelief, Cory put her hand on his arm in gratitude. "Surely you're not serious."

"I most certainly am!"

"Well, the bottom line is this. I hate being so conflicted. It's as though my mind is a chaotic battlefield."

"I give you Napoleon. 'The battlefield is a scene of constant chaos. The winner will be the one—.'" He paused. "Are you listening?"

"Completely."

"'The winner will be the one who controls the chaos, both his own and the enemies.' Pretty relevant, eh? It's about control, Cory—control!"

"But how hard to maintain that!" *I think Abe is completely taken in despite his mental acuity and uncanny gift of discernment, but I do wish I were "the consummate actor," as Jude recently said of Dustin Hoffman's performance in* Rain Man. *That I'm not, nor am I sure who's controlling this conversation! Still my timed tears, flushed face, lowered voice, and cupped hand appear to be deceiving him. Yet I need courage to take that last giant step across the doorsill to make Abe think I'm actually angry enough at Jude to do the horrible thing I'm going to propose. Lord, help—this is so scary!*

"Yes, hard to maintain." He stared at her with his piercing eyes. "Because sometimes the supposed controller is actually the controllee!"

Whatever did that mean? Is he on to me? Is he seeing through me? "Sometimes the supposed controller is actually the controllee." I know I'm on extremely thin ice here, and Abe's eyes are boring into me like lasers. He must see this for the ruse it is! I was so confident up to this point, but now I've lost all confidence, and I can't stop my hand from this uncontrollable shaking!"

CHAPTER 40

As she continued her lunchroom talk with Abe, Cory nervously fidgeted with her hands on her lap.

"I know you're nervous, Cory. Baring your soul like this isn't easy, but I do sympathize with you. As I said before, you can trust me, so please continue."

I surely hope he's serious and not playing me! "One more thing remains, and I'll be done. This has been so therapeutic for me, and I really am grateful to you. I feel better just getting this out." She brushed all the torn pieces of her napkin together and shaped them into a pyramid. "Here it is. I can't forget the photo of Jude and Tina making love. Some people, especially Jude, say those are fake pictures, and I think that too."

Abe coughed as if to clear his throat. "How embarrassing that must have been for you."

"But deep down, I still wonder if it's him, and even when I don't *think* it, I still *imagine* that it is. See the difference? I'm haunted by this feeling that he's more interested in others than me. When I get depressed, I even wonder if he's two-timing me, or if he has a girlfriend back at the university. How can a guy wait for a girl the way he keeps waiting for me? He says he's staying true to me, but is he? Is that kind of willpower even possible for a flesh-and-blood guy? Could a real man even do that? I always imagine him looking at the loose women around here. I can't stand it when he looks at Tina. It's as though his eyes burn right through her clothes." *Jude better not, or he'll hear from me—ha!* She stabbed an uneaten apple with her fork.

"It's as though he mentally undresses her when he talks to her!" She looked helplessly at Abe. "Does any of this make sense to you?"

"Yes, and I've seen that look when you're not around." *Might as well build on this, though I've never seen Jude look lustfully at Tina a single time!* "You'd be shocked, so don't kid yourself. The man is no saint, and it's high time for you to stop being taken in." Abe looked around to make sure no one was listening. "In my opinion, his fantasies are a bigger part of his life than you realize. And it isn't just fantasies. I've seen the flirting." Abe's whisper was barely audible. "Here's the truth. You're far too good for Jude Hepler."

A hurt look on her face, Cory looked in amazement as she digested this comment. "Do you really think he's attracted to other women? Please don't tell me he's attracted to Tina!"

"Are you kidding? He'd roll her in the hay tonight if you loosened the reins a bit. As I said, c'est la vie!'"

"Abe, don't say that! You're killing me!" Cory spoke this in such a loud whisper that a few of the nearby people looked at them.

Abe again spoke softly. "Who's being deceived here? I give you the desideratum of Ludwig Wittgenstein: 'Nothing is so difficult as not deceiving oneself.'"

Cory pulled her seat nearer the table to be closer to Abe and put her elbows on the table. "There are two maybes that bug me: maybe he wants Tina, or has actually done something with her already, and maybe he really was the one who damaged Duke's beautiful car. I haven't talked to you about this, but it's this second thing that's killing me. I can't believe someone damaged Duke's car!" Cory leaned closer to Abe. "If I had proof that he did the latter, I'd—well, I'd be so mad that, under the right circumstances, I'd expose him in a second and probably get back with Duke. How could Jude do that to his classy '57?"

"It was an awful deed."

She looked questioningly at Abe. "I'll clue you in about something that even you may not know." *As if he wouldn't know this!* "Do you realize that most people around here think Jude's the one who banged up Duke's car? But this can never be brought out in the open, so even if it's true, he'll get away with it and continue to play us, and mainly me, as stooges!" Cory looked down at her watch. "Hey, that's a terrible place to stop, but we have to go." Cory rolled the napkin shreds into a ball, pushed her chair back, and stood up.

"Don't be so fast there." Rising from the table, Abe turned his back to the lunchroom to be certain he wouldn't be overheard. *Missy, get ready for this punch!* "I printed Duke's car and know for a fact that it was Jude who damaged his car. Why else would Jude's fingerprints be the only ones on the car? Do you call that an accident?"

Cory pretended to fall backward into her chair, dropped the crumpled napkin ball, and sat back down in disbelief. "You're kidding! I don't believe for a second that you have Jude's fingerprints. I haven't seen any detectives running around here lately." *I feel uncomfortable telling this lie, for I did hear that Jude had been fingerprinted. But the plan, if it's to work, is predicated on Abe's not knowing that we know. Nevertheless, white lies fall into that shady gray area!*

"I do, Cory. I absolutely have the prints."

"Are you serious? How did you get Jude's fingerprints, Sherlock?" She paused as if weighing the significance of this revelation. "Do you realize how important this is? You have the incriminating evidence and do nothing? Are you content to keep me in the dark about my boyfriend and go along with Jude as if everything is just hunky-dory? If he'd lie to me about damaging Duke's car, don't you think he'd lie about other things like his desire for Tina? Or maybe what he's done with her already?" Cory rubbed her temples. "No wonder my deeper instincts have been pulling toward Duke!"

The woman is intensely conflicted! "Of course, I understand."

She again looked at her watch. "Abe, we have to get back to work." She thanked him and started to walk away and then, as though struck by an idea, turned toward him. She looked around to make sure no one was near and cupped her hand to Abe's ear. "Can you bring the fingerprints with you to Pittsburgh on Saturday afternoon?" Abe had an incredulous look on his face. "You're going to the *Hamlet* dress rehearsal, right?"

"Yes, I'm going, but why, pray tell, should I take the prints to the play? What good would they do there?"

"Just do as I say, all right? We might have a use for them. And please bring the fingerprinting kit too. You said it's very small, right?

"Yes, it fits in my pocket."

"Good! Abe, this is important. Don't breathe a word of this conversation to anyone, and just don't ask questions. Promise?"

"Promise."

"I've really opened up to you and told you the kinds of things I've told no one. *No one!* I'm devastated by Jude's behavior. He isn't truthful with me anymore, and he certainly isn't the man I once loved!"

"There's strong evidence that he's been deceitful with you."

They rose and walked together out of the lunchroom. As they approached the personnel carrier, Cory put her hand on Abe's arm. "I wish I would have had time to tell you about the hallucinations I've been having ever since Duke hit me. You know about that, right?"

"Yes."

"I hope another bout of that's not going to pay me a visit! I feel now as if one of those awful fits is coming on me. I hope I'm all right, Abe. Sometimes I worry that these crazy days are too much for me. These woozy feelings are so scary." When Cory faltered for a step as though temporarily losing her balance, Abe reached out his hand to catch her.

Cory had lured Abe into her trap completely. The moist eye was the final grand touch. "Here, Cory. You can dab your eye with my clean handkerchief."

"Thank you." *That last-minute reference to my hallucinations was good since it set up Abe for the Saturday-afternoon play. Maybe I'm a "consummate" actress after all!*

That evening, Cory called Pastor Gabriel on the phone to summarize her lunchroom conversation. "How did I manage to dupe Abe so completely? How could such an intelligent man be so thoroughly blinded?"

"He was blinded by the god of this world—Satan. You recall one of my favorite verses. 'He who is spiritual judges all things, yet he himself is judged of no man.' You remember the apostle Paul's saying that to the Corinthians?"

"Yes. I like the verse a lot."

"The corollary of that is also true. Spiritually unenlightened people cannot judge all things. They don't have the illuminated—I guess I should say liberated—minds they think they do. Their skills of discernment, in fact, are nil."

"I know that's true."

Gabe was leafing through the pages of his Bible as he spoke to Cory. "Recall what the writer of Hebrews says. Here it is. I have it. People of mature faith 'by reason of use have their senses exercised to discern both good and evil.' Abe Badoane, extraordinarily intelligent as he is, cannot discern good from evil. Why was he taken in by your calculated deception? Because, not a believer, he has been duped by Satan. Abe's once astute judgment has become severely clouded over the years. A man like that becomes a shell of what he was. Yes, the serpent is mighty, but God is almighty. Recall what our Lord said in Luke 10:18: 'I saw Satan fall like lightning from heaven.' And his minion serpents will fall too. Rest in Jesus! The Master crushes all serpents under His heel."

"But who am I to go one on one with *this* serpent?" Cory hung up the phone, rolled her shoulder to massage it, and sat on the kitchen floor with Zoe. *Our idea of the mad scene in Pittsburgh scares me to death!*

CHAPTER 41

To this point, Jude and Cory's daring plan had come together perfectly. The only remaining detail was to work out with Charles the logistics of the *Hamlet* scene. Because the staged interlude would be quite complicated, its various intricacies required a great deal of attention. That evening, Jude, Cory, and Charles met at the bridge pavilion in Riverfront Park, Kittanning, to devise their strategy. The first order of business was acquiring the necessary props—the car photo murals, the masks with enlarged photograph faces, the mural poles, and additional items. Jude also shared the handful of added lines which he had composed for insertion in *The Murder of Gonzago* playlet.

"Will you have time to take care of all these details by dress rehearsal?" Charles asked.

"I don't think it will be a problem," Cory responded. "I already have the masks finished, and I've also made good progress with the mural photos. I haven't finish them because, until this conversation, I wasn't exactly sure how to proceed. But now I know."

"What about the poles for the mural?" Jude asked.

"I have them," Charles affirmed. "They're part of the props we keep backstage."

"Good! I'd say we're set.

Oblivious to the spectacle they were on the verge of creating—and the media sensation it would occasion—Jude wrote of their magical evening along the tranquil Allegheny River in Kittanning.

Jude's journal

The river traffic was particularly robust as lots of people had chosen a leisurely ride on the river to while away the hours on this beautiful summer evening. Many strollers and joggers also passed by as we quietly hatched our plan. My favorite part of the evening were the classic cars that lined Water Street and even dotted the park here and there in anticipation of the upcoming car cruise. Truth to be told, the cars made concentration on our improvised *Hamlet* scene difficult. I even made note of the vehicles parked near our end of the park—a '56 Buick Roadmaster, a black '57 Plymouth, a '56 blue Ford, a '56 Lincoln Continental, a '60 powder-blue Ford Falcon, a pink '58 Oldsmobile, a red '65 Pontiac GTO, and my favorite—a white 1959 Ford Fairlane 500 Skyliner with a retractable hardtop roof.

Music coming from the nearby river stage floated through the evening air like a wisp of thistle borne on the breeze. As this was August and the eleven-year anniversary of the month in which Elvis Presley died, the rock group down on the river stage was honoring the king of Rock 'n' roll by playing exclusively Elvis tunes. I jotted down the names of the songs as we worked in the pavilion: "I'm Yours," "Chapel in the Moonlight," "Love Me," "An American Trilogy" (the rendition of "Battle Hymn of the Republic" gave me goosebumps), "One Night," "Precious Lord, Take My Hand," "Playing for Keeps," and "Suspicious Minds." There were others, but I only noted these.

Having completed their plan, Jude and Cory bade goodbye to Charles, departed the Riverfront Park pavilion, and then meandered down the walkway toward the Citizens Bridge. They descended the stairs to the river and walked under the bridge. A large number of pigeons, the abiding inhabitants, cooed as they perched high up on the bridge. "Remember when we stood in the middle of the bridge and threw the roses?" Cory began. "I wonder whatever became of them."

Jude held Cory's hand. "They probably went down the Allegheny River into the Ohio, and then into the Mississippi River. My guess is that the roses washed ashore in Mark Twain's Hannibal, Missouri. I bet Tom Sawyer is picking them up and presenting them to Becky Thatcher at this very moment."

Playing along, Cory smiled. "Tom had a boyish romantic side. I bet he gave them to her in the cave, mischief that he was. Don't you think?" She kissed Jude's hand and cast her gaze to the sunset in the western sky. "Come to think of it, Tom and Becky enjoyed their cave hideaway, which, like ours, had some foreboding elements."

"But theirs was the stuff of fiction."

At the water's edge, they skipped stones across the river as they did when they were children. Picking up a stone, Cory noticed the flowers on the bank. "I'll make you fantastic garlands of these crow-flowers, nettles, daisies, and purple flowers."

"I recognize your line from *Hamlet*, my dearest Ophelia. 'There are pansies; that's for thoughts.'"

"Very good, my love."

They sat on the bank and watched the sun set behind the high bluff on the west side of the river.

If that moment represented sublime tranquility, the afternoon dress rehearsal of *Hamlet,* which occurred on the following Saturday afternoon, was the exact opposite. To simulate an authentic audience, Winston Armrose, the director, had at the last minute asked several of his professor friends to encourage students in their summer courses to attend. A little more persuasive in his request than he intended, he didn't realize that quite a few of the professors had taken his request seriously and, in their zeal to help a colleague, even tied extra-credit writing assignments to the students' attendance, thereby exponentially increasing the number of attendees for the dress rehearsal.

Equally concerned about paltry numbers for the dress rehearsal, Professor Charles Claypoole had also invited a fair number of guests. The result was that instead of the customary small handful of summer-busy, friend-and-colleague well-wishers, the dress rehearsal was packed with many people, including two of the city's noted drama critics.

Taking care of last-minute details with the cast as they neared curtain time, Winston stole a glance at the audience from behind the curtain. "Charles, if these were paying customers, we'd have pulled in a bundle today!"

Meanwhile, Abe Badoane and Duke Manningham, driving toward Pittsburgh from Armstrong County, neared Oakland. As they passed the palatial Italianate dwellings on Fifth Avenue in Shadyside, Abe realized that he had only a few remaining minutes to complete his brainwashing of Duke. *Time for the final bite of poison, but first, some small talk to calm down the big ape since a little bit of sugar makes the medicine go down!* "Can you believe the price of gas is up to ninety-one cents a gallon? Hard to imagine! And did you know that the average monthly rent is now listed at a whopping $420?"

"I can't believe these prices!"

Okay, no more dorking around. Time to convince animal man to do my bidding! "As I said up the road, Cory told me with her own tongue that she's fed up with Jude and wants to get back with you, but she just doesn't know how to tell him to take a hike. If you see Cory in the theater, watch how she looks at you. She wants you in her arms, and I know for a fact"—*he'll love this!*—"not just there." *Ape-man will get my meaning!* "If you get her to start liking you again, that will make her spread, first, the distance between her and Jude and then, second, in that other unimaginably delectable way." He here winked at Duke. *I knew that would get his attention!* "But first steps precede the heavenly plunge!"

"Heavenly plunge or no, I can't believe I'm doing this. I freaking can't believe I'm going to see a Shakespeare play. Just what am I coming to?"

After Duke parked his Chevy in front of Hillman Library on the Pitt campus, the two of them strolled down Forbes Avenue toward the Stephen Foster Memorial theater. The proximity to the theater having made Duke anxious again, he began to puff nervously on his cigarette as they ambled along. Trying to calm Duke, Abe drew his attention to the Carnegie Museum in the distance and the past musical geniuses whose names were boldly embossed across the top of the building.

"Look at the top of the Carnegie. Let me give you a little lesson in architecture."

"I prefer the architecture of those pretty girls standing along the curb in front of us. Look at 34-C there in the pink. That one," he said, slightly nodding his head. "Beside the 36-B in green. They're beautiful!"

"Duke, get your mind out of the gutter."

"Why, man? It's my bread and butter, or buttel, as Bonnie would say." He smiled at Abe. "Like my rhyme? I'm getting as bad as you!"

"Now get serious. See the very top of the Carnegie? In architecture, that top section is called the cornice, and underneath it is the frieze." Duke barely noted the building, enraptured by the females walking along Forbes Avenue on their way to the theater "See it? The small rail under the wide frieze is the architrave. Look at the names under the architrave. Duke, pay attention! That's where the musicians' names are, right? I can see letters but can't make out the names. The old eyes aren't what they used to be. Can you read the names?"

"I'm all about dames, not names!" Duke drew his attention back to the building. "I'd rather feast my eyes on the derriere of Miss 34-C. She gives a new meaning to curves!"

"Cool it, Duke. Now give me the names of those musicians up there on the architrave at the left. We'll play some trivia to settle your nerves and get your mind off the coeds. You're here for important business. Can you read one of the names?"

"Liszt."

"That's Franz Liszt. His dates are…" Abe hesitated a moment, as if retrieving a data file. "His dates are—come on, brain, think—his dates are 1811–1886. He was a brilliant Hungarian piano virtuoso." Abe squinted and look at the names again. "Give me another one of the names up there."

"Dvorak. What the hell kind of a name is that?"

"Yes, Antonin Dvorak, a Czech musician, often thought to be the most versatile composer of his day. He lived, let's see, from 1841 to 1904. Yes, I'm pretty sure those are the dates."

"How do you know all this crap? And here's something else. Who freaking cares? Now look at the rhythm on Ms. Shake Rattle Roll going up the steps over there. That's my kind of virtuoso!"

"Name, give me another name. Forget the dames. I want the names."

"Meyerbeer."

"That's Giacomo Meyerbeer, a German—"

Duke interrupted, "This one has possibility. I like the 'beer' part of his name. Tell me his family made a fine German beer, and I'm good with this dude."

"No, Meyerbeer, who lived from 1791 to 1864, was an accomplished opera composer."

"Now there's yet another freaking interesting fact! How many more, Abe?" Duke halted, grabbed Abe's arm, and stopped him dead in his tracks. "Let me tell you what Huddy and I think."

"What's that?"

"When you were spouting off all the trivia about Armstrong County, the Roman caesars, the Civil War, or some damn thing at lunch the other day, Huddy gave us his theory after you got up and left."

"What is Hudson's theory?"

"That one day you were up in the compost yard when Huddy was turning the ricks of horse manure for the mushroom beds. He said you got too close to the Hi-Lift, and he scalped off the top of your head. Then he poured in a bucketful of horseshit. Guess what?"

"What?"

"We all agreed!" Duke took his eyes off the coeds long enough to ask a question. "How do you remember all this stuff? Your head's full of crap and nonsense! Who cares, Abe? You gotta get with reality, man. Enough with the crap and nonsense and freaking musicians and Shakespeare!"

"Just give me a couple more. Then we'll cross over to the theater."

Duke grudgingly looked back up at the Carnegie. "Rubenstein."

"Yes, Anton Rubenstein, 1829–1894. I think that's right. Yes, that has to be it. He was the founder of the Russian conservatory."

"More crap! I can't tell you how much that fact excites me, Mr. Encyclopedia. I wonder why people call you Einstein." In his most sarcastic voice, he added, "What a mystery that is!"

"Give me another name."

"Chopin." (Duke pronounced this as *chop* as in *chopsticks*, accenting the first syllable).

"Frederic Chopin, 1810–1849, was a Polish virtuoso. He was a pianist of the Romantic period. He's one of my all-time favorites. That man was a true genius. His *Nocturne for Piano 9 in B Major* is really something, and so is his *Prelude for Piano No. 21 in B Flat Major*."

"Abe, shut up! You're driving me crazy! You want to hear what my all-time favorite is? These women! This place is crawling with babes, but I'm not feeling very cool about this. Look how people are dressed, and here I am in jeans. You told me on the way down that I'd like the gravediggers scene in this play. Well, I feel like a gravedigger compared to these college kids and city slickers."

"You'll be fine. Relax."

"You said there would only be a handful of people. Look at this mob of people standing outside. I feel like a hick, man. People in Picksburgh are too classy for me. I don't think I want to go through with this." Duke stopped walking and looked back at his car. "I wish we was going to a Pirates game, or a Stillers game would be better yet."

Abe sensed Duke's increasing nervousness and paused before crossing Forbes Avenue to the theater. *We arrived earlier than I intended since the construction on Route 28 didn't delay us as much as it normally does.* Abe tapped his index finger on his lip. *It's definitely too early to go into the theater. As a way of calming Duke down, I have to find a way to keep him interested, or knowing him, he'll want to bail. That can't happen since it's absolutely imperative that I get him into that theater.* Abe saw a couple blonde coeds ahead of them and dug into his repertoire of blonde jokes. (Note: blonde jokes were the rage in the late '80s and not yet politically incorrect.)

"Hey, Duke, did you hear about the blonde who was stopped by a police officer and was asked to show her license?"

"No! You and your jokes!"

"The agitated blonde responded, 'I wish you guys would get your act together. Yesterday you took my license, and today you expect me to show it to you!'"

Duke gave a nervous laugh.

"Come on, Duke, you tell me one."

Duke looked at the blonde in front of him and, after a moment's reflection, responded, "A blonde was playing Trivial Pursuit one night and was asked the question, 'If you're in a vacuum and someone calls your name, can you hear it?' The blonde replied, 'Is it on or off?'"

Abe laughed uproariously. *I have to come up with another game. And fast!* "We haven't indulged in our rhyming game for a while. Let me say the names of these musicians, and you give me your rhyming wordplay response as we do in the lunchroom. You did that a second ago when you said 'bread and butter' in response to my 'gutter.' Ready? Here goes. I'll give the name, and you tell me the first thing that comes to mind, but your response has to rhyme." Abe squinted and looked again at the top of the Carnegie. "Mozart. What rhymes with Mozart?"

"Jo's cart." Duke nodded to a girl in front of them. "That is one nice cart!"

"I could have predicted that response! Franz Liszt."

"Blondes kiss." Duke looked at Abe. "And don't tell me they don't. That's what I'd like to do to her." Duke gestured to a nearby coed. *For starters!*

"Not bad. I see I've taught you well. Chopin."

"Flo can." A brief pause. "I know she can. And speaking of 'can,' there's a lot of sweet cans around here. When did miniskirts get so short?"

"You need exposure to the ABCs of these geniuses."

"No, I need exposure to the As, Bs, and Cs of these Venuses!" Duke laughed loudly. "Come on, Abe, give me some credit. That was a good rhyme, and fast too. Soon I'll be on a par with you!" Nearing the theater, Duke saw more of the coeds. "I'm not used to seeing so much cleavage. The women at the mines wear sweatshirts and jackets and hide away all the beauty. But I do wonder one thing."

"What's that?"

"When did modesty go out the window?"

"Focus, Duke. You need to spend some time listening to the music these masters have composed."

"Wrong again. No use talking to you." He looked across Forbes Avenue at the women standing in front of the theater. "I'll say it one more time—I didn't know college babes dressed this way. Cory was right. I should go to college!"

"You're a hopeless case!"

As Abe and Duke walked across Forbes Avenue and up the stairs to the theater, Abe reflected to himself, Hamlet, *your time has come! What will this day hold?*

CHAPTER 42

The theater lobby was packed with raucous, weekend-loving, merriment-seeking college students. As they joked and clowned around in the lobby, Duke found their antics hilarious and their jovial mood inviting. Although most were present to fulfill the requirements for a writing assignment, they seized the opportunity, college-student fashion, to blend work with play. "If you ask me, these guys are here to let off some steam!" Duke whispered to Abe.

"They remind me of my salad days when I was green in judgment."

"Whatever that means!"

"Read your Shakespeare! Especially *Antony and Cleopatra*!"

"Don't hold your breath!" The students' rowdy presence lightened the atmosphere and eased Duke considerably. "Heck's fire, they're smiling at me and making me feel welcome." Duke leaned closer to Abe. "Dude over here even shook my hand. I could get along with these geeks and nerds!" Looking around the theater lobby and absorbing the atmosphere, Duke gawked at the coeds more intently now that they were close to them. "Abe, I'll say it again. Are you seeing these women? Tell me if there's ever a wet T-shirt contest down here. Guess who'll be in the front row!"

From Jude and Cory's point of view, all of this bode well for their plan. As Jude shared with Cory on their way to Pittsburgh, "Duke will engage the interlude more fully if he's in a relaxed frame of mind." In the long run, their intent was to expose Abe and enlighten Duke. Their vehicle to accomplish this requisite, if extremely difficult, goal? The improvised scene, which, if executed properly, would catch Abe in a trap as cunning as the trap Hamlet lays for Claudius in Shakespeare's play. Thus, as Jude said to Cory while parking their car near the Carnegie Museum, "To make this work, Duke needs to be emotionally settled but not carnally aroused."

Cory laughed. "The latter, my dear, is *always* an issue with Duke! I can imagine how he'll react when he sees all the lovely women in the theater!"

Jude and Cory entered the lobby several minutes after Duke and Abe. Fortuitously, Cory happened to establish eye contact with Duke as soon as she entered. *Okay, nerves, time to settle and let the games begin!* She flashed a warm smile in Duke's direction, walked cheerily over to him, and gave him a big hug, pressing hard against him.

"Boy, is it good to see you again!" She winked at him, gave him a peck on the cheek, and then whispered to Abe, "Remember how I said I was feeling dizzy in the mines yesterday? My head was spinning like a top on the way down here. I asked Jude why we were headed for New York! Can you imagine that? Maybe I should be at home… or seeing a shrink!"

Duke tenderly put his hand on her shoulder. "I hope you're all right."

Cory looked over at Jude, who stayed near the doorway. "By the way, what's going on with Jude? He barely talked to me during the entire trip. I thought maybe I exaggerated his strange conduct during lunch yesterday. I didn't, not at all!" She looked directly at Duke. "The guy's becoming a jerk. Look at him over there—barely inside the door and already flirting with the pretty coeds. Remember what I said when we were standing by the vending machines at work?" She swept her arm toward him. "Well, there's the proof in living color!"

When Cory walked toward Jude, Abe lightly elbowed Duke to get his attention. "Did you hear that?" he whispered. "Focus, Duke. Quit looking at the broads! Did you hear her? I told you she's on the outs with Hep and wants you. I thought she was going to jump you right here! Did you feel that hug?"

"Are you kidding? She pushed them against me as hard as she could."

"You'll have her if you listen to me. Will you be ruled by me?"

"Okay, I will be ruled by you, but only if this thing ends the way you promise it will. And it better! I can't believe I gave up my day to do this!"

"Good. We need to further think on this."

"Why? The plan's already in place. You won, I lost, and here I am at this loser play!"

"Well, just relax."

Seconds later, while in the middle of the lobby on her way back to Jude, Cory shouted in a loud voice, "God have mercy on his soul and on all Christian souls!" Everybody in the vicinity instantly grew quiet and looked with astonishment at the woman who uttered the strange outburst.

"What's with the mental one?" a college student standing nearby whispered to Abe.

Abe pointed to his head with his index finger.

"Oh, got it!" the student responded in embarrassment. "A nutcase!"

"How do you, pretty lady?" Abe shouted at Cory. He then spoke softly to Duke, "I thought I'd say something comparably dumb to partially cover for her."

At this point, Cory turned away from Jude and wormed through the crowd of people toward the auditorium. Abe and Duke looked in amazement as Cory left the forlorn Jude standing alone.

"Look at Jude!" Abe hissed. "I'm telling you, it's over between them! Would you look at his terrified face!"

Jude's journal

> She was fantastic! Duke and Abe were completely taken in. Cory bluffed them, huffed from me, and like a crazed woman on a mission, puffed to her seat. That's it—bluffed, huffed, and puffed! I was tense as anything entering the theater, but this bit of acting provided some much-needed comic relief. I chuckled to myself. *Cory, you're becoming quite the actress!* I looked at Abe and Duke and

> shrugged my shoulders, as if to say, "That's how she's been treating me lately!" I could tell that Abe was beside himself with joy, though Duke remained a boiling cauldron of hate. The guy stared daggers at me!

Duke assumed that all of this bode well for him and that Cory was, "if I keep my nose clean," his for the taking. "Maybe what you're saying is true, old man."

"The lowest-hanging cherry is the one ripest for picking!" Abe quietly whispered to Duke.

Ah, sweet cherry! "But don't tell me she's going wacko again. Did you see that crazy look on her face when she said that dumbass thing? 'God have mercy on his soul.' Whose soul? Mine? What in the world did that mean? People looked at her like she's mad!"

"Don't think anything about it." *I must distract him!* "It's time to sit down. Lead the way into the theater and sit where you want."

Duke took a seat in the auditorium immediately behind a couple of the smiling coeds. "This might turn out better than I thought," he whispered to Abe. A moment later, a summer-clad, buxom coed bounced down his row and sat immediately beside him.

"Hi, I'm Candy Melonie," she warmly said to Duke, leaning over and offering her hand. "You may like my candy," she said to Duke. She offered him some M&Ms.

"Yes, I'm sure I'd like your candy." *All of it!*

Duke leaned over to Abe and whispered, "Get a load of this. The girl beside me is named Melonie, and she's sure racked with melonies. Did you see her? We're talking melons!" Duke indiscreetly sat back straight in his chair. He cupped his hand to Abe's ear and whispered, "Have a good look!"

Meanwhile, as the three of them—Abe, Duke, and Cory—proceeded into the auditorium, Jude raced out the front door, gathered the props from Joey and Laura, who patiently held them for him, and then dashed around to the back of the theater. Entering the rear door to backstage as previously planned, Jude briefly met with Charles and several designated cast members to go over last-minute details regarding the improvised interlude.

"Greetings, you thieves of mercy," Jude began, a smile on his face. "'I have words to speak in your ear that will make you dumb.' How'd you like my quote?"

Taking an instant liking to Jude, an actor chuckled. "That was cool!"

"Really good!" another laughed.

Jude continued, "Here's the mural photo of the '57 Chevy which Professor Claypoole told you about, and this is the second mural—the one you use *after* the car's been damaged. Charles gave you the necessary details about the interlude, right?"

The actors nodded.

"Good!"

Jude unrolled two large mural-size photos that were attached to poles on the ends. "When you hold up the mural photos by the poles, make sure they're high enough for people to see." He then pulled a hood out of his bag. "Carley, this is the hood with the photo mask of my face, which you'll slip over your head. If you look around a bit while wearing it, everybody in the audience will make the connection. When you"—he continued to point to Carley Metz, who was playing Hamlet—"smash the taillight and mag wheel, be sure to place your hands here and here on the photo very deliberately."

"Okay, no problem."

"Exaggerate your placement to emphasize the location. When you've sabotaged the car and are ready to leave, you might look around to make sure no one saw you and then slink away on tiptoe, burglar fashion. Got it? Any questions? Oh, by the way, were you able to study the speech of some dozen or sixteen lines which we inserted?" The group nodded. "Excellent. You guys will be great. I can't thank you enough, my pirate friends." Jude gave them a wink.

Before Jude departed the backstage area, he drew Charles aside. *Why is he holding his hand to his chest? Are you all right, Chuck?* "When thou seest that act afoot, observe my uncle."

"You're too much, Jude. I swear you've memorized every single line of *Hamlet*!"

"This is important since I want to see if we detect guilt in Abe during this improvisation. My eyes will also be riveted to his face. Later, we'll discuss his reaction. You, Chuck, are the best." He started to walk away. "By the way, Cory and I want to enlighten Duke about Abe's shenanigans. We want you to know that this is every bit as important as exposing the smiling serpent. It's time Duke learns the truth!"

"The whole plan has more than a little craziness to it. You and Cory better do something to recover your wits." Charles smiled as he said this.

"We'll tend to that later at IUP."

"Good idea. Your lunacy won't be noticed there."

"Why do you say that?"

"Because everyone there's as mad as you—ha!"

"You're too much, Charles, but my intelligent colleagues would not appreciate your comment!"

"Even as a joke?"

A moment later, Jude ran around to the front of theater, reentered the lobby, and walked down the aisle to join Cory, seated in the front of the auditorium at stage right. When Jude entered to sit beside her, she flashed an angry look.

"Lady, shall I lie in your lap? What do you think?"

Cory fumed at him and loudly shouted, "I think nothing!"

Jude leaned over and spoke quietly but could still be heard by the people near them. "As Hamlet would say, 'It's a fair thought to lie between a maid's legs.'"

"Get out of here!" Cory screamed. "Sit somewhere else!"

Jude stormed away in anger, but as he did so, he again faced the audience, for whether the plan worked successfully depended on facial recognition.

By this time, everybody in the immediate vicinity was watching the seating fiasco. A man immediately behind Cory whispered to his girlfriend, "Do you agree that Madam Crazy has a few mental issues?"

The girlfriend replied, "What are we in for this evening?"

Duly chastened, Jude stomped away from Cory and took his seat down front at stage left.

CHAPTER 43

Watching the seating drama in front of the auditorium, Abe leaned over to Duke. "Do you mark that?" Duke was talking to Candy and, Abe assumed, not paying attention. Abe elbowed him in the ribs. "Did you see Cory rebuff Jude?"

Duke had taken his eyes from Candy Melonie long enough to look at Jude and Cory. "Yes, I was watching. She must really be mad at Hep." He finished munching an M&M. "Maybe you're right after all."

"What do you mean 'maybe'? Of course, I'm right! I'm telling you, it's down with Jude and up with Duke."

Backstage, Charles went over last-minute details with those cast members who would be part of *The Murder of Gonzago* improvisation. In the meantime, Pastor Gabriel Wyant entered the theater and sat in Cory's row a couple of seats away. The pastor winked at Cory to let her know that he was there to give her support.

Besides the atypically large dress-rehearsal summer crowd, Charles and Winston were surprised that two drama critics were also present. Normally, they would attend opening night instead of dress rehearsal; but in this instance, the critics were present, owing to summer travel plans that preempted the opening-night gala. It was they who later circulated the report of the *Hamlet* performance to the media.

The production was nearly flawless through the opening two acts. The hard work paid off as the actors executed their lines perfectly. Especially effective and believable, Claudius fooled and controlled everyone in his path. Between acts 2 and 3, Charles whispered to Winnie backstage, "The actors are striking a good balance between perfect execution of their lines, which gives the rich Shakespearean poetry its proper due, and the dramatic action, which is building the needed suspense and compellingly advancing the storyline. Do you agree?"

"Totally. They're doing a fine job," Winnie responded.

"I'd say our advice to Claudius, Rosencrantz, and Guildenstern really paid off. Marcel and Austin have the exact right mix—fearful around the mighty king, even fawning at times, yet warmly receiving his obsequious overtures."

"You're right. At one point, Austin's bow to Rick was so low that he almost lost his hat!" He chuckled as he recollected the gesture. "What else, Charles? Any other thoughts?"

"The lighting is superb. Our effort on that paid off as well. Keeping the dim light on Claudius is working. The guy's always in the shadows, another fantastical duke of dark corners."

"I catch your reference to the Duke Vincentio in *Measure for Measure*! Very good, Charles!"

"Seriously, you know what my 'what else' is! The big scene is coming! I just hope it goes okay. Thanks again, Winnie, for allowing us to insert this brief interlude. By the way, have you been watching Abe and Duke out there in the audience? Abe's following along with the rapt attention of a spellbound child listening to a master storyteller!"

"I haven't watched them as much as you, but that hulking animal beside him isn't paying much attention. Geez, the guy is built! I'd say he's definitely more interested in the lovely coed beside him than the play!"

"You have to know Duke!"

The play recommenced and again went well. Rick as Claudius was especially effective with his line delivery, regal bearing, and magisterial interaction with the courtiers. During a pause in the action, Duke whispered to Abe, "I hate the king because he's an SOB! But I'll tell you one thing—that pompous ass is one sharp dude."

"He's a brain, all right!"

"Do you see how he's got everybody wrapped around his finger? Control freaks like that drive me crazy. Why can't those guys see that he's made them into stooges? Compared to him, those dudes have butt-plug intelligence. They might live in palaces, but they're dumb as the torture rack at the bottom of the dungeon!"

"Yeah, you can never tell when a controller is up to something. Claudius sits there plotting away, and even those closest to him don't know it's happening!" *If I swill his brain, it won't be in vain! You're in the dungeon, Duke, and lounging on a nuke!*

During a quick scene change a short while later, Duke again whispered to Abe, "Have you been watching the babe beside me? She'd give Tina a run for her money. Like I said, maybe I ought to give college a try! These are gorgeous women, and this Candy's something else!"

"Don't kid yourself," Abe said, motioning toward Cory. "The one down there is sharper and more beautiful than any woman here. You need to think of your future when you're settled down with a good woman."

"When Candy leaned over to pick up things she dropped, she brushed her velvet thigh against mine. Both times! That was no accident!"

"Focus, Duke. You can tend to your candied dessert later. For now, we're about to watch the great offense unfold, and where the offense is, let the great ax fall."

"I understand about one-third of what you say. What the hell does that mean, 'Let the great axe fall'? Stick to English, okay?" He looked at Candy. *I'd like to let the great ax fall with her!*

Because the evening was so momentous, Cory wrote a longer-than-normal account in her journal.

> As I sat there watching the performance, I was actually quite calm, given the crazy thing I was on the verge of doing. I was temporarily discombobulated, however, when I saw Dr. Buck enter the auditorium and sit on the opposite side near the front. His presence unnerved me, for I feared

he might, during the mad scene, feel responsible for my well-being and, knowing my mental condition, rush up on stage to offer medical assistance. I could just envision him ushering me out before the improvisation!

I scrawled this concern briefly on a note and gave it to Joey, seated beside me, and whispered for him to pass it on to Pastor Gabe. *Help!* I mouthed to Pastor, seated on the other side of Laura. His thumbs-up gesture indicated both comprehension and, knowing him, immediate prayer. That settled me a great deal. Indeed, when I looked at him moments later, his head was bowed, his eyes closed. *What a man of God*, I thought. The picture of him bowed in prayer settled me so much that you wouldn't have known that I was on the verge of doing the craziest thing ever in my life!

At least that was the feeling for a while. I started getting nervous again when we neared the big moment, *The Murder of Gonzago* scene. I knew the success of this scene depended completely on my acting. During the opening acts, it donned on me that I should give a few indications to the audience, especially those seated around me, that I was a mental case. My goofy acting in the lobby had been effective, but apart from some unusually loud head-turning laughter while seated in the auditorium, I gave no warning signs that I was emotionally distraught enough to interrupt the performance with this incredibly insane interlude. I whispered to Joey and Laura, "What crazy thing can I do now that will set the stage for the coming mad scene?"

Joey responded, "Maybe just start talking too loud or stand up and yell 'bravo' at the top of your lungs."

"If I get the courage to do it, pull me down right away as if you're embarrassed out of your mind, okay?"

By now we were at the very end of act 2 when Hamlet was delivering his famous "O what a rogue and peasant slave am I" soliloquy. When he gave that particular line, I stood up and yelled at him, as if enraged, "You ought to feel like a rogue for what you did to that poor woman, you wretch!" Looking at Ophelia, I bellowed at the top of my lungs, "Get away from these men!" People in our area yelled for me to sit down, and all eyes in the auditorium were on me as I interrupted the soliloquy.

Truth is, I yelled louder than I meant to, but it was utterly important that I be heard. The poor guy in front of me nearly jumped out of his seat! Joey jerked me down and loudly whispered to me with horrible, if faked, anger, 'Sit down, you goofball!' The whole thing was perfect for the way it set up the impending interruption. I have to remember to tell Joey that he pulled me down so hard that he actually hurt my bruised shoulder! What luck for me—first, my shoulder's hurt in the car wreck with Duke, I fall on it when I crashed into the tray at work, then Duke smashes me into the side of the car at Beatty's Mill, and now Joey slams me into my seat with his steel grip! What luck!

As we neared the end of act 2, I knew that Jude, in keeping with our plan, would be coming over to see me during the brief intermission. While Hamlet was up there on stage talking about his motive and cue for passion, I was thinking of my own during our brief interaction. Moments later, Jude waltzed up to me as planned and said, with the theatrical swagger of an Elizabethan courtier, "Madam, how like you this play?" Then in normal language, he said in a disgusting tone, "I saw your 'poor woman' outburst. Are you losing it or what? Pretty soon they'll be carrying you out on a bier like the fair Ophelia!"

As Jude spoke, I pretended to be annoyed with his endless blathering. Standing up, I responded, "You are as good as a chorus, my lord!" I held my head as if in anguish, turned to the man in front of me, the man whom I nearly scared out of his skin, and said, "I hope all will be well." I had the nerve to put my hand on his shoulder and said, "We must be patient." The guy wanted to straitjacket me and cart me off to the funny farm right now. And the gentleman behind me, the one who earlier called me "Madam Crazy," said to the girl beside him, "I hope there's a security guard nearby! This could get ugly!"

At this point, I turned to Jude. "And so I thank you for your good counsel." Before I plopped myself back down in my seat, I turned to Duke, whom I had seen earlier, and blew him a deliberate if exaggerated kiss. Duke saw me and reciprocated the gesture with a somewhat subdued wave. It was only later that I learned he had responded sheepishly because he was putting the make on the beauty queen beside him and, feeling awkward, didn't want her to see his wave! No surprise there—Duke is *always* Duke! I sat back down, rested my chin in my hands, and sulked.

But Jude wasn't about to let it go. I knew he'd come up with something because he gave me a fast, if discreet, wink. Something was up his sleeve, and I wondered if he was about to go off script. Oh boy! I thought to myself. Pretending to be very angry that I had blown Duke a kiss, he boomed in a screaming voice, "Hey, are you two-timing me or what? How's come you're waving to that loser back there? What do you think you're doing?" He yelled these lines so loudly that it rattled Duke, who stood up at the "loser" comment.

I stayed in my madwoman persona. "I'm telling you that I'm done with you and that you're too merry, my lord. Just shut up and go back to your palace! I detest that edge of anger in your tone."

"Ha!" Jude loudly retorted. "It would cost you a groaning to take off this edge."

I nearly died when Jude said that. He had even made the slightest hint of a gesture toward his crotch. I couldn't believe it! I'm sure my face went beet red when he went off script this way, and I could barely stay in character. That was so hilarious! I stole a peek in Pastor Gabe's direction, wondering if Jude had stepped over the line of decency with his risqué remark. I was relieved to see Pastor sitting there with his head in his hands and laughing uncontrollably, but that made it harder for me to suppress my own laughter! Gabe later told me that Jude had given the perfect response and, with a wink of the eye, said, "Brevity is the soul of wit!" It took all my effort to stay in my madwoman character!

Jude's journal entry also offers a valuable perspective on the theatrical interruption:

> Cory was again amazing. Her acting as a weirdo was so convincing that she had everyone around her thinking that, truly crazy, she should be taken to a psychiatric unit immediately. I was laughing inside when this suave gentleman, seated in the row behind her and looking all the world like his lordship of very soft society, pompously whispered to me as I stood in the aisle, "Sir, you better take her out. She was manifesting signs of obvious mental distress in the lobby before the play even started." When the lapwing ass spoke to me, I thought of Hamlet's devastating description of Osric, who saw himself as a soul of great article: "Dost know this water fly?"
>
> At any rate, the entire front section, including water fly, had their eyes on us during the intermission. They thought we were fast moving toward a major melee. Our disagreement must have been very convincing, for there were murmurs and cupped-hand whispers all over the place. Again, before taking my seat down left front, I faced the audience when I flashed a look of disgust at Cory, facial recognition being the all-important key.

On his way to his seat, Jude walked by Dr. Buck, who thankfully sat next the aisle, and clued him in on the coming mad scene. "The impending improvisation you're about to see on stage is just an act, so don't rush up there to give Cory medical assistance. Please just stay seated through it since Cory will merely be acting. I'll explain later. Thank you, sir!" Dr. Buck gave him a wink, indicating comprehension.

At the beginning of the third act, Cory again grew very nervous. *The time is coming in act 3 when I will interrupt the production and storm the stage. This has turned out to be more than I bargained for! I thought the dress rehearsal would essentially be a repeat of the afternoon rehearsal and merely add formality, costumes, and a handful of guests, but this big crowd makes me really nervous. I knew the improvisation which we planned in little Kittanning would have me wandering a bit from my secure shoreline, but I never knew I'd be in water this deep! "Too much of water hast thou, poor Ophelia!"—and Cory too!*

Looking over at Pastor Gabriel for assurance, Cory saw him smile and dash off something on a note, which he passed to her (Cory showed Jude the note later): "Have you come to the kingdom for *such a time as this*? This is your *Esther* moment!" He had underlined the key phrase.

Cory jotted a quick response and handed it to Joey, who gave it to Gabriel. "If I perish, I perish, for I promise to proclaim my melodious lay." Gabriel caught Cory's allusion to Gertrude's speech regarding the insane Ophelia, nodded with a quick smile, and sat back in his chair, mouthing as he did so, "All things are possible to those who believe in God!"

The big scene was moments away!

CHAPTER 44

As noted earlier, two drama critics were present for the afternoon dress rehearsal. One of these, Augustus Peabody of the *Pittsburgh Post-Gazette*, offered an illuminating take on the production. A few days after the dress rehearsal, Charles met with him to pick his brain on *The Pittsburgh Hamlet*, as Peabody called it, at the Little Tokyo Restaurant in Mount Lebanon. Far as anyone could ascertain, he was the first to coin the term *The Pittsburgh Hamlet*, which became the customary way to refer to the mad improvisation during the production.

After a couple bites of sushi, Mr. Peabody jumped in, "At the beginning of the improvisation, I thought Cory was truly mental, and I was even taken in by her quarrel with Jude for a while. At first, I thought to myself, 'How embarrassing! The public domain is no place for a private quarrel!' I was sucked in because Cory and Jude's acting equaled that of the best actors on stage! I must say, they were very convincing, and together, you obviously orchestrated every single detail."

"The credit goes to Cory and Jude," Charles replied, sipping his oolong tea.

Mr. Peabody perused his notes. "It was certainly clever that your Laertes mimicked Jude's mannerisms. It was amazing that they acted like brothers. I suppose the same was true of you as well when you were mimicking Horatio, right?"

"What do you mean?"

"That you were closely watching Abe and even copying him, just as Horatio watched and mirrored Claudius. The parallels—Jude to Laertes and you to Horatio—were marvelous. The two plotlines ran along similar trajectories. Did you, Jude, and Cory plan all of these similarities?"

"Yes, it was all part of the plan, though the pastor of our church, Gabriel Wyant, offered some valuable input too."

Mr. Peabody reached in his briefcase. "Here's a draft of an article that will appear in the paper. I'm particularly interested in your take on the accuracy and tone. Mind you, it's merely a working draft."

"I'm more than a little keen to read it!"

"Have at it! I'll tear into this delicious sushi while you peruse it."

Excerpt from theater critic Augustus Peabody's draft article

> A large inner platform on the stage itself had been created where *The Murder of Gonzago* would be enacted. The play and the following improvisation interlude—which led to my calling it *The Pittsburgh Hamlet*—took place on this elevated and spacious inner stage.
>
> The dumb show at the beginning of the playlet completed, Hamlet and Ophelia immediately delivered their lines. When Hamlet said, "The players cannot keep counsel; they'll tell all," Cory Mohney, a young woman from Kittanning in Armstrong County, stood up in the audience—she was seated downstage at right—and snapped at Hamlet on stage in a booming voice, "You're the one that will tell all, blabbermouth!" Joey Mohney, Cory's brother, yanked Cory into her seat amid a chorus of surrounding jeers. Somebody yelled, "Sit down, madwoman!" And another: "Hey, let us watch the play!" People were fed up by this time since Miss Mohney's outburst had several disturbing and unrestrained precedents. Fearing a scuffle might break out, I

actually looked around to make certain security guards were present.

A few moments later, Ophelia delivered her line, "'Tis brief, my lord," to which Hamlet responded, "As woman's love." The last line of Hamlet's speech was Cory's designated clue, I learned later, to launch into her insane interlude. When Hamlet finished it, Cory trampled over Joey's feet and rushed to the stage. Marching directly to Ophelia at stage center, she put her arm around her and compassionately consoled her. "Honey, I suggest you get away from this rat!" sneering at Hamlet during her delivery. "He's no good for you and will destroy you. Have nothing to do with men!" Here she looked angrily at the horrified Jude Hepler, Cory's boyfriend, who by this time had made his way to the stage-left stairs.

People in the audience were shouting and telling Cory to get off the stage. When a loud chorus of boos filled the theater, Jude knew that it was time for him to play his part and attempt to establish control. He walked the rest of the way up the stage stairs; and as Cory, her back to Jude, meandered to center stage with her arm around Ophelia, Jude came to the front of the stage to address the audience. He waved his arms up and down to quiet them. "People, please calm down. I apologize for the interruption, but this woman"—he paused and turned around to make sure Cory wasn't listening—"is mentally… deranged."

He was intensely nervous because of this reference to her insanity when she was mere feet away from him. In fact, his trousers and shirt-sleeve were visibly shaking. Like the rest of the audience, I was so taken in by his acting that I was a nervous wreck for him.

Jude Hepler stole another peek over his shoulder to see if his comment had upset her and, seeing that it apparently hadn't, resumed speaking with great feeling. "Please understand!" He again faced the audience and, wiping a tear, spoke with a lowered but still powerful voice. "We will resume the play momentarily, and we'll get help for my poor girlfriend, but in the meantime, we shouldn't do anything to further upset her as I attempt to escort her out of the theater. Please, I beg you, be patient!" I looked carefully at Mr. Hepler. I could have sworn he was actually crying, and by now his hands were shaking uncontrollably. The rolled-up program in his hand was twitching madly. Talk about acting! I thought later, after I realized that it was an act, that the guy could be on Broadway! Jude then said, "Thank you, good people, for understanding!"

Because his appeal was so effective, the crowd calmed down immediately. I heard a few murmurs around me, but for the most part, people were gracious and taken in by Cory and Jude's superb acting debut on the public stage. During Jude's speech to the audience, Cory pretended to be talking to Ophelia but was merely waiting for Jude to quiet the crowd, at which time she launched full throttle into the improvised scene. The time had come. The readiness is all.

Jude walked over to Cory and tried to usher her offstage. His position in relation to Cory and his manner of speaking exactly mirrored Hamlet's to Ophelia. Astute theatergoers noted the parallel: Jude was to Cory what Hamlet was to Ophelia, each character clearly possessing, and fastidiously copying, that double. The symmetry was fantastic, and I thought to myself, how absolutely brilliant and breathtakingly entertaining! I wondered how many caught the conscious parallel of the two plotline trajectories.

Mounting to a full-blown rant, Cory, at this juncture, tore into Hamlet. "You have no right to speak to this dear woman the way you do! In fact, you shouldn't talk to her at all because you're a jerk!" She started beating on Hamlet's chest with her fists. Carley Metz, a third-year student in Pitt's drama department, was great. He acted as though he was actually being attacked and used his forearms to shield himself from the mad barrage. Ophelia restrained Cory who, separated from Jude, resumed speaking. "I hate him!" she said to Ophelia, flashing an angry scowl, which started on Hamlet but finished on Jude.

This was one of my favorite moments because it was obvious to the audience that she was transferring her hatred of Hamlet to her primary target—Jude. Collectively, we came to see that this was not about Ophelia hating Hamlet in a four-hundred-year-old play; rather, it was about Cory Mohney hating Jude Hepler at this very moment! Cory embraced Ophelia and cold-shouldered both Hamlet and Jude as she, with the demure elegance of a princess, walked toward Claudius. The king smugly sat with his chin propped in his hand, his one leg tucked under his chair, the other extended full length. I looked over at Abe Badoane, who bore a cocky smile like Claudius and exuded the same self-assured kingly arrogance. The parallelism was astonishing—what drama!

The distraught Hamlet and the even more distraught Jude stood helplessly side by side as Ophelia and Cory paraded over to the king. "This man," Cory began, motioning toward Claudius, "is fair and just. I'd trust him completely over that idiot, that moron, that beast!" She gestured at Hamlet, her fierce look beginning on him but again finishing on Jude.

At this point, the cast, huddled like lost sheep on a gale-swept heath, came forward and gathered around Charles and Winston, both of whom had come on the stage. "Our dress rehearsal has been ruined!" one of the actors shouted at Winston in mock frustration. "Get her out of here!" said another. "Why doesn't someone do something? Ophelia acts crazy, but this woman *is* crazy! This whole thing is insane!" The booming voice of a celebrity equity actor could be heard above the din: "I'm going back to Broadway. I've never experienced this kind of madness in crazy New York!"

At this point, Charles walked down stage center to address the audience. "This mad interlude will end in a moment, and we'll continue with the dress rehearsal shortly. In the meantime, we ask you to be civil and compassionate. It's our civic duty to be humane as we deal with this utterly sensitive crisis!"

After the director's poignant—and very effective—appeal, the strangest thing happened. Several of the people in the front row, in the main college students sensing that a good time was theirs for the taking, got out of their seats and boldly walked to the stage so they could hear the improvisation more distinctly. "I can't hear!" Instead of being annoyed by the mad interruption, they were intrigued! "Hey, this is real cool drama!" a student near me commented. "We want to know what's going to happen," another spoke from the stairs. "This is better than a boring Shakespeare play. This is real life!"

The foregoing happened in a matter of a few minutes. It was as though the exposition of Cory's mad interlude was about to give way to the dramatic rising action. We were, figuratively speaking, on the edge of our seats. After Charles addressed the audience, he took his place by Ophelia's side and pretended to whisper something in her ear. Charles withdrew from Ophelia—played by Jan Neale, a third-year drama student at Carnegie Mellon University—and winked at the audience, as though Ophelia had been given instructions on how to handle Cory. Ophelia began the dialogue.

The Pittsburgh Hamlet was about to launch into space!

CHAPTER 45

Peabody's article was not the only written record of *The Pittsburgh Hamlet.* Because the interlude was so utterly unique—and in time, famous—Charles, for his own satisfaction, later transcribed the videotape of the dress rehearsal so that he might possess "the exact language of that extraordinary experience."

The following is a line-by-line transcription of a brief portion of the interlude:

OPHELIA. Do you understand why I'm so angry at Hamlet?

CORY, *nearly shouting.* Yes, of course I do. You have every right to be angry at him! (*Here, she flashed another angry scowl, which, like the others, started on Hamlet but ended on Jude.*)

OPHELIA, *slowly, poignantly—exuding deep pathos.* Why do you understand me so well? No one else does! No one even tries!

CORY. The same thing happened to me once.

OPHELIA. Please explain. Whatever do you mean?

CORY, *stammering as she takes a step away from Ophelia.* It's hard to talk about.

OPHELIA. Can you please tell me? It will make you feel better to get it out.

CORY. I once had a true love—my valentine—but I chased him away when another brute came on the scene. (*Here, Cory takes a step toward Jude and spits at his chest.*) My valentine is gone. (*She lifts her eyes slowly and looks forlornly out in the audience at Duke*). He never will come again, for I chased him away. (*Cory hisses at Jude.*) Young men will do it, if they come to it!

Excerpt from theater critic Augustus Peabody's "rough notes for possible inclusion" in his article

When Cory said that she had a lover once but chased him away, I looked over at Abe Badoane and Duke Manningham since, fortuitously, I was seated near to them. Abe actually slapped Duke's knee and said, "She's talking about you! Did you see her look at you?" He probably meant to say this quietly, but in the hysteria of the moment, he spoke so loudly that those of us in the immediate vicinity distinctly heard his ensuing conversation with Duke. "You see how Cory loves you and wants rid of Jude? This mad scene isn't about Hamlet and Ophelia."

Duke Manningham was apparently listening to Abe, but most likely not to Abe's satisfaction, and indeed I noted that Duke's thigh was wedged tightly against that of the woman beside him. "Duke, focus!" He here cupped both hands at Duke's ear and said something which I couldn't hear. While I thought I made out the word "*Tootsie*" (as in Tootsie Roll), Abe must have chastised Duke for playing footsies with the coed. Charles's citation of Cory's earlier statement flashed in my mind: "Duke is *always* Duke!" Abe hissed, "This mad scene isn't about Hamlet and Ophelia." Here, he grabbed Duke's massive arm with both of his hands and shook it. "Listen! It's about *Cory* and *you*! This is her veiled way of saying she loves you!"

Because Duke replied in a very soft voice—not wanting, I assumed, for the coed beside him to hear—I'm not sure of his response, but it must have been along the lines of, "How can you be so sure?" Abe's retort, on the other hand, was very audible: "I'm absolutely positive. In her hallucination, she has tapped directly into her unconscious mind. She desperately wants to get rid of Jude, but she needs your help!" Abe Badoane stopped speaking at this point and, looking all the world like Claudius planning his strategy, eventually said, "I'll come up with something so that he shall not choose but fall. The point is this: will you be ruled by me? Revenge should have no bounds. *No bounds*!"

"Yes, I'll be ruled by you as long as you don't mess with me. You hear what I'm saying? The Duke gets mad as a hornet when he's pissed with—even by the smiling serpent!" He slammed his fist into his open palm so hard that it made a loud crack. "The thought of getting back at Jude makes me feel good all over!"

Abe responded, "I'm sure it warms the very sickness in your heart."

For me, the most fascinating part of the interlude was its skillful incorporation of Shakespeare's language from the play. All the principal players in the interlude—Abe, Jude, and Cory—adapted actual language from *Hamlet*; and while only Shakespearean aficionados would have noted these clever adaptations of the Bard's actual phraseology (like Abe's reference to the "sickness in your heart" and "revenge should have no bounds" or Ophelia's use of the word *valentine* for her lover), they constituted the single-most brilliant touch of the entire interlude. I eventually detected what was happening: the Jude/Cory/Abe/Duke affair had been superimposed upon the most intricately structured scene in the whole of Shakespeare. The correspondences between the two plots had been forged with mathematical precision.

By this time, more and more people were coming down to the front of the auditorium to listen to the exchange between Cory and Ophelia. "This is so exciting!" a coed shouted. "I can't wait to see what's going to happen!" her friend replied, looking sideways at Duke. "But I'm afraid of that incredible hulk!" On stage, Cory finished telling Ophelia that she once had a true love—she looked again at Duke out in the audience when she said this—and that she, fortunately, discovered how she had been temporarily dazzled by a false love. She scowled at Jude, who, hanging his head, looked angry and hurt at the same time—more fine acting on Mr. Hepler's part.

Another excerpt from Charles's line-by-line transcription

OPHELIA. What did the bloke do that was so bad, and how did you find out?

CORY. I know exactly what he did (*looking out in the audience at Duke*). But my sweet Valentine doesn't. I watched it happen. I saw it.

OPHELIA, *hesitating slightly as she adjusted her earpiece to better hear her cue.* Can you tell me about it?

CORY. Are you sure my telling you won't upset you? You were acting pretty strangely a bit ago, and I don't want to set you off again. Do you know now how little sense you were making? (*She laughed too loudly at this point.*) You scared me out of my wits! As they say up in Kittanning—that's where my manor house is—you were bonkers!

OPHELIA. No, I'm fine. Really. Please tell me.

CORY. Well, I wish I had a way to show you. You know, sort of how we did during rehearsal last Saturday. I mean the improvisation scene. I don't like to talk about things. I prefer to act them out. What we did Saturday was fun because I like to act! A hider plays many parts, his acts being seven ages.

OPHELIA: Yes, I recall. Do you want to do that again? Let me check with our director to see if this is a good time to do it. (*Ophelia, little-girl style, skips over to me [Charles], pretends to ask me if they could stage a brief improvisation, and promptly returns to Cory.*)

CORY, *nervously twirling a strand of hair, she speaks with real excitement and reaches out to touch Ophelia's arm, so keen was she to receive my answer.* What did he say?

OPHELIA: He said he'd love for you to enact the scene. In fact, he wants you to be the director because your improvisation scene last Saturday was the best one. You left before we could tell you that you took first prize in last Saturday's competition. Congratulations! The director suggests that we make this part two of your drama.

CORY. I'd like to enact it very much. Thank you, thank you all very much indeed!

OPHELIA. Professor Claypoole said you should do what you did at rehearsal. Be the director, assign lines and blocking, and instruct the stagehands about props and sets.

CORY. I thank you for your good counsel.

By this time, some of the college students had come up on to the stage and took their place along the periphery, as more and more people simultaneously left their seats and crowded down front. Drama critic Augustus Peabody spoke of this in his *Pittsburgh Gazette* article:

Excerpt from Peabody's "rough notes for possible inclusion" in his article (continued)

When many of the people started crowding the front of the auditorium next to the stage, I decided to join them. I had never experienced anything remotely close to this. Many of us were huddled together in a tight mass, hanging on every word. The whole thing was immensely entertaining to me, though, not knowing at the time how it was going to turn out, I was nervous too. I calmed myself by recalling that this was only a dress rehearsal and that such rehearsals often have rough patches. I knew that calling this a "rough patch" was understatement of the first order!

However, before I was certain that the whole thing was a staged improvisation, I worried that we were being "entertained" at the expense of a person with possible mental issues. My sympathy for Cory Mohney overruled both my desire for amusement and my keen interest in this whodunit. At this point, a Duquesne University professor behind me quipped, "Talk about a play holding the mirror up to nature!" I turned around and commented, "That's only half the truth." Looking at me intently, he asked, "What's the other half?" I said, "Sometimes nature must hold a mirror up to art!" He laughed. "Maybe that's what's happening here!"

By this time, Cory had given directions to the cast members on how to stage the interlude. At her request, the stagehands deftly carted out a large platform and positioned it on the inner stage, making it obvious to the audience that they were seeing a play within a play within a play—

that is, three tiered and separate stages were by now distinctly demarcated.

Ophelia spoke to Cory, "So this is the place where the awful event happened. Right here?"

"Yes, this is the exact place. You see, my valentine has a beautiful coach. Here I can show it to you." Cory gestured toward the mural behind her.

Two stagehands unrolled a large 6×10 feet mural-sized photo of Duke's '57 Chevy hot rod attached to poles. The stagehands stood behind the mural at the two ends. Several audience members gasped when they saw the photo of the beautiful car, which was held up high for everyone to see.

"What a gem hot rod!" one of the college students shouted.

At this point, Duke Manningham viscerally reacted. As I was on the stage by now, I looked back to see Duke standing and shouting, "Hey, dumbasses, that's my car!" Decent manners, even for an uncouth man like Duke, would have normally prevailed in a cultured setting, but the whole rehearsal had by this time descended into chaos. Over half the audience was standing down front, and many were even on the stage to be closer to the action.

Abe Badoane must have known full well that Cory was on the verge of exposing Jude. Beside himself with joy, he had a big smile on his face. He must have thought to himself, *Cory, you're brilliant!* I eased myself to the front seats to hear Duke and Abe more clearly, knowing their exchange would be crucial to the meaning of this unfolding drama.

"Hang on to your arse, Duke," Abe said, pulling Duke back down to his seat. "I think I know what's coming, and it's going to be to your immense liking."

"Well, I don't, and I'm pissed. I can't tell where Shakespeare's frigging play stops and where real life begins."

"It's all part of the play. We're in the play right now. There's no exit from the play."

"Just what does that mean? Why don't you make sense for five consecutive minutes just one time? What do you mean 'no exit'? I'd like to exit right now with gorgeous beside me and take her for a drink!" *What a time for that candied dessert and those gorgeous melonies!*

"Sit tight and see where this thing goes. If I'm right about this, and I'm sure I am, Cory's got the professor by the short hairs!"

Meanwhile on stage, an actor came creeping out, exaggerated burglar style, from the wings. Wearing a KKK-style hood, he kept his head down. In stylized slinking fashion, he tiptoed across the stage, widely swung his head back and forth to make sure no one was watching, and then savagely struck the taillight and mag wheel hubcap on the '57 Chevy. At this precise moment, the stagehands immediately let the second scrolled mural photo of Duke's car drop down over the top of the first, the damage to the car readily apparent.

Duke was immediately out of his seat, trampling on people's feet as he bulldozed down the row, screaming his head off. "Just what the hell is going on here?" He was in the aisle now and running toward the stage, people scurrying to give him room to pass. “What’s going on? Someone’s arse won’t be able to hold the kicks!”

I’ve never seen fury on a face like that—fierce, inhuman! Unable to take my eyes from him, I was totally transfixed, but then the man beside me pointed to the aisle. There came Abe, limping his way to the stage!

I thought to myself, *Are we safe? Just where will this madness end?*

CHAPTER 46

"I want to know what's going on!" Duke screamed at the top of his lungs. "That's my freaking car, and that's exactly what happened. Are you all nuts?" He glared at the cast, who by now were huddled at stage center like frightened elementary schoolchildren during a bomb scare. "What do you think you're doing? I came to watch some halfwit play and not my car get its ass kicked!"

The drama critic later spoke to Charles about this very moment. "I couldn't believe what I was seeing. Duke is a marvelous specimen of a 'man's man,' his muscles bulging beneath his sleek-fitting, button-down shirt, his jeans tight in the thighs, owing to his huge quadriceps, his face red, and his eyes spitfire-scarlet. Like Moses parting the Red Sea, the people on the stairs and stage apron instantly fell over one another to get out of his way. Well, I guess it's human nature for people to reflexively recoil from a charging bull!"

By this time, we had arrived at one of the comic moments of *The Pittsburgh Hamlet.* On the newly installed inner stage, the actor—his name was Roger Edinger—took off his outer hood and revealed the enlarged photo of Jude Hepler embossed on his large mask. To play along with the improvisation, Roger yelled the line which Jude had given him earlier, "Yes, I admit that I smashed your car. I will no longer hide the truth!" The crowd gasped when they saw the connection between the hooded face and Jude who, still on stage, stood by Hamlet. When Jude shook his head back and forth and tightly folded his arms in denial, Roger Edinger, as instructed, followed suit, thereby emphasizing Jude's culpability. At this point, Jude tried to slink away, but several people blocked his exit.

Temporarily confusing reality with fiction by thinking that Roger actually was Jude, Duke ran across the stage, his face contorted in rage. Upon seeing this huge "brainless ape," Roger Edinger thought he was going to be torn limb from limb right on the spot and streaked from the stage like a deer pursued by baying hounds! Professor Charles Claypoole described the moment in his journal: "Roger was scared to the point that he darted out the back door and slammed it so hard you could have heard the windows rattling over at Soldiers and Sailors Hall!"

Later that evening when Roger and his acting cohorts assembled for a post-rehearsal beer at Hemingway's on Forbes Avenue, he spoke of the moment when Duke charged at him. "I'm telling you, I was never so afraid in my life. Did you see the fire in dude's eyes? I thought he was going to kill me! That brainless ape is a brute, and his fist is bigger than my head! Waiter, bring me another beer and make it fast!"

Abe immediately followed Duke to the stage and, wrapping him with both arms, managed to restrain him. "Calm yourself down! Don't make an idiot of yourself!"

"No wonder he's upset!" one of the college students on stage shouted. "The dude in the photo is the guilty guy slinking around back there in the shadows!"

"You're right—the exact same guy!" another student shouted.

By now, most of the people were out of their seats and jammed in the front of the theater to watch the unfolding drama. Some stood on the steps at the two sides of the stage while others formed a circle around the apron. "There must have been a hundred people on stage," according to June M. Samuelson, drama critic with the *Pittsburgh Tribune-Review*. Mr. Peabody agreed with this estimate.

Duke shoved his way through this mass of people, mounted the second stage, and came to the edge of the raised platform where the photos were still being held. "Somebody better tell me what's going on, and I mean right this minute!" Duke examined the mural photos more closely. "This is a photo of my '57!" He took out a picture from his wallet and held it up for people in the vicinity to see that it was the same vehicle. His hand shook violently. "Do you see what I'm talking about? This is a blowup of my car!" He smacked the mural so hard when he gestured toward it that he punched a hole in it. "Why is there a freaking mural of my car on this stage? I want to know right now!"

Cory moved toward Duke, speaking slowly as she ambled along. "My love, I created this play so you could see who the real culprit is."

When she stopped speaking, people waited with bated breath. Watching the drama, Charles thought to himself, *She's the consummate actress who's mastered the technique of the delayed response. How long she waits to reply!*

Very slowly, Cory faced in Jude's direction and, pointing, said, "That rat back there, the guilty-looking one, is the villain who did it. He's the false steward who damaged your coach and stole his master's daughter. I created this elaborate scheme"—here, she swept her hand across the raised platform and the mural photos—"so you could know the truth at last." She paused, walked over to Duke, and lovingly caressed his arm—another bit of superb acting. "My love, I did this for you. Will you be my valentine?"

Jude spoke vehemently, "She's a madwoman! That is not true, and I did not damage your car!" Jude stopped speaking and spoke with great sadness, more great acting. "But I did love her once. I would have eaten a crocodile to prove my love for her." *I hope I'll be safe!* Pivoting, he faced Duke. "I know you hate me, but don't believe what she's saying about your snazzy car," he gushed. "You're too bright a guy to get sucked in by her ploy." Pretending to be fighting off panic, Jude spoke quickly to get his side of the story out there before he was attacked by Duke, still restrained by Abe and, by now, a security guard too.

"I know one thing!" Duke screamed. "Somebody's lying, and I'm pissed bad!"

"By the time I came to the lot that day and saw your Chevy," Jude gushed, "it had already been damaged." The audience reacted to this, some even mumbling in disbelief and clearly siding with Cory against Jude. "She's a crazy, spurned woman who's just trying to frame me because I dumped her. You know the famous quote, 'Hell hath no fury like a woman spurned.'" He pointed at Cory. "Well, there's the spurned woman and"—he swept his arm around him to note the immediate vicinity—"and here's hell!" As though deciding how far to push his luck, Jude stopped abruptly, another perfect example of the timed delay. Slowly he took a step toward the enraged Duke but was still some ten feet away. *Lord, give me strength to confront monster man!* He faced Duke directly and paused, further increasing the drama. *I've never been so scared!* "She's just mad that she lost me"—he stopped and swept his eyes across the audience on stage—"and ended up with this giant loser!" *Lord, protect me!*

Duke violently tore himself away from Abe Badoane and the security guard and shoved past people. He straight-armed and elbowed several out of the way like Franco Harris running off tackle. He blasted over to Jude, curled his hands into fists, and prepared to fight. Hurriedly limping to them, Abe rushed between them to hold Duke back. "I understand that revenge should have no bounds, but not here, not now! Duke, calm down!" His face white with terror, Abe was clearly scared to death. *Duke is not to be messed with! I hope he doesn't attack me!*

Charles's journal entry for this afternoon is a masterpiece of well-wrought prose, one line of which describes his efforts to restrain Duke.

> "How much I had to do to calm his rage!" In using that line, did Abe know that he was quoting Claudius in Shakespeare's play word for word? If so, he was consciously mimicking Claudius, and that raises a much larger question. During the interlude, did he realize that he was to Jude and Cory what Claudius was to Hamlet and Ophelia? Was the man sharp enough to see the symmetry and cast himself, *on the spot*, as Claudius, not so much to enhance the emerging parallelism as to invest himself with the privilege of rank?

Charles completed his journal entry with a final question: "Just how bright is this Abe Badoane?"

At this point, Cory and Jude started into their brief shouting match.

Line-by-line transcription

JUDE. I tell you, I didn't wreck his car.

CORY. You did. You smashed his beautiful coach!

JUDE. Coach? You're crazy. Stop talking like a nitwit. You're just acting. I did not smash his car, witless one, because I wasn't even there!

CORY. Yes, you were. I saw the whole thing.

JUDE. You have no proof, so let's stop this charade right now. Don't you realize you're wrecking this play? (*Jude sweeping his arm side to side.*) These people paid to see *Hamlet*, not a madwoman spout weird whirling words!

CORY. I do have proof positive, punk professor! I can use alliteration too! (*Cory, for a moment, almost broke out of character here. The alliteration exchange "struck my funny bone," she later said to Charles. "And for that brief moment, I let slip a cavorting chuckle but instantly snapped back to character." Jude never broke stride, later explaining, "I was too frightened of Duke to find anything, including your clever alliteration, amusing!*)

JUDE. You don't. No proof exists, so you or nobody else can ever prove who damaged—(*Jude hesitates here, seemingly trying to muster strength; I actually caught him gnawing his lip!*)—ape-man's car!

CORY. Yes, we can. (*Her rather lengthy hesitation here is fantastic. People were dying to know what she meant, and then at last—again like a trained professional—she finally drops the bomb.*) We have fingerprints! (*A collective gasp gushes from the crowd like air from a burst balloon. Cory starts walking over toward Abe, who stands beside Claudius, Rick mimicking both Abe's demeanor and behavior.*)

JUDE. You don't have my fingerprints. I was at the hospital caring for you. (*Screaming*) What an ingrate you are! I loved you, and yet this is how you thank me. Forty thousand men could not, with all their quantity of love, equal the love I had for you. (*Here, Jude pauses and wipes a "tear" from his eye.*) And yet you treat me like this! (*He dabs his eye again.*)

CORY, *speaking to the crowd.* I tell you we have the fingerprints. I don't have them, but somebody does, and he's present now. It's up to him to produce the proof. (*Here, pausing, she slowly turns toward Abe, the drama again breathtaking. She waits an interminably long time and then at last speaks.*) If he chooses, he can do so in a brief moment and instantly settle this madness once and for all.

JUDE. Yes, brief. Nice word. Brief as woman's love. Very brief as your love. (*Shouting*) Very brief as your sanity!

Cory and Jude had baited the mousetrap perfectly. Standing directly beside Claudius, Abe reached in his pocket, smugly pulled out an envelope, and held it up for all to see. Like Cory and Jude, he hesitated before speaking, "Ladies and gentlemen, I have in this envelope fingerprints which were lifted from Duke's classic automobile, that Chevy there on the mural."

Another loud gasp from the crowd, another hesitation.

"They're an exact match to Jude's!" Abe announced.

A college student, eyes red from imbibing spirits, stood by Abe and yelled out in astonishment, "Are you kidding me?" He looked at Abe. "Sherlock, are you telling us that you actually have his fingerprints?" He looked back at Jude. "Then how can dumbass stand there looking so innocent?"

"They are not my prints. That's a vicious lie!"

"They're the same!" Abe waved the documents in the air. "Here are the prints from the car which you damaged!"

"You cannot prove that! It's a lie!" Jude again screamed.

At this point, Candy Melonie, wanting to impress her new hunk friend, came forward and spoke to Jude, "If you're innocent, then you won't mind if he takes your fingerprints right now." She smiled and winked at Duke. When, in a variety of ways, the audience shouted "Fingerprint him!" the raucous college students became even more animated. Drawing strength from this robust affirmation of her idea, the emboldened Candy strutted over to Duke. "Yes, take his prints to see if they match."

Like a defense lawyer in full control of the courtroom, Abe came forward and said to Jude, "Kind sir, what do you say to that? If you're as innocent as you claim, I'm sure you won't mind if we print you right now." Forewarned to bring the print kit, Abe quickly pulled it out of his pocket and held it up for the crowd to see. "May I have a prop, please? Anything will work!"

A stagehand quickly retrieved Yorick's skull from backstage and handed it to Abe. "Jude," Abe requested, "please hold this skull." Abe irreverently tossed it twenty feet across the stage. *That's the exact motion I saw in a recent Pirates game when second baseman José Lind shovel-passed it to shortstop Al Pedrique in a perfectly executed double play. Good job, second baseman Abe!*

"Alas, poor Yorick!" Hamlet and Jude said in unison as Hamlet caught the skull. Peabody described this moment in his article:

> That was my favorite moment in *The Pittsburgh Hamlet*. I could have howled in laughter. The timing exquisite, it was as though the actor playing Hamlet and Jude had rehearsed the toss and the line multiple times! "Alas poor Yorick!" I still laugh when I see that skull twirling in the air and hear their synchronized delivery!

"Alas, poor Jude," Abe quipped, "is what you'll be saying if these prints match!" Abe deftly dusted the skull for Jude's prints as Jude nervously gnawed on his fingers.

A second security officer had come up to the stage by this time to make certain that the confused scene did not degenerate into "a situation." Abe asked them, as independent witnesses, to examine the evidence. "We are fortunate to have men of the law here. Kind sir," he said, speaking to one of the security officers, "could you please examine these two sets of prints? Thank you."

Carefully scrutinizing them, one of the officers stated, "Without the proper equipment, I can't be 100 percent certain, but if I were in Vegas instead of the Burgh, I'd bet big money they're exactly the same!"

Clustered on stage, the gasping crowd immediately reacted:

"Aha! So you're guilty!"

"You *are* the culprit!"

"No wonder this man's angry about his car."

"Look what you did to it. That car's a beauty!"

The crowd hissed at Jude, who feigned guilt and nervousness. Through it all, Charles stood at the side, his face pale, his hand on his heart.

"Yes, they're my prints, all right," Jude remonstrated. "I admit that, but I touched the car *after* it was already damaged. Why won't you believe me? Could someone get me a drink of water?"

"Hell no!" one of the college students yelled. "You made your bed. Now lie in it!" And after a brief pause, "But I do have a beer in my pocket!"

"And a keg at the frat house!" another yelled.

College students across the auditorium cheered loudly.

"Bring it on!" a college student shouted.

"Let the party begin!" another screamed.

One of the officers blew his whistle to quiet the raucous crowd.

"What he said could be true," a lawyer in the audience shouted above the din. The crowd instantly quieted. "This is not incontestable proof. It's circumstantial evidence."

Cory came forward, ushered Abe over to Claudius, and asked Gertrude, seated beside Claudius, if "this kind courtier could recline here." Gertrude graciously yielded her seat to Abe who, thinking the authority gained from sitting in the royal chair may well leverage his case, regally—and pompously—positioned himself beside the king.

Noting Abe's parallel to King Claudius, Jude detached himself from the proceedings long enough to reflect on the similarities. *The casting of the two parallel storylines is now complete: Cory equals Ophelia; Charles, Horatio; Duke, Laertes; Abe, Claudius; and of course, I equal Hamlet. Even more notably, two exact storylines are running side by side, and in each the Machiavellian machinations of two evil villains are on the verge of being exposed through the mousetraps. That will enlighten the idiot Rosencrantzes and Guildensterns around them! Yes, I'd say* The Pittsburgh Hamlet *is in full swing, and the play's the thing wherein we'll catch the conscience of the king.* Jude stole a quick glance at Abe. *But is it airtight enough to catch that wily serpent over there? Lord, we need your grace, for the game we play*—he looked again at Duke's massive coiled fists—*is lethal beyond description, and I could get more than my arse kicked!*

CHAPTER 47

Once it was confirmed that Jude's prints matched those lifted from the car, Duke hit a boiling point. Though the officers restrained him, he broke free, rushed to Laertes, grabbed his metal foil, and ran toward Jude. "Holy hell, this is heavy, but it will still work to cut out your heart!" He was by now a mere ten feet away from Jude. Still standing beside Hamlet, Jude grabbed Hamlet's foil in self-defense and nervously braced himself in case Duke actually charged and swung. Rushing at him with his foil in the air, Duke swung savagely down on Jude's lightweight sword, which he held with two hands over his head. The crashing blow bent Jude's lightweight sword into a ninety-degree angle!

When Abe saw Duke's fury, both he and Claudius stood in unison and yelled, "Part them!" Seeing the perfect opportunity to cite the appropriate line from the play, Claudius yelled, "They are incensed!" Abe joining him, they shouted in unison, "We must stop these mighty opposites!" Their synchronized delivery was precise.

The officers at this point restrained both Jude and Duke and, after a brief struggle, managed to restore order. Seeing this moment of quiet as her perfect opportunity to reassert control, Cory mounted the third stage. She held her temples as though in severe mental anguish, her eyes glazed over like a madwoman's. From atop this stage, she shouted, "Lord, we know what we are, but know not what we may be!"

"What does that mean?" a college student asked another beside him. "Madam Psycho strikes again!"

Cory then hit her fine thespian stride. Pointing to Jude, she said, "This man here proclaims innocence, and indeed some of you lawyers concur that the fingerprints offer mere circumstantial evidence. We respect this expertise and gratefully welcome it. Nevertheless, apart from the fingerprints, irrefutable proof does exist. It cannot be dismissed because it clearly convicts the guilty party."

"What is it?" numerous people shouted.

"What proof?"

"How can you be so certain?" asked another.

"Do you want me to produce the evidence?" Cory asked.

"Yes!" numerous people shouted.

By this time, the entire audience was either down front in the orchestra, on the steps leading to the stage, or encircling the apron of the stage itself. The tension in the auditorium mounted as people were passionately keen to learn of Jude's guilt or innocence.

"I think the guy's guilty!" shouted a coed. "He's been slinking around the whole time. I bet ratso burned Cory like my ex burned me!"

"I don't know," replied a friend. "I'm still not certain."

A few of the audience members were also concerned about Cory's psychological well-being. A theater major, nudging her friend, spoke for many: "Is she mad or acting?"

"I have no idea!" the friend retorted.

Even more, what would be the destined end of the Jude-Duke quarrel? The college students enjoyed watching the antics of a "genuine redneck," as one of them dismissively labeled Duke. "The guy's built like Hulk Hogan!"

Another chimed in, "But his temperament reminds me of Rambo."

"Come to think of it, he's as gutsy as Rocky in the 1985 film," a third added.

Just where was this drama headed? More and more audience members were fascinated by the blurred lines: What was drama vs. reality? What was an ancient Danish fiction vs. an actual current mystery?

"What kind of evidence do you have?" an audience member again shouted.

"We have the film!" Cory shouted. "The film's the thing wherein we'll catch the conscience of the king."

No sooner did Cory say this than Abe, seated by Claudius, immediately squirmed in his royal chair. He had been smugly confident through the proceedings, thinking that he had Jude where he wanted him. *The enraged Duke will not be able to seek revenge in this public place. At least I don't think so, but the truth is, one never knows about Duke Manningham. Nevertheless, it's a given that he'll seek sweet revenge sooner or later. And that bodes well for my larger goal of getting rid of Mr. Hepler once and for all. The idea of a film, however, rattles me. How can there be a film? The only possible video would be that taken by the security cameras, and surely Cory is not referring to that. But if she is, it will show Jude's presence at the gathering of workers by Duke's car after the damage had already been inflicted, thereby weakening—or even destroying—my case.* Abe nervously shifted in his chair. *I don't like this film business a bit, but for the time being, I must smile and smile and be the villain!*

Cory spoke again, "We have the video clip, good folks, and will show it here. Stagehands, could you please prepare the film and lower the screen?"

"How smart a lash that speech doth give my conscience! O, my offense is rank," Abe mumbled to himself but then loudly yelled, "We don't need the film. We already know of this man's guilt. The film could easily be a doctored fake." He waved the envelope of fingerprints in the air. "We have the positive proof here!"

Abe started to leave, but a burly police officer, knowing that it would be best to keep the main combatants in the drama separated, stood behind Abe to block his exit. "Marvelously distempered" (as Jude described Abe in his journal), Abe had no alternative but to sit back down beside Claudius, who then asked, "Is there no offense in this film?" Hamlet shook his head.

Abe inquired, "What do you call the movie?"

"*The Mousetrap*," Jude responded. "We that have free souls, well, it touches us not."

Cory, at this point, asked for the stage lights to be lowered and the video turned on. The screen was filled with a still shot of the mushroom farm parking lot. Cory and Jude had obtained the security film from Morley Spencer, who had located the footage of the day Duke's car was damaged. At Jude's request, Morley isolated Jude's and Abe's presence on the film. He had zoomed in on them, enlarged their images, and then projected it in slow motion. It was this brief loop which Cory instructed the media technician to play.

Cory spoke, "Start the film, please."

When the screening began, Abe again coughed nervously, stroked his hand through his hair, and tried to leave. *On the one hand, I feel exactly like Claudius: "My stronger guilt defeats my stronger intent!" On the other, I feel like Gertrude: "So full of artless jealousy is guilt, It spills itself in fearing to be spilt." And I'm afraid my guilt will show!*

"Carefully note the people in the film," Cory continued. "Can you pick out Mr. Abe Badoane? He's at right center. He's this fine gentleman royally seated here," she said, motioning to Abe.

The crowd nodded. "Yes!"

"Do you see this creep Jude Hepler? He's the one near Abe stroking his chin," she said, tapping the screen with Laertes's foil, which the stagehand had given her.

Again, the crowd yelled, "Yes!"

"Can we safely conclude that the men in the film are the same as these two men here?"

"They are!"

"Definitely!" people in the audience agreed.

"Roll the film, please." The film continued. "Freeze that frame as well. Thank you—yes, that one!" Cory instructed. "Note the blowup of Jude's wrist. Is that the same watch he wears now? Could someone please check?"

Jude attempted to hide his wrist in his pants pocket, but a couple of the college students near to Jude said, "Don't be a coward! Let's see your watch!" Jude reluctantly exposed his wrist and watch. All heads turned toward Jude. "It's the same!" a college student shouted with the joy of an exuberant youthful detective. "It's the exact same watch as in the film!" the student, enjoying the limelight, needlessly added.

His friend beside him turned to Jude and quietly said, "Mister, ape-man is going to kick your ass to Three Rivers Stadium, and it won't be pretty!"

Cory continued, "Thank you. Roll the film."

"You see his guilt!" Abe screeched, leaping to his feet and nearly falling when his bad knee buckled. "Look at Jude squirming over there. Why do we continue this travesty?"

Swayed by Abe's persuasive appeal, people began cursing and hissing at Jude as if a criminal were in their midst. Trying to wrest attention from Cory and recenter himself as the dominant player, Abe paused long enough for people to finger-point at Jude and encircle him. "Officers," he resumed, "don't you think you're obligated to prevent a riot here and take this man into custody?" *This will get them thinking!* "Surely you understand that you're legally responsible for the welfare of these people. A lawsuit would result in a heartbeat if something were to happen." *Here's another great point.* "I don't think your irresponsible way of handling this little crisis would make University of Pittsburgh officials very happy. If I were you, I'd restore order now while you have the chance. If you don't, heads will roll!"

The security guards, obviously taking this to heart, moved toward Jude as if to do so. Abe could not refrain from smiling as one of them took handcuffs from his pocket. He thought to himself, *Serpent, serpent, do your deed. Soon you'll watch Jude Hepler bleed!*

Emboldened by his success, Abe continued, "We need to take Jude Hepler in for questioning and this woman to a hospital. I can't allow my dear friend," he said, motioning to Cory, "to be so abused. This is mental cruelty at its ignominious worst!" He turned away from Cory and lowered his voice. "You can see she's deranged. It's an utter disgrace to delay getting her the help she so desperately needs."

Seeing his impact on the crowd, Abe grew even more bold. *Time to move in for the kill.* "I'm ashamed of all of you. Someone has to show her some love." He again smiled and reflected to himself, *That was a very good serpent bite. Don't ever slight my venomous might!*

"That's right!" an older woman from the left apron shouted. "She needs to be loved and cared for!"

Her friend supported her. "If you loved your girlfriend, you'd be getting her to a hospital instead of selfishly defending yourself here. You ought to be on your knees begging her forgiveness!"

At the back of the stage, Jude hung his head in shame.

Chapter 48

Abe Badoane paused and astutely surveyed the audience. *The woman makes a good point. If I impose a sense of guilt on these useful idiots, as she just did on Jude, I can possibly leverage more of them to my side.* "What's wrong with you people? The longer we dally, the more we aggravate Cory's delicate mental condition. Why be inhumane? Because we have the proof of this man's guilt, this charade is mere madness."

The audience began to jeer at Jude. "He's right!"

"I agree!"

Time to go for the heart! "You are the one who's mad, not Cory," Abe shouted at Jude. "And you and you alone are responsible for putting her in this condition!" People loudly booed Jude.

As much as the tide had turned against Jude by this point, he was nevertheless confident that the next segment of the film clip would yield the incriminating proof he sought and, by now, desperately needed. Still Jude remained wary of Duke. *I'm a nervous wreck, and my knees have distilled almost to jelly with the act of fear! I keep looking at this bent sword in my hand and thinking of the brute force that had so effortlessly crushed it. What would a blow from that fist do to my poor head? Alas, poor Yorick! No wonder Duke has the reputation of being a loose cannon who erupts so violently at the slightest of provocations. And here I am at the other end of his twenty-four-pounder Austrian-made howitzer cannon!*

Jude spoke of this tense moment in his journal:

> For a brief moment, I was scared—scared silly to tell the truth. Before the security guards came

and stood near me, a couple college students had encircled me and started pushing me and calling me some choice words. I don't need to say which ones! Well, one of them—his buddies called him Jared—was a huge tackle on Pitt's football team. When he bumped into me and looked threateningly into my face, I was on the verge of shouting for help but, at the last moment murmured, "Wormwood, wormwood" instead. Then another big college kid grabbed me, the smell of alcohol on his breath, and I muttered, "Angels and ministers of grace, defend us." I knew Shakespeare would be pleased that I quoted this line from *Hamlet*. Through this exchange with the college kids, I never took my eye off artillery man one single time. Duke glowered at me with hate-filled eyes but, for whatever reason, never offered to attack me again.

During the planning of this mad interlude, Cory and I had agonized as to whether or not we would be able to introduce the film in the middle of the improvised interlude, fearing that the whole enterprise would descend into chaos before we had a chance to show it. If that happened, Abe would extricate himself from this mess, Duke would remain deluded, and I would be implicated as the guilty party! Instead, how gloriously it was turning out! The film was playing in all its graphic detail. *When the film zooms in on our hands in the next clip*, I reasoned to myself during the screening, *I'll have Abe where I want him, or as Hamlet would render it, I might "do it pat."*

Desperately trying to regain control, Abe stood beside Claudius throughout this scene. If Abe could have ended the film right there

> and stopped the whole charade, he would have escaped unscathed, and I and I alone would have remained the object of Duke's wrath. That was, from Abe's point of view, the felicitous and destined end to which events were triumphantly leading. The officers continued to stand by me and hold me tightly, especially the big one. What a grip! Cory, the Oscar-winning actress, meanwhile continued to scowl at me. The hate in her eyes was so real that, for a moment, I thought she had, as when overmedicated earlier, crossed the line into real insanity!

Encircled by the students, Jude played the part of the guilty criminal while Duke, like a starved and agitated lion in the Colosseum, waited to pounce on his prey. Moments away from victory, Abe again tried to steer the interlude to a conclusion. "Please, good folks, return to your seats." *That's it! Back to your seats, you idiots!*

The security guards saw their chance to restore order and encouraged people to sit down. One of them shouted to the crowd, "We will resume the play as soon as you're seated."

His colleague joined him, "Please, clear the stage, ladies and gentlemen. This is not a Steelers tailgate party! Back to your seats—please!"

Charles was quite the actor during the debacle as well. To make the interlude even more convincing and not a preplanned inset, he went to the security guards at this point and appealed for their help. "Don't you see that our play is ruined? We'll never live down this interruption if we don't restore order, and Winston and I will be the laughingstock of Pittsburgh. Please do encourage people to sit down. Thank you!" Charles then returned to the wings and watched as people started returning to their seats.

Watching the proceedings from the back of the stage, Jude focused his attention on Charles. *Nice acting, Chuck, but the look of desperation on your face is too real for my taste, though your gesturing hands and quivering voice made for an excellent touch. Yes, you are some actor!* Jude continued to watch him as he stood in the wings. *But what's going on with Chuck? The duress I'm seeing now appears to be real and not feigned. Why is he grasping his chest and clutching his shirt when he's out of sight of people and, therefore, no longer in acting mode? Does this look of panic owe to his desire to play along with our improvisation even when it doesn't seem to matter, or—here's a disturbing thought—is his duress real? Are you, my friend, experiencing actual chest discomfort or not?*

Abe, meanwhile, was thrilled at Charles's onstage appeal for help, and all but gloated. *Victory is moments away. Nothing will extricate the guilt-ridden Jude from my trap. More and more people are taking their seats. I love it when a plan comes together!* "That's it, lovely people!" Abe shouted. "Calmly take your seats, ladies and gentlemen, and the play will resume shortly."

The contrite Jude, meanwhile, stood with his head bowed, a look of shame on his face. When the drama critic Peabody later asked Jude how he, completely innocent and untrained as an actor, could act with such convincing guilt, Jude offered an explanation. "As I stood there on stage, I kept trying to imagine what it would be like to be truly guilty. How do people live with such guilt or handle the horror of being on death row for committing some heinous act? At first, the crimes which I imagined were so general that I couldn't conjure up any authentic emotions, but then it donned on me that if I imagined a truly awful crime, then I could act more convincingly. With that in mind, I looked at my hands and tried to imagine that they reeked with blood from having committed some brutal act, as Ted Bundy did when clear back in 1971 he bludgeoned, raped, and strangled Rita Curren of Burlington, Vermont—that poor, innocent twenty-four-year-old schoolteacher."

"Great idea!" Mr. Peabody said when Jude paused. "Your strategy obviously worked!"

"Well, for a time it did, but to maintain a convincing face of guilt, I came up with an even better idea. I role-played that I was one of the Roman executioners who crucified Christ. This worked so well that, in my mind, I was suddenly at the foot of the Cross at Golgotha instead of on a stage in Pittsburgh. During that strange moment,

I palpably felt the guilt, which the one Roman executioner experienced for crucifying the Lamb who takes away the sins of the world."

"That's an even better idea!"

"Thank you. You say I acted well my part? Well, no wonder! I kept thinking I had Christ's shed blood on my hands, and that was more than a little terrifying! Did you happen to notice that moment when, like Lady Macbeth, I actually flinched when looking at my own hands? That was the moment when I shed that huge tear."

"Yes, I was watching you then."

"It was precisely then that I realized that I *am* that sinner and that my sin *did* kill Jesus Christ as surely as those sadistic Roman soldiers. If I looked guilty standing there on stage, it's because Christ's innocence and my sinfulness hit me like a thunderbolt! For that brief moment, I was at the foot of the Cross and looking at hands—my disgusting hands—which had just crucified Jesus on Calvary!"

"That was a brilliant strategy!"

"Standing there on stage, I remembered Macbeth's lines when he looks at his bloody hands and says, 'This hand…will…the multitudinous seas incarnadine.' I don't need to tell you that he was saying his bloody hands would transform all the seas of the world to pure blood, but I do have to explain that to my students! The point is, I imagined my gory hands making the entire Nile River as blood-red as Moses did during the plagues in ancient Egypt."

All of this transpired in the moments when Abe watched people return to their seats. *Good! Looks as though I'm home free! The poison's done its work as the serpent stings the jerk!*

But then to Abe's profound disappointment, Cory, at this juncture, reasserted her authority. As the security guards shepherded people offstage, Cory demonstrated an unprecedented resourcefulness and loudly shouted, "We haven't seen all the film! You need to see the next part! The film! The film!"

Abe was smart enough to know what was most likely coming next in the film. *They probably will show a close-up of my hand on top of Jude's while we stood at Duke's car! I must divert attention quickly!* Abe screamed above the din, "Is there a doctor in the house? This woman is mentally afflicted and needs immediate help. Can't someone come to her assistance?" *Uh-oh, I'm losing control!* "Ladies and gentleman, please take your seats! We must get help for my dear friend Cory!" Abe again tried to excuse himself but was immediately incased in a sea of flesh. One of the security guards, an officer in the Pittsburgh Police Department, put his hand on his shoulder and forcefully sat him back down on his throne.

"Roll the film again, please!" Cory bellowed.

The crowd instantly hushed and turned en masse to face the screen. Many on the auditorium floor and in the aisles turned around and crowded down to the stage again, several reascending the stage steps.

"In this sequence, note the placement of hands on Duke's car. Observe that Jude is standing beside the car. Now watch what happens. Do you see this man enter the crowd?" Cory again used Laertes's foil to point to the screen. "His name is Bull Chestnut, one of Mr. Manningham's cronies at the mushroom mine. Please watch this sequence closely. We see Mr. Badoane look over his shoulder and motion with his head for Bull to come forward. Bull here enters the crowd. Mark him carefully. With no reason—watch this part—he bumps into Abe, who forcefully flies into Jude. See it? Roll it again. Note how the shove has no provocation—that is, he needlessly bumps into Mr. Badoane. Now watch Jude's hands. See how they fly out on the car when he's struck so unexpectedly from behind?"

The crowd gasped, beginning to realize that Abe had framed Jude. "No wonder Jude's fingerprints are on the car!" someone in the crowd shouted.

"Oh, I get it!" one of the college students said.

"So this smiley guy is a serpent SOB after all," another yelled. "*You're* the rat!"

"Yes, the snake who framed an innocent man!"

Glaring at Abe, Duke tried to squirm free from the men who were holding him. One of the officers moved more closely to Duke in the event he needed to be restrained. Duke screamed, "Let me at that bastard!" He viciously scowled at Abe. "You were behind the whole thing!"

Cory continued, "Watch this next clip. Here, Jude is standing at the center rear of Duke's car. Mr. Abe Badoane comes up behind

Duke to survey the damage to the vehicle. Note his head going back and forth from one taillight to the other, but watch the placement of his hand. See it? Roll the tape again. Note how he places his hand with surgical precision on top of Jude's to firmly imprint Jude's fingerprints. Please freeze it—right there! Thank you." The camera revealed a close-up freeze shot of the two hands, Abe's pressing firmly down on Jude's. The camera stopped, Abe's hand squarely atop Jude's. "Look at the smirk on Abe's face. He's gloating because his evil plan of getting Jude's fingerprint on the car has just succeeded so brilliantly!"

Duke violently shook himself free and charged forward, bellowing at Abe, "You damn liar! You were behind the whole thing!" He went for Abe, but the security guards held him tightly. The whole place erupted into pandemonium when they realized how cleverly Abe had entrapped Duke.

Abe stood up and prepared to speak. Rick, as Claudius, carefully noted this and assumed that Abe might quote the famous line from *Hamlet* when Claudius has been exposed. Abe and Rick yelled in perfect unison, "Give me some light. Away!" The place went crazy.

Violently shaking himself free of the security guards, Abe flashed a hideous look of hatred at Jude and Cory and stormed offstage. He hurriedly limped like a frog with a broken leg down the aisle toward the lobby, his childhood injury flaring again. The audience heard him scream hysterically the whole time, "I'll be revenged on the whole pack of you! Mark me! I will be revenged!"

The animal screams continued until "the big heavy door slammed with an awful crash" (Jude's journal). A ghostly stillness descended on the theater, everybody instantly quiet. Watching Abe storm out of theater, Jude instantly winked at Carley Metz, the actor playing Hamlet, who, recalling Jude's backstage direction, said in unison with Jude, "The king is in his retirement marvelously distempered." The simultaneity was again precise! The place exploded with comic-relief laughter.

Standing onstage, Jude pondered the brilliant but sad man who had just stormed out of the theater. "Yes, marvelously distempered, to say the least!" *But I pity him. Really pity him! What set of life circumstances twists a talented, intelligent human being into a monster like that? I honestly feel sorry for him!*

Chapter 49

That Duke was powerfully affected by the disclosure was evident in his action immediately after Abe's departure. Embarrassed that he had been duped by Abe's chicanery, Duke looked sheepishly at Jude and went immediately over to him. "I can't believe I've been such a jackass. Abe Badoane is as bad as that evil SOB right there!" He flashed a look of disgust at Claudius. "I'm sorry that I blamed you for smashing my car. What a stooge I was! I swear Abe's as ugly and nasty as a fer-de-lance adder! I'm sorry, Jude. Forgive me."

"You remind me of Laertes when he says to Hamlet, 'Exchange forgiveness with me.' I forgive you, Duke. I have done wrong to you too."

When Duke and Jude exchanged forgiveness, the crowd, joyfully viewing the reconciliation, cheered. Jude's and Duke's faces turned red with embarrassment. "I didn't know we were in a fishbowl!" Duke quipped.

"What's past is past," Jude replied, putting his arm around Duke's shoulder to indicate total forgiveness. *Those shoulders are made of granite-hard muscle!*

After reconciling with Jude, Duke started down the aisle in pursuit of Abe, but Jude and a security guard held him back. "Please wait, Duke!" Jude quickly said. "There is a better recourse than revenge."

"I forgive you, but do you expect me to let the snake go free for what he did?"

"Revenge can be curbed. You control it. Don't let it control you."

Jude's comment helped to check Duke's volatility, but it was Cory who, in the end, calmed him the most. Watching Abe storm out, Duke faced the lobby during his exchange with Jude, but then he pivoted toward Cory, who stood alone on the upper stage. He watched her without speaking. *There she stands, alone and heroic and awesome and statuesque…just like Stonewall Jackson at Bull Run!* When she gestured for him to be patient, he instantly calmed down.

Though she spoke softly, Duke managed to hear or lip-read every word. "We'll show you a better way."

Once the film clip had been viewed and guilt determined, order quickly prevailed in the Stephen Foster theater. Winston Armrose took charge as people returned to their seats, and the dress rehearsal recommenced. The remaining scenes of the play were performed without a hitch. Though not feeling well, Charles stayed to the end but excused himself immediately after the play and exited even before the combined postplay debriefing and celebration.

Cory, Jude, Joey, Laura, and Duke, too unnerved to watch the remaining acts, exited the theater after the debacle to reflect and talk. Duke felt the need to ask for forgiveness and explain his conduct over the last months. *I feel like such an idiot. They must think I'm the dumbest ox on the planet, which I am, but the least I can do is apologize, especially to Cory, and I want to do that right away.* "Hey, guys, can we talk? I have a few things I want to say—*need* to say."

"Yes, we can talk," Jude replied. "But much as you hate to hear it, you need to do something else first."

"What?"

"You're obligated to take Abe home. I know, at worst, you want to seek revenge and, at best, leave him stranded in Pittsburgh."

"Sounds great to me. Let the slimy snake find his own way home since that's what he deserves!"

After considerable effort in front of the Foster theater, Jude and Cory managed to calm Duke's violent reaction to the revelation of *The Pittsburgh Hamlet.* Cory took the lead. "Duke, do what's right and forgive Abe. You're trying to reform your ways, and praying for your enemy is the perfect place to start. Remember what Pastor Gabe said last Sunday. If you don't forgive others' sins, then God won't forgive you. One way to show you forgive Abe is to see if he's at your car and take him home if he is. We don't want anything happening to him. You know the guy's not in the best of health, and after the madness in there, he could be in the middle of a breakdown!"

"If he's not around, then join us over there." Jude pointed to Heinz Chapel. "I see it's opened. We can try to impose order on all this chaos in the chapel."

Their suggestion prevailed, and Duke reluctantly went to his car near Hillman Library. But no Abe. Only later did they learn that he had hired an Aire Ride taxi to take him the entire distance to Kittanning. Running from his walk to the car, Duke, out of breath, slipped in the back of Heinz Chapel.

When Jude, Cory, Joey, and Laura entered the chapel, they saw that it was, thankfully, empty and went straight to the front of the sanctuary. Jude and Cory fell to their knees at the altar. "Thank You, God, that Abe has been exposed," Cory began. "May he see the depth of his evil, but more than that, reform his sinful ways. Father, we pray for this intelligent but very lost and sad man."

"We also thank You," Jude joined in, "that Duke has seen first-hand the atrocious evil in which the destroyer has enmeshed all of us. Amen."

The group sat in silence, praying to themselves and praising God for the success of the *Hamlet* interlude. At last, Jude broke the silence, "What can we say? Our mad scheme went without a hitch!" He looked at Cory. "And, Esther, it was your idea!"

When he was certain that they had finished praying, Duke walked humbly to the front of the chapel and joined them at the altar. He turned to Cory and gently touched her arm, very lightly, almost hesitant to do so. "Cory, can you ever…" He broke off, over-come with emotion. "Can you forgive a worthless nobody?" His eyes full of tears, he began to sob. "For what I did to you? For what I am?"

"Of course, I do."

He's a completely broken man, Jude reflected to himself. *But a broken and contrite heart God will not despise.*

Duke turned to Jude and spoke with a quavering voice, "You already said you forgive me, but that don't take away the hurt I did to you and scores of others. I'm a rotten egg and was planning bad stuff against you, Jude. Abe gets in my head and causes me to act like an idiot. The SOB! Oh hell, I shouldn't swear in here. Pops says the church is holy ground."

"We are the church," Jude said, forming a circle with his hands. "The church is people with a relationship to Jesus, not a building where people perform righteous acts."

Makes sense to me. Duke turned to face Cory again. "I'm so sorry. Can you guys forgive me? I mean really forgive me. How can you? I've been so evil." He stumbled for words. "Do you think we can start over again?"

"You know we can," Cory tenderly replied.

Jude and Cory sensed that he had more to say, but for the moment, speech eluded him. Duke threaded his fingers through his hair and ran his right hand up and down the enormous biceps of his left arm. He summoned courage and, looking down, spoke again, "Is there hope for people like me? I'm really messed up." His eyes moist with tears, he drew close to Cory. "May I? I mean hug you?"

"Don't be silly! Of course!"

He gave her a giant bear hug. "I'm so sorry. I really do want to change."

Jude and Cory, in turn, embraced Duke. Cory spoke first, "We forgive you completely. The past is past and is gone forever!"

The scene between the three of them was especially touching, as Cory's journal attests:

> When Duke stood beside me at the altar in Heinz Chapel, he gently put his arm around me, hugged me, sobbed like a baby, and repeatedly begged my forgiveness. He placed his well-shaven cheek against the side of my face as tenderly as one caresses a newborn infant. Saying over and over that he was sorry, he put his head against my shoulder and cried hard. Those hot tears, I thought at the time, were like a soothing balm that medicated my bruised shoulder. I stole a glance at Duke's giant hand and couldn't help but revel in the contrast. With the back of

> it, he stroked my cheek in penitential gentleness whereas, at Beatty's Mill, he had, with that same hand, smashed my face violently against the window and clawed at me like a sex-crazed demon. There, he had been filled with beer and acted foolishly; but in the chapel, he was filled with sorrow and acted penitently. Groping monster, gracious man—the two Dukes! The two contradictory mind-boggling Dukes! Lord, what fools we mortals be!

"Thank you for forgiving me," Duke said as they finished their tearful altar scene. "I feel so bad." He stood up and stamped his foot on the floor. "My mind is a thick grassland savannah, and Abe Badoane slithers through it like a king cobra!"

Nice image, Duke! "Yes, you have reason to feel remorse," Jude said. "We forgive the trauma you inflicted on Cory, but worse than the wrong toward her—and the idiocy of repeatedly falling prey to Abe's machinations—is the wrong you've done to yourself."

Puzzled, Duke looked at Jude. "What are you talking about?"

Jude continued, "You're like most people today: wasting your life in desperate pursuit of nothing and keeping yourself anesthetized to dull the pain of your wasted life." *I can't come on too strong, lest I discourage him, but now that he's in this newfound state of penitence, he needs to face the whole truth.* Jude paused before continuing and then completed his point. "No matter the narcotic you use, you can't stifle the anguished cry of your soul in the dead of night."

"I would have called that psychobabble until just recently. Now standing here and having come face-to-face with my stupidity, I can honestly say, you make perfect sense. 'You can't stifle'—say that again."

"I said you can't stifle the anguished cry of the soul in the dead of night."

"If there was ever bad news, that's it! That's so true. My whole life is one sustained cry of death in a long and lonely night!"

Cory directed Duke's gaze to the front of the chancel and pointed toward the Cross. "Yes, that's very bad news, but up there is the symbol of the *good* news. Because of what He did on that Cross, Christ gives hope to those whose lives are a series of botched beginnings—like yours, like mine. That good news brings light to any dark and lonely life, and what a glorious light it is!"

"I can see God forgiving you guys. You're decent people—moral and good and loving—but He wouldn't forgive me. I am one evil dude." Duke stood up, took a couple paces, and shook his head. "I get sick to my stomach when I think of what an awful wretch I've been." A tear formed in his eye. "I've always been a disgusting sinner, and I have absolutely nothing to show for my wicked life. I really mean that, and it hurts like heck to say it, but it's completely true. I have wasted my entire life!"

"Christ forgives all sinners, Duke. There is no sin so black that He can't wash it clean, and no sinner's heart is so evil that He can't set it free." *I hope my words are a soothing balm to his scorched spirit as his hot tears were to my shoulder.* "Just trust in Him. He is your only hope. He extends grace to all believers, and He wants to be your friend."

"Music to my ears, Cory, music to my ears, but I'll just say that I don't understand grace!"

"Nobody does, but it's divinely beautiful!"

CHAPTER 50

The reconciliation scene at Heinz Chapel was a sweet highlight of that summer. The gushing tears of penitence were followed by rejoicing and praise. As they moved away from the altar, Jude and Cory paused in the center of the chapel to give Duke time to examine the stained-glass windows.

"These are really beautiful." Duke looked in amazement at the windows. "I can't believe any artist can create that sort of beauty! Now this was a man who did something with his life!" *Unlike me!* He stared in wonderment. "Which is your favorite window?"

"Cory, you go first," Jude said.

"I don't know. I like them all, but the Lincoln window has always been a real favorite. Look how Lincoln holds the Emancipation Proclamation in one hand and gestures in a fatherly way to the en-shackled slave. The American flag swirls around Lincoln, for it encompasses the magnificent dream of freedom and liberty for all—a government of the people, by the people, and for the people." She continued to study the window. "To me, the American flag at top left represents the dream because it embodies man's highest and noblest aspirations." She pointed. "See it? There at the top—majestic like a crown. The Emancipation Proclamation at the lower right is the vehicle that ensured liberty and made it a reality. Long live, Lincoln! Yes, I definitely love this window. Charles Connick was a genius."

"I like how you said that," Duke commented. "What about you, Jude? Which is your favorite?"

"I'm like Cory," Jude began. "I like them all, but one of my favorites is also here in the north transept. It's the window to the right of the Lincoln window. See the second one up from the bottom in this left section of the right panel?" He pointed. "Yes, right there. That's the Washington window. It depicts General George Washington at Valley Forge. Our country hung in the balance in those dark days of the Revolutionary War. If it hadn't been for Washington, I don't think the nation would have survived. His troops eked out a miserable existence and died daily in frozen Valley Forge while the British troops partied in aristocratic Philadelphia elegance. The Redcoats made it mighty tough for the rednecks!"

"If there's a redneck window here"—Duke laughed—"I ought to be the centerpiece!"

"Outside of Christ, we're all rednecks!" Jude grew contemplative but said nothing for a moment. Then having formulated his thought, he spoke again, "I see it this way. Washington and the founding fathers created the experiment that spawned the dream, but it was Lincoln who made that dream a reality. Back when the fledgling American nation was like a vast laboratory, the founders theorized that men were created equal, and they wrote the brilliant documents that embodied those sterling truths. But it was Lincoln who forged those ennobling truths into reality on the anvil of his own iron will. What giants those men were!"

The group remained silent as they contemplated the grandeur of the windows. "Duke," Jude resumed a moment later, "did you know the Republican Party was founded to give slaves freedom? That was their platform—offering freedom to the downtrodden, siding with the innocent, taking the part of the oppressed, giving them their day in the sun."

"No, I had no idea, though Pops used to talk about the Civil War and Lincoln a lot."

They continued to look at the beauty of the windows and revel jubilantly that *The Pittsburgh Hamlet* had succeeded so brilliantly. When Duke walked to the windows to examine them more closely, Cory whispered to Jude, "How Duke has changed in a single hour!"

"I agree. The injection of truth into a dark mind works miracles."

They knew it was time to leave, but before departing, Cory looked warmly at Duke. *He loves these windows. I haven't seen him look that admiringly at anything except his car!* "What's your favorite? We haven't heard which window you like."

"I don't know, but I do like this verse from the Bible over here. This is so true of what's happened today."

"Which verse?" Cory asked.

"Over there on the south side. That verse at the bottom left—'And ye shall know the truth, and the truth shall make you free'—how true that is for me! I learned that today, but I sure as heck learned it the hard way!" He continued to look at the verse and marvel at its profundity. "How many other people have been destroyed by their sins? How many fools have been duped by evil people like that malicious dude in the play—what's his face?"

"Claudius," Cory interrupted.

"Yeah, he's the one. There's another snake for you! Why are those courtiers so stupid and unable to see him for what he is? I hate that guy. Does Hamlet get him in the end?"

"We won't spoil it for you." Cory laughed. "But you should see it!"

"You're right. Someday I'd like to see the last acts, but don't dare tell the guys I'm interested in Shakespeare! Huddy would laugh me into next week!"

"I'll say this much," Jude offered. "Hamlet 'gets' him, but he pays a big price. Yes, he wins in the end but has to lay down his life, like a sacrificial lamb, to destroy the evil in the Danish court. I'd say it this way. He destroys evil, but that hard-won success requires his death. That's why the play is such a gripping tragedy."

"That makes me feel bad," Duke said. "I wish he didn't have to die because I really dig that prince. He's cool and likeable and smart as the dickens!"

Cory jumped in, "Does that sound familiar? I'm referring to the sacrificial-lamb business. Have you ever heard of Anyone laying down His life so that others could live?" Cory paused to see if Duke understood. "Of Someone dying so others didn't have to die?" When Duke didn't catch Cory's point, Jude pointed to the Cross at the front of the chapel.

Duke swung around to look at the front of the sanctuary. "Oh, I get it. That's why He died! So that's what you mean when you say He alone gives hope and sets people free?"

"Yes," Cory said. "That's exactly what Christianity is all about—a celebration of the new life that believers have in Jesus."

Duke took his eyes from the Cross and turned to look at Cory. "You're helping me get free from a lot of things that held me down in the past, but you haven't changed my feelings about one thing. Not even close!"

"What's that?" Cory asked.

"My feelings toward Abe. I hate that guy for how he manipulates people. Now I know he was the one behind the sabotage of my car. He's the King Claudius of evil!" The thought again filling Duke with anger, he tightly clenched his fist. "He's going to pay. I'll make him pay! He's like the rattlesnake I saw by the RV in Benezette campground. It just slithered everywhere—just like serpent Abe!"

Standing with Laura some twenty feet away, Joey to this point had been quiet, but he too was a thinker by nature. *Sis's bravery in the theater and these beautiful windows inspire me a lot.* He and Laura moved closer to the Lincoln window and motioned for the others to join him. "Look at the pitiful shackles which control freaks put on the downtrodden," he began. "Here's how I see it. Washington and Lincoln freed people from oppression and tyranny, but look again at the verse Duke pointed at. The great founding fathers of our country liberated the dream of freedom and liberty, but Christ liberates men from the guilt and shame of sin." He paused for moment to see if Duke was following. "Christ liberates the dead heart and brings it to life. Both are obviously very important, but which is more important: liberation from chains or liberation from death?"

"'A dead heart.' Boy, you have me in your crosshairs!" Duke said.

"Very good, you noble philosopher, you learned Theban, you good Athenian!" Jude laughed, appreciating the profundity of Joey's insight.

"I know those phrases!" Cory said. She looked at Duke, who bore the familiar quizzical look on his face during such moments when poetry was cited or esoteric learning invoked. "Duke, he's quoting Shakespeare." She turned to Jude. "*King Lear*, right?"

"You guys amaze me. I'm a nitwit compared to you." Duke sighed. "The jackass of all jackasses!"

"Don't sell yourself short," Cory quickly stated. "You're the one who started talking at lunch the other day about Margaret Thatcher's opposition to centralized decision-making in the European Union. You were over our heads."

Jude jumped in when Cory paused, "You said Thatcher gave a speech about that recently. Where did she deliver that speech?"

"Bruges, Belgium," Duke replied.

"That's it," Jude said. "None of us knew what you were talking about. The guys gave you the same look they give Abe every time he opens his mouth."

"I try to follow the news a little, especially about England. That place amazes me. Pops always talked about English history and got me interested in it from the time I was a little kid. He knew all six of Henry the Eighth's wives. He knew the Tudors better than his own ancestors!"

Jude turned the discussion to the matter at hand. "We're all nitwits as we face *the* challenge before us, bringing Abe to the light of truth and defusing the situation at the mine. That place is a powder keg waiting to explode!"

The talk for the next minutes in the lobby of Heinz Chapel centered on the complex situation at the mine—what could be done, what were the viable options, and what would Abe do?

"He's mad as a hornet," Duke asserted, "now that he's been exposed."

"We know that, but one other thing is equally certain," Cory said, capping the discussion.

"What's that?" Jude asked.

"We have to vow love and forgiveness and denounce hate and retaliation."

For all but Duke, it was reliance on the old creed—"Love conquers all."

Duke reflected on Cory's statement. *To me, this is radical and crazy, but I'm starting to see how love has helped them and how hate has destroyed me!*

On the way down the steps of Heinz Chapel, Jude looked across the lawn toward the Stephen Foster Memorial theater and thought again of the *Hamlet* production. After ambling quietly for a while, he broke the silence. "The play's the thing wherein we'll catch the conscience of the king. Well, we just did! The interlude worked superbly, and Abe was caught in his own trap. Anybody have any guesses as to where act two leads?"

Cory reflected for a moment. "The other night on Vinlindeer, you reminded me that there is a river. You quoted what I wrote to you years ago: 'The river always forges ahead, finds a way, never stops, and knows no defeat.' I hope that's true, Jude, because right now, instead of a shimmering river of glistening gold, I see only darkened corridors of ghastly gloom. Sorry to be so negative, but I'm just telling you how I feel."

Camera-style, Jude slowly panned his head toward the Carnegie Museum. When his eyes settled on the august statue of Shakespeare along Forbes Avenue, the play *Hamlet* again came to mind. "That's true. We definitely have our work cut out, but as the Bard says in *Hamlet*, 'There's a divinity that shapes our ends.' That Divinity—that sovereign, controlling intelligence of the universe—helped George Washington through Valley Forge and Lincoln through the Civil War. Compared to their battles, ours is small potatoes."

"Right, you are!" Cory said, placing her arm in Jude's. "And the arm of the Lord has not grown short. We can't forget that this is our creed. If we trust in it, we'll blissfully cruise that river of glistening gold."

"Yes, beautiful dreamer, we'll float along on its radiant gold!"

Plot Summary for *The Rose and the Serpent*, a Novel by Ron Shafer

This novel is the first in a series of several sequential novels. The Pittsburgh Hamlet is the second novel in the saga.

After a painful five-year separation, Jude (Hepler) and Cory (Mohney) joyfully reconcile but, as in earlier years, are pitted against the brilliant and evil Abe Badoane. More intelligent than Hannibal Lecter and even more scheming, Badoane plots to destroy the lovers as he had five years earlier. Beleaguered by their own emotional devastation and reeling from past traumas, the lovers battle both Abe's evil plotting and the carnal stooges—like macho strongman Duke Manningham, whom Abe uses to do his dirty work.

Though intelligent in their own right and spiritual too, Jude and Cory face extremely difficult odds. After all, how can one stand up against a sinister evil like Abe Badoane? Nevertheless, the lovers learn, through their fire-tested faith, that they not only can withstand but also defeat this terrible evil.

Two subplots inform the fast-paced storyline: First, the events in Jude and Cory's lives mirror the uncanny and recurring rose vision, which wise Old Mary has dreamed across many decades. The one-to-one correspondence between the vision and the lovers' lives greatly adds to the dramatic suspense.

Second, the characters and even the storyline events correlate to the great Shakespearean tragedy *Hamlet*. That correspondence, hinted at in *The Rose and the Serpent*, becomes a full-blown point-by-point remarkably intricate intermeshing by the novel's sequel, *The Pittsburgh Hamlet.*

The Rose and the Serpent ends with Jude and Cory finding out about the highly guarded and utterly private occurrences—two wrenching traumas that had occurred earlier in his life. Feeling exposed and vulnerable because of their find, Abe Badoane vows revenge.

No one, needless to say, stands a chance against Hannibal Lecter, but never has his equal, the wily Abe Badoane, faced Spirit-filled, tough-nosed lovers like Jude and Cory. Despite their failings and their horror-filled adversity, they wage epic battle in this highly dramatic, suspense-filled, lyrically gripping story of love. Who will win this titanic clash of good vs. evil?

About the Author

Dr. Ronald G. Shafer was a professor for over forty years at Indiana University of Pennsylvania (IUP) where he holds a lifetime distinguished university chair. His accolades include a Senior Fulbright Visiting Professorship (to Egypt), Silver Medalist Professor of the Year Award in the Carnegie Foundation/CASE's national top-professor search, citation by *Change* magazine for outstanding professorial leadership, Exemplary Teaching Excellence Award from the American Association of Higher Education, IUP's President's Medal of Distinction, and a flagship grant by the National Endowment for the Humanities. His commendations have taken him to some fifty countries for teaching-abroad stints and invited guest lectures. Shafer has authored numerous scholarly articles, edited two volumes of essays, and presided over the Pennsylvania College English Association. Founder of the Friends of Milton's Cottage, he was executive head of this organization, which helped to restore the home where John Milton completed *Paradise Lost* and which initiated the first two International Milton Symposia. At Milton's Cottage, Chalfont Saint Giles, United Kingdom, Shafer enjoyed "the experience of a lifetime"—audience with Her Majesty, Queen Elizabeth. The three film documentaries he has coproduced and codirected on poets laureate Robert Pinsky and Donald Hall and acclaimed author John Updike have garnered national and international attention. He has written a series of six novels, the first of which, *The Rose and the Serpent*, was published by WestBow Press. *The Pittsburgh Hamlet* is the second installment in this compelling saga. Now in retirement, he continues to enjoy extensive world travel, novel writing, and *the love of his life*—his five granddaughters.